The Longest Year

STAN CRADER

The Longest Year

Published by Wheatmark®
1760 East River Road, Suite 145
Tucson, Arizona 85718 U.S.A.
www.wheatmark.com

ISBN: 978-1-60494-870-7 (paperback)
ISBN: 978-1-60494-879-0 (ebook)
LCCN: 2012946778

THIS BOOK IS DEDICATED TO our men and women in uniform. During the time when I was waiting to turn sixteen and languishing in self-pity, our armed forces were fighting in Vietnam. A generation before them had fought on nearly every continent in WWII and then Korea. That great generation succeeded in preserving our freedoms. And now the present generation of extraordinary warriors is taking the fight to the terrorists.

So long as America is the greatest nation on earth it will be our responsibility to be the world's protector.

Freedom isn't free.

Contents

Contents

Acknowledgements

A BOOK IS SIMPLY THE product of everyone who has had a hand in teaching, influencing, encouraging, or raising the author. Reading is a prerequisite to writing, so I am grateful to my elementary teachers who suffered through my attention deficit days and taught me to read. The disorder was yet to be identified at the time, but I'm sure I had it. Others would agree.

I'm thankful for my grandparents, who raised my parents, who raised me.

Raising our three sons helped keep my memories of my own early driving days crisp and clear. It's amazing how many personality traits are passed on to the next generation. And now I know how my parents felt each time I pulled out of the driveway.

Sometimes an author can be difficult to live with, or so my wife, Debbie, says. She had to endure my hours of staring into space and not responding during conversation. She knows it can't be helped and is patient, most of the time. Since she's my best friend, she also has the responsibility of offering *constructive criticism*, which she did a number of times.

With *The Longest Year*, she enlisted the help of her sisters and mother-in-law (The Miller Girls) to point out "areas of concern" in the manuscript. Two of the sisters have cruel tendencies, which made their remarks most truthful and useful. I'll let the girls try and decide who was cruel and who was not. But their caring comments were of great value. Anyone who writes knows that even the best need a good editor. I needed a team.

A special thanks to Dodi Conrad, whose artistic talent graces the cover of this book. Not only is she a gifted artist, she's also patient. I changed my mind several times during the cover process, going from a portrait of a tunnel to the store with the truck. People too often judge a book by its cover; it had to be just right. And it is. The cover is probably better than the book.

Her painting was done of a Chevy pickup and a building in Marble Hill, Missouri and is where I used to wait for the evening paper. The building is now owned by one of my former school teachers. A big thanks to the Longs who let me borrow their truck and drive it to town to be used for the panting.

The building is the inspiration for Gooche's Grocery. You'll have to read the story to learn the significance of the truck.

I owe an enormous measure of gratitude to the people of Bollinger County, Missouri. It wasn't until I spent some time away that I realized what a special place and time it was to grow up there. Coming of age in Bollinger County was a privilege that I no longer take for granted. All of the people in this book are fictitious, however many of them possess characteristics of those I knew, grew up with, and observe and respect to this day.

Prologue

THE BRIDGE INTRODUCED THE FICTIONAL town of Colby and the band of boys, and caused readers to remember the idyllic days before cell phones, Internet, and texting.

Paperboy helped readers realize that everyone has a redeeming quality—and that some people have an extraordinary and surprising past.

The Longest Year will remind readers of the pivotal role of the automobile and that most coveted possession—a driver's license. The story will make you smile.

Rite of Passage

A FEW YEARS EARLIER, THE boys had met at the stone each day and whiled away the time after school talking adolescent prank strategy that usually resulted in someone getting grounded. In those days they were waiting for the *Colby Telegraph*, but today was vastly different. It was Saturday morning and they weren't waiting for a paper to deliver; a more serious matter was at hand. A life-changing event was about to occur.

Clyde had just endured the longest year in a boy's life. Tommy, Booger, and the band of boys, all younger than Clyde, were huddled around the stone in front of Gooche's Grocery. Clyde was about to take the one exam that all boys looked forward to, one that, if passed, would immediately catapult him into a completely new and envied dimension—that of a licensed driver.

The hour had finally arrived. The boys walked Clyde to the steps of the courthouse and quietly wished him well. They didn't want to get his hopes too high or make a spectacle of what lay before him. There was no farewell, just a nod or two, shoulder shrugs, and some murmuring that might have been construed as an affectionate verbal "good luck."

They stopped a few feet short of the massive double doors. Clyde pulled his shoulders back, took in a huge breath, and then kept moving toward the doors. He exuded confidence; the others, support.

Once Clyde disappeared into the cavernous courthouse, his anxious, envious, suffering devotees ambled back across the street to the stone, hands in pockets, toes kicking at street debris. There was nothing to do but wait.

The Codgers—Bem, Fish, Monkey, and Rabbit—already sitting sentinel over Colby from the courthouse bench, fondly watched the band of boys. Over the years they'd seen countless hopeful, anxious, and apprehensive sixteen-year-olds walk the driver's exam path. This time was different. They'd occupied the bench during Tommy and Booger's paper route days and watched the tightly knit bunch develop from a gang of Clearasil-lathering pipsqueaks into a group of boys inhabiting men's bodies.

"Can you believe it?" Bem asked. Benjamin May's real name had been forgotten by most and never known by some.

"Believe what?" Monkey asked while cleaning his fingernails with the small, well-used blade of a double-blade Case pocketknife.

"That those boys are gonna start drivin', don't cha know," Bem replied.

Monkey, deep in thought, squinted his eyes into razor-thin slits and pooched his thick lips. Montgomery Fulbright had retired as a tree trimmer. He'd trimmed nearly every tree in Colby and done a superb job, as opposed to the crew that came after his retirement and butchered many of the town's largest maple trees, leaving parts of Colby looking somewhat akin to a nuclear test site.

Fish, the elder statesman of the group, also a World War I veteran and a deacon at the First Baptist Church, pointed his finger skyward and chimed in, "I'll add 'em to the prayer list this Wednesday."

Rabbit, with pinpoint accuracy, shot a mouthful of tobacco spit between the exposed roots of a nearby maple tree. He no doubt felt the need to participate in the banter but had to rid his mouth of the murky substance before adding his two cents. "I'm just sayin'," he murmured while wiping the viscous drool off his chin and trying to come up with something to actually say, "they better toe the line. That new state rod don't put up with no nonsense." Rabbit, or Simon James—once known for his speed as a high school football player—was referring to Colby's newest citizen and the area's first resident state highway patrolman.

The boys, oblivious to the Codgers' scrutiny, settled in for the wait and kept a vigilant eye on the courthouse entrance. A stranger might have interpreted their gaze as predatory, similar to a pride of lions watching a herd of wildebeest.

Halfway through a boy's second decade, his thoughts are consumed with girls and driving. Everything meaningful seems to center on possession of a driver's license. The Revolutionary War was about liberty. The westward expansion was fueled by the adventurous spirit that dwells in the heart of man. Driving is the ultimate exploratory gateway. It's the ticket to freedom and the elimination of one's geographical boundaries. It's the first major game changer in a boy's life. To an emerging male in his early teens, driving is everything.

Birthdays are immovable. No matter one's size or intellect, his birth date can't be changed. It's an immutable point in time, and so one must wait his turn to experience the rite of passage. Everyone waits, but time moves excruciatingly slow, and the intensity is immeasurable for boys aspiring to be men.

The days between one's sixteenth birthday and the test date are particularly excruciating. Ailments such as constipation, diarrhea, loss of appetite, and insomnia have been known to occur, sometimes simultaneously, during that span of time. Tommy and the rest of the boys had heard Clyde complain of every sort of ailment at one time or another during his final pre-exam days.

Colby is so small that driver's tests are only conducted during the morning of the first and third Saturdays. Even though it's the county seat, there is seldom a large number of anxious test takers on any given Saturday. There's little fanfare except for those who present themselves for examination. A sixteen-year-old boy without a driver's license is like a cowboy without a horse. Girls are different. They're not consumed with driving; they're a mystery.

Fairview, a much larger town less than thirty miles away and considered a city by its uppity residents, offers the driving test several days each week. Occasionally, Fairview boys, fearful of negotiating city traffic and flunking the driving part of the exam, come to Colby to take the test. They hope to slip in and out without being noticed by locals, and generally that is the case, but not this day. The eyes of those gathered around the stone were ever vigilant.

The written test is simple enough, but fail it and the entire world knows. It's akin to having a nose-tip zit. It can't be hidden. The critical difference is that the zit eventually goes away, but the legacy of flunking the written test lives on forever and is discussed at class reunions forevermore. The pressure to pass causes one to doubt the simplest questions, such as the shape of a stop sign or the color of a yield sign. The driver's written test is a daunting experience, particularly the first time.

Flop finished chewing his last fingernail to the quick and commenced pacing; Tommy watched. Flop's real name was Billy, and that's the name most adults used, but he'd been Flop to the band of boys since the first time they'd seen him with a crew cut. Fortunately, Flop had finally grown into his oversized ears, the root of the nickname. But now his nose was beginning to outpace the growth of his face. Flop couldn't get a break. While he appeared to be disproportioned and emaciated, he possessed a feral-like athleticism.

Booger was removing his boot strings and retying them in a lateral style. Of course, Booger wasn't his real name. His parents had given him Randy, but the band of boys had decided otherwise. Most of the town referred to him affectionately by the name given to him by his band of friends. Even at his mother's funeral, the preacher had referred to him as Booger.

Caleb noticed Booger's new lace pattern. "Hey, that's how the cheer-leaders tie their tennies." Caleb hadn't intended to be hurtful; he'd simply made an observation. But the fact remained, Booger had just emulated the cheerleaders' lacing style, and Caleb's use of the word "tennies" hadn't helped matters.

"I was just tryin' it," Booger said without looking up and then hastily pulled the laces out and retied them in the traditional crisscross pattern.

Tommy began whistling "Last Kiss." It sounded fine to him, but he could tell by their wincing faces that the sound coming out of his pursed lips sounded different to his buddies.

He'd awoken that morning with stopped-up sinuses and described the ailment to his mother as feeling like a floating check valve had been installed behind his nose. When he lay on his left side, his right nostril would clear; when he lay on his right side, his left nostril would clear. But when he stood, both nostrils were clogged and his head hurt.

Tommy's uncle Cletus had recently taught him how check valves func-tion, holding pressure one way but allowing free flow the other direction. Since pressure continued to build in his sinuses, causing his head to hurt and his eyes to feel as if they were about to pop out of their sockets, he imagined a one-way pressure valve lodged in his sinuses. And since the pressure was relieved when he lay one way or the other, he pictured the floating nature of the imagined check valve.

Due to his clogged sinuses, Tommy's voice echoed distorted inside his head, which reduced control of tone in his voice or whistle. Still, his tone control impairment exceeded that which might be caused by a common cold. Tommy's piano teacher was the first to discover—or the first at least to break the news to him—that he was tone-deaf. That didn't stop Tommy from whistling in spite of the sharps and flats that originated from his puffy face.

The "Uncle Sam Wants You" poster hanging in the post office window reminded Tommy of the last time his ears had been so clogged. It was when Gene Hickman had taken him and his dad for their first airplane ride. Tommy was reminded of Gene because it was Gene's wife, Dorothea, who had designed the poster in 1942 and in doing so had won national recognition for herself and Fairview. Since Gene and Dorothea were from Fairview and nice people as well, Tommy concluded that not everyone from Fairview was uppity.

CLYDE HAD BEEN IN THE courthouse too long. "Thing of it is," Caleb began, "I'll bet he flunked."

Tommy flinched at the suggestion and gave Caleb a look, as did the others. They'd all been thinking likewise, but Caleb spitting it out like he did was a jolt to the senses, unthinkable, disastrous. The pink Chrysler in which they all hoped to be chauffeured around by Clyde was waiting next to a sleek new Mustang, which the boys had yet to discover.

"He flunked second grade," Caleb reminded them.

Everett stood but not to fidget. He'd always been larger than the rest, but now stood well over six feet and weighed more than two hundred fifty pounds, very little of that fat. "Shut up, Caleb." Caleb, a habitual smart mouth, glanced Everett's way and wisely did as instructed. Everett, naturally possessed of a gentle spirit, settled slowly back onto the stone but not before giving Caleb a second glare. "I helped him study," Everett added. The rest of the gang grinned. Everett was great on the offensive and defensive lines, but he wasn't perceived as the ideal study partner. He and Clyde, both somewhat pigeonholed because of their size, had less in common than most realized, but they had nonetheless become good friends.

Half glances were exchanged by the rest until the moment of tension passed. Then, almost in unison, they tugged at their pants, rolled their shoulders and stretched their necks—a male thing—and then resumed staring across the street at the courthouse doors. If Clyde emerged with an instructor, he'd passed. Nobody was sure what the flunking protocol was, probably slipping out the back and running home. But Clyde wasn't the running home type. Tommy suspected that an examiner flying out a side window of the courthouse would be a sign that Clyde had flunked. And Clyde wouldn't be doing the tossing; his mom was the real threat in that family. Even Everett knew better than to mess with her.

Until second grade Clyde had been the youngest in his class. Midway through the year, his dad had been killed in a logging truck accident. For Clyde, the loss was devastating and costly. After missing several weeks of school and being unable to catch up with the rest of the class, he'd been retained and suffered a humiliating return to the second grade.

His mom had threatened the entire school board, but the preacher talked some sense into her before any bodily harm was done. It wasn't until sixth grade, when he was promoted from the B class to the A class, that he fully recovered from the stigma of flunking. And now, as the oldest in the class, he was the first to turn sixteen. The tables had fully turned.

Tommy was the first to notice the strange car. "Whose Mustang?" he asked. It was a rhetorical question meant to draw attention to a car that he'd never seen before. The boys had already inventoried and discussed every worthwhile car in the county. They'd have known about the Mustang if it belonged to anyone in the area.

"Probably some Fairview sissy," Caleb replied. The rest of the gang nodded in agreement and took envious notice of the sleek, spotless sports car sitting next to the pink, rust-spotted Chrysler that hadn't been washed since being driven off the car lot some ten years earlier. Clyde occasionally defended the color by saying the window sticker had listed the color as salmon, but the boys, not proficient on the Madison Avenue color chart, saw pink. The Chrysler's paint looked particularly aged while sitting next to the deep, reflective finish of the dark-blue Mustang.

"Can't get many people in that dadgum Mustang," Everett added, his envy sufficiently veiled. Sour grape nods ensued.

Booger noticed Tommy's pained expression. "What's up with you?" he asked, sensitive to Tommy's frequent sniffs. "You look like you just took some cough medicine." Tommy had in fact taken a double dose of Vick's Formula 44, but his distressed look was compounded by a problem that, unlike a head cold, wouldn't soon pass. It would be more than a year before he'd be taking the driver's test. Every single one of his friends would be turning sixteen before Christmas, and he'd yet to celebrate his fifteenth birthday. The cold simply compounded his misery.

"My head feels like it's about to explode," Tommy replied, diverting the real issue but showing clear signs of the stated problem.

Tommy and Booger exchanged sympathetic glances. Booger was sensitive to others in pain; he'd lost his brother in Vietnam three years earlier and had dealt with depression since. But his condition had improved, until the campus antiwar protests ramped up during the past year, and then the shooting at Kent State back in the spring. He'd begun to wonder if his brother had died for nothing. Tommy's uncle Cletus and other war veterans had counseled Booger and assured him that the protestors were loony bin candidates. Nonetheless, Booger had acquired a gift for silence. He usually carried a book with him, an act for which any of the others would have endured endless teasing. Booger's loss put him into a protected class of sorts. Throughout the summer he'd been reading books recommended by Miss Anderson, mostly about the Founding Fathers.

But it wasn't his throbbing head or the fact that he had more than a year to wait before walking the driver's exam path that had Tommy vexed at the moment. His primary ailment was more specific. Melody would turn sixteen in less than a month. How would it work with everyone but him having a driver's license, he wondered. He was sitting on the stone where he and Melody had first kissed. She'd helped him with the paper route during a snowstorm, and on their way home, Tommy had worked up his nerve to make his move at the stone. They'd been sweethearts off and on since.

Flop was rabidly pacing back and forth when Everett noticed something different about him. "Hey," he said, "you shaved."

Flop self-consciously rubbed his fingers up and down the area in front of his ears, which, the previous day, had been flocked with a thick covering of peach fuzz. "Just right here," Flop first said, and then added, "My mom made me." Those four words would be repeated over and over in perpetuity. He'd be reminded of them when friends signed his yearbooks and eventually at class reunions.

"'My mom made me'?" Everett asked, repeating the words exactly as Flop had said them.

Flop looked around sheepishly and then explained. "Last night, after we sat down for dinner, she told me to go wash my face. And I told her I'd washed." The other boys, except for Everett, understood; they'd all had similar experiences. Everett had been shaving at least once per week since sixth grade.

"Well," Flop continued, "she started rubbing my face with a dish towel and then told my dad that it was time for me to start shaving." Flop shrugged and sat down on the stone.

"What then?" Everett asked.

Flop shook his head, disgusted. "We all went into the bathroom, and I shaved while both of them watched." He then pointed at his sideburns. "But just right here."

There were giggles, but with faces in similar stages of maturation, nobody made fun.

The first shave for a boy is always a dilemma. Peach fuzz thickens, then stiffens, and then begins to darken. And one area of the face will mature quicker than another. So, the first shave is usually to remove a small patch of legitimate adolescent whiskers while most of the face is covered in good old-fashioned silky-soft, prepubescent peach fuzz. Booger had only shaved the area in front of his ears and had obviously hoped nobody would notice.

Thoughts of peach fuzz vanished and all ears perked up at the raw, reverberating rumble of glasspack dual exhausts. From the sound, they knew the car before it came into view. All concerns about Clyde or Melody were immediately dismissed and replaced with the visual of Miss Anderson's red '66 GTO. Top down, she came around the corner and rolled to a stop, only feet from the stone. Tommy and the boys had found her electrifying when she'd moved to Colby four years earlier, and the sensation hadn't abated. It wasn't that she flaunted her natural beauty; she didn't have to. It was out of her control. Her femininity radiated. Most of the native ladies of Colby had gradually warmed to her, but there were still holdouts, such as the regulars at Colby Curls Beauty Salon, known more for rumor-cultivating chitchat than achieving beauty.

Flop, having developed into a lithe-footed athlete, won the race to open Miss Anderson's car door. "Why, thank you," she said after emerging energetically from the car. The boys had all been in her class the previous year where they'd studied about George Washington and his penchant for deportment. She looked first at Flop and then scanned the band of boys while pulling her long, thick hair into a ponytail. When she drove with the top down, she always let it blow in the wind. According to the women at Colby Curls, she didn't dress ladylike. When tying her ponytail, the Colby Indians sweatshirt she was wearing pulled up slightly, revealing an inch or so of bare skin, including her belly button. Every pulse surged.

"So, is Clyde taking the exam?" she asked. Tommy swallowed and gulped in a mouth breath. He hadn't taken a breath since she'd tied her ponytail. The combination of Miss Anderson and her drop-top GTO was too much for the senses. His brain had momentarily shut down most of his involuntary bodily functions, such as breathing and saliva swallowing.

Everett of all people, thought to be slow witted, was the first to answer. "Yes, ma'am," he said. It wasn't much of a response, but for two words he was rewarded with Miss. Anderson's full attention. The rest of the boys were immediately envious.

She first winked at Booger and then looked directly at Everett. "So, has he finished the written yet?" Miss Anderson had been seeing Booger's dad for a couple of years. Booger stuck his hands deeper into his pockets, rocked heel to toe, and blushed.

"No, ma'am," Everett replied. Tommy noticed Everett contorting his face, licking his lips, and racing his tongue from tooth to tooth. His mouth too had probably gone dry. It's a phenomenon that Tommy had discovered. When speaking to adults, the mouth either waters too much or not at all. Everett would be swallowing if there was too much saliva. Dry mouth it was, Tommy deduced, and then he rescued Everett.

"He's been in there for about an hour," Tommy said.

"He was most sangfroid when he went in," Everett said, earning him a Miss Anderson wink. She'd gotten on him for using "dadgum" as his standby reply and encouraged him to learn and use new words. None of the others had any idea what he'd just said. Flop frowned. Caleb was momentarily silenced. Tommy figured it was a word Everett had just learned. A few seconds passed and the conversation continued as if nothing had been said.

"Well, he should be coming out anytime," she replied encouragingly, as if she actually knew. "What are the plans once he gets his license?" she asked.

Tommy looked around and replied on behalf of the rest, "We don't have any plans; maybe go to the Houn-Dawg for lunch. Most of us have to work this afternoon." All the boys had jobs, and all had asked off while Clyde took his test. There were no afternoon plans, but they'd given considerable thought to that evening.

The boys jumped when the courthouse doors swung open, but it wasn't Clyde.

"Who's that twerp?" Caleb asked. Miss Anderson grinned.

"I'll bet he gets in 'at dadgum 'Stang," Everett replied.

"Oooh, nice car," Miss Anderson said once she'd seen the Mustang. Her admiration of the twerp's car struck a nerve with the Colby boys. The boy from Fairview was forever marked as a result of Miss Anderson's interest in his car.

The boys were scrutinizing both foreigner and Mustang when Clyde came bounding through the courthouse doors sporting a deeply dimpled smile. He waved proudly and headed for the pink '62 Chrysler.

"He did it!" Everett said and slapped Flop on the back. Flop staggered and then caught his balance. "Oh, sorry," Everett said and then placed his giant paws on Flop's shoulders and gently squeezed. Everett was aware that his body size could intimidate. He used it to his advantage only when necessary, but seldom with his band of buddies.

Nobody cared that the barge of a car had winged rear fenders and that the fender wells were rust ringed. It had four doors and was a veritable mobile living room. And with it, the world beyond Colby awaited them.

In spite of its age spots and river barge design, the Chrysler had a feature that held great promise, and one that the boys were anxious to experience—a convertible top. There was one small problem. The top hadn't been put down since Clyde's father had died, which was a few months after the car had been driven off the showroom floor. There was no way of knowing if it still worked without testing it. And Clyde had mentioned not wanting to put the top down, sort of out of respect for his dad. It was a weird notion, which the boys hoped he'd eventually resolve.

Nonetheless, top or no top, the Chrysler would eventually be their chariot. And that time would be now if Clyde pulled off the driver's portion. The no-nonsense examiner followed, clipboard in hand, policeman-style hat pulled down to the point of almost covering his heartless cavernous eyes.

The examiners were nameless; nobody knew from where they came or to where they returned. To a fifteen-year-old, examiners weren't totally human. They wore brown uniforms similar to those Hitler youth thugs who roamed the streets of 1930's Germany; the boys had seen photos in the encyclopedia.

The Mustang pulled out just before Clyde reached the Chrysler.

"You can do this," Tommy heard Everett whisper. They were all thinking the same thing. In a sense, Clyde was taking the test for all of them. He embodied the aspirations of all. He was the driver's test pioneer, so to speak. New ground was being broken.

They watched Clyde pull away, his hands at ten and two, and head toward the Methodist church where the parallel parking cones were set up. The high-pressure part was over. It would be no disgrace to flunk the driver's part of the test. Rumor had it that the jackbooted examiners liked to flunk the first few drivers of each class, especially boys, just to send a message. Just the same, the pride of the group was on the line. They raced on foot to the back of the church and took positions to watch the most difficult part of the driving portion of the exam, parallel parking. It's not that they wanted to hide from Clyde, but, sensitive to his emotions, they hid from view so as to not disturb his focus.

They were on foot because it was considered bad form for a fifteen-year-old boy to ride a bicycle. A bicycle is at first recreation, and then it becomes transportation. But after a boy's fifteenth birthday, riding a bicycle screams to the world, "I can't drive." Once a driver's license and a car are in hand, then a bicycle is an acceptable option, or as the girls say, cute.

Before reaching the church, the driving exam course snakes through a neighborhood and up Church Hill. The examiners get their thrills by sitting stoically in the passenger seat and observing the victims drive down unmarked streets and deal with intersections, some with and most without stop signs. Crossing the unmarked and imagined centerline or not coming to a complete stop at an intersection is automatic failure. The stopping is easy enough, but the centerline is in the examiners' imagination and anybody's guess. And it's a known fact that if the examiners choose to do so, they can simply say that you crossed the line. Who's to know, and there's no appeal. The brown-shirts have all the power.

And then there's Church Hill. Each car must stop on the steepest part of the hill, back up ten feet, and then proceed. Starting from a dead stop is very difficult for new drivers using a stick, and it's often their demise. It's best to borrow an automatic, but a true rite of passage requires the test be taken in a stick. The question inevitably comes up during one's sixteenth year, "So, did you take the test in an automatic or a stick?" It's important to be able to say, "Stick."

In Clyde's case this didn't matter. His dad had been a log-truck driver. Mastery of the clutch was no doubt a genetic trait gifted to Clyde. He had nothing to prove. The Chrysler, the chariot, the gateway to adventure, featured a push-button automatic. It made no difference. Long live King Clyde and the Chrysler chariot.

Out of breath, the boys peered from their respective hiding places. Conveniently, the first car to arrive at the parallel parking cones was the Mustang. Some things come natural, and the urge to intimidate boys from another town is innate. As if on cue, the band of boys emerged and approached the edge of the street. Their hope was to distract the intruder and cause him to hit a cone. To their dismay, the driver effortlessly maneuvered the short sports car into the center of the cones on the first try.

Slump shouldered they retreated. "That don't seem fair," complained Everett. While his vocabulary had improved dramatically during the summer, his grasp of the irregular verb had not.

"Yeah," Caleb agreed. "Any sissy coulda parked that itty-bitty 'Stang thang."

The pink chariot was in view, and the boys peered out from their hiding places. Clyde slowed to a full stop adjacent to the cones and, at a snail's pace, maneuvered the barge into perfect position. Tommy could see the examiner smiling, a rare but good sign. Maybe the aliens do have hearts, he thought.

The boys raced back to the stone and were waiting when the Chrysler eased into the same parking spot it had left. Clyde emerged from the chariot sporting a molar-exposing grin. His mom gave him a crushing hug and tousled his already disheveled hair. The band of boys reacted by puffing out their chests, repeatedly tucking in their T-shirts, and mentally working through the consequence of Clyde's new possessions—the coveted driver's license, independence, liberty. His passing the test was monumental.

A possibility not considered by the boys was that Clyde had taken the exam before the school class cutoff date; the examiner had most likely sympathetically mistaken him for the youngest in the class. But then Clyde had parked perfectly. It didn't matter; he'd passed.

Tommy tossed Clyde a MoonPie, Clyde's favorite. "Congratulations." The rest of the gang stared in admiration. In the heart of every red-blooded American boy is the relentless desire for adventure. Clyde and his Chrysler were their ticket to new frontiers.

Tommy contemplated the independence that driving represented and how the small slip of paper shrank the world for those who possessed it. But one of the notions that Miss Anderson had impressed upon them during the George Washington studies was responsibility. "With independence comes responsibility," she'd said many times. Tommy began to mull over the consequence of Clyde, the Chrysler, and what lie ahead for the band of boys. For a brief moment his age and the days and months that lie ahead until he'd be taking the driver's test slipped his mind.

First Ride

THE BOYS WATCHED FROM A safe distance while Clyde negotiated permission to take them on a celebratory ride. Clyde's mom, left hand clenched into a fist and resting on her ample hip, and the other shaking a sausage-sized finger in Clyde's face, said, "To the bridge and no farther, buster." They all piled in, and she walked toward the courthouse, where she was the head custodian. Clyde's mom had been letting him drive when she was in the car for a couple of months, or at least until the new highway patrolman had arrived. But Clyde's first time to drive since getting his license would be with a carload of friends.

"Shotgun!" Flop announced and skittered to the passenger side. Tommy and the rest of the boys knew what was coming next.

"Scoot your dadgum bony butt over," Everett said before hip-checking Flop into the center of the front seat.

"That's okay," Caleb said while hopping into the backseat. "Thing of it is, people in the front always die first."

"Where in the heck did you hear that?" Everett asked.

"Everybody knows it," Caleb replied.

"That means he just made it up," Flop said. Caleb flipped him on the ear. Flop grabbed his ear and tried to twist around to get at Caleb but was wedged between Clyde and Everett.

"Don't be such a baby," Booger said. "At least you get to ride in the front." Flop folded his arms and fumed.

"Everybody just shut up," Clyde said. "If mom hears you guys arguing, she'll make you get out." He nodded toward the courthouse doors where his mom, looming like a mama grizzly, stood watching. "Good thing she's hard of hearing," he added.

Tommy sensed Clyde was nervous. He must have had the accelerator flat on the floor, because the engine started with a roar. The fact that connecting rods didn't shoot through the wall of the engine block was a testament to the quality of Mopar engines.

"It started," Tommy said, bringing needed levity to the situation. The engine returned to a rough idle, and Everett pushed the button marked R. Under normal circumstances the boys wouldn't have been caught dead in a car with a push-button automatic transmission. There were no complaints; they'd adjusted.

Just when the car began to roll backward, a loud horn blared. It was Sunny and a carful of half-cheering but mostly shrieking cheerleaders yelling something indiscernible but clearly in support of Clyde. They'd been watching the scene unfold and waiting for the chance to harass the newest driver in Colby. Clyde stomped on the brake, and even though the car had barely been moving, the sudden stop caused everyone's head to snap backward, no doubt making them look like a pack of bobbleheads to Clyde's new fan club. The girl-stuffed Fairlane sped away before Tommy could see if Melody was one of the screaming meemies.

"Is she watching?" Clyde asked, meaning his mom.

Everett had been watching her out of the corner of his eye. "Yeah," he replied.

"Don't look at her," Clyde said.

"Dadgum," Everett said. "She's headed this way."

"Roll the window up so we won't hear if she yells," Clyde whisper yelled and then resumed backing out of the angled parking space. Clyde's mom was wagging an admonishing finger when the boys eased down the street. The boys made their escape, the first of many.

"Put the top down," Caleb said and reached for the brackets that secured the top to the windshield. Clyde gave him a look—the rest took note—and nothing further was said about the top.

Clyde smirked. "She didn't say which bridge." His mother had no doubt meant the bridge on the gravel road to Bird's farm, where the boys had frequently ridden their bikes. Clyde had a different bridge in mind, one that would include a pass over the infamous Seven Sisters. The Seven Sisters weren't sisters but in fact a one-mile stretch of straight highway traversing a geological phenomenon—seven evenly spaced steep contours.

Whenever the subject came up, the Codgers would argue about the origin of the contours. The debate generally boiled down to two schools of thought. One theory was the Ice Age, and the other, the New Madrid earthquake. Both events predated recorded geological history for the area, so the argument was consequently impossible to settle—ideal fodder for the Codgers' intellectually free courthouse bench debate.

"Faster," Caleb yelled from the backseat. Clyde ignored him and kept the not-to-exceed-fifty promise made to his mom. That was fine with Everett, who was gripping the dash with his right hand and unintentionally squeezing Flop's pencil-thin, sinewy thigh with his left. Flop wasn't lobbying for more speed either. He was watching the road, Clyde's death grip on the steering wheel, and the speedometer needle, and wincing in pain from Everett's grip. They were closing rapidly on the first contour, soon to be known as a whoop-de-do.

"Yahoo!" Caleb cheered when the car crested the apex of the first contour and he momentarily went weightless. Clyde let off the accelerator, and the sudden decrease in power, combined with the full weight of the car being returned to the tires, caused the car to swerve a few inches across the centerline. He overcorrected first toward the ditch and then back toward the center and had just gained control of the car when they crossed sister number two.

By then their speed had dropped to below thirty, but nobody complained. Just before reaching the third sister, a car coming from the opposite direction topped the hill with enough speed that the front tires appeared to come off of the pavement. Tommy closed his eyes and braced for the impact. The two cars most likely missed each other by the normal margin, but the boys were certain that an onionskin wouldn't have fit between the Chrysler and the Mustang.

"'At danged Mustang," Caleb said. The driver of the Mustang had no way of knowing he'd just made a challenge and had dug a deeper proverbial grave for himself. Tommy was sure the others were thinking the same as him; instincts had taken control.

High school boys, much like dogs, are territorial. When a stray dog ventures into a new neighborhood, it is met with much resistance by the resident dogs. And if the stray is bold enough to go near a resident female, the resistance turns vicious. A similar phenomenon holds true for boys. The Mustang had penetrated the sacred perimeter which had been protected by generations of Colby's finest hormone enriched adolescent males.

"He'll have to come back this way if he's going to Fairview," Booger said.

"Let's find something to throw at him," Caleb added. Heads shook, and disgusted glances were exchanged.

"Throw what?" Tommy asked. Knowing Caleb like he did, Tommy was sure Caleb would come up with something entertaining.

"Hedge apples," Caleb replied. "Turn around. There was an Osage orange tree before the first sister," he added. Rather than argue, the boys chose the easier strategy: they ignored him.

Clyde rolled over sister number seven at little more than an idle, pulled in at the turnaround, and headed back to town. For slightly longer than a split second, he pushed the accelerator to the floor, kicking in the four barrel and sending the boys into a frenzy. Tommy wasn't sure if the momentary exhilaration he felt was due to the acceleration pushing him into the seat or the fact that they would once again be traversing the sisters.

Clyde chose a new top speed of thirty. Everett relaxed his grip, and blood resumed its nourishing flow to Flop's lower leg. Just after cresting sister two, the Chrysler met the Mustang again. This time both cars were traveling well under the posted speed; both drivers had evidently learned a lesson and survived to crash another day.

"Thing of it is," Caleb began, "good thing that guy is headed the other way."

"Why's that?" Everett asked. It's unlikely he was genuinely interested in any particular answer, but just curious as to Caleb's thoughts.

"'Cause," Caleb thoughtlessly replied.

"Thought so," Everett replied, a bit of sarcasm in his tone.

Sitting half-hidden on a side road between the sisters and town was Trooper Trankler. And that explained the Mustang's slow speed. Thomas Trankler had been quickly nicknamed "Two-T" by the band of boys. But within a week, Two-T had been modified to Tootie, representing both the Trooper's initials and a character in the sitcom *Car 54, Where Are You*. Trooper Trankler was unaware of the given moniker.

The first resident Missouri Highway patrolman had moved to Colby a couple of months earlier. He'd immediately lost favor with the boys after discovering that none of them had driver's licenses and forcing them to stop riding their motorcycles down the county's many gravel roads. They'd appealed to Sheriff Dooley and had learned that the sheriff's primary duty was serving papers and not patrolling roads. And now, there the evil Tootie sat, his net cast, patiently waiting. The boys avoided eye contact as they rolled past.

"That wouldn't be a bad job," Caleb said.

"Except when you'd have to give someone a dadgum ticket," Everett replied.

"I'd just give warning tickets," Caleb countered.

Everett shook his head. "How long you think that would last?" he asked.

Tommy had learned that it was best to stay out of the arguments that often occurred between Caleb and Everett. He noticed through the rearview mirror that Clyde was grinning.

Caleb went on. "I'd go to Fairview and give those idiots tickets." Everett, probably thinking it a lost cause, didn't reply and let Caleb have the last word.

Tommy played the agitator. "Well, at least you'd get to drive a fast car."

"Speedometer in that car registers a hundred and forty," Clyde reported.

"How'd you know that?" Caleb asked.

"I saw it once when he got gas at Burt's," Clyde replied. Caleb frowned, clearly frustrated that Clyde knew something that he didn't.

"Think he's ever shot anyone?" Caleb asked.

Tommy, his thoughts elsewhere, changed the subject. "Where you think those girls went?" he asked.

Caleb, his mind easily shifted from one thing to another, replied, "Let's check the Houn-Dawg first." Clyde set the Chrysler chariot on a course for Colby's hot spot.

Tootie kept his vigil for Saturday cruisers of the Seven Sisters, a magnet for reckless drivers. There he'd write tickets for careless and imprudent driving, infractions which had more costly fines than simple speeding infractions. He would never be in the running for most popular person in the county.

RAILROAD TRACKS SKIRTED THE EDGE of Colby between town and Craggy Creek. The tie yard, feed store, stockyard, lumberyard, coal storage bins, and bulk fuel station were situated adjacent to the tracks. Ground corn tailings blew from the top of the tallest grain silo on the far side of the feed store. Clyde looked both ways before easing the pink chariot across the tracks. A potpourri of aromas and fine dust filled the car—creosote-soaked ties, corn being ground for feed, cattle waiting shipment, and spilled fuel. While familiar smells to Tommy and the band of boys, like many things yet to come, experiencing them while enjoying their new independence in a car inexplicably altered the sensation and felt strangely new.

The Houn-Dawg and Sunny's car packed with cheerleaders came into sight. Tommy was about to say something when Caleb began backseat driving. "Pull up next to 'em," he said. Clyde gave him an "I've about had enough of you" glance and then eased the chariot up next to the Ford Fairlane full of gorgeous girls. If he'd seen them, Henry Ford would have used the girls as models to advertise the car he'd named after his estate. But Henry had never been to Colby; his loss.

The boys sitting next to a window let their arms dangle alongside the car in an effort to look casual, but not Clyde. Clyde kept both hands at ten and two until completely stopped and then pushed the park button and shut down the engine. The throng of girls stunned Clyde by crowding around his window and reaching through to give him congratulatory hugs and cheek and forehead kisses.

Sunny noticed the push buttons on the dash. "Cool," she said and then motioned for the other girls to look. "Clyde's car has push buttons instead of a shifter thingy." And then Clyde had to endure each one of them poking their head inside the car and touching the transmission buttons on the dash.

The words "Clyde's car" reverberated in Tommy's mind like a never-ending canyon echo. The flood of mixed emotions caused him to momentarily feel drowsy. He was thrilled that Clyde had gotten his license—and was now getting the much-deserved attention of the girls—but he was simultaneously envious. He bemoaned the months, weeks, days, hours, minutes, and even seconds before he'd be in position to enjoy a similar reception. And to top it off, he realized that, as the youngest in the class, turning sixteen would diminish to ho-hum status by the time his day arrived.

They all sat outside on the elevated sidewalk that wrapped around the Houn-Dawg taking turns putting money in the jukebox and making small talk. Tommy and Melody were sitting together, a few feet from the others. Tommy's sinuses magically cleared when Melody asked if he planned to go the movie later that night; *Patton* was showing.

"Want to meet at the movie, or do you want to come by?" she asked.

"I can come by," Tommy replied. He'd forgotten about plans to ride around with Clyde and the boys. And for that he'd pay.

She gave him a warm smile. "It's a short walk." Tommy smiled back; she'd read his mind.

Clyde's technique for eating a juicy burger cost him a few adoration points. The attention given to him by the cheerleaders decreased proportionally to the amount of grease dripping from his chin and elbows. Soon, the girls moved to the corner of the building and began rehearsing cheers they'd learned at camp the previous summer, modifying them to fit Colby's mascot, the Indian.

"I need to go," Clyde announced to no one in particular and headed for the Chrysler. "If you want a ride, you better get in."

"Shotgun!" yelled Flop as he sprinted for the passenger-side front door. Everett took his time and again hip-checked Flop into the center of the front seat. It was a scene that would repeat it itself innumerable times. For Flop, the term shotgun was redefined.

They weren't going far. Caleb and Flop were going to the bowling alley, less than a block away, to set pins for the Saturday afternoon league. Tommy and Booger could have walked to Gooche's Grocery, but they all piled into the Chrysler as if to be off on another adventure. The argument over seat selection barely got started by the time they started getting let off.

Tommy had his arm draped across Booger's shoulder while they watched Clyde make the corner and stop in front of the bowling alley to drop off Caleb and Flop. Caleb and Flop watched the Chrysler until it disappeared, headed toward the feed store, where Everett would be let off. A new era had begun.

If they'd waited long enough, they would have seen the Chrysler return to Burt's Sinclair, where Clyde would spend the afternoon washing windshields and checking oil for people filling up with brontosaurus fossil fuel.

Melody

TOMMY HADN'T TOLD THE OTHERS about his plans to walk Melody to the movie. Since she'd mentioned it, he'd decided to do that instead of cruising Colby with the rest of the gang in Clyde's Chrysler. He fretted about how to break the news.

Clyde had made the rounds, picking up everyone except Booger—it was Booger's turn to work until closing at Gooche's—and making a few trips around the loop. Flop was sitting in the back; Everett had simply motioned toward the rear when they'd picked him up.

The loop was a driving pattern, more or less, that had been established eons earlier. Colby cruisers passed through the courthouse square, then through a choice of neighborhood streets, the black-topped ones, back through the square, and then through another neighborhood. Over the course of a typical evening, the same cars would meet each other several times, and people sitting on porches would see the same cars pass by over and over. Waves, nods, and honks occurred repeatedly to the same people. The ritual was part of the Colby culture.

The band of boys were in tall cotton and exceedingly anxious to be seen. Everyone except Clyde waved aggressively to other cars and porch sitters. Clyde never moved his hands from the steering wheel; extending his left index finger was the extent of his waving.

"You told her what?" Caleb blurted out when Tommy began to tell them of his plans with Melody. "Thing of it is," Caleb continued, "everyone's going to the movie. It's the first night for *Patton*. It'll be crowded." He folded his arms in disgust. "This is our first night. Heck, we might talk Clyde into driving up the tracks."

Tommy was grateful for Caleb's mention of the tracks; it diverted attention from him and his plans with Melody. A discussion ensued regarding Caleb's sanity, a topic frequently broached anytime Caleb was around. Caleb had obviously been thinking about the Stephenson gauge, which they'd learned about in Miss Anderson's class.

Frequently, as part of history class, Miss Anderson would cover the origin of a tradition, custom, or standard. By doing so, she'd cleverly arouse interest in different countries and cultures. She was sneaky that way. The previous week she'd covered the controversial origin of the width of railroad tracks. Some say the width stems from the need to fit railroad tracks over ruts made by Roman chariots, but the predominant belief was that George Stephenson, a coal miner, established the width. He chose four feet eight and a half inches because that was the width of horse-drawn carriages, and he wanted carriages to be able to be backfit to travel on his railroad tracks. But the true origin was never sufficiently settled because, for instance, who decided to make horse-drawn carriages a particular width? The answer to that, she'd said, was based on the width of two horses' rears. And she'd been quick to say that she was talking about real horses and not somebody from Fairview.

Caleb, with his way of thinking, couldn't have cared less about the true origin of anything. The tidbit that caught his attention was when she'd mentioned that the width of most cars and trucks were still built to the same standard. Caleb had quickly deduced a car tire would fit perfectly on the railroad track and that by letting a little air out of the tires they could ride the tracks in Clyde's Chrysler. And not only ride the tracks, but ride the tracks to the tunnel, a popular high school couples' weekend hiking spot. The train didn't run during weekends. Caleb's mind never stopped; it seldom ran in a coherent direction, but it never stopped.

By the time they got to Melody's house to let Tommy off, there was a split decision. While they all agreed Caleb's idea was nuts, he'd sufficiently aroused their curiosity. Flop and Caleb were arguing the merits of rail riding with Everett when Tommy jumped out. Clyde's focus was on driving. Melody was sitting on her porch steps.

Tommy thought he'd gotten away with getting out at Melody's until he heard the singsong coming from the Chrysler. "Tommy and Melody, sittin' in a tree, K-I-S-S-I-N-G." He didn't acknowledge them, and soon the Chrysler and the hecklers were out of range.

"Hey," he said after working up the nerve to speak but then noticed Mr.

and Mrs. Hinkebein sitting in the porch swing, which caused his brain to shut down the flow of saliva and increase perspiration to his armpits.

Melody smiled. "Hey back," she said.

"So, gonna see *Patton?*" Mr. Hinkebein asked, stating the obvious.

"Yes, sir," Tommy replied, trying not to sound too much like Eddie Haskell.

"We saw it last weekend in Fairview," Mr. Hinkebein continued. "Don't be late; the opening scene is a speech by General Patton. You don't want to miss that."

Tommy heard Mr. Hinkebein speaking but only made out about every other word because when Melody stood, the breeze caught her glowing auburn hair, maxing Tommy's senses, leaving no brainpower for auditory discernment. Tommy gave the Hinkebeins a nod. Melody was so striking that the simple task of walking without tripping on a sidewalk crack required utmost concentration.

Once they reached the corner and were out of sight of her parents, she took his hand. Even though he knew that the sight of them holding hands would lead to more heckling, Tommy didn't resist. He didn't care. No sooner had he decided that the tingling sensation her touch provided was worth whatever his friends dished out than the Chrysler came into view. Continuing his light grip on her hand was a test of wills: machismo versus romanticism.

In the short time it had taken Tommy to collect Melody and start toward the theater, the boys had stopped at Burt's Sinclair and gotten cigars—Swisher Sweets. Everyone except Clyde had a smoldering cigar protruding from pursed lips. Clyde's cigar wasn't lit. It wasn't even unwrapped and was tucked behind his ear. Flop was coughing, belching smoke with each spasm, and his complexion had already turned pale.

It wasn't Everett's first cigar. He blew smoke rings while tapping off end ashes. "Want a ride?" he asked, his head tilted back gangster-like. Tommy wasn't sure what to do; there was too much to think about. They had only two blocks to the theater, but Mr. Hinkebein had said something about not being late. Melody didn't have permission to ride in Clyde's car, but then she hadn't been told not to either. And worst of all, Tommy wondered, would riding with Clyde diminish Melody's interest in him?

It didn't take Caleb long to chime in. "You can ride in the back with me 'n' Flop, Melody. Tommy, you can ride up front." Caleb's generosity probably stemmed more from wanting to put distance between himself and the coughing Flop than wanting to sit beside Melody.

Everett shook his head disgustedly and opened the door. "I'll ride in the back, and you two can ride up front," he offered. He stepped out, left the front door open, and hip-checked Flop into the middle of the backseat. Flop was fuming, but nobody cared. Not only was he in the backseat but stuck in the middle. Straddling the floor hump in front was acceptable; straddling it in the back was demeaning.

"Sure," Melody said. "Why not?" Tommy followed her into the front seat. Clyde pushed D for drive, and they were on their way.

"They fit," Caleb announced.

After a few moments of silence, Melody asked, "Who fits?"

"Not who," Caleb replied with disgust. "The tires," he continued with gusto and then sat there like he'd just discovered the cure for cancer.

Tommy looked across Melody at Clyde. Clyde shrugged without taking his eyes off of the road. "Let's show 'em," Caleb said.

"Show us what?" Melody asked.

Caleb began to answer but was interrupted by Everett, who explained in half the time that Caleb would have.

"We have time," Melody replied. Tommy realized he'd lost control when she'd taken his hand, long before the Chrysler had appeared.

Clyde took them to the far end of the tie yard, where an old dirt road crossed the tracks. Everett, Flop, and Caleb got out and gave Clyde directions while he maneuvered the car so that the tires were centered on the tracks.

Caleb beamed. "See, just like Miss Anderson said." Melody had to get out and see for herself.

"Now what?" she asked.

"Time to get off these tracks and go to the movie," Clyde answered.

"Aren't you gonna drive it a little ways just to be sure?" Melody asked.

Clyde gave Tommy a quizzical look. "Get in," he said, ignoring Melody's question. Tommy was astonished at Melody's disappointment that they were not going to drive down the tracks; he found that curious, odd, and strangely alluring.

Clyde circled the square. There were a couple of parallel parking spots, but he angle parked at Gooche's. They put their cigars out. Everett laid his on the dash, planning to relight it after the movie.

Booger was waiting in front of the theater and still had his bow tie on. Carryout boys had to wear a clip-on bow tie that read Gooche's down one ribbon and Grocery down the other. It seemed Mr. Gooche thought that shoppers would forget where they were and a quick glance at the carryout boy's clip-on bow tie would solve their dilemma.

"Where'd ya go?" Booger asked.

"It's just like Miss Anderson said," Caleb blurted out. Everett gently but firmly squeezed Caleb's neck and then leaned down and peered into his eyes.

"We cruised the loop," Clyde replied.

Curious, Booger followed up on Caleb's squelched comment. "What about Miss Anderson?"

Tommy nodded toward some nearby adults. "I'll explain inside," he said. "Take that stupid tie off. You're off the clock." Embarrassed, Booger flinched, jerked the tie off, and stuffed it into his pocket.

Tommy let Melody go first; since he couldn't drive and hadn't picked her up in a car, it wasn't a date, so to speak, so he didn't offer to pay her way. "I'll tell you about the tracks inside," he said to Booger and then caught up to Melody at the soda fountain, where she'd ordered a graveyard, a small popcorn, and a frozen Snickers. A graveyard, for those who don't remember, is a blend of every soda available at the fountain.

The theater had two aisles. The seat sections on each side were rows six seats wide; the center section was twelve seats wide. Latecomers had to sit in the seats with cracked upholstery and exposed springs.

An unstated but strictly-adhered-to seating order prevailed at the theater. There were no signs, and nobody had ever been given seating instructions, but the youngest sat toward the front. That worked out well, since the floor was slanted toward the screen: when the little kids spilled stuff, it didn't have far to drain.

The oldest naturally gravitated to the rear. When Tommy was the age of the kids sitting in the first few rows, he figured that old people sat in the back so they'd be closer to the restroom. But since he'd begun to notice girls, and particularly Melody, he realized there were other reasons for sitting in the darkest recesses.

The quirky thing that few noticed was that the Baptists sat on the right, the Methodists on the left, and the Catholics interspersed with both groups. The Assembly of God, Pentecostal, and other long-skirted denominations rarely attended the movies, and if they did, they sat clumped together in the center. And they never ate popcorn, drank soda, or enjoyed a frozen Snickers.

Tommy, raised Baptist, led the way and started down the right aisle. Melody, a Methodist, and naturally drawn to the other side, pulled Tommy into the center section. They'd unintentionally split the difference, but Tommy didn't mind.

Once the side sections filled up, moviegoers were forced to sit in the center, and that created a problem. Those first forced into the center section always chose aisle seats. And then latecomers would have to climb over or scoot by, all the while casting a head-and-shoulders silhouette onto the screen, eliciting heckling and occasionally becoming the target of a peanut M&M.

A poster on the wall leading into the auditorium had explained a new program. Under a "random" selection of center seats would be a coupon good for a free movie. The new policy had enjoyed moderate success, but changing habits was difficult even if it meant free stuff.

"Nice seats," Melody said. The cushions on the center seats were in better condition than the more frequently used ones nearer to the aisle.

Tommy shrugged and began feeling around under his seat for the coupon but found none. "Don't guess my seat was randomly selected," he said sarcastically.

"Oh, I almost forgot," Melody said and leaned over to reach under hers. In doing so her face came within inches of Tommy's. Their eyes locked for a second; he felt her breath and breathed in her Jungle Gardenia. "Me neither," she said.

Booger, wanting to hear more about the railroad tracks, sat next to Tommy; the rest of the gang followed. Tommy leaned forward and glanced down the row at his buddies; Caleb was sitting next to Clyde and bending his ear. The seating arrangement wasn't what he'd daydreamed about all afternoon in anticipation of sitting next to Melody. Here we are, he thought, somewhat disgusted, sitting in the center like a bunch of holy rollers.

The JV cheerleaders, too young to date, usually sat together on the right side. But as if they always sat in the center, which they never did, they marched down the row directly in front of Tommy, Melody, and the rest, and took a seat. It soon became evident why.

One of them turned toward Clyde and smiled. "Hey, Clyde," the one with braces said. "We heard you got your driver's license."

Another one turned, fluttered her eyelids, and added, "We saw your car in the parking lot." They'd clearly conspired before entering the middle section and sitting directly in front of instantly popular Clyde.

So enamored with Clyde, his car, and the railroad tracks, the rest didn't check under their seats, which bothered Tommy. It was his first venture to the center, and he needed confirmation that at least one seat had been randomly selected.

Clyde had no clue as to the reason for his newfound popularity and didn't immediately respond.

The truth finally eked out. "You'll have to take us for a ride sometime." Clyde scanned the faces of the row of adolescent girls who only days earlier wouldn't have shared the time of day with him. Sure, they'd said his name over and over in football game cheers. But he'd never taken that to heart.

"I'll have to ask my mom," Clyde finally replied. It probably wasn't the response the cheerleaders were looking for, but it was the best Clyde could do without having had a chance to be coached by his friends. He'd yet to gain an appreciation for the opposite sex. They couldn't block, tackle, pass, or catch, so he wasn't sure of their purpose.

Tommy was taking it all in and still contemplating the driver's license–free year ahead for him when Melody gently cupped his knee with her soft hand. It struck a chord that caused his brain to malfunction. Before he realized that all she wanted was the popcorn, he'd already drooled and nearly wet his pants even though he didn't need to go.

"Popcorn?" she whispered. Tommy wasn't sure why he'd agreed to split popcorn with her. She liked lots of butter and he didn't. He rarely ate any popcorn, but he found inexplicable pleasure in holding the bag while she dug around.

"So, it really fits?" Booger inquired. Tommy went into detail about how they'd maneuvered the car onto the tracks, and how Caleb had suggested they actually drive down the tracks a ways. Tommy sighed in disgust. "He even said something about driving it through the tunnel."

"No way," Booger said. Tommy responded with a "yes, he's nuts" shrug. "Wonder what the stereo would sound like in the tunnel?" Booger asked.

Tommy realized that Booger was in Caleb's camp when it came to driving judgment.

The Websters—the first and still only black family in Colby—sat down in the row behind them. Mr. Webster was the hat factory manager and was known by all and liked by most. Mrs. Webster's beauty caused each boy to find a reason to turn around and say hello even though the cartoons had already begun and it was dark and whisper-only time. Tommy turned and realized that since the Websters were black, the only thing he could see was the whites of their eyes. It reminded him of one of the many pieces of trivia that Booger had recently read about and shared with the band of boys. It was Israel Putnam who had coined the phrase "Don't shoot until you see the whites of their eyes." He'd done so during the Revolutionary War. It wasn't that Tommy was thinking about shooting anyone; the thought just crossed his mind when he glanced over his shoulder at the Websters.

He glanced again and saw Mrs. Webster showing Mr. Webster a coupon. Satisfied that a coupon had actually been placed under at least one seat, Tommy faced the screen.

George C. Scott, playing General Patton, began the speech that Melody's dad had mentioned. The movie had played a week earlier in Fairview, and many in Colby had already seen it. "Men, this stuff that some sources sling around about America wanting out of this war, not wanting to fight, is a crock of bullshit. Americans love to fight, traditionally. All real Americans love the sting and clash of battle. You are here today for three reasons. First, because you are here to defend your homes and your loved ones. Second, you are here for your own self-respect, because you would not want to be anywhere else. Third, you are here because you are real men, and all real men like to fight."

Caleb had convinced Clyde that they should probably leave the movie early and go cruising. Clyde had halfheartedly agreed, mostly just so Caleb would shut up. But with General Patton's opening remarks, the boys were glued to their seats, eyes trained on the screen.

It's doubtful anyone blinked until the famous speech was completed. Of course the last few words of the speech had been altered, but, given warning, everyone was cued up to read Patton's lips. Nobody had ever heard anything like that at the movie.

Tommy heard the Websters whispering. "You think General Patton really said that?" Mrs. Webster asked.

"I'm sure he did," replied Mr. Webster. "And he was right."

Tommy felt awkward and pretended nothing had happened. He decided to wait to take Melody's hand until his palm stopped sweating, or at least until she'd finished with the popcorn. The movie began; Melody rested her hand on Tommy's wrist. He finished his soda but didn't chew the crushed ice for fear Melody would hear him crunching. Having her so near was both sensational and nerve-racking.

So stirred, few people rose from their seats until the credits had finished rolling. Once the lights came up, everyone slowly moved toward the exit. *Patton* had simultaneously filled the boys with bravado, humility, and patriotism. "It'd be cool to be in a tank division," Clyde said while everyone was piling into the Chrysler. He looked Booger's way. "Think they use tanks in Vietnam?"

Caleb answered, "Too much jungle." Clyde gave him a look. Caleb yielded to Booger.

Booger spoke contemplatively. "I think Caleb's right. There're mostly helicopters in Vietnam, and bombers." He paused a few seconds. "Too many rivers and mountains for tanks."

Clyde, Flop, and Everett were in the front. Caleb, Booger, Tommy, and Melody squeezed into the back. Melody was half sitting on Tommy's lap; he didn't mind. Melody surprised them by joining the military conversation with, "I liked his pistol with the ivory handle." Tommy thought her remark curious and noticed the other boys exchanging eyebrow-dancing looks.

Clyde methodically pushed the R button, and the car began slowly moving in reverse; he was done with talking.

After carefully backing out, Clyde began to ease forward, but their lane was blocked. The Websters were in front of Clyde, and the car in front of the Websters was stopped. Everett stuck his head out and looked ahead. "It's 'at Mustang," he reported. "It's stopped and blocking Miss Anderson's GTO." Miss Anderson and Booger's dad had also attended the movie. Everett stretched his head a little further out the window. "A couple of guys just got out of the Mustang," he continued. It looks like they're saying something to Miss Anderson and Booger's dad."

When the Websters honked, a tall, gangly kid unfolded himself from the Mustang and made a derogatory hand gesture. Mr. Webster stepped out of his car. "Would you mind moving?" he politely asked. The Mustang kid made the same hand gesture again and yelled, "Hey, looks like they got niggers in Colby now."

By that time Booger's dad had gotten out of the GTO and was arguing with the driver of the Mustang, who was making "I don't understand" gestures with his arms. Finally, the Mustang began to creep forward but then stopped, and another man-boy emerged, this one a bit shorter but much beefier. He walked around the Mustang and put his finger to Booger's dad's chest. Clyde methodically pushed the P, for park, button.

Mr. Webster approached the Mustang. The tall one met him at the back of the Mustang. "You better stay out of this, nigger," he said. Mr. Webster didn't appear intimidated even though the punk towered over him.

By this time Clyde and Everett had both gotten out of the Chrysler and were walking past Mr. Webster's car, Clyde on one side and Everett on the other. Clyde gave Everett a nod, the same kind of nod they gave each other immediately following a huddle break during a football game.

Everett tapped the tall one on the shoulder. When the Fairview punk spun around, probably expecting to see Mrs. Webster, he was greeted by someone his height and a large, powerful paw of a hand gripping the better part of his neck. Everett's fingers reached three-quarters of the way around the punk's neck and squeezed.

Tommy watched, knowing that if the tall dude just settled down, Everett would let him go. Everett was slow to anger and would do anything to avoid conflict off of the football field.

Clyde was a different story. He'd spent his early years resenting anyone and everything. He'd mostly recovered and become a bona fide member of the band of boys, but he was still under the influence of a *Patton*-induced adrenaline high. He slipped between Mr. Burger and the Mustang, pausing just long enough to reach inside the window and backhand the driver, and then pushed the punk arguing with Mr. Burger hard enough to cause him to fall backward. He then opened the door of the Mustang and invited the others to step out. By now a sizeable crowd had gathered, including Sheriff Dooley, who had also been at the movie.

Sheriff Dooley, who made it a habit to hang around the movie when it let out on the weekends, came at a trot around the front of the Mustang. "That's enough," he yelled. Clyde was backing away when the punk got to his feet and started for him. Sheriff Dooley grabbed the punk's wrist and twisted it in such a way that obviously caused severe pain.

"Ow!" he yelled. "What you doin' that for?" He looked back at Sheriff Dooley. "That guy pushed me," he complained.

"Why'd you get out of your car?" Dooley asked.

"Let him go, Sheriff," Clyde said. "We can settle this now."

"What's there to settle?" Sheriff Dooley asked.

Clyde shrugged and pointed at the stranger. "I don't know. Ask him."

Miss Anderson put her face within inches of the punk's. "If I were you," she said, "I'd go home." She motioned toward Clyde. "The last thing you want is for this to continue." The punk looked around, surveyed the crowd, saw his friend in Everett's grip, and huffed.

Sheriff Dooley moved between Clyde and the punk, released his grip, and looked at Everett. "You can let that one go, too." Everett's guy started hacking and coughing and gasping for air. Everett looked more scared than the choking kid. Clyde looked amused, like he'd been enjoying himself. Sheriff Dooley looked back and forth between Everett and Clyde. "Call it a night, boys. We need you on the field on Friday nights, not doing community service."

"Yes, sir," Clyde and Everett replied almost in unison, one meaning it more than the other.

Everett tucked his shirt in while the Fairview punks kept mouthing about having done nothing wrong. And in fact they hadn't done anything illegal, just unethical. As they were pulling away, one of them yelled from the safety of the Mustang, "This ain't over!"

Sheriff Dooley waved his arms in a scattering motion. "It's over, folks. Go on home." He walked over to Clyde. "Listen, those boys are looking for trouble. The best thing you can do is go home and don't give them a chance." He looked around and made momentary eye contact with each boy, making sure they'd heard.

"It's late anyway," Clyde said.

Booger's dad and Miss Anderson were standing together. She walked over to Booger and put her hand on his shoulder. "Why don't you ride with us, honey?" she suggested more than asked.

Booger looked toward the rest of gang, who were all watching with envy. "Sure, I'll go," he said.

"Yeah, yeah," Caleb piped up. "Abandon us for a better deal. What are friends for?" Caleb smirked, flashing a grin that said he'd have done the same. "Lucky dog," he said once they'd all piled into the chariot.

"Want us to wait?" Clyde asked Tommy after he'd stopped in front of Melody's house.

"No, that's okay," Tommy replied. "I'll walk home." Tommy still had almost an hour before he had to be home, and he was looking forward to a little porch swing time. He was expecting a catcall from Caleb, but it never came.

Before they pulled away, Everett gave Caleb a look—a frequent form of communication between the two. "Keep your mouth shut." Everett's face was still beet red from his anger having boiled over at the theater. Caleb didn't push it, but, given that he possessed such an animated nature, remaining mute caused him to fidget and squirm more than usual.

Once they'd settle into the porch swing, Melody leaned on Tommy's shoulder and whispered, "I'm worried about Booger." Tommy hadn't come up with anything clever to talk about, but when he did, it wasn't going to be about Booger. But Melody had spoken first.

"Worried about what?" Tommy whispered. Whispering seemed appropriate for a postmovie porch swing moment.

"He doesn't get out as much as you and the other guys. He seems to spend a lot of time at home," she said.

Tommy couldn't tell all that he knew. He wished that he could. A guilt pang settled in when he realized he was wishing Melody would stop talking about Booger.

Eight Track

WHILE WORKING AT BURT'S, CLYDE had managed to acquire a used eight-track and two speakers. His mom had told him he could install the system in the Chrysler once he'd passed the driver's exam. Burt had agreed to let Clyde use the tune-up bay to do the installation. Tommy had watched his uncle Cletus install a stereo in his pickup, so that automatically classified him as an expert in such matters.

Clyde pointed toward the front floorboard and said, "You're smaller. See if you can figure out the best place to mount it." Tommy was about half Clyde's size and fit more easily into tight places.

Tommy was lying on his back looking up at the mess of wires and brackets caked with years of dust. He identified parallel braces that looked sturdy enough to hold the eight-track. "Looks like right under the radio is the best place," he said and then spit out a small particle of something that had fallen into his mouth when he'd spoken. The trick, he thought, would be drilling the holes for the screws without drilling into the radio or any of the many multicolored bundles of unidentified wires hanging under the dash. "Hand me the drill," he told Clyde, exuding confidence which in reality he lacked.

Clyde held a metal screw and a variety of drill bits up to the light, trying to decide which bit was the right size. "Just a minute," he said. He chose what he decided was the right bit, inserted it into the drill, handed it to Tommy, and sat down on the front seat to watch.

While Tommy was drilling the holes and securing the eight-track under the dash, Caleb and Booger walked into the garage.

Caleb jumped into the backseat of the Chrysler, peered over the seat, and then tapped Clyde on the shoulder. "Got a tape?" he asked.

"Where's Everett?" Clyde asked and then reached for a tape laying on the massive Chrysler dash.

"He got into trouble for choking that guy from Fairview," Caleb said and then examined the tape. It was a Beatles tape that looked like it hadn't seen the cardboard protective sleeve since the British invasion.

Half panicked, Tommy said, "I need to get out." He'd stood all he could of lying on his back under the dusty dash. Clyde moved out of the way.

As soon as Tommy and Clyde got out of the front seat, Caleb hopped in and inserted the Beatles *Hey Jude* tape.

"Hell's bells," cried Caleb. "It doesn't work."

Clyde gave him a look. "Don't be cussin' on Sunday."

Tommy used his forearm to wipe the sweat from his forehead and informed the two geniuses of the problem. "It's not hooked up."

Caleb, somewhat indignant, asked, "Whadaya mean, it's not hooked up?" He gripped the eight-track and tried to wiggle it. "It feels hooked up to me."

Booger had been quietly observing. He and his dad had helped Miss Anderson install an eight-track in her GTO. "You gotta hook it up to electrical power, and ground it too," he told a bewildered Clyde and Caleb.

"What kind of trouble is Everett in?" Clyde asked.

"I don't know," replied Caleb. "He just said that he was grounded." Caleb shrugged indifference. "He's probably memorizing more big words."

Meanwhile, Tommy was rummaging around in a shoe box full of parts, the same box that had contained the used eight-track and mounting brackets. "That's what these wires are for," he said, holding up two wires, one red and one black.

While the electrical power epiphany was sinking in on Clyde and Caleb, Tommy began stripping insulation off the wire tips. "You guys can drill some holes to mount the speakers behind the backseat," he told them. He was sure they hadn't stopped to think that the eight-track would need speakers before they could listen to Paul McCartney croon about how money can't buy love and the challenge Lady Madonna faced while feeding her many children. And he was hoping that leaving them to figure out how to mount the speakers would keep them from bugging him while he spliced into a power supply.

Booger winked at Tommy. "I'll help 'em," he said. Tommy nodded thanks before slipping under the dash to begin splicing into the electrical system. He resumed his contorted position, looked up under the dash, studied the mass of wires, and wished he'd paid more attention to how his uncle had wired the eight-track in his pickup. "Red to red, and black attaches to the frame" was about all he remembered. He chose a red wire that looked to be going to the radio and spliced into it. He hooked the black wire to the bracket that held the eight-track.

While Tommy was engineering power to the tape player, Clyde stood holding the speakers, one in each hand, and staring at them, apparently deep in thought. "Where do you think they should go?" he asked.

Tommy wanted to respond but couldn't think of a way to do so without stating the obvious. Booger weighed in. "Well, they should sit on the deck behind the backseat." He paused a few minutes and waited for Clyde to agree. "How about looking in the trunk and seeing if there's one spot better than another?"

Caleb, clearly out of his element, had become unusually quiet, but then Booger's suggestion launched him into action. He jumped into the dusty trunk and, lying on his back, surveyed the bottom of the rear seat deck.

"Well, he—bells," Caleb said and then paused. Of course everyone knew what he'd started to say and didn't. "This thing has holes all over it."

Clyde, excited by the report, said, "Let me see." He tossed the speakers into the backseat and climbed into the giant trunk, forcing Caleb against the fender.

While all eyes focused on Clyde and Caleb sharing the confines of the Chrysler's trunk, Tommy shoved the Beatles tape into the player. The track light illuminated, and he could hear the whirring of the tape player's motor. "Amazing," he murmured to himself, more surprised than he wanted anyone to know.

"They're all nice and round," Clyde said, clearly relieved. "I think they're supposed to be there. And it'll make mounting the speakers easier."

Pleased with himself, Tommy crawled out from under the dash and walked to the rear of the car. Caleb, who'd hopped out before getting smashed by Clyde, was standing next to Booger. They were peering down at Clyde, who was still rooting around in the filthy trunk and studying the underside of the rear deck. "Got any speaker wire?" Tommy asked.

"Speaker wire?" Clyde asked, still lying on his back in the trunk.

"Yes," Tommy replied. "Remember, we have to connect the speakers to the tape player."

"Oh yeah." Clyde nodded. "There's a roll of some kind of wire in that shoe box that the tape player was in." He hopped out and began searching for the wire.

Caleb crawled into the trunk and began drilling holes for the speakers. Tommy motioned for Clyde. "This might be a good time to see if the top works," Tommy said. Sensitive to Clyde's feelings, he was careful to not say "put it down," but simply "see if it works."

Clyde sat behind the wheel deep in thought and glanced at the brackets that secured the top to the windshield. He nodded, but Tommy could tell the decision had been reached after much thought. Clyde reached up and carefully released the bracket on his side; Tommy did the same on the passenger side.

Clyde slowly reached for the small lever with the faded words "Top down/up" next to it. He moved the lever to the down position, but only momentarily, just enough to cause the motor to whir and the top to barely move. When he did, Booger and Caleb leaped from the trunk like a flushed covey of quail.

"What the hell—I mean, I'll be darned," Caleb blurted out.

Clyde still had his finger on the top's control knob when the others stuck their heads inside to see what he was doing.

"Hell's bells." Caleb beamed, again breaking the Sunday code. "Let's put her down!"

"No," Clyde said. His eyes twitched uncharacteristically. "I want to have Burt look at it first." He rubbed one of the many strips of duct tape. "What if the rest of it cracked and split when we put it down?" It was a reasonable concern for which the rest had no argument. He got a sheepish look on his face. "And I need to ask my mom about it." Nobody laughed.

While the boys circled the car and dreamed of the possibilities, Tommy studied the massive dash. Until then he hadn't noticed all of the other buttons; he'd never seen them on other cars. He found the owner's manual in the dash compartment and read about the autopilot knob. Instead of idiot lights, the car had a gauge for everything: amperage, voltage, water temperature, oil pressure. The car was a work of precision.

Realizing that nothing was getting done but gawking, Tommy rallied the band of boys. "Let's get this eight-track installed." He grinned. "Can you imagine how this is going to sound with the top down?" The energy level in the room rose exponentially.

"What about these confounded wires?" Clyde asked.

"Just run 'em down the side of the seat and along the floor, under the front seat, and up to the player," Caleb said.

"Leave the wires exposed?" Clyde asked.

Caleb snickered knowingly; he'd anticipated the question. He pointed at the multiple repair jobs on the canvas top and said, "Duct tape."

While the boys considered Caleb's suggestion, Frank Fritz slipped unseen into the bay. He startled the boys when he asked, "Vere ist Burt?"

The boys turned to see Fritz, a homunculus-sized man, standing in the shadow of the door. Since it was Sunday and the filling station was closed, they hadn't expected anybody to come barging in, let alone someone as strange as Fritz. Fritz was of German descent and wore thick, hazy glasses and a leprechaun-style beard that perfectly matched his diminutive frame.

"I think he and Alison went to Fairview to an art show," Clyde told him. The other boys let Clyde do the talking since he worked at the station and didn't seem intimidated by Fritz. Fritz lived on the edge of town behind a heavily honeysuckled fence. The boys had always considered his home to be more a compound—mysterious and off limits—and Fritz too scary for their curiosity.

Fritz squinted, his already-beady eyes made even more so by the reverse magnification of his glasses. "You haf permission to be here?" he asked.

Clyde morphed into his filling station persona. "Can I help you with something?" He'd dealt with Fritz on a regular basis and had fixed flat tires for him several times.

"Is likely dat you can," Fritz replied with more than a hint of German heritage in his inflection and then stood motionless for a moment. "I neet sum help unloadink a broom machine."

"A what?" Clyde asked.

"Broom machine," Fritz repeated. He then went on to explain that he'd purchased some equipment to make brooms and had it loaded on his truck, and that it would require at least two people and maybe three to lift it off. "I'll pay," he said. "Not much, but I'll pay." With that he had everyone's attention.

"We'll help you," Clyde assured Fritz. "But first we need to finish a job here."

"How long?" Fritz persisted.

"Not sure," Clyde replied and then explained the wire dilemma.

Fritz walked over to the car and pointed at the chrome baseplate strip that ran along under the door that held the floor covering down. "Jus take dat strip up and run the wire unter de floor mat," he said. "Take dose little screws out, and de strip will come up easy enough."

Fritz observed while Tommy removed the front door strip and Booger removed the back. Tommy lifted the floor covering up enough to tuck the wires in and hide them all of the way from front to back. For that he got a wink from Fritz. He then hooked the wires into the player, and the car came alive with Paul McCartney and the Beatles singing "Can't Buy Me Love."

Fritz frowned at the song choice and backed up a couple of steps when Caleb started singing along.

"Give me a few minutes to put the tools away and lock up, and we'll follow you to your place," Clyde said.

"I'll be waiting in de truck," Fritz replied and slowly backed away, all the while keeping a suspicious eye on the tone-deaf Caleb.

About that time Everett walked in. "Thought you were grounded," Flop said.

"I am, or was," Everett answered. "I talked my dad into letting me come help install the eight-track. He convinced my mom that it would be a good experience."

"Here, then," Clyde said. "Help Flop put these back on." He handed Everett the baseplates, screws, and screwdriver. Flop hopped into the front seat, held the carpet in place, and instructed Everett on replacement of the plates.

Once Everett had made his contribution to the project, Clyde backed the car out of the bay and ran back inside to close up. Caleb leaned across the front seat from the back and twisted the volume knob to its stop. "Can't Buy Me Love" was blaring at an eardrum piercing level when Clyde returned. Everett head-motioned toward the backseat, letting Clyde know who'd turned up the volume.

"Paperback Writer" was playing when they pulled into Fritz's ominous-looking driveway. Paul McCartney was belting out, "It's a dirty story about a dirty man, and his clinging wife doesn't understand," when Clyde pulled the tape out.

"Hell's bells!" Caleb cried out in response to the music's abrupt stop. "It was just getting to the good part." He covered his head when Clyde turned around. Clyde shook his head in disgust and got out.

Tommy was more interested in Fritz's compound than Caleb's music protest. "You think he mows and trims all of this himself?" Tommy asked. He looked at the others for a response. All of them were taken aback by the contrast between the outside appearance of the unkempt border fence and the meticulously groomed grounds inside.

Tommy's mind worked overtime. There was no doubt Fritz was odd, and he'd always driven an old army surplus truck and dressed in old and oftentimes tattered clothes. Seeing Fritz's yard caused Tommy's mind to flash images of Fritz from a different perspective. While his beard was pointed and gray, he was always well groomed, his neck and cheeks clean shaven. And his shirts, while old and worn, had always been ironed and tucked in. Tommy then noticed Fritz's boots were worn but well polished.

Fritz pulled back a tarp revealing several pieces of equipment, none of which the boys had ever seen. First, he pulled out a sign that read "*Neue Besen Kehren Gut*" and asked Clyde and Tommy to carefully place it on the porch of his broom shop. Other than the sign, there was only one piece of equipment that required two people, the binding rig. Tommy would learn later that it held the broom while the corn straw was attached to the broomstick and then tightly bound.

Everett held up a bundle of what looked to be a special kind of wheat. "What kind of grain is this?" he asked.

"Broomcorn," Fritz said.

"Doesn't look like corn," Everett replied.

"That's because it's not," Fitz said. "It's broomcorn. It's more like sorghum than corn."

"Interesting," Everett replied.

Several old brooms were mixed in with the equipment. Tommy carried the brooms into the shed where Fritz had asked them to put the equipment. The inside of the shed looked more like a shop or possibly a museum of old tools. One wall held several items, all hanging vertically. Small and large wrenches, a collection of screwdrivers, a variety of hammers—everything hung symmetrically. A collection of handsaws were hanging neatly on another wall.

The boys followed Fritz back to the broom shop where he picked up the sign. "You know what means it?" he asked them. The boys nervously looked at each other and shrugged. Fritz held the sign and looked at it contemplatively and then looked back to the boys. He had an eerie way of making each boy feel as if he were looking directly at them, even when his eyes moved back to the sign. Tommy was suddenly held emotionally captive.

"The meaning depends on the reader," Fritz began. "For me, the words say, 'With new thinking comes new …'" Fritz paused and carefully formed his lips to finish the sentence. "… vision." Fritz had hesitated slightly before saying vision to make sure that he properly made the vee sound. Tommy sensed that he and the boys were witnessing a pivotal moment in Fritz's life. It was no secret that a few years earlier Fritz had inadvertently been mixed up with the Ku Klux Klan and had plea bargained to a lesser sentence that required him to take counseling on dealing with people who aren't white Anglo-Saxon Protestants.

Fritz pulled a well-worn leather billfold from the front pocket of his ironed but threadbare overalls. "I'd like to pay you now."

Simultaneously, as if on cue, the boys took a half step back. "No thanks, Mr. Fritz," Tommy said. Being paid would have cheapened the moment. Tommy sensed that Fritz needed to understand that the boys had helped him out of generosity. Sure, Fritz had offered to pay, but accepting payment would spoil what felt like a rich moment.

Fritz pointed at the Chrysler and asked, "Whose car?"

"Mine, sir," Clyde said, his voice sounding more like Wayne Newton's boy voice than Clyde's baritone pitch.

Fritz held out neatly folded bills. "Here ist five dollars."

"No thank you, sir," Clyde said, his voice almost normal but still nervously strained.

"Please take it," Fritz insisted. "I tink you neet to git a new capsule for the music-making machine." By capsule Fritz was referring to the eight-track tape. "Maybe something by Mozart or Bach," Fritz suggested.

Caleb, probably thinking the standoff was going to last forever, said, "Take the money, Clyde. Get a new tape."

Clyde accepted the money and bowed slightly while doing so. Fritz began vigorously shaking each of their hands and thanking them for their help. He paused when he got to Everett. "You haf an interest in broom making, ya?" he asked.

"Yes, sir," Everett replied, probably not necessarily interested in brooms but wanting to be respectful.

"Would you like to learn how?" Fritz asked.

Everett had no option but to reply affirmatively. "Yes, sir," he repeated.

"I pay by piece, not the hour," Fritz said.

"How many brooms will you be making?" Everett asked.

"As many as the feet store can sell," Fritz replied.

"The feed store will be selling them?" Everett asked.

"Ya, ya," Fritz replied. "But we neet first to make the brooms."

"I work at the feed store," Everett said.

"Not while you're making brooms," Fritz said and grinned. It was the first time any of the boys had seen him smile.

"DADGUM," EVERETT SAID AFTER THEY'D all piled back into the Chrysler.

"I'll say," complained Caleb. "You show up late, don't help with the eight-track, and then get a danged job."

"So," Everett began, "you want to work for Fritz making brooms?" Caleb folded his arms in frustration and fumed all of the way to the Houn-Dawg.

Booger

FOOTBALL PRACTICE HAD JUST FINISHED, and the boys were making their way slowly and painfully toward Clyde's Chrysler. Booger motioned for Tommy to draw near. "I've been working on a new song," he whispered. "I'd like to play it for you." Tommy nodded and then both of them hustled to the Chrysler.

They piled into the cavernous car along with the others. Caleb began his usual content-free ramblings, Booger stared out the window, and Flop, stuffed between Everett and Clyde, took shallow breaths. No matter the temperature, Clyde and Everett, probably because of their size, were always sweating. They'd taken a shower but then put on the same clothes they'd sweated in all day. They were both deep in thought, no doubt contemplating what Coach Heart had told them during his postpractice talk. Flop had chosen the front seat long ago, and there was no getting out of it now. But no matter the stench, he was proud to be sitting next to two football stars.

Coach Heart's career at Colby had gotten off to a slow start. He'd arrived on the scene after earning a degree in kinesiology on a football scholarship and then serving two years in the army, one of them in Vietnam. He was gifted with the ability to play the game, and was full of ideas on physical fitness, but with little coaching experience, he lacked the ability to inspire others.

At first he'd been despised by the boys but had gradually gained their respect, and had taught them to appreciate physical fitness and the value of a balanced regimen, rather than a total focus on weight lifting. He used Flop to introduce the boys to the term hemoglobin and how some are gifted with more of it than others. Flop could run all day long—clearly a person gifted with abundant hemoglobin.

Booger's house was their first stop. "I'll get out here," Tommy said. He followed Booger inside.

After losing his brother to Vietnam and his mother to suicide, Booger had begun seeing a counselor in Fairview. The counselor had diagnosed Booger as suffering from what he termed an existential vacuum, a condition that renders a person feeling worthless or without purpose. As treatment, he'd suggested Booger choose a hobby that required significant concentration. Doing so would fill the void created by the loss of his mother and brother with a specific accomplishment. The counselor, an accomplished guitar player, had pushed Booger in that direction. Counseling sessions eventually became guitar lessons.

Booger had shared the diagnosis with the band of boys and explained the purpose of his piddling with the guitar. At first Booger could only strum a few simple chords, such as the theme song for *Batman* or "Hang on Sloopy," but little else.

Existential was too difficult to pronounce, and only Everett could remember the full meaning. The boys eventually began to refer to Booger's absences as him working on his vacuum. "Is Booger coming?" one would ask. "No," Tommy would reply. "He's working on his vacuum." It wasn't that they needed to know every time Booger was holed up in his room picking away on the guitar. His friends just wondered if he was at home and not coming out at all, or working at Gooche's and possibly available later, or needing a ride home.

Tommy was the only friend for whom Booger would play more than the rudimentary chords. Tommy never asked too many questions, and supported Booger by lending an ear. At first he'd had to feign interest and hold back the yawns while listening to Booger begin a song, mess up, say "no, wait," and then begin again. It had been agonizing, sometimes hearing "no, wait" a hundred times in less than an hour.

Booger eventually mastered the chords. Learning the guitar seemed to have worked; Booger now seldom suffered from depression. His so-called existential vacuum was filled with playing the guitar and the challenge of learning new songs. Tommy followed Booger into the bedroom, where Booger sang and strummed "Yesterday" by the Beatles. Tommy had heard Booger play it before; it was one of the first songs he'd learned to play well.

"Have you played for Miss Anderson yet?" Tommy asked. For months, he'd been trying to convince Booger to play for someone other than himself. As far as Tommy knew, even Booger's dad didn't know how accomplished he'd become.

Before Booger could answer, Tommy asked, "How about I bring Melody over sometime?" Tommy figured that maybe Booger would be more comfortable playing for Melody; they'd mowed her parent's lawn and had been friends with her ever since she'd moved to Colby.

Booger kept strumming chords while he talked. "I don't know."

Tommy decided to try another angle. "Look," he said, "you're good. I think you ought to see if you can play a guitar in the concert band."

"The band doesn't have guitar," Booger replied.

"Why?" Tommy asked.

"I don't know."

"Well, it's because nobody can play a guitar, you goof," Tommy told him.

"We'll see," Booger said. "This is what I wanted to show you." He began to masterfully strum the chords to Mason Williams's "Classical Gas." Watching Booger's fingers bring the guitar to life and knowing why Booger had practiced so hard brought tears to Tommy's eyes. It was one of those moments when one is so mesmerized that involuntary breathing stops. Near the end of the song, Tommy gasped for air, held himself like he had to go, and ran to the bathroom. He dried his eyes, flushed the toilet for effect, and returned.

Booger sat in silence, his eyes looking down at the guitar. He seemed to have amazed himself, and Tommy sensed that Booger was waiting for genuine confirmation. Tommy waited a few moments for his own emotions to further subside; the faux bathroom trip hadn't been enough.

Tommy got control of his trembling chin. "Who knows you can play like this?" he asked.

"Just you," Booger said. "Maybe my dad, but probably not. I usually close the door. He knows I'm taking lessons from the counselor, but he doesn't pry."

"What about Miss Anderson?" Tommy asked.

"No," Booger replied. "I never practice when she's here."

"Listen," Tommy said; it was a warm-up word while he thought of what to say. "I'm gonna bring Melody over and have you play that for her." Tommy waited for a response but got none. "She's constantly asking about you," Tommy continued. "She'd be thrilled to know what you've been spending your time doing. And, it's a beautiful song."

"I don't want to tell anyone just yet," Booger said. He changed the subject with an unrelated but curious question. "You think Coach is right about Everett and Clyde?" he asked.

Tommy gave the question some thought but was more interested in conjuring up a plan to get Booger to play his guitar for Melody, or Miss Anderson, or anybody. He replied the best he could. "I don't know." He sat a moment longer and decided to go along with Booger's effort to change the subject. "They're big," he said, stating the obvious. He paused long enough to chew on the inside of his lip and then continued. "They're fast." He was essentially parroting everything the coach had said.

Clyde and Everett were clearly taller and heavier than anyone on the team. They'd bypassed junior varsity and earned varsity letters as freshman. Even more extraordinary was that only a couple of the skinny little varsity receivers were faster than either of them in the forty. They'd always been big, but God had graced them with speed too. It was a skill that neither had developed through long days at the track but rather one that had been anointed upon them while sleeping or eating a MoonPie. "They've got a future, if they stay out of trouble," Coach had said.

Tommy sensed that Booger's mind was already elsewhere because of his intense expression, which had to have been from something other than Clyde and Everett's athleticism. "Homecoming is coming up," Booger said. Tommy nodded that he knew, but he wasn't sure where Booger was going with it. "You think Sunny would play a duet with me?" Tommy flinched, surprised. The question was unexpected but quenched Tommy's emotional excursion.

Homecoming, a huge event for Colby, was less than six weeks away. Those who'd moved away often returned to visit during the festive weekend. One of the many events held during Homecoming was the music competition. Originally designed as a battle of the bands, it had migrated to smaller acts. The only remaining requirement was that the act had to feature at least two performers. The competition was the main feature on Saturday afternoon and always drew a huge crowd. The town square would be filled with lawn chairs, quilts, and people eating all sorts of deep-fried food.

A few years earlier, Tommy had played a piano duet with Sunny, a girl a year ahead of them in school, at a church recital. The recitals were always a big formal hoodoo with a large crowd, everyone dressed in their Sunday clothes, and even a reception following with dishes that had to be washed. Tommy mentally slipped back to the days he'd spent sitting on the piano bench next to Sunny. He visualized their first and only kiss after a ride on his Honda Mini Trail.

Booger continued, snapping Tommy out of his funk. "I'd play the guitar, and she could play the piano," Booger said.

Tommy's mind reeled. A duet with Sunny? Moments earlier Booger hadn't wanted to tell anyone. Now he was requesting a public performance with the most sought after girl in Colby.

Her real name was Wendy Winchester, but the boys had privately given her the nickname "Sunny." She'd grown into the most striking beauty that Colby had ever produced. *Teen* magazine had discovered Wendy when she was modeling for a ladies store in Fairview. They'd first run a story on her and later put her on the cover when they featured the most beautiful teens of rural America.

During the time of Sunny and Tommy's recital performance, she and Tommy were on the verge of becoming an item. In a rare case of mutual agreement, they'd decided to be friends rather than a couple. Tommy had continued to take piano lessons from Wendy's mother and was the only member of the band of boys with enough nerve to speak directly to her. Any living soul with merely an inkling of male hormone was moved by her beauty.

All of the accolades had caused her to develop a slightly aggrandized attitude. Part of the problem was that others too often yielded to her requests because of both her charm and beauty. She'd been placed by too many on a metaphoric pedestal. It wasn't Wendy's choice. But she'd gradually adapted to the royal treatment and had grown to expect it.

The boys had chosen Sunny as a nickname because the other girls said that she sometimes thought the world revolved around her. One look at her and the boys would agree that the world did in fact revolve around her. Wendy's face brightened the first time Caleb had slipped and called her Sunny to her face. She'd mistakenly accepted the nickname as an endearing description, as if the name implied her to be bright and cheerful, which she mostly was. So, she'd been Sunny since, even to her family.

Tommy nodded confidently. "I'll ask her." Booger's lips pooched slightly, his eyes twitched back and forth, and his head nodded gently in affirmation. After giving it more thought, Tommy continued. "You'll have to first play for Sunny, probably her mother too." Sunny's mother, as the piano teacher, was always in charge of arranging the acts at Homecoming.

Tommy never considered the challenge it would be for Sunny to learn "Classical Gas" on the piano; Booger had not only made it sound beautiful but also easy to play.

Booger's face was set. "Can you call her now?" he asked.

Tommy knew the look; Booger wasn't ambiguous. He sensed that Booger had given the notion considerable thought. Most likely Booger's anticipation of playing a duet with Sunny had driven his passion for mastering "Classical Gas."

Tommy made the call.

While Sunny's phone was ringing, Tommy realized how badly he wanted to tell Melody about Booger. He and Melody had begun to confide their most intimate personal trepidations. Through Tommy, Melody had become acutely in tune with Booger's emotional challenge. She had noticed that Booger was frequently missing when Tommy and the rest of the gang hung out. Tommy had shared many things with Melody about Booger, but, at Booger's request, he'd never told her about the guitar.

Tommy knew Melody would be thrilled to know that Booger wasn't just sitting at home in his room dealing with depression. Booger had found something that provided focus and had perfected it.

Sunny's mom, Mrs. Winchester, answered. Sunny wasn't home, so Tommy explained. "That's wonderful," she said, referring to Booger's guitar playing. "I'll talk to Sunny," she continued and then paused. "She's mentioned Homecoming before, but, other than with you, she's never been interested in playing duets." A sense of privilege momentarily struck Tommy. "I'll have to check out this 'Classical Gas,'" she said. "The music store in Fairview should have the sheet music."

Tommy considered Mrs. Winchester's comment about getting sheet music to be near confirmation that Sunny would agree to the duet. Booger smiled, and his eyes filled with tears when Tommy shared the news with him.

Double Date

Cletus Thornton—Tommy's uncle, or Mr. T to his students—stood outside his science class door and watched kids stream into Miss Anderson's class. He knew too well the look on Tommy's face. He'd seen it time and again. It was the look of a sailor's son watching the ship set sail and being unable to board, the runt of the litter watching as each mate is chosen and carried away, the younger brother watching the school bus pull away, or the youngest in the class watching as his friends, one by one, get their driver's license and ticket to boundary-free adventure.

Uncle Cletus cut Tommy out of the herd of students and pulled him aside. "Penny and I are gonna ride over to the Fairview A&W tonight," he whispered. "Thing of it is," he continued, a line he invariably included in any conversation, "we thought maybe you and Melody would like to ride along."

Tommy's pulse raced. Riding with Uncle Cletus in the pickup was always a treat, especially since he'd installed a Cherry Bomb glasspack muffler; plus, there was the eight-track and a shoe box full of tapes. And since there'd be four of 'em, they'd be smashed together like sardines. Perfect, he thought.

Uncle Cletus read Tommy's mind. "I already spoke to your mother." Tommy grinned. Uncle Cletus smirked and slapped him on the shoulder. "But you're on your own with Melody." The invitation produced the desired results; Tommy's morose face morphed euphoric.

The euphoria erupted into a couple of half-skip steps before Tommy got his happy feet under control. He took his seat next to Melody; class was about to begin. He mustered the courage before leaning over and, stuttering in the process, asked her if she could go.

"You mean like a date?" she whispered and then fluttered her eyelashes. "A double date?"

The phenomena occurred once more. It was happening more and more as of late. His mouth went dry, and his mind went blank. This time another symptom occurred: he found himself staring blankly at his desk with his mouth hanging open. Had there been any saliva, he'd have been drooling.

He hadn't thought of it as a date. He'd never asked Melody, or anyone else for that matter, out on a date. He and Melody always simply agreed to meet at the movie, or sometimes they'd walk together. He wondered if this constituted a real date. He pulled his tongue back into his mouth and was saved by the bell. He'd have all hour to think of a reply.

Melody used her finger to cursively spell yes on her desk. She was smiling and doing a body giggle. Tommy had unwittingly asked her out and she'd accepted. She was ecstatic; Tommy, unsure of what had just occurred, sat dazed.

Miss Anderson wrote MENSURATION in bold letters across the chalkboard. Tommy respectfully called her Miss Anderson at school, but he always thought of her as Bridgett and perpetually did the mental translation. Occasionally he'd slip. Her looks were certainly more in tune with a lady named Bridgett rather than Miss Anderson.

The girls frowned nervously, and the boys smirked questioning smiles. Miss Anderson's class was American History with a special focus on president George Washington. Tommy was curious. He recalled a few years earlier when the girls were shown a film on "personal hygiene" while the boys watched a film produced by the Missouri State Highway patrol showing crash victims who hadn't been wearing seat belts.

She tossed the piece of chalk into the holder and then turned and dusted her hands. "Who can tell me what this word means?" The room fell silent. "Is it something men do?" Tommy looked straight ahead and avoided eye contact with Miss Anderson. "Is it something that women do?" she continued. A few giggle-snorts escaped. Miss Anderson grinned; she knew what she was doing. "Actually," she said, "it's something that either can do." Now she had everyone's attention. She turned, picked up the piece of chalk, and began to write. "Mensuration," she said as she wrote, "is not to be confused with menstruation."

A collective "Ooooh" swept across the class. Tommy glanced at Melody. She'd already looked up mensuration in her little dictionary and had raised her finger-wiggling hand.

"It means to measure," Melody said after being called on.

Miss Anderson concealed very well any sign that she had meant to confuse the class. "That's right," she said. She then went on to explain how President Washington, before becoming president, had explored much of the new world as a surveyor, which at the time required one to have taken courses in what was then known as mensuration. A silent sigh of relief fell upon the class once everyone realized the word didn't involve monthly cycles.

And then came the question Tommy knew she'd ask. "And why?" she continued.

There it is, Tommy thought.

"Why do you suppose George Washington as a young man chose to study mensuration?"

Tommy liked the way she asked the why questions. For example, instead of asking why we *thought* something, she used the word *suppose*. It was a subtle but distinctly different way to ask. Tommy dwelt on "suppose" for a few moments. He'd previously looked up the two words in the dictionary and thought he understood the difference but knew he probably couldn't explain it.

Miss Anderson scanned the class, smiled seductively, and began writing on the board. Her smile sent tingles up Tommy's spine. He was afraid that Melody had noticed. The girls weren't as enamored with Miss Anderson as the boys, and occasionally the girls would be infected with a mild case of jealously over the ebullient GTO- and motorcycle-driving schoolmarm. Tommy avoided looking Melody's way and glanced over at Booger and Everett, the only other members of the band of boys who were in the class. Mr. Franklin, the principal, had had the good sense to keep the boys separated when possible.

Tommy noticed Everett and Booger whispering to each other while Miss Anderson wrote on the board. He wondered what they were talking about—probably something about Everett turning sixteen in a couple of days. Seeing Booger muffle a laugh pleased Tommy. He'd dealt with Booger's fragile emotions and knew that laughter was the best medicine.

And then he began to wonder what would happen when everyone

learned that Booger could play the guitar, and not only play it, but play it masterfully. It dawned on him that the girls would be drawn to the guitar.

The sound of the chalk being tossed back into the tray brought Tommy back to the present. Miss Anderson again turned to face the class and smiled. Since it was September, she still had a dark tan and her blond hair was sun bleached. Tommy could feel his mouth going dry. He swallowed and concentrated on the chalkboard and the quote Miss Anderson had just written. "If you can't find it in Ezekiel, look for it in Israel."

"So, who said this?" she asked. Melody raised her hand, as did nearly every other girl in class.

Dang, Tommy thought. Girls always know the answer. Had he not been so captivated with Miss Anderson, the clear and obvious answer would have been revealed to him as well.

"What's with you boys?" she asked, emphasizing "with." "This is easy." She scanned the class. Tommy knew what was coming next. She was going to call on someone who hadn't raised his hand. She'd picked on Booger the day before. She kept repeating, "Let me see, who should know this?"

Tommy stared at Everett's jaw and ear. His jaw had become elongated, and his ear large and droopy. Looking closer Tommy noticed Everett's nose was looking beaklike. He mentally shivered and realized it was his imagination; there was nothing wrong with Everett except the fact that he would be turning sixteen in a couple of days. He willed Miss Anderson to choose Everett anyway. Good grief, Tommy thought, he's almost sixteen; he should know.

While Miss Anderson was looking at Everett, Melody placed a note on Tommy's lap. He was looking at it when Miss Anderson stopped talking. He looked up from the note; her eyes had stopped on him. "Tommy?"

Tommy's temples throbbed while his mind searched for a name, anything to avoid the dreaded "I don't know" response. The note had the A&W Root Beer logo and a smiley face drawn on it. Tommy's mind was overloaded. He was thinking about the ride to Fairview and scanning the room hoping that somehow the answer would magically appear. His eyes were seeing, but his mind wasn't registering. His mind engaged for a split second when his eyes swept the bulletin board and a large poster of America's first president. He wasn't sure how long it had been since he'd been called on. When stressed, sometimes seconds felt like minutes and vice versa. He battled the paralysis that had gripped his jaw. "George Washington?" he said with an interrogative tone and a slight lisp. The tip of his tongue was cotton-swab dry.

"Very good," she said. Tommy sensed she was being condescending and could feel the girls rolling their eyes. Embarrassed, he glanced at Melody. She was grinning but shaking her head, disgusted but amused.

"It's believed," Miss Anderson began, "that George Washington was impressed with the biblical description of Israel's layout and boundaries, as described in the Bible in the books of Joshua and Ezekiel." She began writing again. "The Supreme Court, in their infinite wisdom, won't allow me to read these passages, but you might find them interesting." She wrote Joshua 13–21 and Ezekiel 40–48 on the board. "These chapters describe Israel and are thought to be the key passages that inspired Washington's passion for mensuration, which is believed to be the impetus for his structured persona."

Miss Anderson was careful to merely suggest the chapters and not assign them for reading. For while she could legally ask the class to read from any number of smut-filled periodicals, since the New York Supreme Court case of *Engle v. Hyde*, the law forbade her from asking students to read from the Bible.

Miss Anderson placed handouts on the first desk in each row. Each person took one and handed them back. While the girls read theirs, the boys sniffed the mimeograph chemicals. Booger carefully folded his into a paper airplane; Tommy followed suit.

"Okay," Miss Anderson said, "these are George Washington quotes. Take 'em home; we'll discuss tomorrow."

Miss Anderson gave Tommy a disapproving look; Tommy unfolded the airplane and feigned studying the handout. One blue mimeographed line stood out; it read, "My mother was the most beautiful woman I ever saw. All I am I owe to my mother. I attribute all my success in life to the moral, intellectual, and physical education I received from her." Tommy worried how Booger would react to the quote and wished Miss Anderson had chosen a different one.

The bell rang. Miss Anderson whacked Tommy on the back of the thigh with her yardstick when he passed her desk. It didn't hurt, but he yelped and faked a limp until through the doorway.

MELODY WAS WAITING FOR HIM when he popped through the door. "What's wrong with your leg?" she asked, genuinely concerned.

"Oh nothing," Tommy said. "It gets stiff when I sit for a while." He knew better than to say Miss Anderson had whacked him with a yardstick. All of the girls were already convinced their history teacher favored the boys. The boys knew it too but considered it a small token toward balancing all the favoritism that all the other teachers since kindergarten had shown toward the girls.

He started to move on down the hall; Melody blocked his path and gave him an effervescent smile. Tommy was anxious to get to seventh-hour PE and get a good locker, but Melody's expression weakened his knees and blanked his brain. "A&W?" she asked.

Tommy looked past Melody for a split second and made visual contact with his uncle Cletus, who was standing in the doorway to his classroom. Tommy got a wink and a thumbs-up. Dry mouth ensued. "Think you can go?" he asked.

"I'll have to ask," she said. "I've never gone on a date." The sound of the word made Tommy dizzy.

Caleb passed by and punched him in the shoulder. "Don't be late to practice." Caleb turned and, walking backward down the hall, continued, "I got the scoop on the train schedule."

Melody frowned. "Train schedule?"

Tommy started down the hall toward the football field. "I better get to practice; last one always has to put the equipment away in that spider-infested shed."

Melody grabbed his elbow. "What time?"

Tommy hadn't thought of a time. They were still within earshot of Tommy's uncle Cletus, who said, "We'll drop by around 6:30." Tommy turned and hustled out the door, partly to get to practice but mostly so he wouldn't have to answer any more date questions.

CLETUS THORNTON, TOMMY'S MOTHER'S BROTHER, had stopped by frequently when Tommy was younger. He had been single at the time and in search of a good home-cooked meal. During the visits he and Tommy had become close. A few years earlier Cletus had married his childhood sweetheart, Penny Lane, who happened to be Booger's aunt and a sister to Booger's deceased mother. So, Tommy and Booger were not only best friends but also related by marriage.

Tommy was shoveling down dinner when he heard the glasspacked pickup roll into the driveway. Uncle Cletus and Aunt Penny, being family, didn't knock and came on in. Uncle Cletus surveyed what was left of dinner. "Uhmm, that looks good," he said and then got a plate from the shelf and started dishing up.

Penny had already begun a conversation with Tommy's mom when Cletus started piling food onto his plate. "You just ate," she protested.

By then Cletus already had his mouth full of mashed potatoes. "Habit," he said.

"You're gonna make them think I can't cook," she continued.

Cletus patted his ample belly, which had grown during their two years of marriage. "Here's proof that you're a good cook, honey," he assured her.

Penny nodded agreement. "And proof you don't need any more to eat."

Tommy's dad looked up from behind the afternoon paper. "Guess the honeymoon's over." He'd said it several times in the past year.

Penny poked Cletus's belly. "Never," she said. Tommy's mom grinned; his dad chuckled to himself.

Tommy's mom put her hand on her brother's shoulder. "Melody's mom called and had a few questions about this so-called date." She smiled. "It seems it's a first for both of them."

Tommy didn't like the direction the conversation was going. "It's not a date," he said and looked at his uncle Cletus for support but got none.

Cletus grinned. "I think it is."

Tommy's mom wiped her hands on a dishtowel and tousled Tommy's hair. "You better be going. She's expecting you."

Tommy vigorously brushed his teeth and was on his way out the door when his mom added, "I think her dad wants a word with you before you go."

Tommy climbed into the pickup and started sorting through the shoe box full of tapes. "What do you think her dad wants?" he asked no one in particular.

Uncle Cletus wasn't any help. "I don't know; I never had a daughter."

Aunt Penny was worse. "He'll probably threaten you," she said only half jokingly.

Tommy looked at the two of them. "What did Aunt Penny's dad say when you asked her out?"

Cletus belly laughed. "He was thrilled … glad she'd finally found a good man." He was referencing the fact that Cletus was Penny's second husband. She and Cletus had been an item in high school before Cletus had been drafted and left Colby to fight in Korea. Penny had married a man from Fairview, but the marriage had failed. Tommy knew that his uncle Cletus and Penny had dated in high school; he'd heard the ladies at Colby Curls talking about it during his tenure as Colby's paperboy.

"No," Tommy said. "I'm talking about when you were in high school."

It was Penny's turn to belly laugh. "He threatened to kill him."

Tommy flinched, wide eyed. "Really?" he asked.

Tommy watched Penny's face morph contemplative. "Well, I don't think he would have used it, but on our first date my dad met your uncle at the door with a shotgun."

They pulled into Melody's drive. Melody was sitting on the steps; her mom and dad were in the porch swing. Tommy didn't see any weapons. So far so good, he thought while getting out of the pickup. Knowledge of Uncle Cletus's first-date experience caused his stomach to churn. On the way to the front porch, he regurgitated some of the fried baloney he'd wolfed down.

The low sun made Melody's hair cast a soft auburn glow. She was wearing sandals, and he could see that her second toe was still longer than her big toe. Tommy had noticed the anomaly several years earlier while mowing her lawn, when she'd frequently supplied him with lemonade. He'd always finished her lawn hot, sweaty, more than sufficiently hydrated, and with an extended bladder.

Mr. and Mrs. Hinkebein stood. Oh boy, Tommy thought, everybody's making a big deal of this. Melody and her mom and dad walked down the steps together. It was as if they were giving her hand in marriage. "Good grief," Tommy said to himself. "We're only going for a root beer float." He regurgitated again; this time it tasted more like green beans. He wished he had some Clove chewing gum.

Mr. Hinkebein did most of the talking, and Mrs. Hinkebein chimed in a couple of times, but Tommy wasn't sure what they'd said. He tried to look them in the eyes as he'd been taught, but he couldn't keep from looking down at Melody's toes. Once he'd been at Hinkebein's Dry Goods when a shoe salesman had stopped by, and Tommy overheard the salesman bragging about having had training on feet and the proper fit.

Tommy had waited until Mr. Hinkebein returned to the front of the store to check out a customer and then had asked the self-proclaimed expert about the long second toe deal; he was careful not to mention any names. The guy had sounded like an authority and explained that the phenomena was most commonly known as Morton's toe, named so after the doctor who identified it as a congenital defect. Tommy, mentally hung up on the word congenital—thinking it akin to genital—hadn't heard the details that followed. But he did remember the salesmen telling how some had thought the long toe a sign of evolution and had called it a grasping toe. Mr. Hinkebein had returned with a couple of boxes of high-heeled zip-up Nancy Sinatra boots just as the salesman had begun to explain that the Greeks had considered the long toe a sign of royalty. And that was Tommy's takeaway.

Lost in big toe thought, and having not listened closely to the father-to-boy-dating-daughter talk, Tommy sensed Melody's mom and dad were waiting for a response. He replied with the most impressionable and still lingering toe-study thought. "I'll treat her like she's royalty," he said. Mr. and Mrs. Hinkebein beamed. Melody took his hand. With her queenly touch, Tommy's stomach miraculously settled.

Tommy and Melody were too self-absorbed on their way to the truck to notice the wordless exchange that occurred between Uncle Cletus and Melody's dad, who'd gone to high school together. Both had served in Korea and possessed an undying mutual respect.

The shoe box full of tapes hadn't yielded the music selection Tommy had expected. He sorted through Boots Randolph's *Yakety Sax!*, first and second edition, *The Best of Dean Martin*, Elvis Presley's *Blue Hawaii* soundtrack, the Everly Brothers, and Patsy Cline. He was looking for the Turtles, the Guess Who, or Rolling Stones. He chose the last tape out of the box, Johnny Rivers. Tommy carefully inserted the tape into the player, and Johnny Rivers began crooning "Summer Rain" with his unique Louisiana inflection.

Penny sang along to the song even though the lyrics were clearly for a man to sing about a girl. "Baby I Need Your Lovin'" played next, and singing wasn't enough. Penny began swaying back and forth. The close quarters left no choice for Tommy, Melody, and Cletus. The movement made its way to the steering wheel, and the truck began to swerve slightly to the music. The song's melody and suggestive lyrics combined with the close quarters of the truck aroused in Tommy a pleasant sensation. An ear-to-ear grin threatened to split his face in half.

The new highway patrolman didn't find it amusing. They'd just crossed the last of the Seven Sisters when the flashing lights closed on them. "Do you know why I stopped you, Mr. Thornton?" Tootie asked.

"No, sir," Cletus replied. Tommy would learn that the first question asked was always the same and to answer just as his uncle had. To do otherwise might be to admit something the trooper hadn't realized you were doing and get you a ticket for something he hadn't originally intended.

While looking at Cletus's driver's license, he said, "You were swerving, sir."

"I may need to have my alignment checked," Cletus responded.

The trooper looked up, leaned slightly so that he could see all four faces, and replied, "Or ask your passengers to sit still." He grinned. "Your call, sir." He handed Cletus his license. "Keep it between the lines and have a good evening, Mr. Thornton."

Penny suppressed a giggle until the trooper pulled away and then exploded into violent laughter. "Well, Mr. Thornton," she said, "I think that's the first time you've been stopped."

"Yes, Mrs. Thornton, it was," he replied. "And you'll notice that I didn't get a ticket." Penny frowned; she'd collected several tickets in her driving career and at one point had nearly lost her license.

Back on the road, Penny reached down and pushed the tape in. "The Poor Side of Town" began to play. Johnny Rivers's rich, melodious voice again flowed from the speakers, "Doot-doo-doo-wah, shoobie doobie." Penny sang along but kept her body movements mostly under control. Her singing became contagious, and eventually everyone was at least moving their lips to the lyrics, even if only slight sounds were being emitted.

Just before reaching the Fairview city limits, Penny pulled the tape. "There's a speed trap just ahead," she warned. Cletus chuckled and was rewarded with an elbow to his ribs.

Curious, Tommy asked, "What's a speed trap?"

Cletus answered, "Well, essentially, it's an area that's heavily patrolled,

Why

and people exceeding the speed limit are given tickets." Penny frowned and feigned a pout.

"Why do they call it a trap?" Melody asked.

"Because," Penny replied emphatically, recovering from her pout bout, "they'll give you a ticket even if you're only going ten or fifteen miles per hour over the speed limit." Tommy didn't understand the logic and was pretty sure Melody didn't either, but neither asked for further explanation. He exchanged a side-eyed glance and grin with Uncle Cletus.

A sky blue '64 Malibu on display in the used car section at the Fairview Chevrolet caught Tommy's eye. "Let's pull in and take a look at that Malibu," he said. Cletus downshifted from third into second causing the engine to rumble powerfully while slowing the truck.

After parking, Tommy and Cletus headed straight for the Malibu. Penny was more fascinated with the landscaping and headed that direction with Melody following.

"Not bad," Cletus said after he and Tommy had done the requisite circling-and-kicking-the-tires inspection. Cletus knuckle tapped the car's side in several places. After repeatedly hearing the sound of sheet metal rather than body putty, he said, "Doesn't seem to have had any bodywork."

Penny began naming the variety of plants that adorned the front of the dealership. Next year's models would be revealed in a few days, and the dealership had recently received a landscaping facelift in anticipation of the curious new-model-year car crowd. Melody nodded politely in response to each of Penny's oohs and aahs but kept looking back over her shoulder at the blue convertible Malibu.

"Think it would be okay to pop the hood?" Tommy asked Uncle Cletus. Cletus shrugged indifference. Up came the hood. "Looks like a 283," Tommy said.

"White leather," Cletus said. "That would be hard to keep clean." Tommy wasn't dissuaded.

"Automatic," Tommy said.

"Bucket seats," Cletus added. The two of them continued to verbalize in single and double word bursts. Penny was describing the flowers, but Melody was paying more attention to Tommy and Cletus discussing the car. Tommy closed the hood and lamented his age.

The girls were finished inspecting the flora and standing next to the pickup. "Ready?" Penny asked. It was more of a verbal nudge than a question. Cletus and Tommy backed toward the pickup but, seemingly deep in concentration, kept their eyes on the Malibu.

Penny elbowed Cletus and then said to Melody, "You're turning sixteen soon. You should get your dad to buy that car for you." She'd meant to tease, but the comment struck mixed chords for Tommy. It was a reminder to him that she'd be getting her license much sooner than him, but the thought of Melody having a nice car was pleasing.

When the A&W sign with the brown oval logo was in sight, Tommy's mouth began to water. The conditional reflex evoked memories of learning about Pavlov's dog. Tommy giggled when the thought occurred to him that had the animal rights people been around during Ivan Pavlov's time they probably would have had him shot.

"What are you chuckling about?" Penny asked. She had no doubt that Tommy was imagining cruising Colby with Melody in her Malibu.

"Nothing," Tommy replied with little more on his mind than the taste of an A&W Root Beer in a frozen mug.

She sighed. "You're just like your uncle."

They pulled into an open slot and began studying the pedestal-mounted menu even though they'd discussed what they were going to order on the way and had already made up their minds.

Penny leaned across Cletus's lap so she could see the menu display. "Let me see."

"Thought you were having a small cone and a root beer," Cletus said.

"I changed my mind." She leaned back. "Okay?" she replied with a sassy tone.

Cletus put his finger on the intercom button. "Everybody know what they want?"

A voice from the scratchy speaker asked, "How can I help you?"

He looked first at Tommy. Tommy said what he wanted, and Cletus repeated it into the speaker. Then Cletus did the same for Melody and Penny. "I'll have a cone and root beer," Penny said.

"I thought you changed your mind," he said.

"I did," she replied, smiled, and then said, "I changed it back."

A horn honked from across the center aisle; it was Sunny and her mother. Everyone piled out of both vehicles and met on the center aisle. Since they were out-of-towners, they got stares from the other, local drive-in customers.

"Guess they're surprised to see that we have teeth," Cletus said. Fairview was much larger than Colby, and Fairview students generally made fun of Colby's rural culture.

"Shopping?" Penny asked Sunny.

"Just picking up a few things," Sunny replied. Her wink at Tommy didn't go unnoticed by Melody.

"Hi, Melody," Sunny's mom said and then patted Tommy on the shoulder. Their recent phone conversation was to remain confidential. "How are you doing, Tommy?" she asked. "Since you no longer take lessons, I never see you." Nobody noticed Melody rolling her eyes.

"I'm fine, Mrs. Winchester," Tommy said. "Thanks for asking."

Sunny was holding a thin song booklet. Penny was curious. "Did you get some new sheet music?" she asked.

"Yes, ma'am," Sunny said. "It's 'Classical Gas' for the piano." She held it up for Penny to see. "Mom's going to help me learn it." Melody let go an audible exhale.

"It's a very difficult piece," Mrs. Winchester added and then lowered her chin and glanced at Tommy.

Sunny and Melody made split-second eye contact—long enough for a rhetorical rattling of the sabers. Had they been felines, their claws would have been fully extended.

"There's our order," Cletus announced. Tommy started digging in his pocket for money.

Penny noticed. "Our treat," she said.

Tommy had learned to graciously accept when adults offered to buy. It was kind of them to do so, they could usually more easily afford it, and all they usually wanted was acknowledgment of appreciation. And it was money saved that he could put toward a car. He bowed slightly, an exaggerated gesture and an attempt at humor. "Well, thank you very much." Everyone giggled except Melody.

The sun had disappeared below the horizon, but shades of red and orange reflected off a sky divinely decorated with a perfect balance of wispy and mare's tail clouds. The setting sun meant that the signal from WLS, the Rock of Chicago, would now reach southern Missouri—890 on the AM dial. Several cars were tuned in. Just like the Houn-Dawg in Colby, patrons at the Fairview A&W tuned their radios to WLS and cranked up the volume. "Green-Eyed Lady" by Sugarloaf was playing. Fairview wasn't so different; it just had more people.

Penny gently hip-checked Melody. "This song's for you," she said and then invaded Melody's personal space by dancing giddily, almost touching Melody's nose with hers and staring into her green eyes. Melody forced a smile.

Cletus got her attention by saying, "That cone is starting to melt." She shot him a look and then began licking the ice cream that was already dripping down the sides of the cone. Cletus leaned toward Melody and grinned. "Let me see those green eyes."

It was too late, but Tommy finally sensed that Sunny's presence had put Melody on edge. He put his arm around her waist. She gave him a "stuff it" glance but then smiled warmly at Cletus and Penny; she was enjoying the attention from them. Tommy had been fretting over whether he should try to kiss her good night after walking her to her door. He stopped worrying about the kiss maneuver, sensing it was probably out of the realm of possibilities.

The Mustang pulled up and parked next to the Winchesters' car. The driver stuck his head out and said, "Hey, there's Miss Teen Magazine." His head was hanging out the window and his face sporting a cocky, toothy smile. "Have you met me before?" he shouted, now slouched and leaning back in his shiny car. Sunny ignored him.

"Maybe we should go," Mrs. Winchester suggested.

Cletus gave the Mustang driver a no-nonsense look and said to Mrs. Winchester, "Leave when you're ready. That guy's not going to be a problem."

"We were about to leave when you pulled up," she said and then looked at Sunny. "Let's go."

"You haven't seen the last of me," the Mustang driver said when Sunny passed by his window. The other boys in the Mustang laughed at his words.

Penny tugged on Cletus's elbow. "Let's go, Clete," she said. "Remember, you're a high school science teacher, not a marine." She pointed at the Mustang. "And he's not the enemy, just a pip-squeak."

Tommy was always proud to be seen with his uncle Cletus, but more so now than ever—his uncle the warrior versus the pip-squeak Mustang driver. But they were easily outnumbered and behind enemy lines, so to speak. Colby and backup—specifically Everett and Clyde—were miles away.

When Cletus turned and headed for the truck, the pip-squeak yelled, "Yeah, you better go back to Colby before they close the gate and roll up the streets."

Cletus turned. Penny blocked his way and pointed at the truck. "Get in that truck." His jaw muscles flexed, but he complied. When he turned toward the truck, Penny walked over to the Mustang. Tommy couldn't hear what she told them, but the cackling from the Mustang seemed to focus on the driver, who'd gone mute.

Cletus was steaming. Melody was distracted somewhat from the brush with Sunny, but a slight edge remained. "What did you say?" Tommy asked Penny.

"Nothing," Penny said.

"You said something," Tommy persisted.

They were a few blocks from the A&W when Cletus broke the silence that had fallen upon the four. "Tell us," he said. "What did you tell those boys?"

"Well," she began, "think about what I do."

"You're a nurse," Cletus replied.

"Yes, and why was I late coming home two days last week?" she asked.

"Fairview football physicals," he replied.

"Exactly," she said. She was leading them on and knew it.

Exasperated, Cletus almost screamed, "What?"

"I recognized those boys, and once I got near the car, they recognized me as the assisting nurse they'd hoped to never see again. I told the driver that I'd share his tiny secret with the world if I heard one more itsy-bitsy peep out of him."

The pickup erupted in laughter. Melody first held her hands to her face as she laughed and then sent violent shock waves through Tommy's body by putting her right hand on his knee. He corrected his slouch, tightened his stomach muscles, and looked at his nose in the side-view mirror to make sure he didn't have a flapper—it had happened before.

"There's Melody's Malibu," Penny said when they passed the Chevy dealer. Melody stretched to see, giggled, and leaned into Tommy's side.

Realizing the good-night kiss was once again a possibility, Tommy began working out the strategy for the maneuver.

The next morning Tommy waited impatiently but quietly for his sister Marsha to finish in the bathroom. He knew that if he let her know he was waiting it would only result in extending the face painting, which is how he referred to her daily application of base, mascara, and eyeliner. "How was your first date?" Marsha asked when she emerged from the steamy bathroom.

Tommy rubbed his eyes. "It wasn't a date."

"Ha," Marsha said. "That's not what I heard." Tommy rolled his eyes, dreading breakfast, where he'd have to endure more questions and listen to Marsha share the latest cheerleading practice revelation.

Tommy took a bite of toast. His mom turned and spooned some scrambled eggs onto his plate. "What's up with you and Mrs. Winchester?" she asked. Tommy chewed and shrugged. "She called last night but said she couldn't say why she needed to speak to you."

"Something about Sunny?" Marsha asked.

Tommy gave her a look. "Why don't you go read a letter from Mickey," he told her. Marsha's boyfriend, Mickey, had joined the navy. Mr. Franklin, the high school principal and a former SEAL, had talked Mickey into going navy instead of waiting to be drafted by the army. Marsha let go a huff that caused her bangs to fly and began examining her fingernails.

Tommy's mom shook her head in amused disgust. "Well, she needs to speak to you."

"I'll stop by after football practice," Tommy replied.

"Better not let Melody see you there," Marsha chided.

Funny Face

CLYDE'S PINK CHRYSLER CAME INTO view with Everett riding shotgun. Tommy walked to the curb. Since Everett lived near Clyde, he always got picked up first and claimed shotgun. However, he probably would have done so no matter the order of getting picked up. He'd be driving soon, and if he got his own car, the pecking order for shotgun would be debated daily.

"Hey," Everett said—his way of saying hello—when Tommy hopped into the backseat. Tommy didn't mind sitting in the backseat alone where there was more room. The others considered it a quirk for which he was regularly made fun of.

Clyde pushed the D button, gripped the wheel at ten and two, and pulled away. He made eye contact through the rearview mirror. "How'd it go?" he asked.

"Okay," Tommy replied, downplaying the evening. "We looked at a nice Malibu parked on the lot at Fairview Chevrolet," he told them and then described the car in great detail.

He paused for a few minutes and then remembered another detail. "Oh, and we got stopped by Tootie." Everett and Clyde perked up and listened closely while Tommy explained.

"I don't think I'd mess with Mr. T if I was Tootie," Everett said.

"I wouldn't mess with him period," added Clyde. Tommy swelled with pride hearing of Clyde and Everett's respect for his uncle Cletus.

"The Mustang boys sure didn't want anything to do with him," Tommy added.

"How's that?" Clyde asked.

"They were at the A&W and were giving Sunny a hard time," Tommy replied.

Clyde frowned at Everett. "You mean Melody?" he asked.

"No, he means Sunny," Everett answered for Tommy. "I saw her too."

"Saw who?" Tommy asked.

"My dad and I drove by the A&W while you were there and saw all of you standing on the center aisle," Everett said.

"What the heck were you doing in Fairview?" Clyde asked. Tommy was wondering the same thing.

"Looking at cars," Everett replied. "My dad saw a car with a For Sale sign and a phone number and wanted to look at it."

"A car for you?" Tommy asked.

"I think he likes the car but is using me as an excuse to buy it," Everett said.

"What kind of car?" Tommy asked.

"An import," Everett replied. The word "import" took the car conversation to a new level.

"An import?" Clyde asked incredulously.

"British, the same company that makes Austins and MGs," Everett said. "I'll tell you about it later." He turned to Tommy. "Let's hear about Mr. T. first."

Tommy was more interested in hearing about the British import but continued with his first-date tale. "Sunny was there with her mom," Tommy explained.

"So what happened?" Clyde asked, somewhat exasperated. "Everett's not going to tell us about the car until you tell us what happened with Mr. T." Tommy told them everything. Clyde and Everett exploded into laughter when he told them of his aunt Penny's role in the escapade.

Caleb was waiting at the curb. He knew that if he wasn't ready Clyde wouldn't wait for him. Caleb always wanted to ride up front, even if it meant sitting wedged between Clyde and Everett. That was about to change.

Just before the Chrysler reached an unsuspecting Caleb, Everett turned to Tommy. "Mind if he sits in back with you?" he asked, still laughing. "He's such a flibbertigibbet."

Clyde, still chuckling, gave Everett a corner-of-the-eye glance. "Been reading the dictionary again?"

"Yeah," Everett deadpanned.

Tommy was processing the long word—he assumed it meant fidgety or something close—when they stopped for Caleb.

A week earlier Clyde had gotten his hands on a new eight-track tape, Donna Fargo's *Funny Face*. Caleb had made it clear that he didn't like Donna Fargo and despised the song "Funny Face." So naturally, Clyde had the tape set to play "Funny Face." He removed his hand from the wheel long enough the push in the tape. "This will drive him nuts." Clyde snickered.

"You're in the back," Everett told Caleb. Clyde was still grinning. His vocabulary was expanding simply by spending so much time with his large friend, the collector of long and seldom used words, the behemoth wordsmith.

Caleb was anything but paranoid. Any normal fifteen-year-old would have wanted to know what the others had found amusing after hopping into a car of guys who were already laughing. "What's so funny?" is what the normal person would immediately ask. Not Caleb. He was too much into himself.

"Funny Face, I love you. Funny Face, I need you," Donna Fargo began.

"Not the funny face tape," Caleb moaned. "Dang! Do we have to listen to that twangy voice saying how much she loves some country bumpkin with a funny face?" he protested.

Clyde didn't particularly care for the song either but found great pleasure in forcing Caleb to listen. "I kind of like her," he lied.

Caleb tried not to let Donna Fargo distract him. "Here's the deal on the train," he said getting settled in the backseat and covering the speaker on his side with a towel from his gym bag. It was the first time all of them had been together since he'd found out some extraordinary information, according to him, about the train.

"Why don't you hold it until we pick up Booger and Flop," Everett suggested. Tommy knew what Everett was thinking. Caleb's plans were always tedious; he didn't want to listen to him repeat it over and over.

"What about the import?" Tommy asked, getting back to Everett's news.

"Everett's getting an import," Clyde exaggerated. "And he was just getting ready to tell us about it." Making Caleb wait to tell a story frustrated him. And leading him to believe that someone else had a more interesting story was both cruel and entertaining.

Tommy noticed that Caleb first rubbed the back of his neck, then shifted from cheek to cheek like he had hemorrhoids, and finally began scratching his ankles as if dealing with chiggers. Caleb had a certain odor about him. His hygiene had always been suspect. Well, it wasn't suspect; it was clearly subpar. During football he was forced to take a daily shower, at least during the week. But it appeared he still brushed his teeth only on special occasions, possibly his birthday or just prior to dental appointments, if he went to the dentist. And his mother, a recovering hippie, was always feeding him volunteer onions and garlic that she picked from the yard or field behind their house. She claimed the natural plants were good for the body and soul. It clearly didn't do anything for the breath, Tommy knew.

Tommy glanced at Caleb and thought of something his uncle Cletus had once said, "A twig grows as it's bent." Caleb's mother still dressed like those shown on the news protesting any number of things—the war, voting age, civil rights. At least she'd begun wearing a bra and braiding her thick, kinky hair instead of leaving it all windblown and looking like an abandoned bird's nest. He was Caleb though, a full-fledged member of the band of boys and, best of all, the originator of the potato gun.

After picking up Booger, who usually had very little to say in the mornings, Clyde stopped for Flop. Everett got out and let Flop in the middle.

Caleb finally realized that he'd been demoted to the rear. "What's up with Flop riding up front?" he asked.

"Change up," Everett said without looking back. Clyde was too focused on driving to participate in the prattle. He and Everett had no doubt discussed the change. Both of them had probably decided that the backseat should share in Caleb's aura and ebullience. Everett calmly turned, looked at Caleb, and simply said, "Train." There's something about large people being able to be completely understood with one or two words.

It was Tommy's turn to be frustrated. He wanted to hear more about Everett's import.

"Thing of it is," Caleb began and then explained the train's schedule. And nobody paid particular attention until he said, "So, we can put this thing on the tracks on a Friday or Saturday night and ride to the tunnel." All heads turned his way. Even Clyde momentarily took his eyes off the road and looked at Caleb through the rearview mirror. "Can you imagine how the eight-track will sound when we're sitting in the middle of the tunnel?" he asked, using all of the drama he could muster. "But not 'Funny Face,'" he quickly added. His complaining would only increase the frequency of "Funny Face" being played.

Caleb had a way of introducing intrigue to the most ridiculous ideas. Tommy watched the faces of the others and noticed the usual transformation. By the time they reached the school and Clyde had pushed P for park, the boys had shifted from absolute dismissal of Caleb's idea to rapt curiosity, and Everett's import had been momentarily forgotten.

The train tracks that ran through Colby and several other small hamlets nestled in the Craggy Creek Valley were known as the Colby Spur because Colby was the largest town on the spur. The tracks followed the course of the creek except along the Craggy Creek Bluffs, where it entered a nine-hundred-foot tunnel.

Legend had it that the hole through the hill had been blasted out by using discarded Civil War cannons. A plaque near the tunnel made no mention of the Civil War cannons but said that the last spike in the spur had been driven in the middle of the tunnel at midnight on August 14, 1869.

The tracks dead-ended at Grissom, a small logging community a few miles beyond the tunnel. Grissom was famous for the railroad turntable and little else. Grissom was so small that the post office was housed in the general store, Grissom Grocery, which was also the filling station and the only commercial building in town. Grissom Grocery, a tie yard the size of a football field, and the famous turntable were all there was to Grissom. Well, there were people, but nobody actually lived in Grissom. Grissom was unique in that it had a population of zero.

The fourth grade field trip traditionally went to Grissom, and students had to ride the school bus down a curvy boulder-riddled gravel road. When Tommy's class had gone, a couple of the girls had puked and the boys had eventually all been moved to the front of the bus where Barbara, the orneriest, most estrogen-starved woman bus driver known to man, could more easily intimidate them with the evil eye.

The turntable looked identical to those included in model train sets except life size and rusty. The train's engine would disconnect from the train, pull onto the turntable, and get spun a half turn. The spin took several minutes to complete, and even though the mechanism was caked with grease, the screeching of metal on metal was evidence that a few spots got missed.

And then there was the sidetrack, a little thing that was rarely mentioned when discussing the famous Grissom turntable. The sidetrack would allow the reversed engine to travel along the side of the track to the opposite end of the train of cars. Sometimes, when the train was longer than the Grissom sidetrack, the engine would simply push from the rear. Only those who had been on the fourth grade field trip could explain why the train sometimes returned from Grissom with the engine in the rear.

Because of the blind spot caused by the tunnel, the engineers—also known as the throttle-jerkers—would use an extra precaution to signal that the train had returned and the track beyond that point had been vacated. Information about the signaling device was not included in anything available to the general public. As a result, Caleb hadn't discovered an important item in his Colby Spur schedule research—how the engineers signaled which side of the tunnel the train has last passed. In time, the gang would all learn this together.

While Tommy walked through the parking lot toward the school, the lyrics to "Funny Face" were stuck on repeat inside his head. Thinking about Melody and the Malibu didn't help. He imagined actually carrying out Caleb's far-fetched notion of riding Clyde's Chrysler on the tracks through the tunnel. Nothing helped. "Funny face, I love you" kept playing over and over in his mind. He began to share Caleb's ill feeling toward the song's brain-clinging lyrics.

Just before Clyde and Everett got out of earshot, Tommy heard Clyde say to Everett, "Flibbertigibbet … good one."

That got Donna Fargo's voice out of Tommy's mind. But another problem pressed even more; Tommy raced to the school library counter and the giant, rarely used Webster's dictionary and searched for Everett's latest word. The dictionary had an odor unlike any other book; it was without a doubt the oldest book in the library—and maybe even the country for that matter. It took a couple of tries at spelling before turning to the right page.

Tommy looked around to see if anyone had noticed him voraciously searching the only book on the counter with its own spinning pedestal; nobody had. He read what part of the definition he could, closed the book, and nonchalantly headed toward his locker. Clearly Everett had gotten his latest word from that very dictionary because handwritten over the definition was "Caleb."

Just before the bell rang, Tommy realized that Everett had never finished telling about the British import.

LATER THAT MORNING TOMMY EXPERIENCED an epiphany that triggered an emotional high. During the hormone-enriched mental excursion, he came to grips with the fact that he and Melody had in fact gone out on a date. And he began to like the idea that he and Melody were now dating. He couldn't put his finger on it, but something was different. He didn't dwell on what it was; he relished the feeling of liberty that the slight nuance provided. Dating had a certain ring to it that seemed to imply driving. His high wouldn't last throughout the day.

The Codgers had migrated from the sentinel courthouse bench and were stationed under the sycamore tree waiting for football practice to begin They customarily found something good to say about each player. The old men were as much a part of practices as the tackling dummies, and on some days the only source of positive encouragement.

The path from the locker room to the practice field passed near where the Codgers sat, which is one reason they chose to sit there. When Clyde and Everett, also known as "the Bookends" among the local football erudite, emerged from the locker room, Rabbit motioned them over.

Rabbit had been all-state while in high school. The Bookends knew that, but in what century it had occurred they weren't certain. Both boys were easily a foot taller and twice the weight of the now diminutive Rabbit. Out of respect, however, they complied with his request and knew that Coach wouldn't make them run for being late if they were talking to the Codgers.

Tommy and Booger were walking by when Rabbit began his admonition. Rabbit first pointed a crooked withered finger at Clyde. "You done gone and got your license. I seen you drivin'." He then turned toward Everett. "And you'll be gettin' yourn next week."

"Yes, sir," Everett said after Rabbit had paused a little longer than normal.

"Well," Rabbit began again, "I'm just sayin'." He again paused, lost in thought.

The other Codgers were watching. "Fizzlesticks, Rabbit," Fish said. "Say somethin' or let 'em go to practice."

What Rabbit had on his mind finally came to him. "We need you both on this team and at a hunert percent if we're gonna win this year," he began. He raised his voice a few decibels and an octave for the next line. "The combination of bein' a football star and havin' a driver's license is a recipe for disaster." He jabbed his finger into the air for dramatic affect.

Tommy and Booger stopped to listen and possibly watch someone have a heart attack. Rabbit was worked up.

"I'm just sayin'," he repeated, "don't pay any attention to those girls. They're just after you because you got a license and you play football."

"Yes, sir," Everett said.

Rabbit started to turn toward his chair under the tree but then thought of something else. "You come to practice and go home and git yer homework done." He looked back and forth from one bookend to the other. "You gotta have good grades to play for a big college."

Rabbit, emotionally spent and out of breath, plopped into his chair. Clyde and Everett continued down the path toward the practice field with Tommy and Booger following. Tommy contemplated the comment about driver's licenses and girls. Sure, he was dating, but his dating was limited and dependent upon someone taking him. His earlier high retreated to a realistic and near-depressing level.

Tommy and Booger stopped by Sunny's house after practice. Since Sunny's mom could play every instrument known to man, and owned half of them, Booger didn't need to bring his guitar. Mrs. Winchester had a puzzled look. "Sunny and I have been looking at the piano score for 'Classical Gas,'" she said. "To be honest," she continued, "it's a very complicated piece."

She reached for a guitar that was in a stand near the piano. "Randy," she said, refusing to use his nickname. Tommy figured she was too proper to use a nickname that resembled nasal discharge. "Would you mind playing the song?" she asked. "I'd like to see what level Sunny needs to match if you two are serious about a duet."

Booger did his usual warm-up routine before stopping to fine-tune the guitar. Tommy had learned that guitar players tune their guitars for much the same reason baseball players pick up dirt and rub it on the bat: there's an ounce of purpose but a pound of routine. Mrs. Winchester was beginning to look something between bored and agitated when Booger finally began the first chords of "Classical Gas."

The longer Booger played, the lower Mrs. Winchester's jaw dropped. Tommy noticed that her bottom lip was on the verge of failing as a saliva dam before she slowly tilted her head back in thought and swallowed. Sunny had reached into her purse for a tissue before Booger was halfway through. She wiped her eyes and sniffed when he finished. Neither of them spoke for several seconds.

"That was absolutely beautiful," Mrs. Winchester finally said and then put her hand on Sunny's leg, tilted her head authoritatively, and, with a slightly cracking voice, continued, "You have work to do."

Sunny, unable to speak, moved to the couch, sat down next to Booger, and gave him an unusually long, warm hug. She looked up at him. "I'll learn it," she said. "This is going to be beautiful."

Tommy's feelings were now mixed. He'd encouraged Booger's duet idea, but part of him regretted having done so. He sensed that once the other girls heard Booger play, they'd respond much the same as Sunny. He was even slightly concerned how Melody would react and then felt a tinge of guilt because Sunny had gotten to hear Booger play before Melody.

Mrs. Winchester had fully recovered and morphed into the taciturn piano teacher. "About practice—" she began.

Booger interrupted her. "I don't want everyone to know that I can play the guitar just yet."

"For whatever reason is that?" she asked.

"I don't want to explain why I took lessons," he replied and then matter-of-factly reminded her why he was learning to play.

"I understand," she said. "We'll just let people think that you're taking piano lessons. We can say that you and Sunny are going to play a duet at Homecoming." She straightened her skirt and then added, "That won't be a lie."

Booger turned to Sunny; their faces were inches apart. "You'll have to keep my guitar playing a secret." She cupped his face in her hands and affectionately kissed his forehead.

Oh brother, Tommy thought and then noticed the postlobotomy expression on Booger's face.

Sunny sat down at the piano and played the first few bars and then gave Booger an "Are you ready?" look. Booger, barely recovered from the kiss trauma, nodded affirmative. An impromptu practice ensued while

Tommy and Mrs. Winchester watched. Sunny had a lot of catching up to do.

Sisyphean task—a phrase that Everett had recently spouted off—came to mind. He'd used the phrase one morning just before picking up Caleb when Caleb's personal hygiene and the need to convince him to use deodorant was the topic. Of course deodorant wasn't natural, so his mother wouldn't allow it in the house.

The phrase had actually occurred to Tommy when he'd first seen the "Classical Gas" score for piano: a blur of notes filled every bar. It was the first time he'd thought of an appropriate use of the ancient word. But he knew Sunny and was familiar with her ability and resolve. For the past four years, he'd watched Booger suffer and experience the true meaning of the phrase. But now a solution had manifested itself. Sunny had no idea that she was about to play a critical role in the crumbling of Booger's Sisyphean dilemma. She probably didn't even know what the word meant; she didn't have learned friends like Everett to teach her such things, just yappy cheerleaders.

Too young to drive and too old to ride a bicycle, the boys walked home. Booger was riding an emotional wave similar to the one Tommy had experienced a few years earlier when he'd worked with Sunny on a duet. Tommy was thrilled for Booger but was simultaneously entertaining sympathetic thoughts for himself. He'd just seen how enamored Sunny had been with Booger's guitar playing; she'd given him a kiss. Tommy had waited months before getting his first kiss from Sunny. And as if that wasn't enough, he knew that after the duet, the other girls, copying Sunny, would be drawn to Booger.

Tommy did a quick personal assessment. He wasn't particularly good at football, and it would be a year before he'd turn sixteen. He'd spent most of the morning at an emotional peak but was heading home mentally and physically slumping.

After leaving Booger's house, Tommy's self-pity lightened when he began to consider the positive side of Booger's time with Sunny and the fact that he himself had already played a duet with her and could talk to her when most boys found her beauty tongue-tying. And anyway, Melody would be turning sixteen soon. He focused on the positive and briefly put the number of days until his sixteenth birthday out of his mind.

It was fried chicken night, and he could smell it before reaching the front door. He rushed to the bathroom and took care of business he'd been holding since football practice. There was no way he was going to use the bathroom at Sunny's. He knew from when he'd taken piano lessons that the Winchester's bathroom didn't have an exhaust fan or a window. He counted to twenty while washing his hands. He'd been doing so since one of the senior football players had come down with a bad case of impetigo.

Marsha knew where he'd been and started in before Tommy came out of the bathroom. During dinner she had to tell what her friends were saying about Tommy's date. Tommy was too hungry to argue, so he endured the convoluted story that had evolved after passing through both the JV and the varsity cheerleading squads.

When Marsha stopped long enough to chew her food, Mrs. Thompson told Tommy, "Mr. Hinkebein phoned. He'd like you to call him." Tommy wondered what he could want. He tried to remember the predate lecture.

Marsha snickered. "It's probably something about racing over the sister in Uncle Cletus's pickup and getting arrested."

Tommy held off on a drumstick long enough to correct her. "We didn't get arrested, didn't even get a ticket, and it's the Seven Sisters." He gave Marsha a look and then took a chunk out of the chicken leg.

He and Marsha cleaned up and did the dishes just as they'd been doing for nearly a decade. "So, how *was* the first date?" she asked. Marsha was always more civil when it was just the two of them.

"It was kind of fun to do something besides walk to the Houn-Dawg or go to the movie," Tommy replied.

"What do you think Mr. Hinkebein wants?" she asked and handed him the frying pan to dry.

"I don't know," Tommy said and slid the dried chicken frying pan into the oven drawer.

You worried?" she asked and handed him a plate.

"No," he said and put the plate away.

She turned and faced him. "You look worried," she said.

"Just curious," Tommy assured her. Actually the Sunny/Booger duet had begun to weigh on him.

"You gonna call him?" she asked.

"I'll probably go by the store tomorrow," Tommy lied. His plan was to wait until she was taking a bath later that evening and then make the call.

Tommy sat on the front porch making small talk with his mom and dad until he heard water running in the bathtub. Perfect, he thought. His parents were on the porch, and Marsha was in the bathroom, her transistor radio blaring. He had the house and the phone to himself.

Mr. Hinkebein answered. "I need to talk to you. Can you come by the store?" he asked.

"I think so," Tommy replied and then nervously asked, "Is this about last night?"

"In a way," Mr. Hinkebein replied. "But I can't really talk here at home." He paused and then continued, "I don't want Melody or Mrs. Hinkebein to hear our conversation."

By then Tommy barely had enough saliva to keep his tongue from sticking to the roof of his mouth. "Is there a problem?" he asked.

"No, no," Mr. Hinkebein assured him. "I need your advice on something. It has to do with Melody's birthday. I really can't talk right now," he whispered into the phone and hung up.

Tommy's mom was coming in from the porch right as he was hanging up. "Was that Mr. Hinkebein?"

"Yeah," Tommy said.

"What did he need?" she asked.

"He couldn't say," Tommy replied. "He wants me to stop by the store Saturday morning."

KNOWING MR. HINKEBEIN WANTED HIM to stop by but not knowing for what reason had kept Tommy awake most of the night, and he found it difficult to pay attention in class until Miss Anderson aroused his interest. A surge of curious energy shot through his body when she wrote an unfamiliar term on the board—manumission. It wouldn't have been unfamiliar had Tommy done his reading assignment. But in a sense it wasn't unfamiliar; she'd written it on the board just before the bell the day before along with a reading assignment.

She continued writing—West Indies, Orphan, Secretary of the Treasury—and then turned and faced the class. "Who can tell me which Founding Father had these things in common?" Most of the girls raised their hands. She called on Everett. He had started to raise his hand but then put it back down.

Everett rubbed his chin. "Dadgum," he said, for which he got a frown from Miss Anderson. "Well … it wasn't George Washington," he said with a trailing-off voice.

"What makes you say that?" she asked.

"Because," Everett said, "Washington had slaves. And that one word means antislavery." Everett thought a few seconds more. "And he wasn't Secretary of the Treasury."

"You're right," Miss Anderson told him. She had a way of bringing value to half-right answers unless they were just way off the subject. "Well, sort of," she continued. "Washington had slaves, but was he proslavery or antislavery?" The raised hands went down.

"We'll talk about Washington in a few minutes." She tapped the board. "Back to the assignment." The girls' hands shot back into the air. She called on Melody.

"Alexander Hamilton," Melody proudly said. "He was born in the West Indies, his father abandoned the family, his mother died soon after, and, like Everett said, he was Secretary of the Treasury. He was also one of the founding members of the New York Manumission Society."

Miss Anderson looked first at Tommy, then at a couple of the other boys, and finally at Melody. "Well, it sounds like you did the reading assignment." She snickered. "Which is more than I can say for most of the boys."

"And what was the New York Manumission Society?" she asked.

"I remember now," Everett blurted out without raising his hand.

"Okay, Everett, let's hear it," she said.

"It was a society established in an effort to abolish slavery," Everett said.

Tommy looked at Everett and figured the little talk that Rabbit had given him was working. Miss Anderson further probed the class on Hamilton and then got back to Washington.

"So, was Washington pro- or antislavery?" she asked. A few hands went up.

"He had slaves," one person said.

"That he did," Miss Anderson agreed and then gave the class a lecture on Washington's effort to emancipate the slaves and how his will included wording that freed his slaves upon his wife's death, which could have put Mrs. Washington in a bit of a pickle after he died. "After the reading of the will," Mrs. Anderson said, "word quickly spread that as soon as Martha Washington died the slaves would all be set free. But she and Washington had treated their slaves more as ranch hands, so her life was never seriously threatened. Although, some say she did consider hiring an armed guard."

Just before the bell, Miss Anderson brought the class back to Hamilton. "So, how did Alexander Hamilton die?" she asked. Like usual, the girls raised their hands. "One of you football players, be prepared to tell the class on Monday how Hamilton met his demise." The bell rang.

SATURDAY MORNING COULDN'T HAVE ARRIVED too soon for Tommy. He arrived at Hinkebein's Dry Goods early; the closed sign was still up, but the door was unlocked. A feeling of apprehension gripped him when he stepped into the empty store. Being alone with Mr. Hinkebein made him feel uneasy.

"Good morning," Mr. Hinkebein said and brushed by Tommy toward the door. "I'll just lock the door so shoppers don't come in and disturb us," he said. Tommy felt a good case of the dry mouth coming on.

Mr. Hinkebein pointed toward the rear of the store. "Let's go toward the back so people can't see us," he said and then led the way. For Tommy, apprehension was turning to fear. On his way to the rear of the store, Mr. Hinkebein turned slightly toward Tommy. "Melody can't know that we've met." Mr. Hinkebein pointed at a bench in the shoe department. "Have a seat." The moisture that had vacated Tommy's mouth gathered on his palms. He wiped them on his pants before taking a seat on the bench.

"Melody is turning sixteen in a couple of weeks," Mr. Hinkebein said. Relief swept over Tommy when he realized the clandestine meeting was nothing more than a precursor to a surprise birthday party. His saliva glands resumed partial production. Tommy began to wonder if he should see a doctor about his malfunctioning salivary system.

Mr. Hinkebein continued, "Melody has never given us any trouble; she makes good grades and works hard here at the store." He paused; Tommy sensed he was searching for how to say something. Tommy began to grow suspicious that something more than a party was being planned. The chance that Melody might have a serious illness popped into Tommy's head.

"Melody told me all about it," Mr. Hinkebein said. "And I drove to Fairview to see for myself," he continued. Tommy still wasn't certain of what Mr. Hinkebein was talking about. "And to be honest, I wouldn't mind having it for myself."

Finally, Mr. Hinkebein just up and asked, "Do you think Melody would like that Malibu you saw on your first date to the Fairview A&W?" Tommy could have focused better had Mr. Hinkebein simply asked about the Malibu, but he had to throw in the extra part about it being a first date and all.

Tommy worked past the first date comment and got the visuals of Melody and Sunny's telepathic exchange of daggers out of his mind. Once focused on the question, the complexity of it made him woozy; he was glad to already be sitting down. He wanted that Malibu but knew it made no sense for him; it would be a year before he could drive. Melody having it would be a dream, so long as they actually began to date.

Mr. Hinkebein snapped him back to the present. "Are you okay?" he asked.

Tommy nodded. "Uh-huh," he replied and quickly assembled his thoughts. "I think Melody would love the Malibu." Tommy could see that Mr. Hinkebein was waiting for more. "That's all she could talk about on the way home from Fairview," he lied. "She'll really be surprised."

Mr. Hinkebein went on to explain how they were going to have a party for her but the car was to be a surprise. "You, me, and Mrs. Hinkebein are the only ones to know," he told Tommy.

"Why did you ask my opinion, Mr. Hinkebein?" Tommy asked. During the conversation Tommy reached the conclusion that he may not be the most qualified person for a parent to consult about purchasing a car for their sixteen-year-old daughter. He also sensed that part of Mr. Hinkebein's motivation for buying the car for Melody was that he wanted the car for himself.

"Melody has convinced her mother that you're a mature young man. Mrs. Hinkebein thinks you know Melody as well as anybody and told me to get your opinion, that you'd tell us if you thought the car too much for her." Mr. Hinkebein patted Tommy on the shoulder and reached to shake his hand. "Thanks," he said. "I'll let Melody's mother know." He smiled. "I think your approval will provide the little extra she needs to give me the go-ahead."

The gravity of the morning meeting slowly settled on Tommy. He now had another secret to keep, and it seemed that he'd just been given partial responsibility for Melody and the Malibu.

The others were already gathered around the stone when Tommy stepped out of Hinkebein's. "What were you doing at Hinkebein's so early?" Caleb asked.

"Nothin'," Tommy said.

The line of questioning would have continued, but Everett and his dad had just pulled up to the courthouse. It was Everett's turn to walk the driver's test path.

Green Goddess

EVERETT AND HIS DAD STOOD in front of the so-called British import and talked for a few minutes. Tommy paralleled how Everett had gotten a car that his dad had wanted, and now the same was about to occur in Melody's case. He found it curious that his friends were driving cars that represented the preference of their parents. What does car preference say about the person? he wondered. Clyde's giant Chrysler, Melody's soon-to-be Super Sport Malibu, and Everett's unique diminutive import. He began to wonder what kind of car his dad secretly wished for.

Everett started walking toward the stone, and his dad headed to the post office. Everett had his head in the driver's exam booklet, occasionally glancing up to avoid tripping. He didn't look before crossing the street, and he was lucky not to get hit by the heavy come-to-town-on-Saturday traffic.

Clyde drilled Everett on the written exam and warned him about the trick questions. The rest of the boys watched with envy while Everett used the time until the courthouse opened to prepare himself for the rite of passage.

The Missouri State Highway Department van arrived, and the team of examiners, clipboards in hand, made their way to the front door of the courthouse. The boys watched, cognizant and fearful of the power that the team of brown-uniformed strangers yielded. The rumor was that driver's examiners were those who had flunked out of highway patrol school, and hence their brooding attitudes.

After a joint high five, Everett crossed the street. The Codgers stood for him and shook his hand when he passed by. An uninformed observer would have thought Everett was going off to war instead of gaining the state's permission to legally drive.

The boys later learned that Everett had made a perfect score on the written test, which wasn't a miracle by any stretch of the imagination; the questions are simple. But the pressure of passing usually caused one to miss at least one, like the color of a yield sign, which tripped up most people. The typical answer was yellow, but the correct answer was red.

The perfect score probably helped him with the driving part. The boys expected Everett to flunk the driving portion because legend held that examiners typically flunked the first few boys each season. But Clyde had passed, so there was hope. Tommy began to question the validity of the legend.

They were huddled around the stone when Everett emerged from the courthouse with a smile so big his fleshy cheeks were pressed into multiple wrinkles. When he saw the boys, he opened his mouth in a silent "Yeehaw!" Tommy thought he saw Everett skip on the way to the car but dismissed it as something totally out of character.

Everett's car was technically a British import, and he had described the car in such a way as to lead everyone into thinking he'd gotten an MG or something exotic, but he'd never mentioned a brand. He'd only said the car had *originally* been built by the British Motor Company, the same company that had built the MG and the Austin.

They'd never seen an MG or an Aston in real life, only in the movies. James Bond had first made the Aston Martin famous by driving a specially equipped version in *Goldfinger*. He and Pussy Galore had made the car famous.

Everett had actually said *Austin,* and the boys would soon learn there was a world of difference between an Aston and an Austin, both British. But it was a car—four wheels and an engine—and when Everett had mentioned that it was a convertible, a serious case of envy spread throughout the band of man-boys. A convertible of any style would be cool.

A couple of days before getting his license, Everett and his mom and dad had gone to Fairview to get the car. So, when the boys had waited at Everett's house for them to return with his exotic import, they were a little surprised to see him pull up in a car not much larger than himself. Everett's dad, Colby's postmaster, was even larger than Everett. The two of them were squeezed into the car shoulder to shoulder and still spilling out on each side. The tops of both heads were slightly higher than the windshield. Tommy wondered how they'd have fit if the top was up.

Everett's exotic import turned out to be a lime-green-over-white convertible Nash Metropolitan, the wheelbase of which was approximately half of Clyde's Chrysler. Caleb's first words were, "It won't fit on the tracks." The boys were seeing the difference between an Austin and an Aston. Austin was famous for the Mini Cooper and other fashion-free cars the likes of which James Bond wouldn't have been caught dead driving.

The car was so short it almost looked square. The fenders covered the top third of the whitewall tires making the already squatty car look even more so. Chrome baby half-moons with a thin lime-green script *M* covered the center of the lime-green wheels. So, the wheels had a chrome center, a green stripe, and an extrawide whitewall on the tire. Nobody had ever seen a car like it before. "Odd" was the word that stuck in Tommy's mind. He'd later use the word "unique" to describe the car to others.

During the walk-around, Flop noticed the chrome Metropolitan adornment on the front fender. "Metropolitan," he said, "just like the ice cream."

"Good one, Flop," Everett said and laughed, as did the others. Everyone except Flop understood the humor.

Everett showed them how the spare tire mounted on the rear of the car had to be removed to access the pint-sized trunk, which was barely larger than Everett's football helmet and duffel bag.

Tommy sensed that something was missing, but exactly what escaped him. Finally, Flop made the observation. "Where's the backseat?" he asked.

Everett stated the obvious. "It doesn't have one." He further explained. "Convertible Austins don't have backseats, only trunks." They'd all seen what Everett had called a trunk, which was nothing more than a giant shoe box. It was clear that Everett saw the car from a different perspective than the rest.

"It only has two seats?" Flop asked.

"Yep," Everett replied and then chuckled. "One for me and one for a cheerleader." The rest of the boys snickered. Everett had never had a girlfriend let alone been on a date. The modeling agencies weren't exactly making a path to his door, and neither were the Colby girls. He was one of those guys with which girls liked to be "just friends."

On further inspection the boys had noticed the hood ornament, which was easily seen from a distance, but they'd been distracted by the diminutive topless neon car overflowing with two extra-large bodies. The ornament, a winged voluptuous mermaid, was mounted on the front of the hood. The mermaid's body was chrome, and her translucent wings, which lit up when the headlights were on, were tinted lime-green to match the car.

The boys quickly got over the shock of the actual car versus their expectation, and, based on the striking color and provocative hood ornament, they named it "the Green Goddess."

The license examiner circled the Green Goddess while Everett worked the turn signals and headlights and honked the horn. The brown-shirt, satisfied that the go-cart on steroids was safe to drive, opened the passenger-side door to get in. Before doing so he said something to Everett and motioned toward the rear. Everett got out, and the two of them put up the top. There must have been a rule against taking the exam in a convertible with the top down.

Cozy is the adjective used by American Motors in the literature for the car. A tight squeeze is a more accurate description. With the seat all the way back, Everett's arms were still bent at a ninety-degree angle while his hands rested at ten and two. The brown-shirt had to remove his hat; the top of his head was devoid of even the tiniest sliver of hair. There was barely room between his lap and the dash of the car for the ominous clipboard, so he had to drape his bent elbow out the window in order to fit. Everett's expression was anxiously proud; the examiner's was one of frustration and embarrassment.

Before pulling away Everett adjusted the mirror on his side and asked the examiner to do the same on the passenger side. The mirrors, tiny silver-dollar-sized things mounted on the rear of the front fenders but reachable from inside the pint-sized car, were by any measure more for decoration than function. But Everett knew that mirror adjustment was an item on the clipboard.

The boys didn't bother to race to the school to watch Everett parallel park. An idiot could park the tiny car.

"Melody is next," Booger said while they waited. The boys exchanged contemplative nods.

"Think she'll get a car?" Caleb asked.

"I'll bet she does," Booger added. "The Hinkebeins have only one car now." Tommy sat frustrated and picking at a hangnail, unable to share all he knew on the subject.

The boys were speculating and debating possibilities for Melody's car when Sunny pulled up in her Fairlane. "Hey, Boogs," she yelled. The abbreviation didn't go unnoticed. "Get in," she said when Booger started nervously her way. While Booger was getting in, Sunny smiled and waved. "Hey, guys," she called. Booger, somewhat in a state of shock, seemed hypnotized and rode off without a wave, nod, or anything resembling a good-bye.

"'Get in'?" Caleb said after Booger and Sunny pulled away.

"'Boogs'?" Clyde asked. "What's up with that?" Booger had just been hailed by the most beautiful girl in Colby and arguably the prettiest girl in the entire state.

Tommy was exponentially exasperated. Another friend was getting his driver's license, Booger's guitar playing had earned him the attention of Colby's most coveted girl, and Melody was about to get the car of his dreams.

Sunny's drive-by pickup of Booger had left the boys speechless, but the Green Goddess coming into view snapped them out of their state of delirium. Everett had just made history by being the oldest boy in the class and passing the driving part on the first try. Clyde had been excluded in the band of boys' record keeping due to his birthday falling before the school cutoff date and the chance that the examiner might think him the youngest.

Tommy figured Everett's success was due to a couple of things. First, the car's size and maneuverability made it easier to comply with each and every element of the test. But that hadn't kept others from failing. Second, the chrome-domed brown-shirt probably didn't want to be seen again in the Green Goddess.

Dorcas

CLYDE HADN'T MISSED A SUNDAY since getting his license, and he had been bringing the rest of the boys with him. Church attendance was mostly an excuse to drive, and they'd make a morning of it by first taking in the Seven Sisters and two quick trips around the loop.

Everett getting his license introduced a new dimension to the Sunday morning routine. The Houn-Dawg was closed on Sunday mornings, but the central location and highly visible parking lot made for a perfect rendezvous spot for those wanting to be seen in a car. Clyde had picked up Tommy and Booger first and then Caleb so that the personal hygiene-free Caleb would have to sit in the back. Providing proof to the accuracy of the axiom that opposites attract, skinny, feral Flop and Everett the giant had become car buds.

Clyde pulled into the parking lot from one direction and Everett from the other so that the two cars came to a stop facing opposite directions. Psychologists have postulated that men park in such a manner so as to keep a vigilant eye in all directions and that the behavior is engrained and left over from a time when ferocious dinosaurs lurked about. In Clyde and Everett's case, the maneuver was nothing more than putting the driver's side of each car adjacent with the other and making conversation between the two drivers easier.

When the top-down Green Goddess pulled into the parking lot, Tommy looked at the size disparity between Everett and Flop and was reminded of Fred Flintstone and Barney—a skinny Barney. Apparently, Flop had found a pair of his dad's sunglasses; they were too large for him. His head was gangster leaning, and one arm dangled down the side of the door.

"You're late," Clyde said. They'd agreed to meet at 8:30, giving them time to do some cruising before church; it was past 9:00.

"My mom had to give me the safe driving speech," Everett said. "And then Flop's mom wanted to make small talk while she walked around and inspected the car."

"Who's the idiot behind the Foster Grants?" Clyde asked, slightly modifying the sunglass company's famous slogan.

Flop removed the boxy-looking shades and said, "It's me."

"I'll be darned," Clyde deadpanned. "Sure is." Flop grinned and slid the glasses back on and resumed his cool posture. Clyde looked at his watch and said, "We need to get going."

"We'll follow you," Everett said.

There are no signs, but everybody is supposed to know not to park in the area near the front of the church that's covered with chat; that space is reserved for visitors. The rest of the parking lot was either covered with a thin layer of creek gravel or hard pack clay with exposed shoe-toe catching rocks protruding here and there. And then there's the dilemma as to precisely when someone who attends church on a regular basis, but has yet to officially join, loses their visitor status and has to compete for a parking spot.

The Codgers were gathered around a giant maple tree near the front of the church and policing the unmarked visitor parking area. The spaces between the massive maple's roots were packed with decaying cigarette butts and remnants of spent chaw.

Parking spots weren't assigned, but they may as well have been. An unspoken but well understood reason for the creation of the visitor parking area was to avoid the confusion and conflict that too often arose as a result of visitors parking in a space normally occupied by a regular member. After Mr. Koch passed away, the Websters began to park near the front door in the Kochs' regular spot, but little was said because they always gave Mrs. Koch a ride to church.

Clyde arrived first and parked in visitor parking. The Codgers, rather than encouraging Clyde—a frequent visitor—to park elsewhere, had told him it was okay. The Codgers circled the Chrysler and welcomed the boys. Tommy wasn't sure in which the Codgers were most interested, the spiritual growth of the boys or their football prowess.

Tommy could hear the Codgers arguing as they approached the car. Monkey, a deacon at First Baptist, was complaining to the others about Brother Baker. "He's on another danged savatican."

Fish raised his finger and jiggled it toward Monkey. "He's on sabbatical."

"That's what I said," Monkey replied. "Savatican." Fish motioned a "forget it."

The only thing Tommy could figure was Monkey believed the Vatican had something to do with whatever Brother Baker was doing. Monkey was confused, and Fish knew better than to try and set him straight.

Bem added his two cents, which even at that price was an overvalued opinion. "I heard he might be lookin' at another church, don't cha know."

Fish raised his finger again, this time a little higher and slightly waving it back and forth. "It's a fancy name for a retreat. All the Baptist preachers in the southern Missouri association are there. They're going to elect a representative to attend the national convention."

Bem, sounding defensive, added, "Well, I heard it at Clemo's Barber Shop; Clemo told it for the truth, don't cha know."

"With that many Baptist preachers in one spot, I'll bet they fry every chicken in the county," Monkey added.

Rabbit hadn't been involved in the exchange and was the first to notice Everett pull up. "Fizzlesticks," he said. "Would you look at that."

The arrival of the Green Goddess stopped the squabbling. It was their first up-close look, and they acted as if a spaceship had just landed.

Bem proved his power of observation. "It sure is green."

"What is it?" Rabbit asked.

"It's a car, don't cha know," Bem replied.

Fish, already stooped over—his natural stance—noticed the emblem on the side. "Metropolitan," he said. "Who makes it?"

By this time Everett had gotten out and was standing with the rest of the gang. "The British Motor Company," he announced.

"Ain't it a Rambler?" Rabbit asked.

Everett had done a little research. "It's imported and sold by American Motors," he replied. Tommy could tell that Everett liked connecting the car to British Motors; that was certainly more exotic and unique than Rambler, a common American brand.

Rabbit scratched his chin. "Well, I'll be," he replied.

The Codgers circled the car a couple of times. Bem pushed down on one fender and tested the shocks and springs. He looked at Everett and then back at the car. "You fit in this thing?" he asked.

Rabbit gave Bem an incredulous look. "Bem," he said, "he just drove up in it."

"I know that," Bem snapped.

"I'm just sayin'," Rabbit responded.

Fish looked at his watch. "It's time to go in," he said.

Sunday School had been cancelled since an interim speaker was filling in for Brother Baker. Interims tended to show little regard for the pot roasts cooking at home or televised Sunday afternoon football. Their job was to speak to the congregation in ways that the local preacher couldn't without stepping on toes. This one didn't disappoint.

Tommy and the rest of the boys took a seat in the back row, which, except for them, was normally occupied by those who didn't have a regular pew. Sunday School being cancelled meant he'd missed the chance to visit with Melody between services. Since she was in the choir, they couldn't sit together in church. The choir was singing "Bringing in the Sheaves" while the congregation took their seats. The other boys must have been watching Melody because when she gave Tommy a twinkly-eyed smile he got an elbow from Booger and winks from the rest.

The Browns, a family that had left the Pentecostal Church over a dispute about women wearing head coverings in church, were sitting across the aisle. They occupied the entire pew, the father on one end, the mother on the other, and six kids—four boys and two girls—in between. The oldest, a girl, was twelve and wore buckle shoes. Her sister, the youngest, was still in diapers. The four boys wore black trousers, white shirts buttoned all of the way up, and white socks to set off their black Sunday shoes.

Pentecostals were known for being fundamentalist, and their choice of biblical names for their children was proof. The oldest was named John, after Jesus's disciple. The next two were named for rivers: Jabbok and Jordan. When being introduced, Jabbok was invariably understood to be Jacob. He would no doubt spend his first few years of elementary school correcting his teachers. It would have been so easy to have named him Jacob and been done with it. The youngest was named Jericho, which, to his parents' eventual consternation, would likely be shortened to something simple like Jerry or just Jer.

When naming the girls, they'd introduced an unnecessary complication. The oldest girl had been named Bethlehem, after the town where Christ was born. Her name was mercifully shortened to Beth. And that's a good thing, because the second girl's name was Bethany. Bethany would likely develop a complex of invincibility, being named where Lazarus was raised from the dead and Christ's ascension occurred. Beth was the oldest child and Bethany the youngest—Alpha and Omega in a weird sort of way.

The Browns were a lively bunch and introduced a worship style not typical of the traditional Southern Baptist. Tommy had heard the Codgers referring to the new family as the glory group.

The interim speaker looked swollen. He was fat, but no fatter in one area than another. His wrists were so chubby that his french cuffs threatened to cut off circulation to his sausage fingers. His neck expanded to enormous proportion as it descended to his shoulders. Tommy estimated the angle from the bottom of the interim's ears to where his neck met his shoulders to be approximately forty-five degrees. When he paced back and forth, Tommy could see that he was as thick as he was wide. He would have made a good center or point guard, Tommy figured.

Typical of a Baptist evangelist, the rotund interim began the sermon by talking about where he was going to eat after the service and what he'd been promised would be served. He'd patted his belly and smacked his lips while describing the expected menu. Tommy could never understand why evangelists began a sermon by making people long for its conclusion so that they could rush home and eat.

His tongue must be swollen too, Tommy thought, because his voice sounded like he had a cold. On the bright side, Tommy continued in thought, he looks like an eater, so maybe the sermon won't drag on. The interim's name was listed in the bulletin as Russell Ralston. It was hard to say without making a slight whistling noise; Rotund was easier.

Rotund's right hand held the podium, and his left jabbed a stubby finger toward the ceiling. Left-handed, Tommy figured, and he began to pity the person who had to sit next to him at a dinner table.

"If you are strangers to prayer, you are strangers to power," he began.[*] He paused long enough to look around and make eye contact with several

---

[*] Billy Sunday Quotes.

on the first row. He looked Fish's direction. "Yank some of the groan out of your prayer and put in some shouts," he said with a crescendo ending.

"Glory," yelled the father of the glory group.

"Yes, glory," repeated several of his clones. The oldest daughter began convulsing until the mother reached over and pulled her arms down.

Tommy figured the prayer remark was aimed at Fish, who had announced last week's and this week's attendance and last week's offering, welcomed the visitors, and said a prayer that mentioned all of the old people too sick to attend church, Brother Baker's sabbatical, Brother Russell, and the boys turning sixteen. When Fish had paused for a second, Tommy at first thought he'd forgotten to say amen, but Fish had only stopped for a breath before he resumed his monotone droning. The back of Tommy's neck had begun to ache before Fish finished his all-encompassing prayer.

A rogue thought struck Tommy. Since new drivers who didn't otherwise attend church began to do so after getting their licenses—and usually brought their friends—the driver's license examiners should be encouraged to be more lenient. At least those who thought it important that teenagers attend church.

Rotund stepped to the side of the podium and leaned forward. "Going to church doesn't make you a Christian any more than going to a garage makes you an automobile." Tommy had heard Coach Heart make a similar statement except using football practice and football player in place of church and Christian. What Coach Heart lacked in coaching skill he made up for with little quips.

"Amen, brother," shouted the father of the glory family.

"Yes, yes, amen," repeated the male clones of the group.

It's said that there's something for everyone in a sermon for those who listen. Rotund didn't disappoint. "Turn to Acts 9:36," he said and then waited for the congregation to find the passage; the glory group had already done so. Others, sensing the purpose of the pause, turned to a random page in their rarely read Bibles. Those without Bibles grabbed Hymnals and feigned searching for the passage.

"Here we see how after prayer a disciple was raised from the dead." That got most people's attention. "And it was a woman disciple at that," he said with an emphasis on "woman." Now he had everyone's attention. It's likely that few remembered there being a woman disciple.

"Now there was in Joppa," he began, "a disciple named Dorcas." The boys snickered, evidence that they were listening. Rotund paused momentarily to see if anyone had noticed that the scripture actually read Tabitha, which when translated meant Dorcas. The glory group was exchanging affirmative nods; they'd been obediently following along. Rotund's swollen-tongue translation had been missed by the rest.

The reading of verse twenty-nine is where it got interesting. "So Peter rose and went with them to the upper room. All the windows," it sounded like he'd read, "stood beside him weeping and showing tunics and other garments that Dorcas had made while she was with them."

The glory group exchanged frowns while the rest of the congregation smiled blissfully, waiting for Dorcas to be raised from the dead. Rotund continued reading, and since it was a long passage, he began pausing frequently for mouth breaths. A whisper began with the father and then swept through the glory group; nods followed each whisper. "Widows, not windows," Tommy could hear them saying.

Rotund, out of breath and pleased with himself, stopped reading at the end of the chapter. The women had heard that there was a woman disciple. The boys had learned that someone in the Bible was named Dorcas. Several were perplexed by a visual of Peter being surrounded by and talking to garment-draped and weeping windows. The glory group hadn't learned anything except the interim couldn't enunciate. Their enthusiasm was beginning to wane, evidenced by their lack of verbal response.

Rotund concluded by saying, "Sometimes when you hit the devil square in the face, he runs like he's been hit in the mouth," which, to Tommy, didn't seem congruent with the story about Dorcas. Tommy figured that most of the men probably felt like running, but not because they'd been hit in the mouth.[†] The St. Louis Cardinals and L.A. Rams noon game was being televised.

The drowsy congregation, as if to have been themselves raised from the dead, came to life during the doxology, grabbed their things, and went forth. The women, emboldened by Dorcas's apparent defeat of death, left with a new and sporting attitude and their noses jutting skyward.

---

† Rams and Cardinals actually played on Friday, September 18, 1970; Rams won 34–13.

Libby

CLYDE'S MOM HAD INVITED THE boys over to watch the game. She liked to cook and, judging by her size, frequently sampled her fare. Clyde's house was on a hill just outside the city limits and secluded enough that the boys could pee off of the porch, shoot guns, and do all kinds of things not allowed in town. He and his mother had lived alone since the death of Clyde's father, when Clyde was only seven. The house was only a few years old; the town had raised money to build it after the original house had been destroyed by fire.

Since Clyde's mother was an experimental cook, she was always trying new recipes and inviting the boys over to enjoy her culinary trials. She generally amended every recipe with copious amounts of sugar, lard, or butter. Her productions were always quickly consumed by the ravenous teenagers, who brought her exceeding delight and encouragement to cook more.

Her kitchen skills far exceeded her acumen for landscaping. Their yard consisted mostly of scattered areas with grass mixed with unidentified broadleaf weeds and bare areas in which the only thing growing were the exposed roots of the nearest tree. Her bizarre collection of yard ornaments was unmatched. Many of the ornaments, standing alone, would have been the perfect accessory, such as the metal spinner with the dipping bird and windmill blades, or the copper butterflies that fluttered when the wind blew, or the metal silhouette of a couple holding hands. But then there was the plywood cutout that looked like a lady bending over, the little gnome who looked more evil than happy, and the assortment of glittery rainbow wind-helix things she'd proudly acquired at a yard sale in Fairview.

"Too much" would immediately come to a normal person's mind when passing by.

"In need of counseling" would likely be the first thing a passing psychologist might think.

Her most recent addition to the yard was a tall tower topped with a rotating TV antenna, making TV signal strength at their house better than anyone in all of Colby. In spite of the bright-colored ribbons of silk with which she'd adorned the tower, Clyde was proud to bring it to everyone's attention. The boys were anxious to watch the game on a crystal-clear screen.

Flop hopped into the Green Goddess with Everett; the rest piled into Clyde's Chrysler. Flop and Everett, each the antithesis of the other, had become good friends. Flop, the thin, nervous accountant-looking one was actually sloppy, carefree, borderline naive, and, at best, an average student. Everett, the large grizzly-sized one, was nervous, self-conscious, meticulous, and scholarly. Both were good at football; they had that in common.

So many people wanted to look at Everett's car that they couldn't get away from the church until after Clyde and the others had left, but they caught up with the Chrysler at the railroad crossing. Clyde was once again maneuvering the behemoth car onto the tracks with help from Caleb and the boys.

Everett stopped and Tommy walked over. "Caleb talked Clyde into putting the car on the tracks and driving to the other side of the yard."

"In broad daylight?" Everett asked. "Dadgum," he said in amazement.

Tommy shrugged. "Caleb convinced Clyde that everyone would be watching the game."

"Like we should be?" Everett replied. Tommy shrugged again.

Once the car was situated on the tracks, Caleb ran to the front tire. "Let a little air out of each one," he yelled. The rest of the boys watched as Caleb moved from tire to tire complaining about nobody helping.

Once he had all four tires draping over the rails, he walked to the driver's side. "Put it in low, take your hands off the wheel, and don't touch the brakes."

"How do I slow down?" Clyde asked when in fact he should have protested when Caleb began letting the air out of his tires. It was as if Caleb had cast a spell on him.

"Well," Caleb said and then paused in thought. "Tap the breaks lightly and don't let the wheel turn."

"How do I do that without putting my hands on the wheel?" Clyde asked.

"Want me to drive?" Caleb asked.

"Sure," Clyde said, obviously not thinking clearly. Caleb hopped into the driver's seat and started down the tracks. The rest of the boys jumped out and joined Everett. Since the tracks were guiding the car, Caleb was free to hop from side to side and monitor the car's progress.

The boys watched, amazed. A few minutes earlier they'd been on their way to Clyde's house for a feast and televised football. And now they were standing in the empty tie yard with Clyde watching the Chrysler ease along the tracks with Caleb inside, jumping back and forth like a spider monkey looking for a place to pee.

Once the car reached the crossing on the other side, Caleb had the good sense to stop the car and push the P button. He jumped out smiling and looking satisfied. "See, nothing to it." Caleb had planted a seed when he'd previously proved to the boys that the car would fit on the tracks. But he'd significantly aroused their curiosity with the track travel demonstration.

Everett broke the trance when he asked, "Clyde, did your mother fix one of those pot roasts?" Everyone's focus immediately shifted from track travel to food and football.

THE CARDINALS LOST, BUT EVERETT and Clyde were too absorbed in analyzing the game to let the loss bother them. Tommy was amazed at their eye for the skill of the offensive line protecting Cardinal quarterback, Jim Hart. Flop had focused on Roger Wehrli, who had been a standout at the University of Missouri and a first-round draft pick by the Cardinals. Flop, like Wehrli, was a natural at cornerback, albeit nearly a hundred pounds lighter.

Clyde's mom had fixed enough food for a small army, and the boys had consumed every last morsel, which delighted her. Itching to drive somewhere, they decided on the Fairview A&W. "You can't still be hungry!" she exclaimed.

Caleb, always talking before thinking, blurted out, "They just want to check out the Fairview girls."

"What's wrong with the Colby girls?" she asked.

"Mom," Clyde said and gave her a look. "We just want to drive somewhere."

"I don't know," she said with a worried expression.

Tommy called his uncle Cletus and talked him into going. Clyde's mom finally agreed when Tommy reported that his uncle Cletus and aunt Penny were going. Everett called his mom and asked if he could drive to Fairview and said that Tommy's uncle was going too. The rest of the boys made calls and used the same everyone-else-is-going logic to gain permission for the trip to Fairview.

Uncle Cletus and Aunt Penny were waiting for them at the tie yard. "Cards lost," he said when Everett pulled up.

"Wehrli had a good game," Flop responded.

Uncle Cletus grinned. "The Rams scored thirty-four points. Wehrli can't do it all." While they were talking, Clyde and the rest pulled up. Aunt Penny waved from the truck. "How about we go first," Uncle Cletus suggested. Tommy figured Uncle Cletus was thinking he could keep Clyde and Everett from speeding if he was in front.

The caravan commenced. Uncle Cletus's pickup led the way, followed by the Green Goddess and then Clyde's Chrysler. They crossed the Seven Sisters at less than fifty miles per hour, but even at that speed there was a moment of near weightlessness on each apex. Flop almost lost his hat but was able to catch it because of his lightning-fast reflexes.

Tommy noticed Booger discreetly playing the air guitar on the way. He appeared to be lost in thought, but Tommy knew better. He was strumming down the side of his right leg while his left hand practiced frets on the other leg. To the uninformed, it looked like he was either nervous or had an itch.

A couple of Cessnas were in the pattern when they passed the Fairview airport. Since Miss Anderson was still instructing, Tommy figured she was probably in one of the circling planes. She'd told the history class about Ira Biffle, Charles Lindberg's first flight instructor and also a long-ago and rarely-heard-of native of Colby.

The Malibu was still sitting on display at the Fairview Chevrolet. Tommy hadn't heard from Mr. Hinkebein, so he didn't know for sure if Melody was going to get the surprise of her life the following week. He was too awestruck by the car to say anything.

"Nice car," Caleb said. He was looking out the rear window. The others turned quickly to see what had gotten Caleb's attention.

"Sky blue Malibu," Booger said. "Cool." Tommy wondered if Booger was thinking about the Chevelle Malibu that his brother, Johnny, had planned to buy when he returned from Vietnam. "Let's stop there on the way home," Booger suggested.

Clyde nodded but was concentrating too much on driving to engage in conversation. The other boys kept an eye on the Malibu until out of sight.

The A&W wasn't too busy; there were three slots together. A Thunderbird full of Fairview girls pulled in behind them; evidently they'd seen the caravan—or more specifically, the convertible Green Goddess—cruise through Fairview. The Green Goddess was dwarfed by Cletus's pickup on one side and Clyde's massive pink Chrysler on the other. The girls parked across the aisle from Everett and honked. Arms and waving hands poked through every window.

There's something mysterious about girls and boys from one town being interested in those from another. Maybe it's because they haven't known each other since grade school and are consequently unaware of each other's quirks. Or possibly it's the grass is greener phenomenon. No matter the reason, intercity teenage courting leads to trouble.

Neither Everett nor Flop was a candidate for male model, and the reason the girls were drawn to them was no mystery. What Tommy had anticipated was playing out before him. The girls poured out of the Thunderbird and crowded around the Nash Metropolitan. "Nice car," one of them said while she twirled her hair. "What kind is it?" she asked.

Everett had developed lockjaw. Flop answered. "It's a British import." He'd been schooled by Everett, who looked frightened; Flop, however, looked to be in his element. His self-confidence exceeded reason.

"Oooh," the girls cooed.

"Convertible," one of them said, stating the obvious.

Cletus's truck and Clyde's Chrysler were of no interest to the girls. Cletus, Penny, Tommy, Clyde, Booger, and Caleb had front-row seats to the fawning. So focused were the girls on the Green Goddess and the boys on the enamored girls that no one noticed the Mustang full of Fairview boys make two passes around the A&W before speeding away.

"Like I said," Flop began, "we're from Colby." He then continued with a bravado that indicated being from Colby carried magical powers. Tommy watched the girls exchange glances, no doubt thrown off slightly by Flop's "Like I said."

"Are you on the football team?" one of them asked.

Everett managed to eke out a response. "Yes, ma'am," he said an octave or two higher than normal.

"Dang," Flop said. He pointed both hands, palms up, toward Everett, as if to be introducing royalty. "This is Everett Fluegge; he was all conference last year on both sides of the ball." Fairview, being a much larger town than Colby, was in a different school conference, so they only played each other every other year. In over fifty years, Colby had won once. The girls had no clue as to anything Flop was saying and knew nothing about Colby football or the players.

Another girl who had been sitting in the middle of the backseat of the Thunderbird got out. Tommy noticed that she and Everett had locked eyes and were oblivious to the exchange between Flop and the other girls.

"Hi, Libby," Everett said. As it turned out Libby and Everett had met at the previous year's regional Beta Club meeting. Libby, like Everett, was large. She was proportionate, but large. She had a pretty face that uniquely blended exuberance and humility. Tommy's first impression of Libby was that she was perfect for Everett.

Their order came, and all the girls except Libby returned to the Thunderbird. Everett looked relieved when they left, but Flop kept winking and waving every time he made eye contact with one of them. His smile threatened to split his face in half.

"Your car?" Libby asked.

Everett clutched the steering wheel for security and nodded. "Uh-huh."

"Nice," Libby said. "I've never seen one like this."

"It's a British import," Everett said.

The rest of the Colby gang witnessed the exchange. The girls in the Thunderbird were still digging into their order and oblivious to Libby and Everett's close encounter.

"Pretty," she said and then giggled. "I like the hood ornament." Everett looked through the windshield at the likeness of a nude chrome goddess and blushed.

"I better go," she said. "Do you still have my number?" she asked. Everett didn't answer. "Here," she said and scribbled her number on a napkin. "Just in case you lost it." She handed the napkin to him and returned to the Thunderbird, glancing back over her shoulder several times on the way.

Clyde was laughing and looking down at Flop from the Chrysler. "Guess we know who the Casanova is," he said. "And it sure ain't you, Flopper."

"Since you guys are celebrities, why don't you lead the way?" Cletus yelled from the truck.

"Hey, Everett," Clyde said. "These guys want to stop at the Chevy dealer and look at a Malibu." Everett looked toward Cletus, who nodded approval.

Everett took the lead and pointed the Green Goddess toward the Chevy dealer. Uncle Cletus had to wait for a couple of cars before pulling out from the A&W; Clyde was behind him. By then the Green Goddess was a few hundred yards ahead of them, just enough to make it through a light at which Cletus and Clyde had to stop.

The locals in the Mustang had been watching the strange lime-green poor excuse for a car that had attracted the attention of *their* girls. An implicit rule known by all boys but not necessarily understood by the girls is that the single female population of a given town is the property of the local boys. It is strictly verboten for boys from another town to sweep in and attract their attention, let alone affection. They're forbidden fruit.

Everett pulled into the Chevy lot and parked the Green Goddess next to the Malibu; he and Flop hopped out to take a closer look. They popped the hood of the car and were too absorbed in the four-barrel carburetor to notice the Mustang pull up.

The driver of the Mustang got Everett's attention when he yelled, "Hey, you the driver of this fruit loop-looking box of a car?" The tall kid that Everett had choked in the parking lot after *Patton* and two others were standing next to the mouthy driver.

The tall kid poured what was left of his cup of soda into the front seat of the Green Goddess, dropped the cup into the slushy mess, and smiled at Everett. "What'd you do that for?" Everett shouted. His slow fuse had been lit. He began chewing nervously on his bottom lip; the Fairview boys mistook Everett's building anger as a trembling chin. The Fairview boys were clustered between Everett and his car. Rushing to his car to inspect the mess would have meant rushing them and certain confrontation. Everett fumed.

Flop was taking it all in. He hadn't seen the likes of the Fairview rabble since moving to Colby from Chicago a few years earlier. Flop didn't show any fear. His courage may have been based on his Chicago rearing, or it could have been that he'd noticed Cletus's pickup and Clyde's Chrysler pulling into the lot. And of course there was Everett, who was larger than any of the Fairview punks. "If you know what's good for you," Flop began, "you puppies will go on your way." He took a step toward them when he spoke.

"The little one has some guts," the smarmy driver said.

"The big one is about to cry," the tall one said. "You're not so brave when you don't have your little podunk town behind you." He rubbed his neck while his smile slowly shaped into an evil grin. Everett, gifted with patience, bode his time and continued to avoid physical confrontation; the others would be there soon. Tommy's uncle Cletus would know what to do.

Clyde had seen what was going on before pulling into the lot. He sped toward the group and pushed P for park before the car had completely stopped. The grinding of the transmission got everyone's attention. He jumped out and walked confidently toward the Fairview gang. The fact that there were four of them didn't faze him. "What's up?" he asked and chest bumped the tall dude. It was clearly a rhetorical question. He squared off between the Malibu and the Fairview boys.

Tommy and the rest of the gang approached more cautiously, moving podlike toward the Malibu. Tommy noticed a Sold sign on the windshield but didn't take time to process the implication.

Flop, emboldened by the arrival of the Colby gang, stepped up beside Clyde and pointed at the tall one. "Slim Jim here poured something into Everett's car," he told Clyde. The Fairview boys stepped aside when Clyde moved toward the car.

Clyde looked at the taller one and said, "Clean it up."

"With what?" Slim Jim asked.

"Your shirt," Clyde said and then pointed at the others. "And their shirts if you need 'em." A man-boy with whiskers and a protruding forehead that shaded wide-set eyes, who looked to be slightly taller and heavier than Clyde, got out of the Mustang. He was the same boy that Clyde had back-handed a few nights earlier in Colby. Clyde pointed directly at him. "Use the Neanderthal's shirt; it's big enough to clean the entire car."

The Fairview gang was clearly perplexed. They'd no doubt intended to intimidate a couple of strangers, and the tables had been turned.

Rhetoric had ceased and intense stares were being exchanged when Cletus and Penny walked up. They'd heard the exchange. Penny looked toward Smarmy, held up her pinky finger, and asked, "Remember our tiny secret?" She grinned. "I'd start cleaning up whatever mess you've made."

"That's okay," Everett said. "I don't want their greasy paws touching my car." The Fairview punks scattered when Everett started toward the Green Goddess. "Give me a shirt," he told no one in particular.

The Fairview boys hesitated for a second until Clyde snapped a head and shoulders fake like he was going to rush them. They all jumped back and began frantically removing their shirts and tossing them to Everett.

Everett used the cup to scoop up the ice and the nicest shirt to wipe up the rest. He then surprised everyone by slinging the cup of ice through the Mustang's open window. The speedometer and sport gauges caught most of the slushy goo.

The Neanderthal started around the car, and the smarmy driver puffed out his chest. Aunt Penny waved her wiggling pinky finger. "Good-bye, boys," she said.

"Let's get out of here," the driver said. The shirtless emasculated boys got in and gave Everett a hard stare before speeding out of the car lot.

Uncle Cletus put one hand on Everett's shoulder and his other on Clyde's. "You boys need to settle this on the football field," he said. "If either of you can get to that Mustang-driving quarterback, you'll shut down their entire offense." He then looked at Flop. "With your speed, if you've learned to catch over the summer—" He paused and did a visual sweep of the others. "Colby just might pull off a win against the high-and-mighty Fairview."

Football aside, Everett hadn't seen the last of the Fairview boys.

Party

Marsha answered the phone, sighed, and then yelled for Tommy. "It's for you."

"Who is it?" their mother asked.

"Mr. Hinkebein again," she answered.

Tommy had begun to dread phone calls at home. Since the only phone was located on the wall between the living room and kitchen, there were no confidential conversations.

"Hello," he said, barely audible. When nervous he found it difficult to force wind across his vocal chords. A mumbled conversation followed.

After Tommy hung up, Marsha pried, "What did he want this time?"

"None of your business," Tommy replied. That would have been his reply no matter the subject, but in this case it really was none of her business. Marsha huffed and went into the bathroom.

Tommy thought of a logical purpose to explain the call. "He just wanted to remind me about Melody's birthday party," he yelled through the bathroom door. Tommy's synapses were overloaded. Melody was turning sixteen, and now this. Paralyzed, he lingered in the narrow hallway outside the bathroom door. Even though he and his sister constantly argued, he inexplicably found comfort in Marsha's interrogations.

"Why didn't you just say that to begin with?" she asked.

"I don't know," he replied. He heard bathwater running and left her alone.

Mr. Hinkebein had confirmed that he'd bought the Malibu and wanted to know if Tommy would ride along later that evening after the birthday party to pick it up. The dealer, knowing the car was a surprise sixteenth birthday gift, had agreed to meet them after hours. Melody would be thinking that they were going to the A&W for a root beer float, her favorite.

While walking to Melody's house, Tommy hoped that she'd gotten over the episode in Miss Anderson's class earlier that day. She must have, he figured. Otherwise, he wouldn't still be invited. And then it dawned on him she couldn't have easily uninvited him; her mother wouldn't have allowed it. His anxiety built as he recollected the virtual death spiral he'd experienced earlier that day.

They'd first discussed Alexander Hamilton's death, which was due to a gunshot wound suffered during a duel with then vice president, Aaron Burr. And the class had agreed that contemporary politics were relatively boring.

And then Miss Anderson had broached women's rights and the origin of the women's movement to gain the right to vote, when Tommy had asked, "Why were women trying to get the right to vote?" The question had evoked dirty stares from all of the girls, including Melody. The question he'd meant to ask was why didn't women already have the right to vote, but it had come out wrong.

Before he got a chance to explain his question, Miss Anderson had gone on a long diatribe about early American women, including Mary Katherine Goddard, who printed the first copy of the Constitution, and Susan B. Anthony, who was first a school teacher and then a women's rights advocate. It was as if Tommy's question had opened the proverbial Pandora's Box of women's suffrage. Tommy got cold-shouldered and chin-upped looks from Melody and the other girls each time Miss Anderson noted a significant attribute of a woman.

Miss Anderson was finally letting him explain himself when the bell rang. The girls had left in a cluster talking about how early American women had been mistreated.

"Nice job," Booger had said sarcastically while walking toward football practice. Tommy, lost in thought, didn't respond. "Think we're still on for tonight?" Booger had asked.

"Hope so," Tommy had replied.

At Melody's request, her sixteenth birthday party was only family and Tommy. Melody's uncle Lester was already there when Tommy arrived. Everyone except Melody knew about the Malibu.

Mrs. Hinkebein answered the door. "Melody's still getting ready," she said. She took Tommy through the house to the back patio to join Mr. Hinkebein and Melody's uncle at the barbecue grill. Her uncle, who was from Fairview, was talking about the high school football team when Tommy walked out.

Lester extended his hand. "Hey there, Thomas," he said and then patted Tommy on the shoulder and continued to shake his hand longer than was comfortable. "You must feel special." He snickered. "You're the only non-family member invited to the big sixteen."

Tommy recalled that Melody had mentioned family only and then rolled her eyes after learning that her mother had invited Uncle Lester. "We're his only family," Melody's mother had told her. "He's been married a couple of times, but, in his words, is presently between wives. Mom knows he's crude but considers him her personal project," Melody had told Tommy and then again rolled her eyes and huffed.

"How's the football team looking?" he asked and then went on to bloviate about the Fairview team. "Heard a couple of your big guys were in Fairview trying to pick up some our cheerleaders," he continued.

Lester was a little taller than average and thin every place except his belly, which protruded like he'd recently swallowed a small melon. He suffered from every gastrointestinal problem known to man and was constantly expelling gas from one end or the other, always with great fanfare.

He stopped talking long enough to hike his leg and let go a doozy. He looked behind him as if expecting to find something. "Dang, Arnold," he said to Melody's dad, "sounds like you've got a frog problem." Melody's dad grinned, but Tommy could tell he wasn't amused.

He turned back to Tommy, his mouth drooped open in thought, and waved a half-closed fist and dangling finger. "Yeah," he began. "Our golden boy had to run those boys back to Colby."

Lester treated himself to a proud pause and tucked in his shirt; it was always coming out both in front under his bulbous belly and in the back since he had no rear end and his pants, large enough to fit his belly, hung loose and baggy.

Tommy worked up the nerve to ask, "Who's your golden boy?" Melody's dad winked and kept the grin but now looked sincerely amused.

Lester staggered backward, dramatizing the notion that everyone knew the golden boy. "Greg Golden," he responded indignantly. "He's young, but he's good."

"What position does he play?" Tommy asked.

"Quarterback," Lester responded. "He moved in from someplace, probably Florida, I don't know. He's a sophomore, but he's already sixteen. Coach says he's fast, got an arm, and knows football."

Tommy stared contemplatively at the bulbous-nosed uncle and drew his own conclusions. The Mustang driver had a name: Greg Golden, or better yet, "Golden Boy." He was anxious to let Clyde and Everett know how the story had been spun in Fairview.

A devious thought came to Tommy, and he smiled. Pester would be a good nickname for Lester—Lester the pester.

Pester took a sip of whatever it was he was drinking. Tommy figured it was something with alcohol in it since Pester only sipped it and was talking louder than necessary. But then he always did that; maybe he needed a hearing aid.

"What's so funny?" Pester asked.

"Just thinking about the golden boy," Tommy replied. And before he could exercise better judgment, a string of words for which he'd given little to no mindful thought spewed forth. "I hope he likes lying on his back, because that's where he's gonna be when he plays in the pit."

Tommy was thinking about the biennial competition that was played alternately at Colby and then Fairview. This year the game would be played in Colby.

Pester dramatically staggered backward again. "Don't let your mouth overload your ass there, little man," he said. Mr. Hinkebein shook his head, gave Lester a look, and flipped the burgers.

Tommy was still contemplating the involuntary comment he'd made and didn't give Pester's language a second thought. His mind was developing visuals of Mr. Mustang's, or Golden Boy's, head bobbling as Clyde or Everett or both sent him crashing to the turf. He decided to tell his uncle Cletus, who'd know how to tell Mr. Franklin and Coach Heart.

Coach Heart's career as a football coach had taken a turn for the better when Mr. Franklin had offered to assist and Coach Heart had accepted. Mr. Franklin, the high school principal, was legendary. He'd arrived in Colby after having served in the Navy SEALs and had gained popularity with the band of boys with his no-nonsense demeanor—and with a little prank he and Tommy's uncle Cletus had played on a mouthy football player a few years earlier.

"So," Pester began, "when are you turning sixteen?"

It was an innocent question, but the cumulative conversation had caused Tommy to begin to churn with contempt. He didn't have any alternative but honesty. "I'm only fifteen," he replied. Tommy had turned fifteen a few weeks earlier, but in light of the jubilant sixteenth birthdays being celebrated by friends, he had let his fifteenth pass with no celebration.

"You some kind of prodigy?" Pester asked.

"No," Tommy replied. "Just a late birthday."

The question caused Tommy to contemplate a dogged dilemma with which he perpetually dealt. His friends, and worst of all, his girlfriend, were turning sixteen nearly a year ahead of him. Being ten when the others were eleven was of no consequence. But the rules change at sixteen. And he'd be miserably captive at fifteen for at least another year.

Melody's mom stuck her head out the door. "We're ready in here," she said.

Mr. Hinkebein had already begun to take the burgers off of the grill. "We're ready here too," he said. He and Mrs. Hinkebein made momentary eye contact. Mr. Hinkebein nodded toward Pester and shook his head in disgust.

Once inside, Pester gave his sister, Melody's mother, a side hug and slobbery kiss on the cheek. She wiped it off when he turned to take a seat at the head of the table, the place where Mr. Hinkebein no doubt usually sat. Tommy, sensing that Pester was tolerated by the family as somewhat of a sympathy case, was reminded of the saying, "You can pick your nose, you can pick your friends, but you can't pick your family."

Pester held his refreshed drink high and after a muffled burp said, "Cheers to the birthday girl." The others held their glasses of iced tea and said, "Cheers!"

Pester had already reached across the table and grabbed a burger when Mrs. Hinkebein asked Mr. Hinkebein to say the blessing. The Hinkebein's custom was to hold hands during the prayer. Pester awkwardly laid his hamburger down and then offered one hand to Mrs. Hinkebein on his left and the other to Melody's dad on his right. Tommy was doubly happy that he wasn't sitting next to the greasy-pawed Lester the Pester.

During Mr. Hinkebein's long Baptist prayer, Tommy sneaked a peek and saw that Pester had a sheepish look. After the blessing Pester looked around and saw what everyone else was drinking and then asked, "Could I get some of that iced tea?"

Once Lester reeled himself in and ceased his endless chatter, a verbal void filled the room. The occasional sound of a chirping Cardinal was the only sound. Tommy, mentally consumed with Booger's upcoming performance, the car, and the prospect of Melody's lingering disdain for his earlier classroom comments, couldn't think of anything worthwhile to say. The sound of people chewing their food was almost as annoying as fingernails on a blackboard.

Finally, Pester broke the silence with, "What do you think about the Russian cosmonauts spending seventeen days in space?"

"Not the same as our moon landing," Melody's dad replied, with a defensive tone. And Pester nodded agreement.

"The shooting at Kent State was a tragedy," Pester added. Heads shook, some in remorse and others wondering what had moved Pester to make such a remark. Mrs. Hinkebein marched in with a candle festooned cake, rescuing the rest from further Pester proclamations. Pester, still under the influence of inhibition inhibiting alcohol, began the singing.

Evidently stirred by the singing, Pester resumed his boisterous behavior, back slapping, and offering hugs that lingered just a little too long. Mrs. Hinkebein finally suggested he head home before dark.

Just before everyone stepped outside, Melody's mom gave Tommy the high sign; he'd cleared Booger's surprise debut with her. While everyone was outside saying good-bye to Lester the Pester and pretending to be sorry that he was leaving, Tommy called Booger and let him know the gig was on.

Tommy had yet to speak directly to Melody. And while he'd looked her way several times during dinner, she'd looked away each time. The buildup to Booger's performance hadn't gone as planned, and he hoped that Booger wouldn't notice. When he saw Miss Anderson's car pulling up, he mustered the nerve to say, "Melody, I have a surprise for you." Still miffed, she forced a smile.

Mrs. Hinkebein let them in. Booger's dad, Miss Anderson, and the Hinkebeins visited while Booger removed his guitar from its case and began tuning. Miss Anderson gave Tommy a wink, a sign that she wasn't holding any women's suffrage grudge.

Melody was visibly surprised but still not talking to Tommy. Booger was hiding his nerves by focusing on his guitar. Tommy pulled Melody aside and got right to the point. He whispered, "I know you've been worried about Booger spending too much time at home and that he's become a recluse. Well, you're about to hear what he's been doing while everyone else has been lollygagging around."

Booger played a few chords to no particular song, and everyone's expression said it all: his playing was great. Their expectations were so low that they thought that was the best he had. Tommy remembered thinking the same thing. Booger finished playing the warm-up chords, and everyone clapped. Tommy was watching Melody's reaction; she was smiling.

Booger, oblivious to the clapping and accolades, made one last twist of a tuning key and then began. Except for an occasional lip twitch, his face was stoic, but his fretting fingers moved with measured passion. "Classical Gas" demands a slow start but rapidly builds into a blurring tempo. Tommy scanned the room and watched the faces as Booger's fingers worked their magic. Smiles turned to awe, and then eyes began to well with tears of joy.

The three-and-half-minute musical feast shocked and emotionally exhausted everyone. Silence held everyone captive for nearly a minute. "That was for Mom," Booger first said and then locked eyes with Melody. "Well, for you too, Melody." His lip was quivering.

Melody moved to the piano bench. "Oh, Boogs," she said and gave him a long hug.

Booger's dad knelt beside him and with a trembling voice said, "She would have been so proud of you." He regained his composure and continued, "And so would Johnny."

Melody's mom was equally touched; she retrieved a box of tissues and shared them with Miss Anderson. "Homecoming is coming up," she said. "You should play in the music competition."

Booger glanced first at Tommy and then turned to Mrs. Hinkebein. "I've thought about it," he said and then strummed a few chords. Tommy had warned him against talking about the duet with Sunny.

Melody stood. "Well, Boogs," she said. Tommy had never heard Melody call Booger by the abbreviated nickname, and he was sure she hadn't been talking to Sunny. "Tommy said he had a surprise for me." She looked at Tommy. "That was the best birthday present ever," she said. "Nothing could top that."

Booger brought much-needed levity to the room when he said, "Tommy didn't do a thing. I played the dang guitar!"

"That's right," Melody said and gave Tommy an affectionate smile.

Tommy grinned. "The day isn't over."

Melody's dad winked at Tommy and turned to Melody. "Hey, I promised you an A&W float."

A TWO-CAR COLBY CARAVAN HEADED toward Fairview. Melody opted to ride with Tommy and "Boogs" in the drop-top GTO. While Melody hadn't said so, Tommy sensed that she'd forgiven him. And the look on Melody's face said she was sure the day couldn't get any better.

Melody's mom and dad followed in their Galaxy 500, the same one Tommy had ridden to the emergency room in after a roller skating injury four years earlier when he'd cut his forehead and wet his pants.

While Melody was enjoying her float, Mr. Hinkebein got Mr. Burger's attention. Tommy watched Mr. Burger's eyes widen about the time Melody's dad must have told him the real reason for the trip to Fairview.

The top on the GTO was still down; the night air was cool. Melody snuggled close to Tommy as the car gained speed and headed home toward Colby. "The day's about over," she said, hinting that she'd yet to receive a gift from him.

Tommy chuckled. He could see the Malibu sitting all alone in the lot; Melody's mom and dad had left the A&W a few minutes before them and tied a giant red ribbon around it. It took Melody a few seconds to realize the car was for her.

She walked around the car not really sure what to do. Finally she hugged her mom and dad and emotionally thanked them. Once she recovered, Tommy opened the door. "Look inside," he said.

Melody looked inside and saw a wrapped gift sitting on the front seat. "What's this?"

Tommy grinned. "I couldn't give it to you until now."

She ripped it open. "An eight-track!" she said and gave Tommy a lingering hug. "You'll have to install it since you're the eight-track expert."

Tommy was warmed by Melody's misconception that after he'd watched an eight-track installation, and then managed to get Clyde's installed without short-circuiting anything, he was an authority on the subject.

Mr. Hinkebein dangled the key. "Happy birthday," he said. "Start her up."

Her hand was shaking when she insecurely guided the key into the ignition and twisted. With a throaty rumble, the engine came to life.

Tommy and Booger hopped into the backseat, and Mr. Hinkebein got in the passenger's seat. "Let's go," he said.

"Where?" Melody asked.

"Home," Mr. Hinkebein said.

Melody pointed at herself. "Me drive?" she asked.

"Sure," her dad replied. "I saw that new state rod leave town this morning with a bunch of camping gear in his truck. Tommy and Booger looked at each other with raised eyebrows and smiled. It was always humorous to boys when they witnessed adults evading the law.

Tommy and Booger watched Melody. She paused for a few seconds and then went through the driver's ed class routine, first adjusting the seat, then buckling her seatbelt, and then adjusting the mirrors. And then she did something she'd never done in the driver's ed car; she reached for the lever that controlled the convertible top.

After putting the top down, she scanned the mirrors, looked all around, and gently pushed the accelerator pedal. The engine's RPMs increased slightly, but the car didn't move. Mr. Hinkebein winked at the boys. "You might want to put it in gear."

Melody grinned and reached for the gear selector on the column; it wasn't there. "It's a Super Sport," her dad said and pointed at the console between the bucket seats. She reached for the large steel ball. "You'll have to push that button on the top of the ball to get it into reverse." She pushed the button with her thumb. "Brake," he reminded her.

The car shifted into reverse with a powerful thud, the engine RPMs lowered, and the sound dropped an octave; it was as if the car had a mind and was saying, "Let's go." Melody backed the car out of the parking space with a series of no brake, full brake, no brake, full brake. They probably looked like a carload of bobbleheads while she got the car into position to head for Colby.

Finally on their way, Mr. Hinkebein, Tommy, and Booger let their arms dangle along the side of the car. Mr. Hinkebein ran his fingers through his thinning hair. Tommy and Booger did the same even though they both had crew cuts, a football requirement. Melody's hands were at ten and two, her auburn ponytail dangling over the back of the seat.

Once past the Fairview city limits, Mr. Hinkebein encouraged Melody to speed up. She'd been used to the driver's ed car, a four-cylinder Ford Maverick. When she mashed down on the Malibu accelerator and kicked in the four-barrel, the front of the car rose and everyone was pressed into the back of their seat. "That's good!" her dad shouted. Melody and Tommy made momentary eye contact through the rearview mirror. She grinned.

At highway speed and with the top down, the wind noise was too loud for talking. Everyone was left to their thoughts. Tommy mentally replayed the day. Melody had turned sixteen, the magic age, the renaissance year. He fast-forwarded through Melody's acerbic uncle, Lester the Pester. Booger had moved everyone, including Melody, to tears with his guitar playing. And it was only a matter of time before the rest of the cheerleaders knew of his new chick-magnet skill.

Tommy had a flash of reality. He was riding in his dream car, except it was Melody's. Well, really her dad's, but she'd be driving it. He wasn't a football standout. He could play the piano but not very well. The exuberance he'd felt earlier in the day slowly slipped away. An emptiness enveloped him when he contemplated the twelve long months until his sixteenth birthday. It had been a bittersweet day.

Quarterback

THE CODGERS WERE SITTING SENTINEL on the courthouse bench discussing football.

"The best quarterback we've had in a long time graduated, don't cha know," Bem opined.

"We're sure gonna have a good line," Monkey said.

"Don't do no good to have a line if there's nobody to protect," Bem replied.

"I'm just sayin'," Rabbit said.

While the Codgers were talking and saying very little, Coach Heart and Mr. Franklin pulled into the Houn-Dawg. It had become part of their daily routine. They'd open the gym for the football players around 5:00 AM. Mr. Franklin would work with one group in the weight room for an hour and then switch with Coach Heart, who put his group through an exhausting aerobic workout.

While the exhausted boys languished in the locker room, Patty Pope, proud owner of the Houn-Dawg and a fervent Colby football fan, treated the coaches to breakfast and coffee. She'd just served Coach Heart and Mr. Franklin plates loaded with eggs, bacon, and hash browns when the Codgers came shuffling in. They settled in at the table next to the coaches and ordered their usual—coffee, black.

Bem looked toward the coaches and tried to act casual. "Say," he began. "What're we gonna do for a quarterback this year?"

Both coaches knew what was being said around Colby. Two of the most promising linemen in the state had nobody to guard. Coaches were expected to call great plays and make great players out of whoever showed up each year to play. Some years were better than others, but some years the talent for quarterback just didn't exist. This was one of those years.

"I think you'll be surprised," Mr. Franklin said between bites.

The Codgers exchanged suspicious glances. They'd been discussing the quarterback position since last season and had come to the conclusion that there wasn't a candidate worthy of the Bookends, Clyde and Everett. It had been a frustrating summer for the Codgers.

"I'm just sayin," Rabbit began, "it's gonna be a shame if we don't have a quarterback to put behind those two big boys."

Ben Franklin was half amused and half aggravated at the Codgers. But he knew that the same attitude prevailed throughout the community. Apparently part of the coach's responsibility was to pull talent out of thin air.

"We're gonna be strong at the quarterback position," Mr. Franklin said. Coach Heart looked at him with a raised eyebrow.

Ben Franklin knew something that none of the others did, including Coach Heart. If things worked out the way he hoped, Colby football would be solid; Clyde and Everett would have a prize to protect.

His confidence aroused the curiosity of every Codger. They sipped their coffee and exchanged contemplative stares. They knew Ben Franklin as both a resourceful and no-nonsense man. Their hope was boosted, but their worries persisted.

Patty eavesdropped and recollected another conversation she'd helped herself to a few days earlier.

THE FAIRVIEW COACH WAS DEALING with a different set of problems. Quinton Clarence had been the number two quarterback for two years. Tall, lanky, fast, and smart, Quinton was outstanding in any of the skilled positions. He'd lettered both his sophomore and his junior year playing on both sides of the ball, mostly as tight end and defensive end. Since Fairview's starting quarterback had graduated, Quinton was a cinch for the slot, except for two things. First of all, he was black. Fairview had never had a black quarterback, and there was already talk.

Quinton's family had moved to Fairview from Chicago three years earlier. His father had been recruited by Carter Webster, the manager of Colby's hat factory. Quinton's father was an engineer, and Carter had recruited him to install and maintain a line of automated sewing and embroidery machines. Rather than move to Colby, the Clarences had decided to locate in Fairview so that Quinton could play football for a larger high school and stand a better chance of being seen by a Division 1 college recruiter.

The second problem was that during the early part of the summer, a family had moved to Fairview from Florida. And with them came their son, a football prodigy. He was mature beyond his years and a natural leader. Except for his acerbic nature, he was the total football package. Giving in to pressure from several of the football boosters, the coach had announced that Greg Golden would be the next Fairview quarterback.

Quinton's father and Carter often spoke of racial challenges in rural America. Both men had done well and were well respected while on the job. But away from work, there was a definite stigma that prevailed. When Quinton's situation came up, Carter had suggested they move to Colby.

Carter, knowing of Colby's football team deficiency, had contacted Ben Franklin directly. Ben had scouted Fairview the year before in anticipation of the upcoming biennial game. He knew well Quinton Clarence's potential and had already begun to dread playing Fairview with him leading the team. Carter and Ben had met in the parking lot of the Houn-Dawg earlier that week to discuss the situation.

"Whadaya think those two are talking about?" Bem had asked, sitting across the street with the rest of the Codgers. Few things went unnoticed in Colby by the octogenarian sentinels.

"Could be anything," replied Fish.

"Probably nothing," chimed in Bem.

"Has to be something," argued Fish.

"Yeah, probably," agreed Bem. It was early; they resumed chewing and whittling and didn't give the coaches any further thought.

While taking out the trash, Patty Pope had seen Carter Webster and Ben Franklin talking. Her curiosity aroused, she had lingered out of sight around the corner of the Houn-Dawg.

Carter had explained the situation and then asked, "What are the rules in a situation like this? Can he play if they move?"

"It's complicated," Mr. Franklin had replied.

"How so?" Carter asked.

Ben thought for a moment. "Well, a student can't transfer for athletic reasons, which Quinton would be doing, but he can move with his parents and be immediately eligible." Ben finished speaking, but his expression indicated there was more.

"Doesn't sound complicated to me," Carter said.

"Oh yeah?" Ben continued. "What are the Clarences going to say when asked why they're moving? His job hasn't changed."

Carter scratched his chin. "I see what you mean. It's not like this town is recruiting black families."

The two men stood there in silence for a few minutes. Finally Ben struck a contemplative pose. "That Koch memorial is coming up."

"That's right," Carter agreed. "I've been asked to speak to how Mr. Koch helped us bridge the racial gap when we first moved to town."

Ben nodded in conspiratorial agreement. "Uh-huh, and the Clarences could be moving to Colby because you shared with them how warm and welcoming Colby is."

Carter scratched his balding head. "And I could change his hours for a month or so to add to the validity of his needing to live closer to the plant."

"I think that'll pass the smell test," Ben said.

"Back to the first question," Carter said. "Will he play if they move?"

Ben headed toward his car. "This conversation never happened."

Patty Pope had sensed the confidence in Mr. Franklin's voice. She'd overheard factory workers talking about the black technician who lived in Fairview and whose son was a standout football player. And she'd heard the players talking about the Fairview golden boy. A smile spread across her face when she'd connected the dots. She immediately began plotting to use the information to have some fun with the Codgers.

PATTY WATCHED THE COACHES LEAVE and then grinned. Her grin was no doubt caused partially by contemplating the addition to Colby's football program, but more so because of the taunting that was about to occur.

After Coach Heart and Ben Franklin left, the Codgers stared at the door and then each other and continued to sip their coffee. "What cha think they've got up their sleeve?" asked Bem.

"I'm just sayin,'" started Rabbit, "that Mr. Franklin has an odd air about him."

"Special forces and all that," said Monkey.

They sat there nodding in agreement, although it wasn't clear on what it was they were agreeing.

Sporting a smirk, Patty brought a fresh pot of coffee to the table and began topping off each cup. "I've got a hunch," she began.

"About what?" Bem asked.

"The quarterback," she snapped back, feigning surprise that there was anything else that might be on her mind. The men looked at each other as if to insinuate that they doubted the value of her so-called hunch. "Want to hear it?" she asked. The men shrugged indifference. "Okay then," she said. "Never mind." She walked back toward the kitchen knowing full well that they'd beg to hear it.

"Well, fizzlesticks," Rabbit blurted out. "You gonna tell us or what?

"Quinton Clarence," she said. The Codgers exchanged blank stares. "Do I have to explain it?" she asked. None of them responded. "Fairview's got that new kid, the one from Florida; he's supposed to be a football phenomenon or some such thing." The Codgers nodded as if to be agreeing to something they'd long ago figured out. "The Fairview coach just announced that the new kid would be the starting quarterback and not that Quinton kid. And did ya know his dad's the machine tech at the hat factory?"

Bem gave Patty an "Are you from Mars?" look. "How do you know all of that?" he asked.

"The soda delivery guy," she said. "He's a big Fairview football booster." Patty had in fact spoken to the soda deliveryman about the upcoming football season.

"The Clarence kid isn't happy about not getting his shot at quarterback," she continued. "It's my guess that he's going to move to Colby."

"Can he do that?" asked Bem.

"Sure," replied Rabbit. "So long as he's living with his parents, he can play." Since Rabbit had been a high school football standout decades earlier, the others yielded to his comments on the subject.

"Does he live with his parents?" Monkey asked.

"Who else would he live with?" Rabbit asked.

"Do his parents live here?" Bem asked, getting to the point.

"Not yet," Patty said. Her expression was full of implication. She watched the Codgers; one by one it clicked.

"Tall, lanky boy, ain't he?" asked Fish.

Monkey nodded agreement. "Black too."

"Fast," added Rabbit.

Patty dampened the moment with, "Don't tell anyone."

"Why?" they asked in unison.

"Secret," she said.

"You know," Bem protested.

"It's just a hunch, remember," she said.

The Codgers slumped like the air had just been let out of their wrinkled bodies. "What about the soda man?" Bem asked.

"He didn't say anything about anyone moving," she replied.

"You just dreamt that up?" Rabbit asked.

"Sorta," she said.

"Whadaya mean, 'sorta'?" Rabbit asked.

"It's a hunch," she said. "A hunch is kind of a sorta."

Fish looked confused. "Is he moving or not?"

"Nobody knows," Bem said.

"Somebody knows," Fish argued.

"Well, probably so," Bem agreed, frustrated. "But we don't."

"I'm just sayin'."

The Codgers nodded agreement, and then each left a dime for coffee on the table, shuffled out of the Houn-Dawg, took up position on the courthouse bench, and prepared to face the day.

SEVERAL OF THE FOOTBALL PLAYERS came regularly to the Houn-Dawg between the morning workout and school. Patty was known for her heaping-helping breakfasts for the football team. The band of boys pulled into the Houn-Dawg and watched the Codgers slowly making their way across the street to the bench. They were so deep in thought that it appeared they were on a death march.

"What's up with those guys?" Caleb asked Patty.

"They're in a quandary," she said.

"A quandary?" Caleb asked.

"Yeah," Patty said and then turned to attend to the griddle loaded with grits, hash browns, and scrambled eggs.

Before anyone could inquire as to the Codgers' quandary, Caleb asked Everett, "What exactly is a quandary?"

Flop, having been riding with Everett in the Metropolitan for nearly a week, took a stab at it. "It means puzzled." He was guessing and looked to Everett for confirmation.

Everett squinted his eyes and scanned the room as if to be studying the water stains on the ceiling. "A quandary," he began, "is more of a predicament than a puzzle." He looked at Patty and asked, "Are they in a predicament?"

"No," she said. "Actually they're puzzled."

"Told ya," Flop blurted out.

Flop was sitting on the stool next to Everett. Everett leaned down and whispered. "If they were puzzled, then they weren't in a quandary." He then lowered his whisper even more. "Mrs. Pope used the wrong word." Everett then gently patted Flop between the shoulder blades. The rest of the boys were too consumed with watching the food on the griddle and salivating to give any thought to Flop's dilemma over the finite definition of quandary.

"You look like you need to eat," Patty said and placed a sizzling plate in front of Flop. Flop's emaciated appearance fooled many. His strength and agility had improved over the summer, but his body remained too lean to look healthy. Coach Heart occasionally called him Feral Flop.

"Thanks," Flop said and then shoved as much food as possible into his mouth after asking, "What was their quandary?"

"They're worried about who's going to be quarterback this year," she said and then turned from the griddle and solemnly faced the boys. "I am too." She stood there for a moment waiting to hear what they knew—nothing.

It was a dilemma they'd been discussing all summer. Several had stood in at throwarounds, but nobody had exhibited sharp passing skills. The receivers had had to deal with wobbly, too-high or too-low passes all summer. It wouldn't be the first time that Colby wasn't able to field a team with skill at every position.

CARTER WEBSTER'S OFFICE PHONE RANG, and he picked up. Mr. Franklin got straight to the point. "I called the state office," he said. "A student must be enrolled within the first ten days of the semester in order to play sports."

"Didn't school start last week?" Carter asked.

"Wednesday," Ben replied.

"This is Monday," Carter thought aloud.

Ben did the math. "He needs to enroll by next Tuesday." There was silence on the line; both men were thinking. "They'll need an address inside the school district," Ben added.

"I was thinking that," Carter replied.

"Look," Ben said, "this is as far as I can go on this."

Carter gave an understanding nod even though he was alone in his office. "I'll get the ball moving," he said.

"I look forward to Colby's first black student," Ben said.

"Black quarterback," Carter added.

"That too," Ben said.

Carter walked out onto the production floor and found Wendell Clarence adjusting the needle timing on a sewing machine. He gave Wendell a sign and kept moving. He and Wendell were sensitive to people thinking that Carter might play favorites since they were both black. They'd agreed to keep their personal conversations to a minimum.

Wendell finished the adjustment and performed a test while Carter made his way through the busy production area. Carter was waiting for Wendell when he returned to his tool cabinet.

"There's no guarantee," Carter whispered. "Quinton will have to earn a spot."

"That's almost the same as a guarantee," Wendell said while wiping down and putting away his wrenches.

"Here's the deal, though," Carter began. "You've got to move inside the district by this weekend." Wendell froze momentarily. Carter continued. "Quinton will need to be enrolled in school by next Tuesday with a home address inside the school district."

Wendell frowned. "I'm not sure that's possible."

Carter nodded confidently. "Call me tonight." Wendell returned a nod. The conversation had taken less than thirty seconds.

TOMMY AND EVERETT ARRIVED TOGETHER. Miss Anderson was at the blackboard. She'd written two words on the board: iconoclasm and manumit. While the boys took their seats, she wrote two names: Washington and Lafayette. Everett began thumbing through the pint-sized dictionary that Miss Anderson had given him the week before. Melody was fanning through the pages of the five-pound history book. Tommy pulled his book from under his seat and turned to the index. He found iconoclasm in the index; there were several pages associated with it.

Miss Anderson turned to face the class, rubbed her hands together to get the chalk residue off, and then waited for everyone to be seated before taking attendance. It was only the second week of school and she'd already been giving homework assignments. Tommy recalled the halcyon days of sixth grade, when Miss Anderson was new in town and had coddled them like they were her treasure. However, on the first day of class this year, she'd made it clear that her job was to both educate them and prepare them for college.

Everett now had his history book open and was rushing from page to page with one hand while his giant fingers held multiple places open in his miniature dictionary with the other. Tommy couldn't find manumit in the index. He found the other words, jotted down the pages where they could be found, and noticed that a couple of the pages matched. He jotted down the page numbers for Washington and Lafayette. He turned first to the pages that were associated with both words and both names.

By now Everett had the fingers on one hand holding several places in the history book and the other hand holding several places in his dwarf dictionary. Everett's enormous size struck Tommy. While the desk chair was scaled perfectly for someone Tommy's size, it was almost comical to see how Everett had to squeeze into his. Together his forearms were nearly as wide as the desktop, and the chair back reached less than halfway up his back. Everett had always been big for his age, but now he was big for *any* age. Tommy sensed something else. Everett wasn't simply looking for the answer to please Miss Anderson; he was truly interested in the answer for himself. He'd inexplicably taken the Beta Club Ambassador position to heart, possibly inspired by Libby.

Miss Anderson was watching Everett feverishly scan the pages he'd finger-marked. Tommy couldn't tell if her expression was one of sympathy, compassion, or exuberance. No matter, he got the call. "Everett," she said. He looked up. His expression was one of either surprise or interrupted focus. "Let's begin with you," she continued. That was her way of letting the rest of the class know that they weren't off the hook. "What do these people and these words have in common?"

Everett had worked up a sweat racing through his five-pound text book and palm-sized dictionary. Or maybe just being stuffed into a chair made for someone half his size somehow caused the sweat to ooze out. He wiped his forehead with the back of his hand. "Well," he began, "both generals were opposed to slavery." He paused a second and tapped his temple with his pencil. "And since slavery was popular at the time, that made them iconoclastic."

"What about manumit?" Miss Anderson asked.

Everett looked perplexed. "Slavery," he said. "They were both opposed to slavery."

"So," Miss Anderson said, "manumit means opposed to slavery?"

"Sure," Everett replied. He shrugged as if to imply that everyone should know that plain as day. In reality, it's possible that, other than Miss Anderson, Everett may have been the only person in the room who had ever heard of the word.

Miss Anderson turned to the rest of the class. "Washington had slaves until the day he died." Everett raised his hand. Miss Anderson grinned. "We'll let someone else respond."

Melody had kept reading while Everett had been talking; she raised her hand. Miss Anderson nodded. "He changed," she said and then read from her book. "During the shaping of the constitution he grew to oppose slavery. But he feared that to say so would divide the delegates representing the states."

"How do historians know that?" Miss Anderson asked.

Everett's bear paw was the only hand in the air. Miss Anderson smiled and nodded but didn't call on him, probably thinking that Everett had done enough talking. "Remember," she said, "his will specified that after he and his wife died all of their slaves would be set free."

Miss Anderson spent the remainder of the hour discussing Washington and Lafayette's lifelong relationship. Just before the bell rang, she issued a thought challenge. "Be thinking about something I mentioned earlier," she said. "Washington's will specifying the release of his and Mrs. Washington's slaves upon both of their deaths was read at his death." She paused and made sure everyone was listening. "Think about the quandary that Mrs. Washington was in when her slaves knew—" The bell rang before she could finish her thought but not before using the Q word and leaving everyone looking forward to the next day's class.

AFTER PRACTICE, FLOP THREW HIS duffel bag into the Green Goddess's tiny trunk. Everett first straightened Flop's bag and then placed his bag and several textbooks beside it. Few things got by Flop; he'd noticed the anal-retentive rearrangement of the bags and the pile of books Everett was taking home to study.

Tired from an intense conditioning football practice, they both grunted when they settled into their seats. Flop turned to Everett. "You're just a nerd in a giant's body."

Everett, unlike Flop, thought before he spoke. "Is that good or bad?" he asked.

"Neither," Flop replied. "It is what it is."

"Nerd," Everett said, more to himself than to Flop.

Flop gave Everett a look of disgust. "Good grief, Everett," he said. "Don't tell me you're going to do a word study on nerd."

Everett didn't respond; he'd already mentally moved on. His mind was on the phone conversation he'd had with Libby. Everett wasn't a nerd in the true sense of the word. He wasn't singularly focused and obsessed about any particular thing, and he was sociable. Confident but shy was the best way to describe Everett. But he certainly had nerdlike tendencies. In light of the confrontations that had occurred between the Fairview and Colby boys, asking a Fairview girl out on a date and then taking her to a restaurant in Fairview bordered on stupidity. Innocent or naive was probably a more accurate description of Everett, but Flop had never been known for his word power. Nerd would have to do.

The night before, Everett had pulled the napkin sliver with Libby's number on it from his billfold where it had been safely stored and treasured for nearly a week. He'd waited for his parents to start watching *Mary Tyler Moore* before dialing. He'd fretted all day over how exactly to ask a girl for a date. He could figure the area of a concave polygon but didn't have a clue when it came to chitchat with girls.

A woman's voice answered. "Hello?" Everett was fairly certain it wasn't Libby. "Hello," he said and then realized he needed to clear his throat. "May I speak to Libby?"

"May I say who is calling?" the lady on the other end asked. Everett assumed it was Libby's mother.

"Everett Fluegge," he replied. "We met at—" Everett started to say but was interrupted.

"Oh, we've heard all about you," the motherly voice began. "Libby said you'd be calling." Everett was simultaneously relieved and curious. Libby expecting his call brought comfort and confidence, but acute curiosity shot back and forth behind his eyes.

Everett was still processing the fact that Libby had told her parents about him and that they had listened, when another voice came on the line. "Hey," Libby said; her cheerful voice was feminine but strong. If she sang in a choir, she'd be an alto or lower. "I thought maybe you'd lost my number," she continued.

"Well dadgum," Everett said, half in disgust. "Football practice, homework, my job," Everett began, making excuses for not calling.

"You have a job?" she asked.

Everett would regret having said it. "Yeah, two. The feed store, and a guy who makes brooms."

"You talkin' about that guy featured in the paper?" she asked.

"Uh-huh," Everett replied.

"Why weren't you in any of the pictures?" she asked.

"I hadn't started working for him yet."

"Cool job," she said. "My parents won't let me get a job. They want me to study and practice my piccolo."

Everett recalled Libby's enormous hands and tried to visualize her holding the minuscule instrument. "You play the piccolo?"

"It's a hoot," she said. "I'm the biggest girl in the band and play the smallest instrument." She giggled. "My dad said I'd have a better chance of getting a music scholarship if I played an instrument that no one else did." She giggled again. "I might have to switch to the flute because my hands are almost too big for my stupid piccolo."

The conversation, although mostly one sided, was going much easier than Everett had expected. He was particularly impressed that Libby was comfortable with her size. He'd wondered if large girls were self-conscious. Like him, she'd probably always been large and didn't know any other way.

Everett had written several questions down just in case he got nervous and couldn't think of anything to say: favorite color, TV show, movie, school subject. "What's your favorite restaurant?" he asked.

When she answered, Everett liked her even more. "Pig's Tail," she said. Everett told her about the first time he'd been there, when he and his friends had helped move the bowling alley. "I remember that," she said. "I wondered what happened to those old machines."

"They're here in Colby," Everett proudly said.

"I hope the guy who owns the bowling alley in Colby is nicer than the goofball here in Fairview," she said. "He's gross; thinks he's a ladies' man."

"You're right. I remember," Everett agreed. "When we came to move the alley, he had on a big necklace and his shirt wasn't buttoned."

"So, when are you coming to Fairview again?" she asked.

"I might be coming to the Pig's Tail," he replied.

"Really? When?" she asked.

"I was thinking about going on Saturday night," he said, cautiously uncommitted and controlling his voice so as to disguise his nerves.

"Saturday night?" she confirmed.

"Uh-huh," Everett replied. The conversation wasn't going like he'd planned. Somehow he'd gotten to the Pig's Tail without Libby.

"Who're you going with?" she asked.

"Well, I'm not sure," Everett replied. His greatest fear had come to pass: his mind had gone blank.

Libby's forward nature was the answer to prayer. "Why don't you drop by and pick me up, and we'll go together," she suggested.

"Sure," Everett said. "I could do that."

"Then it's a date. What time?" she said.

She'd skipped through the part where she'd have to ask her parents, a crucial step that Everett had been told to expect, and the part where she'd either think up an excuse to say no or convince her parents to let her go.

Before Everett could respond, she continued. "It gets crowded after six," she said. "Why don't we try to go before then?"

"Okay," Everett said. "I'll be by around a quarter to six."

"Make it five thirty," she said. "My parents want to meet you. My dad will probably give you some sort of speech."

"Okay," he said. Now he was getting nervous again.

"My mom knows Peggy," Libby said.

"Peggy?" Everett asked.

"Yeah, the lady with the patch over her eye at Pig's Tail," Libby said. "She calls herself Peggy the pirate. My mom plays cards with her," Libby continued. "She has a drifting eye. Peggy does, not my mom," she said, clarifying.

After the call Everett sat at his makeshift desk struggling to get his mind wrapped around geometry. Postulates, theorems, obtuse and acute angles: the geometry glossary blended into a blur. He put the book of dimensions away and reached for American history.

Since a regular desk was too small, and a large desk was too large for his bedroom, Everett's dad had improvised. Everett's desk was an old door supported on one end by a dilapidated filing cabinet and two four-by-four posts on the other. Since he'd helped his dad shorten the door and attach the posts, Everett was proud of the custom-built setup.

Miss Anderson had mentioned that George Washington had been credited with being the first American mule breeder. And since the mule was Missouri's mascot, Everett was intrigued. His history book was turned to a page with a drawing of President Washington standing with a donkey. The drawing's caption read "Washington and his prize jack, Royal Gift, a gift from King Charles III of Spain." Everett read where King Charles had given Washington a pair of prize jacks. One of them had died at sea, and the other is credited with siring over fifty super mules. And the lineage of most prize mules throughout the United States could be traced back to Royal Gift.

After reading for a while, Everett rubbed his eyes and pondered the gift of a donkey from the King of Spain and also Washington's friendship with Lafayette, all the way across the Atlantic. Everett froze momentarily on the notion that he knew few people outside of Colby. He looked up George Washington in the index and read everything in the book about the first president of America before falling asleep at his desk.

New Kid

FLOP WAS WAITING AT THE edge of the road when Everett pulled up. He carefully placed his duffel bag in the trunk next to Everett's bag and neatly stacked textbooks; he'd learned. He got in and, typical of Flop, began the day announcing a plan. "Caleb called and said he had Clyde talked into goin' road hunting Saturday night."

"I have a date," Everett responded.

He said it in such a nonchalant way that the weight of the event didn't at first register with Flop. Within a few seconds, however, the full impact of Everett's reply had coursed its way through Flop's synapses. "A what?" he asked.

Everett grinned. "A date."

"With whom?" Flop asked. Everett had been studying the Strunk and White book on grammar given to him by Miss Anderson and sharing tips with Flop; the occasional corrections were working.

"Libby," Everett said. "One of those girls we saw at the A&W."

"Oh yeah," Flop said. "The big one?" Everett tilted his head slightly and glared. "She's pretty too," Flop quickly added. "They all were. But you got to admit she's big for a girl." Flop and Everett were good enough friends that Flop could say anything. And it's a good thing they were because Flop knew no other way.

"I guess she's a pretty good size," Everett admitted. "I just didn't notice at first."

"Her parents big?" Flop asked.

"I'm meeting them Saturday," Everett said.

"Oh." Flop chuckled. "Must be serious. Already meetin' the parents."

"No," Everett said. "You have to meet the parents before going out on a date." Flop looked at him in disbelief. Everett continued, "I think her dad wants to give me the 'keep my daughter safe' speech."

"I'll bet her dad's big," Flop said. "I'll bet he's got a big belly, bulbous nose, and crooked teeth from eating too much."

"Why would you say that?" Everett asked, annoyed.

"I don't know, just popped into my head. I'll bet her mom is a good cook," Flop added. "Big people are usually good cooks."

"Like my mom?" Everett asked. Flop didn't answer.

"Libby doesn't have a big nose," Everett said with an air of uncertainty.

"I'm trying to remember her exactly," Flop said. "It seemed like she had a pretty face and loud voice. Where'd you meet her at?" he asked. Everett gave him a look. Flop corrected himself. "Where'd you meet her?"

"At the regional Beta Club meeting."

Flop chuckled. "Oh, so she's got a big brain in that big head."

There was a moving van parked in front of the duplex where Mrs. Koch lived. "Looks like someone is moving into the duplex next to Mrs. Koch," Flop said. Everett slowed to a crawl but saw nobody stirring. The new people would have to remain a mystery.

They pulled into the Houn-Dawg and stopped beside Clyde's Chrysler. "Everett has a date," Flop said first thing.

"Who?" nearly everyone asked simultaneously.

"Libby the giant," Flop announced. Everett faked a backhand toward Flop. Flop flinched and then said, "Libby the *gorgeous* giant."

Everett shook his head and grinned. "You're hopeless." Everett couldn't be upset; he was too happy about the date.

"From Fairview?" Caleb asked.

"You gonna bring her to Colby?" Tommy asked.

"We're going to the Pig's Tail," Everett said.

Caleb laughed. "Pig's Tail?" he asked. "Really? Aren't you supposed to go for a stroll in the park or do something where you hold hands?" Everett was beginning to come down from his date-induced high. "Has she seen you eat?" Caleb continued.

Everett changed the subject. "Hey, it looks like there's someone moving in beside Mrs. Koch." The boys exchanged glances. Nobody knew anything, which was odd for a small town. People just didn't appear out of nowhere without somebody saying something beforehand.

"Who is it?" Caleb asked. Everybody shrugged.

THE BOYS WERE ON THEIR way to Miss Anderson's room. History wasn't their first class for the day, but they liked to hang out there before school. She'd tell them stories about flying or where she'd ridden on her motorcycle. And they simply enjoyed looking at her. Recently Everett had begun to ask her questions about American history, which cut into the storytelling time.

Quinton Clarence and his family were standing in the principal's office when the boys walked by. The hall was abuzz; word had spread instantly. Some saw a black student—a first for Colby. A few of the girls a saw a tall, athletic, good-looking guy. The band of boys saw a quarterback. It took Tommy a few seconds, but he made the moving van connection.

"What's he doin' here?" Caleb asked. It wasn't a racially charged question. The boys knew Quinton from football and that his father worked at the hat factory.

Tommy hoped that what he was thinking was right. "Looks like he's enrolling," he said. Clyde and Everett both looked momentarily at Quinton, then at each other, and then at Tommy.

Tommy knew what they were thinking. "That's who you guys will be protecting this year." The rest of the boys looked at Tommy with a "How do you know?" frown. "Melody's creepy uncle said that the Mustang jerk is supposed to be a hotshot quarterback, and the coach just announced that he'd be starting, not Quinton."

The boys huddled around Tommy. "Well, he didn't call him the Mustang jerk. His real name is Greg Golden. Anyway, he's the Fairview quarterback. I'm guessing that Quinton is coming here so he can play football, and I'm hoping quarterback. Everyone and his brother must surely know by now that we don't have one."

"His sideburns are thicker than yours, Everett," Flop said. The rest of the gang took notice of Quinton's thick sideburns, which extended below his earlobes. The awestruck man-boys inadvertently touched the sides of their own faces.

Coach Heart was making his way through the crowded hallway. Quinton was beginning to draw a crowd. A new enrollment was rare in Colby; the population was stable—in reality, stagnant would be a better description.

Caleb could be described many ways, but bashful wasn't one of them. "Is he gonna play quarterback," Caleb asked the coach.

Coach Heart surveyed the band of boys. His expression looked like he'd just learned of a death in the family. "Follow me," he said. He hip-checked his way through the hallway to Miss Anderson's classroom. He closed the door after the boys shuffled inside.

He wiped the sweat from his forehead. "Is this gonna work?" he asked. Tommy was slightly amused by the desperation in Coach Heart's voice. Quinton was exactly what the team needed, but Coach Heart needed their cooperation.

"First game is Friday," Everett said. Everett's words were telling. In four words he'd said all there was to say regarding Coach Heart's concerns. Quinton would be accepted, but more important than that, he needed to get up to speed on the plays.

Coach Heart studied each face; he looked nervous. "Okay, I'm only going to mention this once," he began. "We don't have much time, and I can't really talk about this race thing without getting into trouble. Quinton Clarence is transferring to Colby." He paused and took in everyone's response. "Today is critical," he said. "Quinton will be the first black student here at Colby. You boys will have the most influence on how he's accepted."

Tommy hadn't thought about the race issue until Coach mentioned it. He recalled the days when the Websters had first arrived. It had been a big ordeal, but the Kochs had invited them into their home, and in doing so, they had set the example for the rest of Colby.

"So, is he gonna play ball?" Clyde asked, looking for an absolute answer.

Coach Heart couldn't read Clyde's expression. "I haven't spoken to him yet," Coach replied, which was true but obfuscating. He tested the waters. "I certainly hope so."

Clyde nodded, deep in thought. "We could use him," he said.

"You dang betcha," agreed Flop.

Clyde looked at Flop. "Maybe he can throw the ball so that even you can catch it." All of the boys except Flop laughed.

"Okay," Coach said with a questioning smile. "So, I can count on you guys to help him feel welcome?"

The boys looked each other and shrugged. "Sure," several of them said.

"So long as he's not a big jerk," Flop said.

Everett gave him a gentle shove. "Look who's talking."

Coach Heart had already left. The boys lingered a few minutes but were moving toward the door when Miss Anderson walked into the room and flipped on the light. She held her nose. "Pee-yew," she said. "You guys really stink up the place." Everyone pointed at Caleb.

"His mom fixed gingerbread again," Clyde said. "She usually burns it."

"Doesn't anyone use aftershave anymore?" she asked.

Everett grinned and nudged Caleb. "You gotta shave first," he teased.

"Have you heard?" Tommy asked. In fact, Ben Franklin had called her the night before and filled her in.

"Yes, I heard that a student from Fairview is moving to Colby," she said, playing it naive regarding race or football.

"You know what this means?" Clyde asked.

Like Coach, she wasn't sure how to take him. "Not really," she answered.

"We have a quarterback!" he exclaimed with a level of enthusiasm rare for Clyde.

Miss Anderson grinned. "Did Coach say that?" she asked.

"Coach couldn't decide if he was worried about Quinton being black or excited about him playing football," Clyde said. "I don't care what color he is. I just want to win."

Tommy had been thinking and finally connected the dots. "There was a moving van in front of the Mrs. Koch's duplex this morning," he said. "I'll bet that's where they're going to live." The rest of the boys nodded in agreement with Tommy. Tommy recalled the one-sided conversation he'd had with Lester the Pester. "I'll bet he's moving here just so he can play football," Tommy added.

He looked at Miss Anderson with suspicion. "You think Coach knows that already?"

She wisely played it down. "It doesn't make any difference now," she said. "Quinton's family is moving to Colby, and he's now a student." The boys were distracted by her smile. "We can only hope that he'll be at football practice today."

She waved toward the door and squinted her nose. "Now get out of here before one of you has another gastro expulsion."

First Game

THE FIRST GAME OF THE season was traditionally against I-Mack—short for Immaculate Conception—a private Catholic school from Fairview. The two schools had about the same student population, but the private school had the entire town of Fairview from which to pull talent. Most of the students were Catholic, but it wasn't a requirement, especially if one was gifted athletically. I-Mack's primary focus in sports was soccer, because that's the premier sport at most Catholic colleges.

The Codgers began their Monday over coffee at the Houn-Dawg, as usual. Monkey's golf cart—the bag holder replaced with a bench so four could ride—was parked near the door. Each year he'd added a new Colby Indian decal. There was something on nearly every flat surface. Some had said it was the decals that held the contraption together. The decals and the fact that the cart appeared at nearly every football practice and game had earned it the moniker "Spirit Cart."

New for this year was a giant spear attached to the top. Joe-Bill, a local metal sculptor, had suggested it as a joke. The mistake he'd made was doing so in front of witnesses; Monkey had accepted. Joe-Bill's spear was essentially a piece of art and contrasted sharply with the rest of the decal-riddled Codger-carrying contraption. Monkey had discovered that the spear made the golf cart top-heavy, so he had to go slow when making a turn—a small price to pay for such a fine school spirit adornment.

Since it was football season, the primary topic was Friday night's game. They took their regular seats at the Houn-Dawg, and Patty brought a pot of coffee and then set a Fighting Indian coffee mug in front of each curmudgeon. Rabbit looked like he'd developed indigestion. "Those I-Macks are gonna kick our butt this year," he began. The two teams were usually competitive, the score close, but Colby had won eight of the past ten games. Those were years with superb quarterbacks.

Patty smiled; they hadn't heard, which was rare, and she was enjoying the moment. "That's no way to start your week," she said.

"I'm just sayin'—" Rabbit replied and then took a double take at Patty. "You're awfully happy today," he added.

"You freeloaders don't want to miss practice today," she said.

They all looked up from their coffee. Rabbit asked, "Why's that?"

She gave Rabbit a wink and replied, "I'm just sayin'."

About that time Jupiter Storm walked in. Jupiter was arguably the nosiest person in town. He never lingered in one place very long; he'd stop only long enough to share the latest gossip or to inquire about matters that were generally none of his business. He was both intriguing and annoying. The Codgers most likely envied Jupiter's penchant for finding out things first even though his technique was aggravating.

There was no hello or good morning; he just blurted out, "Who's moving in beside old lady Koch?" The Codgers exchanged blank stares.

"You mean Mrs. Koch?" Fish asked, and he did so in a way to imply that Jupiter shouldn't refer to the town's matriarch as "old lady."

Jupiter ignored Fish but noticed Patty grinning. "She knows something," he said.

"She knows you're a pain in the rear," Rabbit said.

Jupiter nodded as if to agree and then said, "Maybe, but she knows something else." All of the Codgers turned toward Patty. Those with stiff necks were slower in turning than the others.

"Don't look at me," she said. "All I'll say is you can find out for yourself." She nodded her head as if to say, "And that's final," but then continued. "You might go offer to help whoever it is that's moving to town and find out that way." She glared at Jupiter. "You gonna order something or leave?" Her expression made it clear that he needed to do one or the other.

"I'll have a cup of coffee," Jupiter said and then pulled a chair up to the Codgers' table. In doing so he'd violated any number of implied but unstated social rules held sacred among the courthouse bench elite, of which Jupiter was not a member.

"Joe-Bill make that spear for you?" he asked. Monkey nodded but didn't make eye contact. Like everyone else in Colby, Monkey had learned that if you pretended he wasn't there, he'd go annoy someone else. It was the same strategy used for bear attacks, and equally difficult to do. "Thought so," Jupiter said, getting back to the question about the spear.

Patty, wearing an impish grin, watched the Codgers' table while cleaning the grill. She was no doubt amused by the unusual lack of conversation. The Codgers, normally boisterous and arguing about multiple issues, were all staring into their coffee, mute, while Jupiter scanned the table and wondered why nobody was talking.

"I'm gonna run over and see who starts unloading stuff off that moving van," Jupiter finally said, and it was clear he was looking for a response. When he got none, he stood up to leave.

Fish finally spoke. "Let us know what you find out." It was a rhetorical remark; everyone knew that Jupiter would soon be making the rounds and telling everyone who was moving to Colby. And that was one of the pluses about Jupiter: he was a community crier of sorts.

Jupiter tossed twenty cents onto the table for everyone to see and left without closing the door. Patty shook her head and closed the door and then turned to the Codgers. "Okay," she began, "I wanted you to have to find out for yourselves, but since Jupiter is on the prowl, I'll tell you now so that he won't be the first to be blabbing it around town."

She didn't tell them how she knew, but she told them what she knew. It was as if she'd cast a spell; the Codgers were all deep in thought but beaming.

Rabbit's question seemed odd at first. "Think Mrs. Webster will be helping them move?" he asked.

"You think just because the Clarences are black that Mrs. Webster is gonna be there?" Fish asked.

"Could be," Rabbit replied.

The rest of the Codgers frowned. "So what if she is?" asked Monkey with a tone of sarcasm.

"Well," Rabbit began, "if Mrs. Webster is there, and the Clarences are moving in beside Mrs. Koch, then—"

Monkey finished the sentence, "Where there's Mrs. Koch and Mrs. Webster, there is sure to be homemade brownies." And without any further words spoken, the Codgers hustled to the spirit cart.

QUINTON CLARENCE HAD MOVED WITH his family from Chicago to Fairview four years earlier, and they'd moved once before that, so he had a little experience with being the new kid. And he was used to being black in a mostly white population. But Colby's rural culture would prove to be new to him.

The boys at Fairview, particularly the athletes, had always dressed similarly: the same brand of jeans, always pressed with a crease down the front of each leg, and button-down oxford shirts with the little loop in the back, which they called BDs.

Boys at Colby wore jeans, but they weren't pressed. And there was no uniformity with regard to shirt choice. A few BDs were seen moving through the hall, but there were also the colorful shirts with snaps for buttons, and a couple guys had work shirts with their name above the chest pocket, like something seen at a filling station. Colby lacked any discernible dress code.

Quinton stood out for two reasons: he was black, and he was dressed in Fairview fashion. He had one of those mouths that never completely closed, revealing a set of perfectly uniform pearly-white teeth. He was tall but not imposing. He moved with a charismatic aura that invited kindness.

Kids, unless taught otherwise by their parents, aren't typically racially biased. The Websters had moved to town and were now totally integrated into every aspect of the community. Colby had never had a race-related problem. Nobody had any reason to be racist from personal experience. Quinton's first day began without a hitch. The girls swooned over his looks and his attire. Quinton's athletic prospects caused the boys to embrace him with equal but different enthusiasm. None of the students questioned his motive for moving from Fairview to Colby. Since his dad worked at the hat factory, the move seemed natural and wasn't questioned.

MISS ANDERSON HAD GOTTEN WORD about Quinton and modified the study plan. Rather than continue discussion of Washington, Lafayette, and their notions about slavery, and run the risk of making everyone uncomfortable, she decided to cover elected officials in general. On the board, she had written "Congress" in letters two feet tall.

Tommy walked in, saw how the chairs had been rearranged, and frowned in confusion. He got a wink from Miss Anderson. The chairs had originally been arranged in five rows of six chairs. There were now six rows with five chairs.

Booger didn't notice; he took a seat in the third chair in the second row, same as always. Clyde didn't notice either. Tommy watched Everett scan the room and dip his chin six times as he counted and then look toward Miss Anderson. She had gotten tickled by watching students arrive and take what they thought was their regular seat.

School had been in session for less than a week; there weren't assigned seats, but students had already claimed a seat, not unlike the typical church scene. Tommy had soon figured it out. A seat choosing calamity was about to occur, but it wouldn't be Quinton's doing. When Quinton walked in with Flop, Tommy motioned for him. Flop frowned but followed. "Let's sit over here by the windows," Tommy said. Quinton shrugged indifference and took a seat.

The students who normally sat in the back of the class walked one by one to the end of the row and then looked around bewildered. Most of them ended up in the sixth row near the windows.

After everyone had finally taken a seat, Miss Anderson asked, "Notice anything different today?" All heads turned toward Quinton. Smarty-pants Everett raised his hand.

"The desks have been rearranged," Miss Anderson smiled. Several of the kids hadn't figured it out; students now sitting in the sixth row looked perplexed.

She asked Quinton to stand and, after introducing him, said, "Welcome to American History." She spent several minutes asking Quinton about himself: what his favorite sport, TV show, band, and song were; if he could, what animal would he be; and more. At first Quinton looked embarrassed, but Miss Anderson asked the questions in such a way that he began to comfortably answer. And when appropriate, she pointed out someone in the class with a similar interest. She was skilled at integrating new people into a new environment. "You may sit," she said after asking him everything except his blood type.

"Today we're going to discuss how our government leaders are chosen." She turned and wrote "Robert Morris" on the board. "Who was Robert Morris?" she asked.

Flop raised his hand. "The inventor of the Morris code?"

"That was Samuel Morse," she said. No one else was brave enough to take a shot. "Robert Morris was one of the very first senators," she said. "Now, how was he elected?"

Melody was the only one to raise her hand. "By popular vote?" she asked more than answered.

"That's how it's done now, Melody," Miss Anderson said and then continued. "Before the Seventeenth Amendment to the US Constitution, senators were chosen by each state's legislature—two from each state."

"What we now have is probably a better system," one of the brownnosing front row students offered.

"One would think," replied Miss Anderson, "but not exactly." The brownnoser's smirk morphed into a frown of disappointment. "The Seventeenth Amendment also gives the president the power to appoint senators when for any reason a sitting senator leaves office. And that gives the president more power than was originally intended by the Founding Fathers." The bell rang before Miss Anderson could elaborate.

Tommy and several of the players were waiting with Quinton at the locker room door when Coach Heart gave him his equipment. Tommy could see that Quinton was a little disappointed. He thought that maybe Quinton didn't like the number he'd been assigned. Some players are very particular about the number on their jersey.

Booger had saved a locker for Quinton and Tommy. "Here ya go," Booger said and pointed at the lockers, which were first-come, first-served except for Booger's. He always used the locker that had been dedicated to his older brother, who had been a high school legend before being tragically killed in Vietnam.

Tommy noticed that Quinton had lost the spring in his step. "What's up?" he asked.

Quinton held out the equipment for Tommy to see. "This stuff is used," he said.

"Everyone's is used," Tommy told him. "We always get reconditioned stuff." Tommy nodded toward Clyde and Everett. "They got new helmets but only because their heads are so big."

"Fairview gets new stuff every year," Quinton said.

"This ain't Fairview," Booger told him.

"Everyone's is used?" Quinton whispered to Tommy and Booger. They both nodded. And that seemed to satisfy him. Coach Heart and the rest of the team were gathered under the goalposts when Quinton, Tommy, and Booger came out of the locker room.

"Gentlemen," Coach Heart began. He always called the boys "gentle-men" when he had something to say that he thought was important. He pointed at Quinton, who was sitting with the band of boys. "We have a new addition to our roster." Nearly everyone snickered. It had taken less than two minutes for the news of Quinton Clarence's enrollment in Colby to spread throughout the student body seven hours earlier. And he'd just gotten dressed-out with the rest of the team in the locker room in full view of Coach Heart.

Mr. Franklin was grinning too. Seeing that Coach Heart was slapping the football and searching for what to say next, he took over. "Here's the deal, boys," Mr. Franklin began. "We know two things." He held up his hand with one finger extended. "During throwarounds this past summer, nobody stood out as an automatic for the QB position." He paused and scanned the eyes of nearly every player. After letting the assertion sink in, he then extended two fingers. Mr. Franklin looked at Coach Heart before making his second point. He looked nervous. "And second: Quinton here would be the starting QB for Fairview if his parents hadn't decided to move to Colby."

Customarily, it was not acceptable to speak when the coaches were making one of their grandstand speeches, but Caleb's outburst was fit-ting. "Their loss is our gain," he said. He didn't yell, just said it matter of fact-like.

Caleb's comment startled both coaches. They looked at each other, and while doing so, several other players chimed in. "That's right," another said and others agreed.

Clyde stood up. "I heard that 'Stang-drivin' punk is gonna be their QB this year."

Both coaches were visibly relieved that the team supported Quinton joining the team and taking the QB position. Mr. Franklin capitalized on the moment. "There's only one game that matters this year." He set his hands on his waist and struck a commanding pose.

Coach Heart saw what was happening. "That's right, gentlemen," he said. "This is *our* year." Quinton was grinning.

Mr. Franklin added, "Fairview will be gunning for us. They're a bigger school and favored to beat us. This year will be different." He pointed the hand that was holding a football at Quinton. "We have their quarterback."

He looked directly at Quinton. "Their line will be gunning for you." He passed the ball to Quinton. "Let's see what you got."

Everett and Clyde stood and held Quinton between them. "They'll never touch him," Everett said and turned to Quinton. "You won't even need to wear pads when we play them," he said. The rest of the team rushed the three of them and formed a rowdy scrum.

Coach Heart blew his whistle. "Positions," he yelled. The team ran toward the field and split up into their individual practice squads.

Flop hit Quinton on the shoulder. "Follow me," he said and then headed toward the receivers.

Word of Quinton's transfer had reached every nook and cranny in Colby. Codger's Corner was packed. Even though Quinton had never held the starting position at quarterback while at Fairview, the word of his coming to Colby had been incrementally embellished as it went from person to person. Many showed up expecting to see a football phenomenon. Quinton had been elevated to legend before stepping onto the field. Expectations were high.

Quinton didn't disappoint. His passes were perfect spirals and on target. They were so easy to catch that Flop was snagging them one-handed. And there seemed to be no end to how far he could throw. One pass traveled over fifty yards in the air before being easily caught.

Frank Fritz had placed a Be Back Later sign in the window of his broom shop. He'd joined the crowd in frequent cheers when a receiver caught one of Quinton's long passes. Fritz's participation in the revelry was proof that his counseling on racial prejudice had been a success.

QUINTON WAS SOON TO BE eighteen and, like many students, didn't have a car, which wasn't unusual. But he had yet to take his driver's exam, which was. The boys were leaving the locker room and headed toward the parking lot when the car and driver revelation occurred.

"You have a car?" Tommy asked.

"My dad does," Quinton replied. It was one of those responses that doesn't directly address the question but provides a probable answer.

Clyde and Everett were always the last ones out of the locker room, so the band of boys never got in a hurry to leave; it was of no use. When the two lumbering creatures rounded the corner of the gym, the only two cars remaining in the parking lot were the diminutive Green Goddess and Clyde's Chrysler.

Flop bebopped toward Everett's car. Tommy noticed Quinton grinning when they reached the car.

"I saw this car this morning when my mom brought me to school. And then at practice, after watching you dart around, I knew it had to be yours."

Everett placed his bear paw on Quinton's shoulder. "Well, actually, it's mine."

Quinton gave Everett an up and down, looked at the car, and then glanced back at Everett. His mouth was working, but no words were coming out. "You serious?" he finally managed to say. He pointed at the behemoth Chrysler and said, "I figured that was your car."

The rest of the boys, including Clyde, had gathered by then. "Faded pink is my favorite color," Clyde said, joking. Quinton, speechless, shook his head and stomped one foot. "Want a ride?" Clyde asked. "We usually stop by the Houn-Dawg after practice."

"Houn-Dawg?" Quinton asked. He knew football, but he had a lot to learn about Colby.

By Wednesday the practice crowd had grown to the point that Mr. Franklin and Coach Heart considered having practice on the playing field. Since the first game with the I-Macks would be played in Fairview, the field would have time to recover. But they eventually decided against the notion, worried it might bring bad luck; they'd never practiced in the pit.

Quinton had picked up on the offense so quickly that it was as if he'd been playing at Colby since grade school. He'd become familiar with the players and was already using their nicknames. The coaches had agreed that Quinton was a godsend, not something that either of them deserved but more likely justice for Quinton. Rather than dwell on providential reasons, they got back to discussing football and winning.

High school football is steeped in tradition and elicits more community discussion than any other sport. A likely reason is that so many are involved. Field preparation begins as soon as the previous season ends, and there's always a debate on seed choice and soil treatments. Everyone with a lawn considers himself an expert in this area and offers his unsolicited opinion.

The marching band raises money for uniforms and better instruments. Civic clubs lobby for which games they'll get to run the concession stands.

Everyone loves to offer an opinion regarding the depth chart order and play choices and to speculate about the prospect of a winning season. These discussions never end but begin to pick up momentum with summer throwarounds. And they become serious during preseason practice.

The rock-solid Colby fans began gathering in the I-Mack stadium long before the first I-Mack fan arrived. Friday night football is an obsession, akin to a religion for some. A few fans disappear each year along with a player who has graduated, but they're replaced with the family of a new name on the roster. Those faithful to the Fighting Indians fill the stands no matter the prospect of winning or losing.

The I-Mack's mascot is a Golden Griffin, a mythical half-lion, half-eagle creature, but few outside the I-Mack student population can describe it. Sitting atop their media box is a four-legged animal with a lion's body and an eagle's head, or that's what it's supposed to be. It looks more like a dog with the face of a gargoyle. In the back of the end zone is a statue of the Virgin Mary holding a baby Jesus. Behind her is a crucifix mounted on the outside wall of their basketball gymnasium. The I-Mack stadium is an eerie place.

In full view of the I-Mack mythical creature, the Virgin Mary, baby Jesus, and a crucified Jesus was a Colby student circling the field in elaborate Indian regalia and working the Colby crowd into a frenzy.

Coach Heart had gathered the Fighting Indians around a dilapidated chalkboard. He was twirling a whistle tied to a dingy shoelace; he had the team's rapt attention and knew it. The only problem was he'd mistaken their focus as keen interest in his pregame speech. In truth, the boys were waiting for the inevitable: when the twirling whistle collided with Coach's jaw bone. They knew better than to laugh when it occurred; they could do that later.

"The I-Macks won't be a pushover," Coach Heart began and then explained in too many words how the small private school had everything to gain and nothing to lose. He then turned to Mr. Franklin.

The pregame motivation talks had taken on a new dimension since Mr. Franklin had started doing them. Tommy listened and sorted the real stuff from the metaphorical and hoped the others were able to delineate as well.

Mr. Franklin's expression became solemn when he said, "Gentlemen, remember the fundamentals." He paused and took a breath. "The most important play is the next play. We'll talk about botched plays tomorrow. Always focus on the play that's being played." Tommy was sure that those words were real and should be taken literally.

Mr. Franklin's expression morphed into that of an insane person. He looked at the defensive backs. "You need to rip the hearts out of those Golden Griffins and leave them beating and bleeding on the field." Tommy was sure that those words were metaphorical.

Moments later, Tommy followed Caleb out of the locker room. "Rip their hearts out," Caleb growled and then forearmed a defenseless locker door.

Everett turned to Caleb. "Save it for Fairview Public," he said, referring to Fairview's public high school. "This is a superpractice." He started walking again. "Let's win but not show all of our cards."

The Colby crowd, led by the marauding Indian mascot in a tomahawk chant, had reached a fever pitch by the time Colby took the field. Two abreast, the team trotted from the locker room to near midfield and then curved toward the visitor's bench. Their entrance was relatively anticlimactic when compared to the roar of the crowd. Downplaying would rule the night.

Super Fan, mentally deficient, but one of Colby's treasures, hadn't gotten the downplay message. With his arms extended, as if to be a human airplane, he was following closely behind the Indian mascot. When the team finally emerged, he abandoned the roving mascot and zoomed near the team. He customarily bought new jeans, shoes, and a Fighting Indian jersey at the beginning of each year. This year he'd opted for red Converse All Stars instead of the more traditional white canvas. Evidence that he was now living on his own was the large cardboard tag still attached to his dark blue and stiff Tuff Nuts, which still had the fold creases. One of the cheerleaders got him to hold still during the national anthem and pulled the tag from the back pocket where it had been stapled. Super Fan's expression was of pure delight while the cheerleader tugged around on his rear end.

Super Fan had his issues as everyone well knew, but lack of knowledge of the team and the individual athletes wasn't one of his deficiencies. His new jersey always included the name of the player he thought to be the year's standout. He'd chosen Quinton Clarence. Anywhere Quinton was, Super Fan was orbiting nearby, avoiding direct eye contact but constantly making adoring side-glances at the new quarterback.

Flop, Clyde, and Everett met the Griffin captains at midfield. Having grown up with the two massive man-boys, Tommy had become accustomed to their enormous size. Seeing Clyde and Everett standing at the fifty in their pads next to the others brought their size into perspective. Each of them made two of Flop, and Flop, in his pads, dwarfed the zebra-suited referees.

Colby won the toss and chose to defer. Tommy never understood why the winner always chose to defer, which meant the loser of the toss usually got the first possession. Both teams took the field. The Griffins were set to receive.

Caleb was running in place and talking to himself. Tommy watched and listened and hoped that Caleb had forgotten the part about ripping out a Griffin heart. The Griffins on the field were mere humans, not mythical creatures as represented by the deformed-looking thing on top of their press box.

What the kickoff lacked in distance it made up for in height, which gave Colby, and particularly Caleb, plenty of time to penetrate the Griffins' line. An unsuspecting I-Mack received the kickoff. Had he called for a fair catch, the Griffins would have begun the game on the thirty-five yard line, good field position. As it was, Caleb hit the I-Mack with enough energy to light up a small town. The player collapsed and didn't move again until the coaches helped him off the field. The ball bounced toward the end zone and was picked up by Flop, who ran it in for a touchdown.

And that was the only time Flop touched the ball for the entire game. He'd been making spectacular catches all week, but no pass plays were called against the Griffins. Even more interesting was that Clyde and Everett allowed Quinton to be sacked four times.

The team celebrated their first victory by flipping each other with wet towels and putting their jockstraps over the heads of JV players. And for first-year JV players, there was another tradition. Few JV players risked taking a shower, but those who did were rewarded by having embarrassing items stuffed into their duffel bags. Since Colby was the visiting team, they'd dressed in the girl's locker room, where female personal hygiene items were available in a vending machine. The JV players would eventually have their duffel bags taken away and emptied during the bus ride home and then asked to explain why they needed the little surprise package. Seasoned JV players never took showers at away games.

Coach Heart let the boys do what boys do and then blew his whistle to stop the melee. He explained the strategy. "Congratulations, gentlemen," he began. "We played well on both sides of the ball." Tommy had noticed that when the team played well, Coach Heart used the inclusive "we," and when they lost, he used the exclusive "you." He was glad that tonight it was "we."

"You might be wondering why we didn't pass," he said, and several players reacted by affectionately punching Quinton and making remarks about the passing game. "And you might have noticed that Quinton got sacked four times tonight."

"Yeah," Caleb yelled. He looked at Clyde and Everett. "What's up with that?"

Coach Heart handed the game ball to Mr. Franklin. "Mr. Franklin will explain."

Mr. Franklin's face looked sinister. He slapped the ball with a ferociousness that got everyone's attention. "Fairview Public had plenty of scouts here tonight," he said. He pointed at Quinton and continued. "I've heard that they don't like the fact that we got their quarterback." He scanned every face, making sure he had everyone's attention. "They know Quinton can pass, but they don't know we can catch." He pointed the ball at Flop. "And now," he said and pointed at Clyde and Everett, "they think our offensive line is weak. Big but weak."

"Caleb," Mr. Franklin said and then paused momentarily. "That was a legal hit, but you could have given that kid a concussion; it wasn't necessary. You won't get a chance to do that against Fairview Public." Caleb's face expressed disappointment.

"We won, but we didn't show our hand." He looked at Clyde and Everett. "I know it was tough letting those clumsy-footed chubs go through; it's not in your nature." He looked at Quinton. "Thanks for not showing how you can scramble." Quinton nodded. Tommy remembered Clyde and Everett's pregame comments.

Mr. Franklin's next statement was a half shout. "There's only one game that matters this year." The team erupted into a frenzy of chest bumps, high fives, and towel flips.

Coach Heart blew his whistle. "Bus leaves in fifteen minutes." Deodorant spray fogged the locker room; half of the team hadn't bothered to take a shower. The stench would remain on the bus until Monday morning, when it would be replaced by the odor of thirty sweaty kids—a different odor, but an odor nonetheless.

Cruising Colby

ONE OF THE SUPERSTITIONS SURROUNDING the driver's test was the propensity to flunk the test if taken the first Saturday after one's sixteenth birthday. In truth, only a couple of others in the class besides Everett and Clyde had turned sixteen, and all had taken the test on the first Saturday. Contrary to legend, all had passed. Melody wasn't terribly superstitious. She'd walk under ladders and step on the cracks in the sidewalk, but she didn't take any chances when it came to the driver's test. She'd waited until the second Saturday after her birthday.

Melody had asked Tommy to go with her to take the test, so Tommy had gotten to Gooche's early in order to get in a couple of hours before taking off for her exam. Leo Goolsby, the butcher, had already arrived and was making cuts of meat for the Saturday shoppers. Tommy first checked the most frequently shopped canned goods aisle. The store was arranged that way so that the heaviest stuff was first, except for the bread, which was always near the front door. He didn't fool with the bread aisle; the bread-truck men took care of that area themselves. Tommy had never understood why the bread wasn't situated near the checkout so that shoppers wouldn't have to keep moving it around each time they added something to their cart.

He'd stocked the shelves so many times he knew what to expect. The chicken noodle soup, pork 'n' beans, and kidney bean displays needed the most attention. He figured people were starting to make chili after he noticed the canned tomato inventory had gotten low. After making a list of items needed, he grabbed the two-wheel dolly and headed for the storage room.

Mr. Gooche hadn't arrived, and Tommy was growing more anxious by the minute. He'd called the previous evening before Tommy had gotten home from practice, but Marsha hadn't told him until morning. Mr. Gooche hadn't left a message except to say that he'd speak to Tommy the next day.

A few minutes before Gooche's opening time, he saw Melody standing on top of the stone peering into the still-closed store. He quickly hung his apron in the produce room and returned the Garvey price marker and holster to Mr. Gooche's office. Leo let him out the rear door.

Melody was still on the stone and looking for Tommy inside the store when he came around the corner. She was doing the toe-to-heel thing, and Tommy could tell by her breath that she was nervous. The driver's exams wouldn't begin for another thirty minutes, but she'd wanted to get there early and be the first. Her dad had parked the Malibu in the space provided for those taking their test.

Tommy took her hand; it was clammy, another sign of nerves. He tried to think of something that would help her relax. "Listen," he began. "What's the worst that could happen?"

She gave him a wild look. "Why, flunking, of course!" she said.

"That's right," he replied. "And what happens if you flunk?" he asked.

"I have to wait until next week to take it again," she replied as if Tommy didn't already know.

"That's right," he said. "Now here's the deal. You waited an extra week, and you know this stuff; we went over it last night." By then they'd reached the front doors to the courthouse. Tommy turned to face her, put his hands on her shoulders, and looked directly into her green eyes. "You're gonna pass. Just pretend it's you and me doing the practice test."

"What about the driving part?" she asked.

Tommy considered that a good sign. Since she'd moved on to worrying about the driving part of the exam, it meant she was confident of the written. "That's the easiest part," he smiled and told her. She believed him even though he'd yet to take the exam and wouldn't for a long time.

They both heard the front doors of the courthouse being unlocked from the inside. She turned her head toward the door, but her body remained facing Tommy—a clear sign she didn't want to do it. "Did you know Everett has a date tonight?" he asked her, an attempt to ease her mind. Everett had only told a few people.

"A date?" she asked. "With who?"

"A girl he met at a Beta Club meeting."

Melody smiled. She too had attended the meeting in Fairview. "I bet I know who it is," she said.

Melody struck a pensive pose, finger-tapped her chin, and grinned mischievously. "Maybe we'll have to go on a date too," she said. She did the eyelid flutter that always sent tingles up Tommy's spine.

Tommy put his hands on her shoulders, turned her toward the courthouse, and whispered in her ear. "First you need to get your driver's license." He gave her a gentle push toward the double doors.

"So, Everett is going on a date," she said and gave Tommy a wink just before she disappeared into the cavernous building.

Tommy, so engrossed with Melody's parting comment and gesture, hadn't noticed the Codgers, who were perched on the courthouse bench and watching Tommy and Melody's every move. They'd been watching since Melody had stepped onto the stone and started looking for Tommy inside Gooche's; they hadn't missed a thing.

"Another one turned sixteen?" Monkey asked. Tommy nodded.

"That her car?" Bem asked, pointing toward the Malibu. Again, Tommy nodded. He'd helped Melody wash and wax it the night before. He'd spent over an hour shining the mag wheels. Had the car belonged to anyone else, he would have been envious at the least and more than likely resentful.

"When are you taking the driver's exam?" Fish asked with a tone of sympathy.

Tommy sat down on the bench next to them, leaned back against the faded ad for Rexall Drugs, and thought about the question. It was a question he'd grown weary of answering. "Not for another year," he said.

Monkey stopped whittling, spit a string of tobacco juice, and looked up, bewildered. "Not for another year?" he asked. Tommy nodded. "Why?" Monkey asked, incredulous.

The other Codgers looked at Monkey like he'd lost his mind. "'Cause that's when he was born, you idgit," Bem said. "You can't get yer license 'til you're sixteen."

Tommy listened as the Codgers continued to criticize Monkey for his gaffe. It was clear to Tommy that Monkey had figured he was turning sixteen along with his other friends and simply didn't understand why a red-blooded American boy would delay taking the driver's exam. And the other Codgers probably understood that as well, but they weren't about to let it pass.

The bantering was another scorching reminder to Tommy that it would be a year before he'd be entering the courthouse doors on his way to the freedom and liberty that a driver's license brings. He walked over to the Malibu. The daydreaming bliss he'd been enjoying while stamping prices on canned goods and visualizing Melody getting her license had been supplanted with sorrow when he contemplated the notion that he'd be sitting in the Malibu's passenger seat, not the driver's. It wasn't a revelation of any sort, just a brutal realization of the unfortunate timing of his birthday.

"Why didn't they pass more during the game last night?" Rabbit asked Tommy. Tommy shrugged, indifferent. His mind had entered that state of depression one experiences when faced with an inevitable long-term and suffering circumstance. Monkey, unfazed by Tommy's apathy, looked to the Codgers for their opinion on the matter.

Tommy had sufficiently bathed himself in self-pity, a disease with no cure, when Melody emerged from the courthouse. But unlike the jubilant expression worn by one who had passed the written, she was sporting a grimace. Tommy's heart sank to a new depth, but for her instead of himself.

An involuntary smile took control of his face almost before his brain got the message when Melody turned, started toward the Malibu, and gave him a thumbs-up. Tommy was momentarily confused until the examiner who would be riding with Melody emerged from the courthouse. She was built like a bullfrog, with small pixie feet and thick ankles that supported a body as wide as it was tall. There was no evidence of a neck; her head, which was mostly jaw, was attached directly to her shoulders. Her chest appeared more like that of a man with highly developed pectoral muscles than that of a buxom lady. She walked with a powerful gait, swinging her feet more out then forward—probably necessary due to the size of her more than ample thighs. She was neither masculine nor feminine, just hard and angry. Her uniform was stretched tight at every seam.

Tommy didn't know her real name, so he conjured up one for her. Her shape resembled a bullfrog, but because she was female, that wouldn't work. While he was thinking, a toad jumped out from under the Codgers' bench. Toad it was. He'd learn later that Toad had warned Melody that she didn't like it when driver's applicants had an audience.

Toad, frowning and pooching her thick lips to the point that her upper lip almost touched her snubbed nose, circled the car while Melody tested the headlights, turn signals, and brake lights. The Malibu rocked when Toad settled into the passenger seat. By then Tommy had nonchalantly moved closer and watched as Toad tugged at the male end of the seat belt and expanded it to its full length. It wasn't a particularly hot day, but Tommy could see that Toad's face was flushed and that sweat was dripping from her chin.

Tommy watched them pull away and then walked toward the Codgers; they were still talking football. "I ain't sayin' he ain't a good quarterback," Monkey was explaining, talking about Quinton Clarence. "It's just that if he thought he had a chance of starting at Fairview, they wouldn't have moved to Colby, don't cha know."

"What's your point?" asked Fish.

Monkey explained, "Well, we've been watching practice, and the Clarence boy is dang sure the best quarterback Colby has seen for a long time, but," he hesitated and shook his head in doubt, "the new boy over at Fairview must be better. The Fairview game is going to be a tough one. Always is." The Codgers exchanged glances, each of them in silent thought. Monkey continued. "And ... and ... and," he stuttered, "Fairview is gonna be gunnin' for us, since our quarterback is from there." He slapped his knee, leaned back, looked toward the sky, and sighed in disgust. "Even if they weren't gonna start him."

Tommy's morose feeling began to subside after the Codgers mentioned Quinton. He remembered Quinton saying he didn't have a driver's license, and he was nearly eighteen. Tommy surmised it was possible to survive without a driver's license.

He stopped paying attention to the Codgers when Melody's Malibu came into view. He could see she was sporting an exam-passing smile when she pulled in to park. He waited for Toad to complete the driver's license application and hand it to Melody before he approached. Melody waited until Toad had disappeared into the courthouse before waving the application around excitedly while rocking back and forth heel to toe.

When Tommy got close to her, she went slump shouldered and feigned a frown. "Miss Terry told me that I can't drive until I take this to the license bureau," she said. The thought that immediately crossed Tommy's mind was how the name Terry worked for either gender; Miss Terry, Terry the Toad, had been appropriately named.

The license bureau was nothing more than a separate drawer in the main counter at Gooche's Grocery; they headed that way together. Melody was now on the other side of the divide between those who have their driver's license and those who don't, and Tommy wondered how their relationship would change.

"So," she said, "Everett has a date?"

"Yeah," Tommy said, lost in thought, contemplating the coming adventure.

"Probably Libby," Melody said. "At the Beta Club meeting, we were calling her large Libby, but not to her face. She's tall like Everett; they spent a lot of time together at the meeting."

Velma, the main checkout lady at Gooche's, had watched Tommy and Melody cross the road. Velma was also the license bureau clerk; she'd put a closed sign on her checkout counter and was waiting for Melody when she walked in.

Velma glanced at Tommy. "Mr. Gooche wants to talk to you before you clock back in," she said. Velma's comment compounded Tommy's anxiety. He'd begun to worry that Mr. Gooche wasn't happy about him taking off on a Saturday morning. He'd forgotten about the mysterious phone call last night, but it was now fresh in his mind. He reached for a piece of Clove chewing gum so that his saliva could compensate for the juices produced by his churning stomach.

Melody handed Velma the application and then began nervously working her lips and tapping the floor with first one foot and then the other. Velma meticulously checked the forms and, to Tommy's thinking, took longer than usual. She looked at Melody and smiled. "Congratulations. For fifteen dollars we'll make it official."

Melody unfolded the damp-with-sweat ten- and five-dollar bills she'd been holding since finishing the exam. Velma laid them aside, wrote out a cash receipt, and handed the papers to Melody. "Until you receive your license, you'll have to keep this application with you when you drive," she told Melody, but she did so in a kind voice—much different than Toad's tone.

Tommy walked Melody back to her Malibu. Melody looked at the folded application. "It's not as cool as an actual license," she said. Tommy gave her a look of disgust. Melody nodded, indicating she understood that Tommy would give his right hand for what she was holding.

She caught Tommy by surprise when she said, "My dad said I could have the car for a couple of hours tonight."

Tommy, still lathered in self-pity, hadn't completely considered the obvious consequence of Melody getting her license. Mr. Hinkebein had so much as admitted that the car was for himself, not Melody. Tommy nearly swallowed his tongue when she asked, "Want to drive around a little and go to the Houn-Dawg?"

"Sure," Tommy replied, but, still stunned, it came out more like "thure."

"What time?" she asked, which Tommy thought curious since she was doing the asking and would be doing the driving. "What time do you get off work?" she asked.

Tommy made sure his tongue was wet before answering. "Seven," he said.

"Perfect," she smiled. Tommy had the feeling that she would have said perfect no matter what time he'd told her. "Should I come by Gooche's or your house?" Before Tommy could answer, she continued, "I have to be home by nine."

"Come by Gooche's," Tommy said without mentioning that he'd have to call home and get permission—another reminder of his lack of independence.

As he watched her pull away, a surreal feeling swept over him. Later that night, he'd be cruising Colby with Melody, in her Malibu, if his mom said it was okay.

When he turned to walk toward Gooche's, he saw that the Codgers had been watching. They were grinning. Monkey spit, pulled his shoulders back, and made an attempt to puff out what had once been a muscular chest. "She's a keeper," one of them said when he walked by. "If looks were measured in inches, she'd be a country mile," another said. Tommy wasn't sure which Codgers had spoken; he was still in a daze. He heard words but not voices. He nodded at them and kept going.

His dreamy, out-of-body moment was displaced with another bout of anxiety when he started toward the store and began to contemplate what was on Mr. Gooche's mind. A moment of pleasure shot through his mind when he passed the stone, the spot where he and Melody had first kissed four years earlier on a cold, snowy night.

The Truck

MR. GOOCHE WAS WAITING FOR him. "Follow me," he said and then walked with purpose toward the rear of the store. Tommy followed him through the storage doors and onto the loading dock, worry supplanting the blissful memory of the first kiss. When they reached the loading dock, Mr. Gooche stopped and pointed at the truck. "I'm thinking about getting a cardboard baler," he said and handed Tommy a piece of literature with photos of a machine that crushed cardboard boxes. "We can get over a week's worth of boxes into a single bale of cardboard," he continued. "There's a company in Fairview that will pick up the bales for free. They recycle or some such thing."

Tommy didn't immediately understand what the cardboard baler had to do with the truck. Mr. Gooche kept looking at the truck and talking about the boxes. "We won't need to burn the boxes," he continued. His roundabout approach wasn't working. Finally, he spun and faced Tommy. "We won't be needing the truck."

Since Tommy was waiting for Mr. Gooche to get on with the reason for wanting to speak to him before work and his mind was still partially preoccupied with Melody and the Malibu, he was slow to realize what Mr. Gooche was trying to say. Finally Mr. Gooche handed the virtual talking stick to Tommy. "So, what do you think?" he asked.

Tommy hadn't been paying close attention and wasn't sure how to respond. "Well," he began as he collected his thoughts. "The baler will be handy," he first replied, thinking Mr. Gooche surely had to be proud of the new cardboard smashing machine. It was possible that nobody in Colby had ever seen one. But he noticed Mr. Gooche making a face as if he'd expected a different reaction. Tommy thought back on the thrill of driving the truck to and from the incinerator when he was only twelve. "But the carryout boys are going to miss driving the truck around in the lot." He smiled at Mr. Gooche. "That was always the highlight of my day back then."

Mr. Gooche chuckled when Tommy brought up the history of the truck and the prepubescent carryout boys. "Let me ask you something," he said. "How many carryout boys do you think have had that same experience in this truck?"

Tommy thought for a moment and remembered all the past carryout boys—some now in their thirties—who had shared with him their memories of driving the Gooche's Grocery truck. "Oh, Mr. Gooche," Tommy said, "I don't know. Lots."

"How many of them, do you think, would like to have this truck?" Mr. Gooche asked.

Tommy did a couple of heel bounces and replied enthusiastically, "All of 'em, I'm sure."

Mr. Gooche put one hand on Tommy's shoulder and pointed at the truck with the other. "Mrs. Gooche and I discussed this at length last night. And we decided that we'd like you to have the truck."

For a moment Tommy couldn't respond. His voluntary functions had ceased. He couldn't feel his feet and wasn't sure he was touching the ground. Could this possibly all be a dream: Melody, the Malibu, the truck, everything? His mouth had gone dry, and his tongue was stuck to the roof of his mouth. He was literally rendered speechless.

Mr. Gooche jostled him. "So, what do you think?"

Tommy couldn't process all the thoughts that were colliding inside his head. There were countless cars that he'd dreamed of owning, but cost had been the primary barrier. The truck was old; he hadn't seen anything that old for sale anywhere and had no idea how much Mr. Gooche would be asking or if he'd finance it. "How much are you asking for it?"

Mr. Gooche rubbed his chin. "Well," he began, "in order to make it legal, there has to be a transaction." Tommy nodded as if he understood, but he didn't. "We'd like to sell it to you for one dollar." Perplexed, Tommy squinted his eyes. "Look, Tommy," Mr. Gooche explained, "the truck isn't for sale. There's no telling what I could get for this thing if I tried to sell it. We want you to have it."

He turned and faced Tommy. "I know that you won't be getting your license for a long time." That was something of which Tommy needed no reminding. "You can take this thing to your dad's shop," he said. And while sympathetically patting Tommy on the shoulder, he continued, "Mrs. Gooche and I know you'll take care of her, and fixing it up will give you something to occupy your mind while you wait to turn sixteen."

The reminder of the driver's license wait didn't register because Tommy had already begun to consider the possibilities. His dad's shop had painting equipment; it was for tractors but would work on trucks. He could paint his name on the door, but it would just be Tommy Thompson, not Tommy Thompson and sons, like the farmers around Colby. Maybe he'd put something clever like "Thomas Thompson—General Contractor." After all, he did a variety of jobs, many of which required him to give people a price before performing, such as lawn mowing. Tommy didn't think it, but the subconscious notion that he'd be the envy of every former Gooche boy had to have existed somewhere deep in the recesses of his hippocampus.

All of these thoughts and more swept through Tommy's mind in a split second, and then he snapped to and realized Mr. Gooche was waiting for a response. "Really?" he asked. He realized a one-word response was inadequate, and worse than that, he was fairly certain he'd muffed it by uttering "weally" instead of "really." He wrung his hands and tried to look directly into Mr. Gooche's eyes like he'd been taught, but he was in a daze. "I ... I don't know what to say, Mr. Gooche." Then, in a split-octave voice, he said, "Thank you, thank you."

The truck gradually began to look different to Tommy. He opened the door, and, instead of seeing a dusty dash and bench seat with exposed springs and stuffing spilling out, he saw a vintage truck that with a little work would be a one-of-a-kind Colby classic. He came to appreciate even more that all of the truck's windows were still intact. Nobody in the school parking lot would have something so unique. He looked under the dash and immediately saw a perfect spot to mount an eight-track. He wasn't sure if he'd spoil the vintage interior by installing a stereo, and would discover later that the old truck had a 6-volt system—not easily adaptable to the eight-tracks designed for the more modern 12-volt alternators.

Mr. Gooche interrupted Tommy's mental excursion by saying, "The cardboard baler will be here this afternoon. You can take the truck home anytime after that." Tommy, still in shock, nodded that he understood. Still stunned, he continued to study the truck from the new perspective.

Knowing what was going to occur, Leo Goolsby had been watching from the loading dock while smoking his umpteenth cigarette of the day. He stood there wiping his hands, amused at Tommy's bewilderment. "You better snap him out of his little funk before he wets his pants," Leo told Mr. Gooche.

"Follow me," Mr. Gooche told Tommy and headed toward the door. Tommy did as instructed but, while looking back at the truck, tripped on the first loading dock step and nearly fell.

Mr. Gooche had already gone through the dock doors when Leo stopped Tommy. "Listen, sport, you better treat her right or I'll cut your you-know-whats off," he said and pointed toward Tommy's groin. "You'll be singing soprano the rest of your life."

Tommy, anxious to both catch up with Mr. Gooche and put some space between him and Leo, nodded and trotted away. Leo's words continued to echo in Tommy's mind. Tommy was sure that countless other former Gooche boys, now men, probably felt the same way. He'd just been bestowed the honor and responsibility of caring for an item sacred to many in Colby.

Mr. Gooche had the bottom drawer of his corner file cabinet open and was searching through what looked to be some very old files when Tommy reached his office. There were several cabinets, and none of them matched. He'd clearly added them as needed. The one he was looking in was against the wall, the oldest, with the thickest stack of dust-covered papers on top. "Here it is," he said and pulled out the folder that had kept the truck title safe for over twenty years. He handed it to Tommy.

Tommy examined the title to the sacred truck. He read the front of the title with the same reverence as a preacher reading scripture might. He saw where the owner was listed as Gooche's Enterprises, which made him wonder what other businesses Mr. Gooche owned or had owned. The year of manufacture read 1949.

"Got that dollar?" Mr. Gooche asked.

Tommy pulled a damp, crumpled dollar from his pocket and laid it on the only uncluttered spot on Mr. Gooche's massive oak desk. "I'll need to fill out the seller's section," Mr. Gooch said and carefully pulled the fragile title from Tommy's grasp.

Tommy thought for a moment and said, "I guess I should call home and make sure that it's okay."

Mr. Gooche grinned. "I spoke to your parents last night."

That explains the call, Tommy realized.

Mr. Gooche looked up from his desk and smiled. "Now, Thomas Thompson, as soon as I sign this title, the truck is yours." It was a surreal moment for Tommy. "Your mom and dad will be here when you get off work to take the truck to your shop."

Tommy was immediately conflicted, and Mr. Gooche noticed. "Is there a problem?" he asked.

"Sort of," Tommy said. "Melody is coming by at seven."

Mr. Gooche chuckled and put his hand on Tommy's shoulder. "That's not a problem, Tommy," he counseled. "That's a situation, and there's a perfect solution." He went on to explain how Tommy could include Melody in moving the truck from Gooche's to the shop.

"I still need to call home," Tommy said.

"That's fine," Mr. Gooche said. "But your parents know about the truck."

"I know," Tommy said. "But they don't know about Melody's plan to take me to the Houn-Dawg."

Mr. Gooche grinned and laid his hand on Tommy's shoulder, "You're a busy boy," he said and then handed Tommy the price marker. "Now get back to work, but double-check the price on the marker," he cautioned. "You're going to have a hard time focusing today."

Tommy paused long enough to swallow and get his vocal chords under control. "Thank you very much, Mr. Gooche." This time he was able to get the words out without sounding like a blend of cowboy and choirboy.

Tommy had made his way to the cereal aisle before leaving to walk with Melody. He double-checked the price on the marker before stamping each box and placing it on the shelf. His mind played Tony the Tiger saying, "They're grrreat!" when he put Frosted Flakes on the shelf. And next he visualized the Lucky Charms leprechaun chanting, "They're magically delicious." But the lion's share of his mind kept alternating scenes of him cruising Colby with Melody in the Malibu or fixing up the truck. He thought it curious that his mental excursions regarding the truck weren't of driving but of working on it.

He'd catch himself sitting in an aisle staring blankly into an empty box, saliva about to drip from his mouth, and then snap to when a shopper needed to get by. Mr. Gooche had been right; he needed to focus. He even spot-checked a couple of items that he'd price marked earlier to make sure he'd gotten the correct price.

He made several trips to the storage room, most of them unnecessary. He'd stop at the loading dock and gaze at the truck, a myriad of memories and possibilities flooding his mind each time. And each time he'd see something about the truck he hadn't noticed for a long time. On one trip he noticed the electric wire woven through the stock racks. He and the band of boys had decorated the truck one Christmas by putting a string of lights along the top of the stock rack.

It seemed like forever until lunch when he'd tell the others the news.

THE BAND OF BOYS HAD planned to meet at the Houn-Dawg for lunch to collect on the free burger, fry, and drink that Mrs. Pope always gave them after a football game. It didn't matter if they won or lost, she'd treat them to a combo. And if they won, she'd top it off with a milk shake. The Chrysler and Green Goddess were already there.

Chances were the news of Melody passing her test had already reached everyone in Colby, but Tommy figured the boys would want to know the details. Tommy could see Caleb's animated expression through the window and mistakenly figured he was talking about the previous night's game. He'd have to skip through the details of Melody's test taking and get to the news about the truck.

"Are you serious?" Quinton was asking Caleb when Tommy stepped inside. Tommy was surprised to see Quinton sitting with the others. It wasn't a problem for Tommy, but the band had been the same group of boys for several years, and Quinton's quick addition wasn't yet natural.

"You can drive a car on the railroad tracks?" Quinton asked Caleb.

"Thing of it is," Caleb said, "the width of a car's tires is the same as a train's wheels."

"Dadgum," begged Everett, "don't ask him to explain. It's true."

"Hey, Tommy," Booger said and motioned to a chair beside him that he'd saved. The boys had moved two tables together and had already eaten. Tommy took a seat and anxiously waited for a chance to tell about the truck.

Mrs. Pope brought him a mixture of Orange Crush and Pepsi, his favorite. "I'll have your burger and fries in a jiffy," she said. She patted him on the back. "Good game."

"Thanks," Tommy said. He'd only kicked a couple of extra points. He took a long draw from the straw, did a carbonation-induced burp, and then waited for his chance to speak.

Because Caleb never stopped talking long enough to take a breath, Tommy had begun to think that Caleb could breathe through his ears. Mrs. Pope affectionately squeezed Tommy's shoulder when she put the basket holding a burger and fries down in front of him. She'd probably noticed Tommy's anxious expression.

"So, it's a plan?" Caleb asked. He'd finally paused for a response, but Tommy's mouth was full of grilled beef and onions.

By the time Tommy swallowed, Caleb had resumed talking about his plan for Clyde to take the Chrysler down the tracks to the tunnel that night. Driving to the tunnel had been a perpetual subject, but occasionally Caleb decided that it needed to be done right then. Tommy was suspicious that Caleb was trying to divert attention from Everett having a date or Melody getting her license. Caleb wouldn't be getting his license for another month.

Tommy finally got his chance. "Melody passed the test," he said. He'd decided to get their attention with Melody's news and then make the unexpected announcement. Everyone turned toward him; Caleb slumped slightly and folded his arms in disgust.

"Hey, that's great," Booger said. "I was so wrapped up in Caleb's train tunnel scheme that I'd forgotten. Tell us about it." The boys who had yet to take their driver's test winced when Tommy described Toad.

Before Tommy could tell them about the truck, Flop started making fun of Everett for having a date. "Like I said," Flop began, "while we're cruising down the tracks, Everett will be spending his hard-earned money on some Fairview girl."

Caleb looked at Everett with a suspicious expression. "Why would you ask out a girl from Fairview?" he pried.

"How many times do I have to tell you, Caleb?" Everett began and then quickly added, "Never mind. I know that memory isn't your strong suit." Laughter erupted. "I didn't ask her, she asked me."

"I'm not a memorizer," Caleb said after the laughter subsided. "I'm a doer." And just to get back at Everett, he added, "I heard she's a big girl."

Everett grinned. "She's about your size," he said and then put his finger to his chin. "No," he continued. "She's a little taller." Caleb didn't press it since Everett had him by more than six inches and a hundred pounds.

By the time the boys were getting up to leave, Caleb had brought the conversation back to driving Clyde's Chrysler on the railroad tracks.

Tommy started to tell them his latest news but then decided to wait until later so he'd have their full attention. The boys each thanked Mrs. Pope for the free lunch before they left.

Quinton left with Everett in the Green Goddess. It had taken only a couple of sessions in Miss Anderson's class for Everett to discover that he and Quinton had a common interest—history. Quinton's focus was more specific than Everett's, and he'd clearly studied American history beyond that which was required in the classroom.

Mrs. Pope had asked Tommy to wait a minute; she wanted to give him an order. The others were walking out when she handed him the order for ground beef, onions, and paper towels. Tommy was looking at the note when she said, "You looked like you had something to tell them." Tommy was always amazed at the innate ability of adults, especially mothers, to read minds. He told Mrs. Pope about the truck.

She tossed the towel she'd been using to wipe down the tables across her shoulder, planted one fist on her skinny hip, used the other to prop herself against the counter, and then tilted her head in amazement. "That's really something, Tommy," she said and stared deep into his eyes. "You'll need to take good care of her," she continued. Mrs. Pope then stared introspectively out the front window of the Houn-Dawg. "Seeing her on the streets again will bring back a lot of memories for people who were around when she used to make home deliveries."

Tommy was intrigued by Mrs. Pope's affectionately referring to the truck in the female gender. He began recalling those who had shared with him their Gooche's truck stories. He was convinced more than ever that he now possessed a true Colby treasure, and the door art design became a forgone conclusion.

BY LATE AFTERNOON WORD HAD gotten around about the truck sale, and a competition of who knew it first began to shape up. People compared the time of day when they first learned and who'd told them. In Colby it was important to be on the leading edge of important gossip; the sale of Gooche's truck was a seminal event.

After clocking out, Tommy walked to the loading dock to take one last look. Milton's golf cart was parked in front of the truck, and the Codgers were standing there, hands in their pockets and rocking back and forth on their heels.

"What cha gonna do with her?" Monkey asked.

"Take it to my dad's shop," Tommy answered. He noticed that cars with people pointing at the truck were slowly cruising by. A surreal emotion remained; he hadn't fully grasped the levity of the truck transaction.

"Gonna paint it?" Bem asked.

"Probably," Tommy answered. By then a small crowd was beginning to gather.

"You need to keep it 'riginal, don't cha know," Bem told him.

"You better not sell it," Rabbit said.

"Why would he sell it?" Bem asked.

"Fizzlesticks, Bem. I was just sayin'. I'd hate to see him sell the thing to some yahoo collector from Fairview or some such place."

"I'm gonna fix it up and drive it," Tommy mustered the nerve to say. The crowd had caused his saliva glands to cease functioning.

"Got yer license?" Rabbit asked.

"Not yet," Tommy said.

"Can't drive 'til you get your license," Rabbit said, stating the obvious and an unnecessary reminder for Tommy.

"He knows," Bem said and then gave Tommy a sympathetic nod.

The Chrysler pulled up, and the Green Goddess was close behind. Everett punched Tommy on the shoulder. "Dadgum," he repeated several times while circling the truck. The rest of the band surrounded him and stared at the truck in awe.

"Thing of it is," Caleb said, "you don't even have your driver's license."

Tommy began doing the math and counting the days until his sixteenth birthday. He was beginning a slow descent from his all-day high when Melody emerged from the crowd. "But I do," she said and then leaned her head through the truck's driver-side door. "Wow," she whispered and then slowly shook her head. "Unbelievable. She's one of a kind."

Tommy's truck-induced high resumed; he needed no further confirmation of the truck's magical appeal.

"You drive," Tommy's dad said.

"Really?" Tommy asked.

"Sure. Dooley and Tootie are at the shooting match."

"Hop in," Tommy's dad told Melody. She jumped in and scooted to the middle.

"Nice," Tommy's dad said after Tommy double clutched and put the truck into first gear before coming to a full stop at the first stop sign. "Where'd you learn how to do that?"

"Going back and forth from the dock to the burn pile," Tommy said.

"Most men my age can't downshift to first without grinding the gears," he said, clearly impressed.

Tommy's right foot momentarily shoved the accelerator pedal to the floor when Melody patted him on the thigh. She smiled at Tommy. She wasn't sure what a double clutch was but sensed it required driving skill and was infatuated.

Nephilim

WITHIN A WEEK OF QUINTON Clarence moving to Colby, Everett and his broom-making employer, Frank Fritz, had an unexpected conversation. "Ya, Mr. Fluegge," Fritz said. Everett noticed that Fritz frequently mumbled, mostly to himself, and paying attention to what he was saying wasn't generally necessary. It wasn't unusual for Everett to show up at the broom shop and resume what he'd been doing the day before and work for half an hour before Fritz would do more than nod. He was a man of few words. But when he had something to say that needed to be heard, he'd call Everett by his surname. Then it was time to listen.

Everett stopped binding a broom and gave Fritz his full attention. "Yes, Mr. Fritz." Everett found Fritz's strict German etiquette contagious and had become accustomed to being referred to as "mister." And it wasn't a chore for him to do the same with Fritz.

"Dar's a new boy," Fritz began. "He's blick." Everett nodded that he knew whom Fritz had in mind. "I'd like to meet him." Everett was momentarily dazed. Of all the things Fritz may have said, asking to meet Quinton was the least likely.

Few things are kept confidential in Colby. And even though few spoke of it, most knew that Fritz was seeing a counselor who was helping him deal with his Nazi leanings, and particularly his racism.

"I vould like to meet dis younk man," Fritz said. Everett was at a loss for words. He'd known Quinton for little more than a week but was fairly certain that meeting a person of Mr. Fritz's background wasn't something Quinton would easily agree to. "Ja know dat I haf changed my mind about Negroes," Fritz said.

While holding a new broom, Fritz explained his motivation to Everett in a way that only Fritz could. Fritz's counselor had suggested that he take the time to get to know a Negro. Fritz confided that he'd considered approaching Mr. Webster at church, but the right opportunity had never occurred. "Besides," Fritz had said, referring to Mr. Webster's intonation, "I've heard him speaking; he's not a normal Negro anyway."

Everett was pondering Fritz's notion of a normal Negro when Fritz finished the short but strange conversation with, "Don't mention why you're bringing him to me." Fritz paused in search of a word. "Let's make it look like a kone sigh dent." He emphasized a sigh and meant coincident.

Everett grinned. "Sure, Mr. Fritz. It will be our little secret."

"Ya, ya." Fritz nodded. "A *geheimnis*." Everett had to assume that Fritz had momentarily reverted to his native tongue.

Everett's thick, fuzzy hair, heavy facial features, and large, boxy body had too often fooled people into thinking he was dull; his reserved and contemplative demeanor was easily mistaken as a sign of thoughtlessness. In fact, Everett's mind was always working. For instance, he knew broomcorn wasn't really corn; it's actually sorghum, even though most people called it straw. He and Fritz would exchange a wink when a customer would admire their new handmade broom and comment about the quality of the straw. Straw, Everett knew, was the stalk left from harvested wheat. A half-wit could see that broom bristles don't resemble wheat straw, Everett had quickly surmised. "The world was full of half-wits," Fritz frequently reminded him.

Everett carefully placed a new broomstick into the binding machine and wrapped it with "pearl" that had been soaking overnight in a solution of water with a carefully measured addition of bleach. Pearl is the highest quality broomcorn and is what's missing on cheap brooms. He then added a layer of broomcorn too coarse to be classified as pearl, followed by another layer of pearl, and then carefully worked the foot pedals causing the broomstick to rotate and wrap the binding wire tight.

Fritz had at first stood over Everett and criticized every move. It was important to use just the right amount of straw, two pounds. Two pounds was the standard weight that people had grown to expect—any less and the broom felt cheap, any more and broomcorn was being wasted. Fritz had allowed Everett to make a broom for his mother with 100 percent pearl and no filler. That broom certainly lived up to the sign on the door: *Neue Besen Kehren Gut*, a new broom sweeps clean.

Everett stood the broomstick with the shapeless bundle of broomcorn bound to one end into the stand that Fritz had made. The stand held three brooms, and Everett's job was to keep at least two brooms in the stand at any given time, working fast enough to have three in the stand before taking a toilet break. Fritz had determined that it took the same amount of time to thresh, stitch, and trim the brooms as it did to use the toilet. Fritz's constant calculating kept Everett entertained. Fritz finished the brooms by placing them into a press that shaped them and held them for stitching. The last step was cutting the broom to make a uniform end edge.

Everett had developed an idea for a small hand broom that could be used for cleaning shelves, cars, trucks, and hard-to-reach places. He'd priced the store-bought kind and noticed they sold for almost the same as the bigger brooms. The smaller broom would require less broomcorn, the most difficult to come by material in broom making.

He'd intended to bring his idea up, but Fritz had gotten him mentally off track by talking about Quinton, and then there was his first date with Libby. He pushed the notion of the hand broom aside. Thinking about the date with Libby caused him to crave Pig's Tail barbecue; his mouth watered, which make him realize he needed to use the toilet. He got busy, got ahead of Fritz, and placed a third broom in the box before heading to the outhouse.

EVERETT SLATHERED ON THE JADE East before heading for Fairview. When he passed the Colby city limit sign, he realized that, except for short trips around Colby, he'd never driven anywhere alone. A feeling of exhilaration swept over him. The euphoria was tempered by first-date anxiety. And Fritz's request to meet Quinton nagged at him. He tried to focus on the date and what to say. His phone call with Libby had gone well but only because she'd led the conversation.

Wanting to be as inconspicuous as possible while driving through Fairview, he'd left the top up. He failed to realize that inconspicuous was an impossibility in a lime-green-colored diminutive foreign car. People in Colby had gotten used to seeing it and rarely pointed anymore. Fairview would be a different story. The Nash Metropolitan was an eye-catcher.

A Nash Metro's dash is simple; normal-size push/pull knobs that operate the floor vents and heater are logically located. A speaker grill is located in the center of the dash, with a giant volume knob on the left side and a matching tuning knob on the right. The knobs are so large it's as if they were meant for a large truck rather than a subsized car. The only gauge, a large round speedometer, is centered above the steering column.

The Nash's radio was tuned to KXOK, a popular St. Louis station, but when the sun went down he'd change it to WLS, a Chicago station. WLS played the same songs as KXOK, but listening to a station farther away was in vogue. It wasn't that he felt the need to be in vogue, but he wanted Libby to know that he knew what he was supposed to do, as if he cared about such things, which he didn't, or so he thought. Everett's mind worked similarly to most boys who cared about what people thought but pretended that they didn't.

The teachers liked to think that their students were inspired to continue thinking about the subject matter beyond the classroom; that was rarely the case, except with Miss Anderson's students. Regarding school, the band of boys frequently discussed topics learned in American History, such as George Washington's penchant for deportment and proper behavior, at least when they weren't talking about football.

In reality, girls and cars dominate the mind of a teenage boy. If thinking was music and thoughts could be scored, every other note would be a girl, usually a specific girl but not necessarily, sometimes just the last one to smile in their direction. Igniting a boy's hormone blaster requires very little effort on the girl's part.

After hours of inspiring classroom lectures and countless football field drills, and in spite of raging hormones, while girls are at the core of their consciousness, cars generally dominate boys' discussions. It's within their comfort zone. Psychoanalysts call it metaphoric substitution or the existential gap. Grandmothers call it "boys being boys." While discussing cars, the notion of burying the needle often comes up. Burying the needle, for those who have led a sheltered life, is reaching the speed in a car at which the speedometer needle completely disappears. There's nothing untoward or metaphoric about burying the needle; it's simply and utterly about speed. This only applies to speedometers that display horizontally.

Since the Nash's speedometer is round, the needle never goes out of sight, so it's impossible to technically bury the needle. With round speedometers it's possible to do what's known as pegging the needle. In this lesser feat, the car must reach a speed at which the needle lies tight against a little peg that's positioned just beyond the highest number on the dial. It's a lesser feat because the needle stops advancing and remains in sight, the sensation of speed far beyond that which is displayed is lost, and the perceived increase in risk and peril is diminished. Pegging the needle doesn't garner the accolades of burying it, but it's nonetheless a goal and must be regularly attempted with a carload of witnesses.

The fastest speed Everett had ever reached was forty-five; maximum speed on his car's round gauge was eighty-five. Forty-five was at the top, dead center. Speed had never been associated with the Green Goddess, and since Everett usually had the top down, forty-five had always felt plenty fast. In the case of a convertible, pegging or burying the needle was not a prerequisite to manhood.

Before reaching the Seven Sisters, Everett increased his speed to sixty-five, the posted daytime limit; reflective tape would cause the posted limit to change to sixty after dark. With the top up the car's sound was different. Wind whistling through the window seams and the tightly wound sound of the engine replaced the swirling blasts associated with an open canopy. Everett pushed the pedal to the floor; it was almost there anyway. The car's engine didn't race or lurch, but the pitch changed.

Feeling more engine vibration through the steering wheel than he'd ever experienced, Everett glanced at the speedometer; the needle was vibrating and creeping past seventy-five. Everett's natural inclination was to press harder on the pedal in an effort to peg the needle.

At seventy-five miles per hour, a car travels over a hundred feet per second. He was closing quickly on the first sister. Everett had only taken his eye off the road for a split second, during which time the car had traveled nearly a hundred feet, when the right front tire centered a large pothole that would have been easily avoided at forty-five miles per hour.

Everett looked up in time to see the pothole but not in time to avoid it. His overcorrection and the force of the impact caused the car to swerve violently to the left and into a side skid. Just before reaching the left shoulder, the rear of the short car passed the front causing the car's skid to drift back toward the right side.

Physics were working in Everett's favor. Since the car was so small and light, the skidding was able to quickly arrest the high speed. The fact that the skid marks veered to the left and then back to the right, rather than continuing off into the deep ravine for which it was headed, had nothing to do with physics and everything to do with providence.

Less than five seconds after Everett had glanced at the vibrating speedometer, the car came to a stop just short of the crest of the first sister. Everett was stunned; for a moment he wasn't sure where he was. He stared straight ahead but saw only through his mind's eye. His pulse resembled a drumroll, and he felt as if he'd suddenly developed a fever. With a gasp, he finally resumed breathing.

Once he'd regained his bearings, he jumped out to see if there was any damage. When he stood up, he could see over the crest of the first sister. Sitting partially off the road just a few yards ahead he saw a Volkswagen bus surrounded by Girl Scout Brownies singing "Michael Row the Boat Ashore" and watching their troop leader, who was staring hopelessly at a flat tire.

"Glad you stopped," one of the girls said, and the rest stopped singing and stared at him. Everett nodded; his vocal chords were momentarily inoperative.

The troop leader, a lady of Miss Anderson's beauty, looked frazzled. "Would you mind parking on the top of the hill there and warning oncoming traffic?" she asked. Everett nodded and made a hand gesture; he was still rendered mute.

After straightening the car, he surveyed his skid marks and quickly circled the car. One of the hubcaps was missing. "This thingy came rolling over the hill just before you stopped," said an angelic voice. Everett turned and a tiny Brownie, not much larger than one of his thighs, handed him the missing baby moon.

"Thanks," he said not much above a whisper. She smiled and bounced back toward the disabled microbus. He snapped the baby moon back into place and started toward the bus to help the damsels in distress.

Everett had found the spare tire and was rigging the jack when Tootie pulled up, lights flashing. The troop leader had the girls lined up single file along the highway on the crest of the hill. She'd told Everett she thought it best to keep them in a highly visible spot. Tootie first spoke to the troop leader and then approached the bus.

"Those your skid marks?" he asked. Everett nodded; by then he'd been cranking the jack lever and raising the bus. "You might want to have your brakes checked," Tootie went on. "Looks like they caused you to swerve."

"Yeah," Everett agreed. "I'll have Burt check 'em." He was relieved that Tootie didn't question him about speed.

"Where you headed?" Tootie asked. After he explained about going to Fairview and his first date, Tootie offered to finish changing the tire.

"Thanks," Everett said and started up the hill toward the Green Goddess. The drive to Fairview had moments earlier caused exhilaration; now he was light-headed and weak in the knees.

The leader pointed at the Green Goddess and said, "Cute car."

The girl who had returned the hubcap, and the most delicate-looking one of the bunch, asked, "How do you fit in it?"

Everett grinned, causing a sharp spasm in his jaw muscles. "I wear it," he replied. The girls all giggled.

After passing the row of Brownies and before reaching his car, Tootie announced. "He's got a date." The leader smiled, and the Brownies giggled louder.

His hands were glued to the wheel at ten and two, the radio was silent, and the needle never passed forty-five the rest of the way to Fairview. Everett's mind kept exploring the possibilities of what could have happened had he not hit the pothole and skidded to a stop. The smiling face of each Brownie swept through his mind. He prayed and made all the typical post-trauma promises. His stomach was upset, and the thought of food made him nauseous.

EVERETT HAD WORRIED ALL WEEK about being nervous and not knowing what to say. It wasn't until he pulled into Libby's driveway that he realized he hadn't given the date an inkling of thought since leaving the waving Brownies behind. His jaw muscles, sore from clinching, gave way to a giant smile when he saw Libby sitting on her front porch. Her large size was explained when he saw her parents, who were spilling over both ends of a porch swing hanging by chains that looked to be twice the normal size.

He apologized for being late and explained how he'd helped a Brownie troop with a flat tire. He didn't see the need to mention the skid. Libby's parents were impressed that he'd stopped to help. "Chivalry isn't dead after all," Libby's mother said. Her dad, as tall as Everett but thicker in the chest, shoulders, and waist, nodded approval.

He stood to shake hands; his massive hand swallowed Everett's. Everett couldn't remember the last time he'd shook hands with someone who had a bigger grip than his. "LB," he said, introducing himself. "My real name is Robert. Everyone used to call me Bob, until another Bob moved to town. Then I became Large Bob, but now I'm just LB." Libby's gift for gab came honestly.

Everett opened the door for Libby, but since her hips were wider than the seat, he let her close the door. The "How do you fit?" comment made by the angelic Brownie came to mind while Everett made his way to the driver's side. Libby started by calling the car "cozy" and then never stopped talking all of the way to Pig's Tail.

"It's not your fault," Libby said when they pulled up.

"What's not my fault?" Everett asked, his first chance to speak since pulling away from her house.

"Parking lot is full," she said and then huffed. "Remember, I mentioned that we'd need to get here early." Everett noticed that her cheerful attitude had developed an edge. "We can eat in the car," she said. Everett frowned; there wasn't room for a breath of air, let alone a sack of sandwiches. Libby picked up on the frown. "Yeah, I see what you mean," she said, even though Everett hadn't spoken. "I know," she began. "We can order at the window and wait for a seat."

Everett didn't care; his appetite had returned with a vengeance. He'd experienced the phenomenon before. Just before football games he'd lose his appetite and then following the game eat the equivalent of two meals of burgers and fried onions at the Houn-Dawg.

Mr. T had explained how being nervous could cause the stomach to produce extra acid, which either emptied the stomach or sent signals to the brain telling the body to eat. Either way, Everett was hungry.

They were ordering at the window when a table for two opened. The table was for two normal-sized people. Everett and Libby's knees were touching, and when they placed their elbows on one side, their hands dangled off the other. It could have been romantic, but at this stage in their relationship, it was simply crammed. Libby didn't seem to notice, so Everett tried to relax.

Each table had a menu attached to the napkin holder. It was easy to tell who wasn't local; locals never looked at the menu. Anyone heard ordering anything other than BBQ sandwiches received piercing side stares. The lady known as Peggy the pirate waited on them, and Everett found it nearly impossible to keep from looking at the patch.

"There's an eye under there," Patty offered without being asked. "It drifts, kinda like the eye on that humpback of Notre Dame feller," she added. It was a visual that Everett didn't need just before ordering. "Regular or combination?" she asked.

"One of each," Libby said.

"Me too," said Everett. He'd wanted more, but after glancing at the prices on the menu board posted on the wall near the cashier, he wasn't sure he had enough money. Someone else had always paid, and he hadn't given any thought to the cost.

"Fries and coleslaw too," Libby said.

"How about you, sport?" Peggy asked.

Everett had done the math and reached into his pocket to double-check that he still had money. "Yes, ma'am," he said.

"Just Peggy," she said. "Don't nobody call a one-eyed lady ma'am. Drink?" she asked with an attitude.

"Tab," Libby said and winked at Everett. "I need to watch my figure."

"Mountain Dew," Everett said. "It'll tickle your innards," he added. The words no sooner left his mouth than he wondered what had possessed him to say the soft drink's jingle. He'd never said the jingle and couldn't remember having ever drank Mountain Dew. It was confirmed; he'd lost control of both thought and speech.

He ate while Libby talked and ate; she was able to do both simultaneously. They each had two sandwiches, but Libby finished hers first and had never stopped talking. They sipped their soda-flavored crushed ice and nibbled on the remaining fries. Everett was ready to leave, but he wasn't sure where they'd go.

"How's Quinton doing?" she asked. Before Everett swallowed and had a chance to answer, she began talking about Fairview's Beta Club and then asked another Quinton question. "He's gonna start, isn't he?" she asked just after Everett took another bite. And again, before he swallowed, "That new guy we got for quarterback is a creep," she said and then shared with him what the cheerleaders were saying about Fairview's prized athlete. She kicked him under the table and then whispered, "I hope you guys beat us like dogs," and then glanced around the room to make sure nobody had heard her blasphemous remark.

Libby's incessant prattling didn't bother Everett. He began to enjoy her rattling on, frequently changing topics, and never needing a thoughtful response. Her mention of Quinton reminded him that he needed to figure out a way to get him over to Fritz's. He thought the remark about Fairview's new quarterback telling, and he hoped to make her wish come true. She seemed to be enjoying herself, and Everett had time to think.

When Everett took his last bite, Libby said, "We need to be going; there are people waiting for a table."

IT TURNED OUT THAT FAIRVIEW had a cruising loop too. But being larger than Colby, Fairview's loop had more options. The main artery traversed the city park and then branched out through a variety of neighborhoods. The park was central, and no matter the choice of neighborhood, every car packed with hormone-enriched teenagers crisscrossed the park several times in a given night.

Libby continued her Fairview ramblings, pausing only when she needed to tell Everett where to turn. Everett did as told. She finally talked him into putting down the top, whereupon she began waving wildly at every car they met. It was easy for Everett to imagine that she knew everyone, but he was wishing that she didn't.

"There's the creep," she said, pointing. Everett had recognized the Mustang earlier; they'd met it a couple of times already. He looked in the rearview mirror and saw that it was turning around. "Wanna get an ice cream?" she asked.

"Sure," Everett said without thinking. What he should have done was get out of Fairview; Libby had him both enamored and annoyed, but peculiarly curious.

"It's up here on the right," she said and pointed to a neon sign that read Dairy Queen. "Let's live a little," she said, mimicking DQ's latest slogan.

When they got closer, Diana Ross could be heard singing "Ain't No Mountain High Enough." Libby began to wave her arms to the music; Everett could feel her gyrations through the car's steering wheel. The parking lot was full, but there was plenty of room for the Green Goddess, which soon became a spectacle. Libby knew almost everyone, and even the ones she didn't were interested in the uniquely shaped and odd-colored car. People of all ages were there: kids, parents, even grandparents.

Everett, having never seen a DQ and not watching enough TV to have seen a DQ commercial, didn't know that the DQ was a franchise. He figured that the owner's name must have been Dilly, as nearly half the items on the DQ menu began with Dilly. He chose a Dilly Bar because it was the least expensive and looked simple. It was no surprise to him when Libby ordered a Hot Fudge Sundae Delight; it wasn't the most expensive item but was enjoying some sort of celebrity status, with its own poster plastered directly above the order window.

Libby headed toward a covey of cheerleaders crowded around the lone picnic table; Everett dutifully followed. "I'll introduce you," she said. He sensed someone staring and then noticed the Mustang parked next to another car full of guys; they were all looking his way.

"This is Everett," Libby announced when they reached the girls. "They're cheerleaders," she said in such a way as if to imply royalty.

The girls looked Everett's way. Those with drinks began sipping through their straws, and those with ice cream took a bite. Everett noticed the unison movement and figured it was an auto-response. He'd read where people frequently take a bite or drink so that they don't feel the need to say something.

After an awkward silence, one of them asked, "You play football for Colby?"

"Sure," Everett replied. "And other things too."

"Like what other things?" another asked and then giggled.

"I'm studying for the MCAT," Everett replied without thinking. It was as if someone had taken control of his mind and mouth. Recently, at career day, he'd heard a doctor talking about medical school and the standardized medical college admissions test. He'd never given the MCAT or medical school a second thought since career day. His response surprised him as much as it did the cheerleaders.

"Really?" another said after licking the back of her spoon. "What kind of doctor do you want to be?" she asked.

"You didn't say anything about being a doctor," Libby interrupted, saving Everett from the need to expound on a subject for which he'd given very little thought.

"I doubt he's said much of anything, Libby," one of the Fairview girls said with more than a hint of playful sarcasm.

Libby's expression was a mix of smile and frown. "They think I talk too much." She put Everett on the spot. "Do you think I talk too much?"

"You have a lot to say," Everett replied. "So far it has all been interesting." The girls giggled. Libby wasn't fazed.

"Did you see his car?" Libby asked.

They all perked up as if being reminded of a forgotten appointment. "Oh yeah, the green convertible," one of them said. "What kind of car is it?"

"It's a British import," Everett responded with more than a hint of pride in his inflection.

"What's the deal with doctors and sports cars?" asked a cheerleader.

Libby had been silent for nearly a minute, possibly a record. "They need something fast so that they can race to emergencies," she answered.

Everett listened, the incongruence of fast, race, and Nash Metropolitan striking him as humorous, but he didn't correct them. He realized their impression of him was off base, but he savored the notion that they thought of him as medical school material. A seed had been unintentionally planted.

"You should be a chiropractor," one of the girls suggested with a demure tone. "Then you could give massages with those big, strong hands."

Libby glared at the twiggish cheerleaders, finished her sundae, and tugged on Everett's elbow. "We should go."

LIBBY LIVED ON A CUL-DE-SAC. Everett had never heard of such a thing until getting directions; he'd looked it up rather than ask her to explain on the phone. He walked her to the door, and before he'd had the chance to give it any thought, she stopped talking for a second, grabbed his shoulders, and planted a quick kiss smack-dab on his unprepared lips.

"I had a good time," she said. Everett was stunned. She continued, "You're kind of quiet."

"I don't mind listening," he mustered the control to say.

Libby smiled. "We're a good match then," she said. "I'd ask you in, but my parents are gone. I saw them pulling into the DQ with my aunt and uncle when we were leaving."

"I need to get back to Colby anyway," Everett said. "Wanna do this again sometime?"

"We better," she said using a threatening tone, implying that Everett had no choice but to call again. "Next time let's not be late so that we can get a big table."

"Okay," Everett said, and Libby disappeared into the house. The date ended as abruptly as it began.

The Mustang and another car, parked crossways in the street, had the only way out of the cul-de-sac blocked. The Mustang driver, along with several others, was standing outside the cars.

"Think you can cruise into town and have your way with our ladies?" Fairview's new quarterback asked. He was holding a small baseball bat and pointed it threateningly. Everett's first thought was to spring from the car and grab the bat. The top was still down and he might be able to pull it off, but he wasn't sure.

Smarty-pants started circling the Green Goddess and tapping his hand with the bat. "How're we gonna settle this?" he asked. A car pulled up on the other side of the Mustang. Everett figured it was more reinforcements and was giving serious thought to putting his car in reverse and making a run for it, but he'd eventually have to face these guys or sit in Libby's driveway until they left.

Two men had gotten out of the new car. The headlights of the car made it difficult to see anything but large silhouettes. Oh no, Everett thought, two giants. He reached for the shift knob.

"You clowns have the road blocked," one of the nephilim said. Everett recognized the voice; it was Libby's dad, LB. The other had to be her uncle. She had mentioned having an uncle but nothing about him being a twin. When the Fairview boys turned their attention to the large men, Everett sprang from the car like a cat and snatched the bat from a surprised, bewildered, and now trembling punk.

Everett's swift move took them all by surprise. The boys had just seen a split-second preview of Everett's gifted athleticism, unusual for someone weighing an eighth of a ton.

Libby's uncle kept his eye on the backups. LB watched Everett. "You're agile for a big guy," LB said and then moseyed in Everett's direction. "Well, you should have figured that you couldn't come to Fairview and go showboating around town with one of our girls without stirring up trouble." Everett's confidence began to wane. LB held out his hand. "Give me the bat," he said.

He turned to the others. "Now," he began, "looks like there's a bit of a mismatch." He paused a few seconds and continued. "Mismatches are good on the football field, but they're not so good in a street fight." He held the fat end of the bat and pointed the thin end at the Fairview gang. "So, one at time, gentlemen," he said and pointed the bat toward Everett. "Who's first?" he asked.

He pointed the bat at the Mustang driver. "How about you, batman?" He tossed him the bat. "Here, since you're such a shrimp, you can have the bat." Everett struck a defensive stance, which caused the boys to step back.

Mustang man let the bat dangle at his side. "We were just messing around," he said, his expression half smile and half grimace.

LB chuckled. "Thought so." He shook his head in disgust and looked at his brother. "So much for the big street fight."

The clone chimed in. "Guess nobody wants to tangle one on one."

"Guess not," LB said. "Well, how about moving your cars so I can go home then," LB told the deflated street fighters. The boys piled into the two cars. "I'll take that for now," LB said, pointing at the bat; Mustang man handed the bat over. LB tapped the Mustang with it. "No more messing around tonight," he said. "You understand me?" The driver nodded. "I'll keep the bat for now," he said. Nobody argued.

It was just the three of them standing in the middle of the street. "You should have known better," LB advised. "You okay?"

"Dadgum," Everett said. He'd gone all night without using his fallback word. "I'm glad you showed up," he continued. "I was worried for a minute."

The clone spoke. "You looked a little scared when LB tossed the bat back to our star quarterback."

"I was," Everett nervously confessed.

"Of what?" LB asked. "You didn't have any trouble taking the bat away the first time."

"I only know one speed," Everett replied.

"How's that?" LB asked.

"Well, I don't know gentle," Everett said. "If I'd have hurt him, then my football career might have ended. I'm counting on a football scholarship for college."

"We've heard that about you," the clone said. "You and the other big one; I think his name is Clyde." The twin clone extended his hand. "By the way, I'm Richard," he said.

"Let me guess," Everett said. "They call you LR?"

Both men laughed. "Yeah," LR replied. "We're not known for clever nicknames here in Fairview."

"It's a good thing we're playing Colby the last game of the season," LB told his brother. "I've got a feeling this guy is gonna be a handful for our O line."

LB punched Everett lightly on the shoulder. "Kinda fun to knock the snot out of those smart-mouthed punks, isn't it?"

Everett grinned. "Yeah, it's definitely gonna be more pleasurable after tonight." LB and the clone were grinning. "I like to look 'em in the eyes when I take 'em to the ground."

"Well, don't hurt him too bad," LB said. "Hopefully we'll be headed for districts after playing you guys."

"We'll follow you out of town," LB offered. "Put the top up though. You look like a giant clown in that green thing." Everett turned and started toward the Green Goddess. LB added a parting note. "Another thing," he said. "For the record, we don't like the way the coach handled Quinton's situation. We're glad he's getting a shot at Colby."

LB and LR followed Everett to the edge of town. The sky was overcast, and once outside the city limits, the streetlights ended. The car's headlights functioned more like spotlights, making two bright spots on the road but not illuminating much else. The speedometer's faint glow was the only light inside the car. Everett had never driven at night alone on an unlit highway. The solitude gave him time to think.

He reached the conclusion that it wouldn't go well if a Fairview football player came to Colby and cruised around town with, say, Melody or Sunny. And then he remembered the time an out-of-towner had taken Sunny's older sister Beth to the movie. That guy had left town with a swollen lip, broken headlight, and bashed-in hubcaps. He remembered the event being sixth grade playground fodder for weeks.

Everett was nearly to the Seven Sisters before he realized that, deep in thought, he'd driven all of the way from Fairview with the radio turned off. He twisted the volume knob to on and turned the dial to WLS just in time to catch the psychedelic chord prelude for Kenny Rogers and the First Edition's "Just Dropped In."

I woke up this mornin' with the sundown shinin' in
I found my mind in a brown paper bag, but then ...
I tripped on a cloud and fell eight miles high.

Alone with only his thoughts and the incongruent lyrics of sundown in the morning and tripping on a cloud, he smiled. Crossing the apex of each sister added a physical dimension to the music.

He slowed to a crawl near the last sister, the one where he'd nearly wiped out a Brownie troop. The skid marks were still clearly visible; he'd have to show the guys. For a moment he wished he had Caleb's imagination so that he could concoct something more interesting than a pothole as the cause.

After passing the Colby city limit sign, he felt his body relax. It wasn't until then that he realized how tense he'd been all night. He'd never forget his first date, and the primary memories would have little to do with the girl. Colby had never looked so good.

Clyde's Chrysler was at the Houn-Dawg. Everett pulled in; he was sure the guys were anxious to hear how the date with Libby from Fairview had gone. When he opened the car door, he was hit full-force by the Houn-Dawg's distinctive odor, a major league whiff of frying burgers and onions. The aroma and familiar scene filled his senses; he blinked slowly and smiled. He was glad to be home.

Provocation

Tommy saw Everett and discreetly nodded at him from across the room. Tommy, Melody, Clyde, Flop, Booger, and Caleb were crowded around a four-place corner table. The Houn-Dawg was packed. Tommy watched Everett gently squeeze between crowded tables and head their way.

The usual after-movie crowd were nearest the door; they'd just seen *Airport*, which was what the band of boys would have seen had they not succumbed to Caleb's persuasiveness and survived a misadventure of their own.

A group of boisterous old men who'd had too much to drink at the American Legion's first Saturday of the month shooting match were seated in the center. Tommy had made an earlier observation regarding alcohol's effect on voice volume, hearing impairment, or both.

A large family of Seventh Day Adventists occupied two tables. They resembled the Glory gang that had started coming to First Baptist, but this family had a bigger selection of stair-stepped kids. Since Adventists worshiped on Saturday, their after-service meal was on Saturday night. They were focused on a man with long wavy hair, which was piled on top. He wore a double-breasted suit and was waving his arms wildly about, and when he spoke, his booming voice filled the room. The Saturday worshipers hung on his every word, which were countless. He was no doubt a visiting speaker. Every church had them in from time to time: a boisterous, self-righteous, self-proclaimed heavyweight who would swoop in and tell it like it is the way a local couldn't do, at least not without running the risk at never again getting invited for Sunday dinner.

They probably hadn't counted on sharing a space with the rowdy shooting match drunks.

Caleb saw Everett and began vigorously motioning for him to make his way through the mix of shooting match vermin and holy rollers. "You're not going to believe it," Caleb said when Everett got within what should have been hushed-tone earshot. In his wild-eyed excitement, he showered his side of the table with saliva during his attempt at whispering.

Clyde, sitting next to Caleb, wiped something off of his ear that had shot out of Caleb's mouth and pointed at Tommy. "You tell it." He gave Caleb a "shut up" look. Caleb wiped his mouth on the inside of his elbow.

Everett looked at Tommy. "Tell what?" he asked.

Caleb took another bite and then couldn't control himself. "We did the tunnel," he whispered, but with such force that he again showered Clyde with a mixture of saliva, ketchup, and bits of french fry.

"Dang it all, Caleb," Clyde said. "Settle down and let Tommy tell it."

"Well dadgum," Everett said. "Why didn't you wait for me?"

"Couldn't," Caleb said; he couldn't control himself—not a first for Caleb.

"Caleb," Clyde said, "if you don't shut your confounded trap, I'm gonna stick a dirty sock in it. Besides, we didn't get anywhere near the tunnel." Caleb closed his mouth, and the unspent energy immediately manifested in whole-body fidgeting.

Tommy began, "We'd planned to see *Airport*, but when we got to Caleb's, he had a spotlight, pellet rifle, and an idea."

"Idea?" Everett asked.

"Road hunting," Clyde said. Caleb was rocking-back-and-forth beside himself; he so wanted to do the talking. Clyde gave Caleb a look and added, "Road hunting for rabbits: that was his first idea."

"Hunting rabbits with a pellet rifle?" Everett asked and then quickly grinned. "Oh, I see. An ulterior motive."

Caleb's face spoke for him. "A what?" he asked.

"Never mind," Everett said.

Clyde side-glanced at Caleb and then nodded for Tommy to continue. "We headed out toward Bird's farm. Booger and I were sitting on the hood, and Caleb was shining the light."

"It was plugged into the cigarette lighter," Caleb blurted out.

"What were you going to do with a rabbit if you got one?" Everett asked.

"Yeah, I know," Tommy said. "It sounds stupid now, but Caleb made it sound like fun and said it was legal."

Everett held his hand up slightly higher than the table's top and waved a finger signaling that he had a question. "You were planning to shoot rabbits, at night, from the hood of a car, with a pellet rifle?"

Tommy shook his head guiltily. "I know, I know, when you say it like that it sounds really stupid."

"Can it be said in such a way as to not sound stupid?" Everett asked sarcastically, using his special grammar.

"That's not the best part," Clyde added. Caleb was grinning, clearly proud of himself.

Tommy continued. "When we reached the railroad crossing, Caleb produced a train schedule and convinced everyone that the train wasn't running tonight."

Caleb leaned into the table and rattled off, "That's when Melody decided she wasn't gonna do it." He then leaned back and with a satisfied expression popped a ketchup-laden french fry into his mouth. Clyde immediately began loosening his bootlaces. Caleb put both hands over his mouth and frowned.

Everett looked at Melody. She gave Tommy an unapologetic glare. "I know, I shouldn't have encouraged him," she said.

Clyde, still working on getting his boot off, looked up. "It was Caleb's idea; of course it didn't make any sense," he said.

Tommy smiled at Melody and continued, "Melody and I helped direct Clyde onto the tracks."

Clyde finally got his boot off, revealing a once white but now clay-colored sock with a big toe poking through. Caleb quickly pulled a paisley bandana from his pocket and gagged himself. Melody helped him tie it. It wasn't the first time Caleb had carried out a self-imposed sentence, primarily to avoid a worse fate at the hands of Clyde.

The boys were used to such a display and continued listening to Tommy without giving Caleb's routine a moment's notice. However, it was likely the first time the Adventists had seen someone gag himself. The youngest, a chirpy-haired boy wearing a suit that had been prematurely handed down, pointed first at Caleb, then at the traveling evangelist, and then at his mouth. He was mocking a yawn when his amply girthed mother squeezed his neck hard enough to make the miniature comedian's eyes bug.

Everett was getting impatient. "And then what?" he asked and then said, "I can't believe you drove through the tunnel." He shook his head in amazement.

"That's just it," Tommy said and then pointed at Caleb. "Einstein there hadn't thought about what to do once we passed the tunnel."

Everett slapped his thighs in exasperation. "You take forever to tell a dadgum story," he said. "So what happened?"

Tommy was giggling too hard to talk. Melody had an "I told you so" look. Booger took over. "I was still on the hood; Tommy and Melody were sitting on top of the backseat when Melody asked where the tracks went to after the tunnel."

"Good thing I didn't touch the confounded brakes," Clyde said.

"Why's that?" Everett asked.

Booger shook his head and was slow to answer. "Clyde punched the neutral button, and the car slowed to a stop."

By then Tommy had recovered and was able to talk. "Clyde put the car into reverse, and everything was going okay until we reached the crossing." He shot Clyde a grin. "When Clyde tapped the brakes …"

Clyde added his two cents. "I thought it'd be okay since we were on the danged crossing."

"Anyway," Tommy continued, "when he put on the brakes, the front tires turned just enough to cause them to come off the tracks." Melody's "I told you so" nod got more enthusiastic. Caleb made a noise through the bandana gag. He was probably trying to say brakes, but it's impossible to make a B sound when your lips won't touch.

Everett frowned. "So you didn't make it to the tunnel?"

Clyde was shaking his head in disgust. "We didn't make it fifty feet from the crossing."

Tommy chimed in. "Since the back tires were on the crossing, we were able to keep backing even though the front tires were off the tracks and having to cross each tie."

Clyde did a "boy howdy" head nod. "It's a darn good thing the back tires were on the crossing when the front tires came off," he said.

"So much for the tunnel idea," Everett said and began sipping the cherry freeze Patty had brought him. He hadn't ordered it like he always did, and he wasn't going to since he'd spent all of this money feeding large-Libby from Fairview.

"On the house," Patty whispered, further proof that she was clairvoyant and aware of Everett's postdate destitute financial condition.

Caleb jerked the bandana off. "Tomorrow," he said, and then began re-tying it so as to avoid Clyde's filthy sock.

"Tomorrow?" Everett asked.

"After church," Booger whispered.

Clyde pointed at Caleb and explained. "The train schedule that Einstein got had a map of the spur, and it shows all of the crossings. There's a forest access road crossing just beyond the tunnel."

Melody had heard enough train track talk. She winked at Everett. "How'd it go with Libby?" she asked.

He first told them about the Brownies but managed to modify the story without lying, leading them to believe that he'd first seen the disabled van before making the miraculous hockey stop.

Up until that point, Flop had been too busy eating a large basket of french fries bathed in half a bottle of ketchup to talk. A loud lip smack followed a last cleansing lick of the side of his palm. "Let's go see the skid marks," he said. Caleb was nodding and making grunt noises.

"Tomorrow," Everett said to Flop and then continued. He told them about Libby's giant parents and her dad's twin. "I saw the Mustang kid," he said and then paused. He looked at Clyde and then the others. "We really need to beat Fairview this year." He spared them the details of the blocked road incident.

"You can take the gag out, Caleb," Clyde said. Caleb reached for his soda and made several straw-collapsing draws. The sudden shower of carbonation made his eyes water.

Everett, still intrigued by the tunnel, asked, "Have any of us even seen the tunnel except in photos?" Uncomfortable glances were exchanged.

"Caleb?" Clyde asked.

"What?" Caleb answered, feigning ignorance.

Clyde looked sternly in Caleb's direction. "You've wanted to go to the tunnel since the first day I got my license. Have you ever seen the danged thing?"

Melody saved Caleb further embarrassment. "Maybe we should walk to the tunnel first and see what it looks like," she suggested. It was a logical suggestion and one for which nobody had a good argument.

"Walk?" Caleb asked, dejected.

Tommy frowned; Melody noticed. "What?" she asked.

"Dad and Uncle Cletus were going to help me work on the truck tomorrow," he said.

"Shoot, Tommy," Caleb said and then reminded Tommy of something for which he needed no reminding. "The truck can wait; it's gonna be almost another year before you get your license."

THE INCREASE IN DECIBELS OF the chatter of a full room grows deceptively slow and isn't noticed until the noise suddenly ceases, which is what happened when Quinton stuck his head through the Houn-Dawg's door. The shooting match crowd stopped talking first, which set off a chain reaction when the Seventh Day horde followed suit and looked to see what had silenced the drunks. The band of boys turned to see what had shut up the evangelist.

The only sound was that of the Kink's "Lola" coming from the jukebox. Moments earlier it couldn't be heard; now it sounded too loud. The Seventh Day mom put her large and probably greasy hands over the chirpy-haired little boy's ears. She didn't see fit for him to hear Lola going on about making a man out of an innocent boy. He squirmed, but she had a lock on him.

Quinton was visibly relieved when Tommy motioned for him to join them. Tommy realized he hadn't given Quinton a call and included him in the group's Saturday evening plans. He made a mental note to make a better effort at including Quinton.

Quinton carefully made his way through the crowd saying, "Excuse me," several times along the way. Tommy had asked Quinton about being black in an all-white community. Quinton had explained that he felt as though white people were more uncomfortable with him than he with them, which was the reverse of what Tommy expected. Tommy witnessed that play out while Quinton made his way across the now chaotic maze of tables and chairs to the far corner to join Colby's self-appointed societal epicenter. Quinton was smiling, but everyone else had a look of fear or consternation.

Finally, one of the shooting match drunks broke the tension with, "Hey, there's our new quarterback." He held his coffee mug high to propose a toast, spilling a good deal of the contents on the napkin holder and the salt and pepper shakers in the process. "Here's to ... what's your name, son?" he asked.

"Quinton, sir," Quinton answered and kept moving.

"To Quinton Sir," the saliva-spraying drunk said. The rest of the room repeated after him but not as enthusiastically as the table of inebriated shooters, who then became the focal point.

"Where you been?" Melody asked.

"Watching TV," he replied and then looked at Tommy, who was still moping from Flop's driver's license remark. "You were going to call."

"Sorry," Tommy said. "I forgot."

"No problem," Quinton said. "I'm the new kid. Dad was driving us around town, and I saw the Green Goddess and the Chrysler and asked if I could get out. Can one of you guys give me a ride home?"

"Sure," Everett said and then scooted his chair back to make room.

Quinton pointed at Everett's glass. "That looks good. What is it?"

Everett held up the tall, frosty glass. "Cherry freeze; it's my favorite."

Melody giggled. "You can tell by looking at Flop that he likes the fries."

"Or at least the ketchup," Quinton said and handed Flop a napkin. Nobody had bothered to tell Flop that he had smudges of ketchup on both cheeks. It was an everyday occurrence for Flop, wearing evidence of past meals. They liked to see how long he'd go without wiping it off.

Melody looked at Tommy. "What are you doing to the truck?" she asked.

"I've been sanding off the rust spots," he said and then perked up. "But tomorrow we're gonna remove the head so we can give it a valve job."

"Who is we?" Quinton asked.

"Me, Booger, my dad, and Uncle Cletus," Tommy replied.

Quinton looked at Booger and scrunched his nose. "Is that your real name?"

"No," Booger said. "It's Randy, Randy Burger. But I've been Booger since first grade."

Quinton's expression indicated Booger's reply was a partial answer. "Don't ask," Melody said. Quinton grinned and didn't ask about Flop's nickname, the reason being somewhat evident, although not as much so as when Flop had first been given the tag.

Caleb's eyes were dancing. "You're gonna take the engine apart?"

"Just the head," Tommy said.

"Can you see the pistons when you do that?" Caleb asked.

"Sure," Tommy said.

Caleb's eyes began twitching. "Uh-oh," Clyde said.

"Why 'uh-oh'?" Quinton asked.

"Caleb is thinking," Clyde replied. "That's never good."

The group shared in telling Quinton what had transpired that evening. Quinton repeated the word unbelievable several times while the story unfolded.

"Everett had a date with Libby from Fairview," Melody told Quinton.

"Really?" Quinton asked. "Big Libby? Did you meet her dad?" he asked. Everett nodded affirmative. "Libby always lights up the room wherever she is," Quinton added.

"Her dad said he'd rather have you as quarterback," Everett told Quinton.

Quinton's face became dead serious. "Seriously?" he asked. Everett then shared the details of the roadblock and how it had ended and what Libby's dad and uncle had said about Quinton. Quinton was deep in appreciative thought and visibly stirred by Everett's words. With a contemplative expression, he said softly, "Golden, he likes to be called Golden."

"Who?" Everett asked.

"The Fairview quarterback. His name is Greg Golden, but he likes to be called Golden."

"Sounds to me like he thinks he is golden," Tommy said. Quinton just shrugged.

A thought crossed Caleb's mind, and out of the blue it came forth in a burst, "Shoot, heck with the tunnel or that old truck. Let's go to Fairview tomorrow and kick some butt."

"Caleb," Clyde said, "put a sock in it." Quinton was the only person at the table that didn't know that Clyde's order to Caleb wasn't metaphorical. Clyde's complexion had washed red; he turned to Everett. "You didn't tell us that part."

Everett shrugged. "I was gonna wait until game day, but I changed my mind when I saw Quinton."

Clyde looked first at Quinton, and then he and Everett locked eyes. Each knew what the other was thinking.

"I was thinking the same thing," Everett added. "I can't say the same for the Mustang kid, or Golden whoever." Everett thought for a moment and then said, "Provocation." He grinned eerily. "The act of provoking. And in this case, providing motivation to build momentum."

Quinton looked at Everett and half frowned. "You some kind of wordsmith?" he asked. "I can see why Libby would like you. She's always coming up with words too."

"I have an idea," Melody said, changing the subject. "How about we help Tommy with the truck for a while and then walk to the tunnel?" She emphasized walk.

"What's with this tunnel?" Quinton asked. "You country people have some sort of tunnel fetish?"

"Ever seen a train tunnel?" Flop asked.

"On TV," Quinton replied.

"Didn't you ever want to see one in real life?" asked Caleb.

"Not really," Quinton replied. "Should I?"

"What would you do on Sunday afternoon if you were in Fairview?" Tommy asked.

"Probably go to the DQ and sit in cars," Quinton said.

Melody smiled. "Well, in Colby, we get to take apart truck engines, sand down rust spots, and go lurking around old train tunnels."

"What's with this old truck?" Quinton asked. "You guys get all goofy when Tommy mentions anything about some old truck." When he got no response, he added, "Sounds like it needs a lot of work."

"It's more than a truck," Melody began. "It's kind of a ..."

"Shrine," Everett said, finishing her sentence.

"Shrine?" Quinton asked. The boys explained. It would be the first of many facets of Colby culture that would need explaining.

"Trucks, trains, and tunnels," Quinton said, shaking his head. "Sounds like a song."

"So, tomorrow we work on a truck, then walk down the tracks to a tunnel?" Quinton asked.

"Church first," Melody said.

Quinton grinned. "Perfect. Church, trucks, trains, and tunnel—

that's definitely a song in the making." He looked at Caleb, who had sounded the most enthusiastic about going to the tunnel. "How many times have you been to this tunnel?" he asked.

"Counting tomorrow?" Caleb asked; he'd never been and everyone knew it. The band of boys' table erupted in laughter loud enough to cause the drunks and holy rollers to curiously look their way.

Church, Truck,
Train & Tunnel

A DUST DEVIL OF LEAVES was making its way across the church parking lot when Tommy, his dad, and Marsha pulled up in the Scout. Marsha was driving, and his dad was sitting in the front passenger seat. Tommy was unusually quiet in the back.

Marsha probably thought her driving had improved since Tommy wasn't giving her constant feedback on her every move. He hadn't even commented when she'd ground the gears by inadvertently trying to shift into reverse instead of second, a frequent mistake by novices. Tommy had noticed, but his mind was occupied with the day ahead. He was looking forward to working on the truck, but the tunnel adventure was struggling for mind share.

"How'd I do?" Marsha asked after backing into the Thompson's unofficial parking spot.

Tommy looked himself over. "I'm not bleeding, so I guess you did okay."

His dad did an amused headshake. "You did fine," he said. "Take your time shifting and you'll get the hang of finding second easier."

Tommy jumped out and headed for the visitor parking spot. The Clarences were already there, waiting in their car for the Websters. Before moving to Colby, they'd been attending a Baptist Church in Fairview that had a small, exceedingly expressive, and primarily black congregation. The Websters had talked them into visiting Colby First Baptist. The Clarences had been made to feel welcome by everyone, including Frank Fritz.

On their first visit, they'd happened to sit in front of Mr. and Mrs.

Brown and their kids—John, Jabbok, Jordon, Jericho, Bethany, and Bethlehem—and appreciated the large, disciplined family's demonstrative worship style. And while Brother Russell Ralston's stirring and borderline accusatory messages were considered meddling to most, Mr. and Mrs. Clarence, as well as the Browns, found his provocative words inspiring, so they'd decided to return.

Quinton saw Tommy and got out of his parents' car. "Let's watch for Melody," Tommy said. While they waited, Tommy asked, "Why didn't you ever get your license?"

"Can't afford it," Quinton replied.

"It's only twelve dollars," Tommy said.

"That's to get your license," Quinton responded. "But then your insurance goes up."

"Insurance?" Tommy asked. He'd never thought about insurance. The only additional costs he'd considered were for an eight-track, speakers, and tapes.

"If I get my license, then the insurance on Pop's car goes up," he explained.

"Really?" Tommy asked.

Quinton continued. "If I had my own car, which we can't afford, then I'd only pay insurance on that car. Either way, if I get my license, the cost of insurance goes up. The insurance company figures the cost of insurance based on the number and age of drivers in the household."

Tommy noticed that Quinton explained the situation without shame but as a matter of fact. His family couldn't afford for him to drive and that was that. He wondered if Quinton had ever thought of getting a job but decided to wait for a better time to ask.

Tommy was processing the insurance tutoring and Quinton's job prospects when Melody finally arrived, driving so slowly that he could hear the sound of each individual stone crunching while the car crept thought the parking lot to the spot where the Hinkebeins had been parking for over a decade. While he watched Melody slowly back into the spot, he thought about how honest and unashamed Quinton had been about his family's financial limitation.

The three of them walked to the front of the church and waited for the others. Tommy's mind was processing too many thoughts. He'd awoken early thinking about the truck, looking forward to learning about the engine and visualizing what the truck would look like once it was painted. The tunnel trip interloped among the truck thoughts. And then Quinton had shared the reason he didn't have a driver's license. Everyone in Colby tested for their license as soon as possible; it was automatic. Tommy hadn't thought about the cost of insurance but was now curious.

"Is his nickname because of his ears?" Quinton asked when Flop and Everett pulled up.

"Oh yeah," Melody answered. "You should have seen them when we were in grade school," she said as if that time had been eons earlier instead of only four years.

"What about the nose?" Quinton asked.

Melody sighed sympathetically. "That's new."

"His head is kind of shaped like a lightbulb," Quinton went on. "But he can run like a deer."

"Everett called him an anomaly," Tommy said. "And it made Flop mad until Everett explained what the word meant and that he was referring to how strong and athletic he was in spite of being nothing but skin and bones."

The Codgers had gathered around the maple tree and were making their way toward Melody and the boys when Clyde's Chrysler and the rest pulled up. Tommy saw the Codgers headed their way. "Looks like they've got something on their minds," Tommy said. "Rabbit has that frown he gets when he wants to ask a football question."

By the time Clyde, Caleb, and Booger had gotten out of the car, the Codgers had traversed the twenty feet or so across the parking lot; Fish had his finger up indicating he had something to say, but before he could get his breath, Rabbit looked directly at Quinton and asked, "You gonna tell us all the Fairview plays?"

"I could, sir," Quinton replied. "But I'm not sure that's ethical, and the coaches haven't asked."

Fish, a World War I veteran and First Baptist Deacon, had finally gotten his breath. "That's what I've been trying to tell them," he said, thumbing at the other Codgers.

"We know all of their plays," Everett said and then crossed his thick arms across is barrel chest and stared down at the Codgers. "They've had the same coach and have been running the same stunts for years."

"Well, fizzlesticks," Rabbit said. "I just thought it would be nice to have an advantage and win for once."

Bem pointed at Clyde and Everett. "Looks to me like we got the advantage, don't'cha know," he said.

"I'm just sayin'," Rabbit said, "they got that hotshot kid from Florida or some such place, and he's supposed to be good."

Quinton spoke up. "Golden is new," he said. "Everybody here knows Fairview's plays better than him."

Everett stepped forward and put his bear paw on Rabbit's bony shoulder. "Don't worry, sir. We're gonna win this year. The golden boy won't be a factor." The band of boys and Melody knew exactly what he meant. Everett's exuded confidence injected the Codgers with a smidgen of hope.

"Why do we eat meals?" Brother Russell began.

"Amen," a younger Brown boy yelled. The rest of the Browns gave him a look for shouting out at the wrong time. It wasn't his fault. Since Brother Russell, referred to by the boys as Rotund, had begun his interim stint, he'd started each sermon with an interrogative statement that invited a congregational response. The little Brown was only mimicking what he'd heard the previous three Sundays.

"I'll tell you," he began. "Turn to Luke 14," he said and then, looking over his glasses, scanned the congregation. Those with Bibles began flipping pages in search of Luke. The few without Bibles received an admonishing glare from Brother Russell. Most had learned without being told that taking a Bible to church was a must when Rotund was speaking, but some never learned and regularly suffered the wrath of Russell.

"God could have made us so that we don't need to eat," he said.

"Amen," said Mrs. Brown. It was rare and probably against some Baptist article for women to shout out, but Mrs. Brown was no doubt moved by the concept of not having to feed a horde of kids. Several women were nodding agreement. The men were frowning.

"But he didn't," Rotund continued. "Meals are meant as a time of sharing and receiving physical and spiritual nourishment," he said. "Now with all of this talk about eating, I'm sure that many of you are already thinking about dinner. I'll keep this sermon short." He rubbed his hands together and grinned. "Please stand for the reading of the scripture."

Everyone stood while he read the first fourteen verses of Luke 14. He paused after verse eleven—*For whosoever exalteth himself shall be abased; and he that humbleth himself shall be exalted*—and chuckled eerily. "How many of you want to be exalted?" he asked. Everyone should have known it was a trick question, but nearly every hand shot up. "Now listen," he said before reading the remaining three verses. "Please be seated," he said once he'd finished reading.

Everyone sat and listened as Rotund expounded on the reading. He made sure that everyone understood how they could come to be blessed according to Luke 14:13: *But when thou makest a feast, call the poor, the maimed, the lame, the blind.* The smiles that had spread across the room when he'd announced a short sermon slowly faded with each fist-pounding of the podium and sweat-wiping swipe across his forehead. He offered a long list of reasons, some scriptural, to invite the less fortunate to share a meal. He only paused when taking a gurgling sip of water from a giant mason jar.

True to his word, he ended the sermon ten minutes early, but it had felt like longer. After they'd filed out, Tommy heard an older man say, "Kind of makes me want to start hobbling around or wearing an eye patch." An older cane-wielding lady responded by jabbing the toe of the grumbler's shoe. There was a wince, and no further comments were made.

TOMMY, HIS DAD, AND UNCLE Cletus were at the shop and had already removed the hood when the others began to trickle in. Melody offered to start drawing what she thought should be painted on the door. She and Tommy had discussed the truck's door art at length. They considered a variety of ideas, and it wasn't until then that Tommy realized how repetitive his name sounded—Thomas Thompson. They'd decided to go with T Thompson.

Melody was happy to sit at a bench and sketch while the boys crowded around the engine compartment. Tommy repeated to them what he'd just learned himself while listening to his dad and Uncle Cletus. "It's a 105-horsepower 235," he said. He told it in such a way that everyone should have been impressed, so they were.

Tommy's uncle Cletus, or Mr. T to the boys, was considered a genius. Anyone who had memorized the 118 elements on the periodic tables and knew the atomic structure of each could do anything, at least in their minds. Tommy's dad, on the other hand, had his pilot's license. So, for the boys, deciding which man was smartest was akin to choosing who would win a battle between Batman and Superman—an impossible conclusion to reach.

The boys were crowded around the engine compartment staring at the in-line six-cylinder engine; nobody wanted to miss the taking apart of an engine. The plan was to remove the head so that the valves and valve seats could be ground, a routine maintenance item for older engines. Tommy was wiping away the grease, revealing bright, new-looking paint with each swipe. The only rust spots were near the exhaust manifold where the heat had burned away the oil and grease. The boys were anxious to see the bowels of an engine.

"First we'll remove the valve cover," Uncle Cletus told them.

"Here's a 7/16," Tommy's dad said and handed Uncle Cletus a socket wrench with a 7/16-inch socket already attached. Tommy was always amazed at how mechanics could eyeball a bolt and know the exact size. He usually had to make at least two attempts before getting the right size socket or wrench.

Uncle Cletus removed each valve cover bolt and tossed it into a Folgers coffee can, and then he slowly lifted the valve cover off revealing the rocker arm assembly. Tommy had seen the rocker arm on a tractor before, and Clyde had seen several while working at Burt's. They made room for Booger and the others to get a good look.

"You want to see how the rocker arm works?" Tommy's dad asked. The boys were too amazed to answer. "Stand back a little," he said and then told Tommy to start it.

"Wow, you can start it with the valve cover off?" Caleb asked.

"You wouldn't want to drive down the highway," Uncle Cletus said, "but, yes, the engine will obviously run with the valve cover removed." He explained how the camshaft, located on the side of the engine block and driven by the crankshaft, was pushing up the pushrods, and they in turn were pushing up the valve tappets, which were pushing down on each valve at precisely the right moment.

"They're called tappets," he explained, "because they make a 'tap, tap' sound while operating the valves. Listen." They all tilted their heads slightly to listen even though the tappet sound could have been heard from across the shop.

"Next," Uncle Cletus continued, "we're going to remove the linkage from the Rochester one-barrel carburetor." He spoke to them as if they were in class; it was his natural voice around kids. He could have simply said carburetor, but that wouldn't do for someone who could explain how glass is actually liquid in a solid state.

The tappet display had gotten Melody's attention, but when Mr. T started talking about carburetors, she returned to the bench and the sketch of the truck's door art. She'd finished on the letters to Gooche's Grocery and had begun working on a drawing of a carryout boy, which Tommy had not requested. And she'd decided on something for the tailgate—*Facta Non Verba*.

"Shut it down," Uncle Cletus yelled and then removed the six bolts holding the rocker arm assembly, tossed them into the Folgers can, lifted the rocker arm off, and pulled the pushrods from their respective slots. The engine disassembly class continued until the head had been removed. It was the moment they'd been waiting for.

Melody heard the boys oohing and aahing and came to see. She peeked in between Tommy and Clyde and saw a dirty iron cube-looking thing with a shiny, flat top and six cylindrically shaped holes. Uncle Cletus was twisting the crankshaft pulley causing the pistons to slide one by one to the top of the cylinder. The boys would verbalize a response each time a new piston came into view. Melody, unimpressed, again returned to her sketch, being the only one in the group, other than the men, who had actually done something.

"That's about all we can do until you get the valves ground," Cletus told Tommy. Tommy and Booger carried the head to the bench next to the valve-grinding machine. The others put the tools away, making sure to match each tool to the outline on the pegboard. Tommy's dad put the Folgers can, now overflowing with engine parts, into the bed of the pickup and asked, "Where you all off to now?"

"The tunnel," Caleb answered before anyone else could. The two men exchanged grins. Caleb picked up on it and said, "Thing of it is, the train doesn't run on Sunday."

"Oh, we know," Tommy's Dad said and then asked a rhetorical question. "Have you been there before?" Everyone shook their heads. Hiking down live railroad tracks was not an appropriate family outing. Mr.

Thompson had not taken Tommy nor had any of the other parents taken their children. The first trip to the tunnel was another Colby rite of passage and was traditionally done as couples after driving.

Mr. Thompson walked to a shelf holding an assortment of partially used quart cans of paint and soaking brushes. He wrapped a paintbrush up in a shop towel, chose what looked like the oldest can of paint, and handed it to Caleb. "Here. My guess is you're gonna wish you'd had this when you get there."

"What for?" Caleb asked.

"You'll see," both men said almost in unison.

"Thanks for taking the head off," Tommy said before they left.

Tommy was almost through the door when his dad called out, "See if 'CT loves PL' is still on the tunnel wall."

The comment stopped Tommy in his tracks. It took a couple of seconds to process and then it dawned on him—Cletus Thornton loves Penny Lane. "Really?" he asked.

Uncle Cletus was grinning. "That was a long time ago," he said. "I doubt it's still there."

"You'll hear about it tomorrow if it is," Tommy said.

Cletus looked at Tommy's dad and grinned. "Thanks, Ted." Tommy's dad matched Cletus's sheepish grin and shrugged indifference.

When Tommy finally emerged through the shop door, Caleb stopped pacing momentarily and stood rigid. "We need to get going," he said. "Thing of it is, it's gonna get dark."

"Probably so," Tommy said and winked at Melody. "It does every day."

Flop was already climbing into the Green Goddess with Everett. Whenever Everett took his own car, Caleb commandeered shotgun in Clyde's. Tommy, Melody, Booger, and Quinton squeezed into the backseat. It was a tight squeeze, but no one wanted to sit in the middle in front and get sprayed on with each of Caleb's outbursts.

Caleb slapped his knee. "Brother!" he protested. "We're never gonna get there." He reached down and shoved the eight-track tape into the play position.

Clyde first gave Caleb a look and then pulled the tape out before gently returning it to the play position. "How would you like it if I treated you like you do my tapes?" he asked. Caleb twitched but didn't answer; he'd gotten the not-so-subtle message.

After a moment of uncomfortable silence, Melody cheerfully announced, "To the tunnel!"

To which Caleb, now recovered from Clyde's admonishment, added, "And beyond. To the tunnel and beyond."

Clyde gave him a side-glance and grinned. "You're weird."

Caleb responded, "Well, we *are* going past the tunnel."

Melody patted Caleb on the shoulder. "You just make our little walk sound so poetic." With an eye twitch, Caleb frowned, clearly not certain if Melody's comment was a compliment or a criticism.

AFTER PARKING AT THE CROSSING, they started toward the tunnel. Something they hadn't noticed previously, probably because it was dark, was that the track curved slightly leading up to the tunnel; the tunnel wasn't visible from the crossing.

Railroad ties are laid every two feet, which is just slightly less than the average person's gait. In order to walk on top of the ties, each step must be slightly shorter or a lot longer than what is natural. Walking along the side of the track is an option, but the incline beyond the tie ends can be steep and hard on the ankles. Each step requires focus.

Caleb was the first to notice the entrance. "There it is," he shouted. Everyone stopped tie hopping and looked up. Still over a hundred yards away but in clear view was the opening to the tunnel. "It's smaller than I thought it would be," Caleb added, sounding disappointed.

"Can the train fit through there?" Flop asked. Nobody answered.

"My dad said they blasted it with a giant cannon," Melody said.

"Really?" Caleb asked.

"It's solid rock," Everett chimed in with an incredulous tone.

They proceeded cautiously, alternating between tie hopping and stopping to admire the fern-covered hillside, the hole blasted through it, and the perilous drop-off on each side of the track.

A wide and deep ravine preceded the tunnel entrance. Rather than build a long trestle to maintain a consistent grade, the ravine had been filled with tailings from the tunnel blasting. The result was a large pond on the uphill side and a short trestle that spanned the pond's narrow overflow. The track bed dropped steeply on both sides. One side dropped down twenty feet to the pond's edge; the other side dropped much further into a brushy, viper-infested abyss.

Melody took Tommy's hand when they reached the area with drop-offs on both sides. She pointed toward the tunnel and said, "Look, you can see the other end." Once they'd gotten close enough to the tunnel's entrance, the light at the other end was visible.

The tunnel entrance was little more than a hole blasted into a hillside that appeared to be a monolith covered with a layer of soil barely thick enough to support ferns, thistles, and wildflowers. A sparse mix of oaks and maples grew miraculously from the giant rock and had already turned to their various shades of fall hues. Without the tracks leading to it, a casual hiker would have easily missed the tunnel.

Once they were within a few yards of the entrance, Caleb shielded his eyes, peered inside, and remarked. "That's farther than I thought it would be."

"Eight hundred ninety feet," Melody said.

"Looks longer," Caleb said.

"It was built over a hundred years ago," Melody continued. "They drove a ceremonial spike in the center of the tunnel at midnight on August 14, 1869."

"How'd you know that?" Caleb asked.

"Says so on this plaque," Melody said. Only then did the rest notice the engraved iron plaque mounted on the tunnel's wall a few feet from the entrance.

"Doesn't look like the time of day makes any difference," Everett observed. "It's probably always dark in the middle."

"It's still there," Melody said; she'd begun to study the graffiti.

"What's still there?" Caleb asked.

"CT + PL, right over there," she said and pointed at the faded but still visible initials.

"Those are twenty years old," Tommy said.

"Did anyone remember the dadgum paint?" Everett asked. Tommy held up the can and the brush.

"What should we paint?" Quinton asked.

"TT + MH," Caleb replied, stating what he thought to be obvious, and then took the paint and brush from Tommy. Melody blushed; Tommy suddenly became preoccupied with a hangnail.

"We need to paint something that represents the entire group," Booger suggested.

"What?" Caleb asked. He'd already dipped the brush into the paint and was ready to begin scribing.

"Let's all think about it while we walk through the tunnel," Clyde suggested.

"Walk through?" Caleb asked.

"Sure," Clyde said. "Remember? The tunnel and beyond," he replied.

Everyone waited for Clyde and Everett to lead the way.

"I can't see," Caleb complained and then inexplicably sat the paint can and brush down.

"Once your eyes adjust, you'll be okay," Everett assured him.

"It's cool in here," Clyde noticed.

"Feels good," Everett added.

Huddled together, they crept along one tie at a time. The further along they went, the darker and colder it got, and the more frequent the drips from the groundwater seeping through the tunnel's jagged rock ceiling.

"How far have we gone?" Caleb asked, his voice echoing.

Clyde chuckled. "Not very far; look back." The opening they'd just entered still loomed large; the tracks leading in were still visible, but the other end was just a small retina-piercing bright hole surrounded by damp darkness.

The darkness drew them closer. Tommy was gripping Melody by the waist, and she had her arm across his back, her hand cupping his shoulder. The damp ties were slick; each step had to be carefully negotiated. The boys had long abandoned the implied personal space rule and were huddled almost as tightly as Tommy and Melody.

"Dadgum," Everett began, "it's dark in here," repeating what everyone had said several times along the way.

"Anybody bring a flashlight?" Caleb asked.

"I have one in my car. Why don't you run back and get it?" Clyde responded sarcastically, bringing some much-needed levity.

"Stop," Everett said. "Try this. Don't look at either end, just look at the wall of the tunnel." Everyone did as instructed. "Use your hands to shield your eyes from the light coming in from either end."

"The wall is really jagged," Melody said.

"There's water standing alongside the track," Tommy noticed. The group quietly examined the interior of the hundred-year-old legendary tunnel.

"What's that on the wall?" Melody asked. The rest looked to where she was pointing. With their hands cupped on each side of their faces, they could make out in faded letters *Et Lux in Tenebris Lucet*.

"Weird," Caleb said with an ominous tone.

"Wonder what it means," Melody said.

"We'll have to ask your uncle Cletus, Tommy," Booger added.

"Yeah," Caleb agreed. "He's knowledgeful." Everyone knew what he'd meant.

Caleb made a *shh* sound. "What's that noise?" he asked.

The huddled group stood motionless, staring at the tunnel wall and listening.

"I think that's water dripping from the ceiling," Melody said. Everyone's breathing slowed so that they could tune in to the dripping sound.

"Thing of it is," Caleb began, "that's not the sound I heard." He'd no sooner got the words out than there was the sound of something splashing in standing water. "That!" he whisper-yelled.

"Let's keep moving," Everett suggested. He and Clyde began moving again.

After they'd been moving a minute or so, Caleb said, "This thing must be a mile long."

"Melody said it was 890 feet," Tommy told him.

"How long is a mile?" Caleb asked. Nobody answered. Caleb's questions were oftentimes allowed to float off into infinity, especially when he got into one of his nervous chatterbox moods.

Tommy's eyes had adjusted to the point that looking at the light coming in from either end caused slight ocular pain. The thin puddle of water that ran between the track and the jagged tunnel wall came into view. Looking back, the tracks, puddle, and tunnel wall disappeared into the darkness. Looking ahead, while shielding his eyes from the exit light, everything turned from dark and barely visible to a gray hue.

He and Melody were still clutching each other. He could smell her hair—Prell. When she turned to look at the wall, her head blocked the light coming from the exit. Her nose, lips, neck, and ponytail shaped a delicate silhouette.

Everyone else's eyes had adjusted too. The closer they got to the other end, the quicker the pace and the more space the boys put between themselves. At one point they'd all been touching each other lightly on the forearm or shoulder, but the boys instantly put that out of their mind upon exiting the tunnel. Tommy had enjoyed the experience with Melody and had no plans to purge the memory.

Everyone was stumbling around and squinting when Caleb asked, "Now what?"

"We're looking for the next crossing," Clyde reminded him.

"Thing of it is," Caleb began with a hint of nervousness, "I'm not sure it's such a good idea to drive through this thing."

Melody chuckled and said what everyone else was thinking. "It was your idea in the first place, Caleb."

"Thing of it is," he repeated and then paused for the longest time. Everyone knew that he hadn't thought of what to say next and out of curiosity let him struggle in thought. "What if the train came?" he asked.

Everett didn't let him off the hook. "You've got the schedule in your pocket. You talked about it at the depot. The train doesn't run on the weekend."

"It's straight as an arrow," Clyde said, pointing back at the tunnel. "Driving through it shouldn't be a problem." Caleb didn't respond.

Quinton's eyes were the first to adjust to the bright sunlight. Since he was new to the group, rather than be part of the Caleb heckling, he'd looked ahead. "Is that the crossing?" he asked. Caleb's map had shown an abandoned crossing just beyond the tunnel.

They were so focused on the crossing ahead and the promise of a trail to the county road that nobody noticed the small packet. A few yards from the tunnel's entrance, one track had something the diameter of a half-dollar coin and half an inch thick attached to the top of the rail. If they'd noticed it, they would have seen the word written in faded red: *Danger*. They didn't notice it then, but they would later.

They all stumbled along until they reached the spot that Quinton had seen; it was a crossing primarily used by the forestry department. They followed the access trail in the direction they hoped would lead to the county road.

"Dadgum," Everett said and began wiping his boot on clumps of weeds. Melody looked where he'd stepped. "Gross," she said.

Everyone was standing over the pile of scat, now mashed flat from Everett's size 15 Redwing work boot. "Coon crap," Clyde said and then, after side glancing at Quinton, clarified, "Raccoon crap."

Curious, Melody leaned over and took a closer look. "How do you know it's raccoon crap?"

"Persimmon seeds," Clyde said.

"Coon … er … raccoon crap always has persimmon seeds," he said.

Quinton eased the vernacular tension. "'Coon crap' is easier to say than 'raccoon crap,'" he said, mostly for Clyde's benefit. Clyde nodded nervous agreement and grinned. His forehead was beaded with sweat. Quinton shrugged indifference. He had assimilated with the group and didn't find it necessary to talk incessantly.

"Dadgum coons," Everett said. During his frantic scraping, he'd missed the subtle exchange and clarification.

"For the record," Quinton said, "I've never eaten a persimmon." Everyone chuckled. Everett, however, wasn't particularly amused. After wiping the small beads of sweat from his forehead, he picked up a small stick and began poking at the last pieces of scat that seemed to have magically adhered to the double stitching on the side of his heel.

When they reached the county road, Clyde looked back and said, "The Chrysler could make it down this trail."

Despite the temporary bouts of fear experienced while deep inside the tunnel, Tommy sensed that Caleb would eventually get his original wish, whether he liked it or not.

Everyone stopped and looked back toward the tracks when Melody said, "We forgot the can of paint."

"Caleb had it last," Tommy said.

"I don't know what happened to it," Caleb said. Everyone believed him.

A shroud of dread fell heavily upon Tommy. Two choices came to mind, and neither was to forget about the nearly empty quart can of paint and well-used brush. It was the principle of leaving something behind that vexed him. One option was to walk back through the tunnel, and the other was to walk down the track from the other end. The thought of either sucked the breath out of him.

Melody noticed; she put her hand gently on his slumped shoulder. "I have an idea," she said.

"We can get it when we drive the Chrysler through the tunnel," Caleb said before she could. His confident tone caught Tommy by surprise, and probably everyone else too. But adhering to the code, nobody reminded Caleb that only moments earlier he'd suggested that a drive through may not be a good idea.

Clyde and Everett, both impervious to fear, exchanged glances and shrugged agreement. Tommy's suspicion was confirmed; it hadn't taken the seed long to germinate.

On the way back to town, Melody asked, "Can anyone remember the words we saw on the tunnel wall?" The discussion evolved from few saying anything to everyone's memories being sufficiently jogged so that each was defending their version at the top of their lungs. The argument was never settled; it just ended when everyone went their separate ways and headed home.

Civility

Before Miss Anderson began teaching at Colby, American History had been a relatively easy class to pass. With minimal effort, a good grade was a cinch. The most challenging part of the syllabus was the US Constitution; the passage of which was a graduation requirement. The graduation stipulation cast an ominous cloud over the class; it had to be taken seriously. It was feared almost as much as the driver's test.

The pupils had been filled with mixed emotions when on the first day of class Miss Anderson had explained the new syllabus, which wasn't a state requirement, she explained, but hers. Tommy felt no fear; he looked forward to the challenge, if only to be in her presence.

Miss Anderson's looks provoked visceral emotions deep in the soul of every male student and probably most of Colby High's male faculty—and maybe all of Colby, for that matter. She could single-handedly raise the heart rate of an entire gymnasium with a simple smile. But she was so kind that her natural gifts of beauty, perfect complexion, and proportion didn't breed contempt among the female population, except for Mrs. Cain and the regulars at Colby Curls.

"I don't know why she feels the need to change things," Mrs. Cain complained to Mr. Franklin. Her grievance should have been with Mr. Franklin, who had instituted the change that was the root of the problem. Before Mr. Franklin had arrived, Mrs. Cain's job was to answer the school's phone, dole out classroom supplies, and keep her fingernails manicured. She was now given the occasional task of providing clerical assistance to the teachers under Mr. Franklin's purview. She was typing up a worksheet for Miss Anderson while complaining.

"Who benefits the most from the changes she's making?" Mr. Franklin asked. He'd seen the handwritten worksheet consisting of the first ten of 110 rules of civility that President Washington studied as a child.

Mrs. Cain surely knew the answer but couldn't bear to admit it. "I'll bet the students aren't happy with her," she said, fabricating a concern and verbalizing a hope.

"Have you gotten to number six yet?" Mr. Franklin asked. His office door was open. He looked at the wall that separated him from Mrs. Cain and chuckled. She begrudgingly read rule 6, written in Miss Anderson's impeccable handwriting, and then made a face from the other side of the wall. Rule 6 read, in part, *Speak not when you should hold your peace.*

"Let me know when you have them mimeographed," he said. "I'll take them to her."

"Oh, I'll run them to her," Mrs. Cain replied. Mr. Franklin grinned. He loved it when reverse psychology worked. Even though Mrs. Cain despised Miss Anderson and loathed doing anything for her, Mr. Franklin knew Mrs. Cain would deliver the copies if for no other reason than to keep him from visiting the teacher who had all of the boys talking.

Miss Anderson's looks hadn't gone unnoticed by Mr. Franklin, and he'd allowed Mrs. Cain to think the worst when, toward the end of the previous school year, he and Miss Anderson had spent what could easily be perceived as an inordinate amount of time in his office with the door closed. Closing the door wasn't a necessity for their conversation; he'd done it simply to provoke the curiosity of Mrs. Cain.

And it had worked. But Mr. Franklin's wife and Miss Anderson had become good friends and had discussed Mr. Franklin's penchant for the fomenting of rumor. It was a trait that had surfaced after moving to Colby. Mrs. Franklin credited Mrs. Cain for sparking the devious behavior. Mr. Franklin and his wife had discussed the closed-door sessions, not so much for the door closing aspect, but more for the content of the discussion.

It was during those sessions that Miss Anderson had proposed and explained her idea for a major change to the American History syllabus to focus on the character of the Founding Fathers, particularly George Washington. The previous lesson plan required students to memorize a lot of events and dates but allowed little time for the discussion of the significance of each.

Mr. Franklin had studied Miss Anderson's detailed recommendation and had been interested in Washington's renowned invincibility as a soldier, particularly his role in the battle of Monongahela during the French and Indian War. Even though he had several horses shot out from under him, Washington was the only officer not shot.

After reading Washington's 110 rules of civility, Mr. Franklin had asked Frank Fritz to make a wooden plaque of rule 81, *Be not curious to know the affairs of others, neither approach those that speak in private.* He'd hung the plaque above his office door and in clear view from Mrs. Cain's desk. Mrs. Cain had evidently presumed the rule was meant for others and not her.

Mrs. Cain didn't realize it, but her delivery of the fill-in-the-blank test sheets didn't work out as she'd hoped, which was for the test to breed contempt for Miss Anderson. Mrs. Cain was greeted by smiles and thought they were for her. But the smiles were caused by the mimeograph smell, which was an elixir of sorts. She was on her way back to her office lair with a smidgen of a smile when the class realized what was on the addictive sheets, whereupon Mrs. Cain became the object of numerous evil thoughts.

Everyone understood that the test questions had been prepared by Miss Anderson, but Mrs. Cain had delivered them. The unfair notion was akin to a patient holding a grudge against a nurse who gives a shot ordered by a doctor. It didn't help that Mrs. Cain had handed the test papers to Miss Anderson while holding her lips so tightly together that they'd almost disappeared into her grimacing face.

Miss Anderson had the knack of sharing the stress of test taking with her students. Tommy noticed how the general sentiment of the students was that Miss Anderson wouldn't give tests if some higher power didn't require her to do so. Since Mrs. Cain delivered the test, she represented that higher power and appeared to enjoy anything that had to do with rules and guidelines for student behavior.

Miss Anderson handed the first person on each row a stack and didn't have to tell them to take one and pass the rest back. Everyone knew. There were no surprises; it was a simple fill-in-the-blank covering the ten rules she'd handed out the previous Friday. She planned to cover ten rules each week and be finished before Christmas break. The boys had found the rules curious, limiting, and certainly fodder for debate.

Rule 3: *Show nothing to your friend that may _____him.* Tommy thought for several seconds and then filled in the blank with *affright*, and while doing so, he thought of when he and Booger had tricked Flop into jumping into the ice-cold Craggy Creek in late winter years ago.

While memorizing rule 7—*Put not off your clothes in the presence of others, nor go out of your chambers half-dressed*—he'd wondered how that worked with the locker room.

And rule 8 confused him. *At play and at fire it is good manners to give place to the last comer, and affect not to speak louder than ordinary.* He understood being a good sport and showing respect for the loser. Flop had pointed out that the rule didn't specify which place, but only a place. "Could be last place," he'd said.

And there was the speaking part of the rule. Since it was fall and the Fairview game was approaching, Tommy related everything to football. He considered the notion that the cheerleader's primary purpose was to entice the crowd to be loud. And he'd observed Miss Anderson cheering after a touchdown. He'd seen the bulging veins in her neck when Everett and Clyde had once doubled up on a quarterback sack. But maybe at a football game, loud was ordinary.

Miss Barbara's bus rides came to mind, and he wondered if Miss Barbara would be a much happier person if everyone obeyed rule 8 while riding the bus. After further contemplation, he crossed off that notion; there were days in which nothing could have altered Miss Barbara's disposition except maybe hormone therapy.

Tommy's daydream excursion was interrupted when Miss Anderson stood and said, "Pass them to the front." The test wasn't particularly difficult and didn't require precise memorization, but some of the blanks were for words not commonly used in today's language, such as chambers and affright.

After football practice Everett took Quinton to meet Frank Fritz. He'd filled Quinton in on Fritz's background and prepared him for the visit. Quinton had done a little homework too.

Quinton extended his hand to shake. "Pleased to meet you, sir."

Fritz stopped wiping his hands with a shop towel long enough to shake Quinton's hand and mumble, "Zo, you're dis new quarterback that Bem, Rabbit, Fish, and Monkey are always yakking about." Fritz's quick glance at his hand didn't go unnoticed by Quinton. He was used to people looking to see if any of the black had rubbed off. Fritz resumed wiping his hands with the shop towel, but that was his nature; if he wasn't using them, he was wiping them.

"Yes, sir," Quinton said. "Well, at least I'm the quarterback. I'm not sure what is being said about me."

"Everett tell you why you're here?" Fritz asked, getting straight to the point.

"Well, sir—" Quinton began but was quickly interrupted by an impatient Fritz.

"I got mixed up wit de KKK and developed zome notions. A lady in Fairview," Fritz began, referring to his therapist as simply a lady, "zuggested I get to know vat she kalt a person of color."

"Everett says you can make anything," Quinton said, no doubt trying to ease the tension.

Fritz was already standing erect, but Quinton's remark caused him to strike a rigid pose. A smile lurked beneath his softened grimace. "I like to verk vit my hands," Fritz replied and then said, "I show you."

Fritz started toward the door to his shop and Quinton asked, "What about the brooms?"

"I show you dat last," Fritz said and motioned for the boys to follow. "Dis way." He pointed out the diesel generator that allowed him to be totally self-sufficient if necessary. "I even haf my own vater," he said and opened the cover exposing his well.

He then led them to his largest shop building, where rows of assorted contraptions were sitting as if on display. He turned, rested his hands proudly on his hips, nodded toward the contraptions, and proclaimed, "Here for repair."

"What's that?" Quinton asked and pointed at what looked to him to be a mess of pans connected by a dizzying array of braces.

"Dat," Fritz began, "belonks to da feet store. It's for sorting eggs."

"How does it work?" Quinton asked.

Quinton's question was a call to action. Fritz tucked the shop towel into a hip pocket and moved closer to the contraption that looked like an erector set project gone bad rather than a machine with a specific purpose.

"First," Fritz said, "it's broken. Zo, it doesn't verk." He then pointed a finger skyward and continued, "But if it did, dis is vat it vould do."

"You gently lay de eggs here." He pointed at a large round collection tray. "And ven it spins, first go the small eggs and den last go de bik eggs."

He then pointed at the spindle that spun the round tray. "It's broken, and the parts are no longer awailable."

"You make the parts?" Quinton asked.

Fritz snapped to attention, and the smile that had been struggling to leap forth finally spread across his bony leprechaun face. "I make special," he said and then planted both fists on his hips.

"Come," Fritz said and motioned for the boys to follow. "I show you." He led them to an area with several machines.

"That's a nice drill press," Quinton said.

"You know for vat it is?" Fritz asked.

"Sure," Quinton replied. "My dad is the machine technician at the factory."

Fritz pulled at his beard. "Dat is right," he said. "I hadn't put the two and two together. Zo," Fritz continued, "you know how about the drill press." He pointed at a more complicated-looking piece of equipment. "You know for vat this is?"

"It's a lathe," Quinton said.

Fritz was visibly impressed. "You know how verks it?" Fritz asked with a hint of suspicion.

"I know what it's used for, but I don't know how to operate it," Quinton said.

Fritz smiled again. It was the first time Everett had seen him smile twice in the same day. "I teach you," Fritz said. They stood there for an awkward moment and then Fritz said, "But not today."

Fritz motioned for them to follow and started toward the door. "Today is broom day." He held the door for them and then locked it securely before walking toward the broom shed. "Friday and Saturday morning is only for brooms," he said. "Quality requires focus. All day on Friday and the morning of Saturday I only make brooms."

He stopped short of the broom shed door and faced Quinton. "You need a job?"

Quinton looked at Everett, and the two of them shrugged. "Here?" Quinton asked.

"Ya, of course," Fritz replied. "Vere else?"

Fritz nodded at Everett. "Dis one has a good job at the feet store," he said and then reached up and patted Everett on the shoulder. "And he's too bik." Fritz pointed at the confines of the broom shed. "Ve're always bumping into each other." Fritz had resumed wiping his hands with the shop towel. "Zo, you vant to learn how to make brooms?"

Fritz pointed at the sign hanging above the door—*Neue Besen Kehren Gut.* "The saying has many meanings."

Everett shrugged and chuckled. "I guess I just got fired."

"No, not fired," Fritz protested. "Fired is bad; you're a good younk, bik man. You are making room for dis one." He pointed at Quinton. "Your name is too hard to say." Fritz pulled at his beard. "May I call you Q?" Fritz misunderstood Quinton's wince for an approval.

"*Danke,*" Fritz said and bowed slightly. "You start today?" he asked. Before Quinton had a chance to clarify, Fritz motioned for him to follow. "It's time to learn."

"We have a game tonight," Everett said.

"I know," Fritz said, sounding frustrated. "That's all the old guys dat sit and sit at de courthouse know to talk about." Fritz paused in thought. "Let's make one broom and den you can go play."

Realizing they didn't have a choice, the boys followed Fritz into the confines of the shed. Fritz explained about soaking the broomcorn overnight to make it pliable. While attaching the broomcorn to the handle with binding wire, he again explained that the broomcorn wasn't really corn but more like sorghum grass.

Fritz stopped pedaling the binding machine and looked at Quinton. "Vat is Homecoming, Q?" Quinton didn't answer; he'd soon learn that most of Fritz's questions didn't require answering so long as he listened. "Who's coming home?"

"People who used to live here, I guess," Quinton replied. He looked at Everett and made a facial plea for help.

"There's a Homecoming king and queen?" Fritz asked. "Of vat are they king and queen?"

"Homecoming?" Quinton replied with a tone of insecurity.

Fritz moved to the threshing machine and knocked the grain off the ends of the broomcorn. When finished he asked, "Again, vat is dis Homecoming?"

He moved to the broom handle vise. "Are you paying attention, Q?" he asked.

"Yes, sir," Quinton said.

"Good. Making a broom is simple, but it requires focus. You can't be thinking about being a king of de Homecoming vile making a broom." Fritz placed the broom in the vise and ran four rows of stitching through the straw.

After trimming the ends of the broomcorn, he then handed the finished product to Quinton and asked, "Tell me, Q, which is of more walue today, dis broom or de Homecoming king and queen?"

When Quinton didn't immediately answer, Fritz continued, "It's not a good question, Q." He began wiping down the machines. "It has no easy answer. The walue of dis Homecoming is different for everyone." Fritz pointed at himself. "For me de Homecoming has no walue, but to others it's very important." He pointed at the broom. "But the broom has walue for everyone." Fritz pointed at the door. "Now go. And vin the game for your king and queen."

Everett and Quinton watched Fritz cover the vise and binding machine with a well-used piece of canvas and then headed out. The boys got in the car and sat in stunned silence. Everett started the car and before putting it in gear looked over at Quinton. "That was the most esoteric thing I've ever heard from Fritz."

"Esoteric?" Quinton asked.

"Yes, Q," Everett said, "mysterious, perplexing."

"Q?" Quinton asked.

Everett grinned.

"'Q' stays here," Quinton said.

"Not on your life," Everett said. "Quarterback Q." Quinton crossed his arms and slumped. Everett leaned over and shouldered him. "Have you read next week's rules?"

Quinton tightened his crossed arms. "No. Why?"

"Rule twenty," Everett began. "'The gesture of the body must be suited to the discourse you are upon.'"

"Your point?" Quinton asked.

"You just won approval from the most difficult and judgmental person in the county, possibly on planet earth. And he gave you a job. Be happy."

"Got a new name too," Quinton mumbled with pouty lips and then sat up and looked at Everett suspiciously. "Was the job part of the plan?" he asked.

"No way," Everett replied. "Getting fired wasn't part of any so-called plan."

"No," Quinton disagreed, "he made it clear that you weren't fired." Quinton chuckled and unfolded his arms. "What did he call it? Making room?"

THEY PULLED INTO THE HOUN-DAWG just as everyone else was getting ready to leave. Clyde had a carload; Everett pulled alongside. "How'd it go?" Clyde asked.

"Fritz gave him my job," Everett replied, sounding remorseful, which he wasn't.

"Your job?" Caleb asked from the middle of the front seat.

"That's not all," Everett said. Once he had the attention of everyone in the Chrysler, he continued, "Someone has a new name."

Caleb sat up from a slumped position. "A new name?" he asked.

"You know how Fritz is," Everett continued. "He's got that accent and all. Well, right away he shortened Quinton to Q." Quinton began rubbing his temples. Everett elbowed him and whispered, "Rule twenty, Q."

"Yeah," Everett said. "Fritz said that I needed to make room for Q."

Clyde frowned. "Make room?"

Everett laughed. "It was Fritz's way of telling me that he was giving my job to Quinton." He again elbowed Quinton lightly. "I mean Q."

"Well," Caleb began, "it's not like you'll miss making brooms."

"Where's Tommy and Booger?" Everett asked.

"Working on Booger's vacuum," Clyde replied.

"On a game day?" Everett asked

Clyde shrugged. "Guess so."

"We're supposed to be in the locker room in less than an hour," Clyde said.

After they'd pulled away, Everett confessed, "I'll miss making brooms." He tilted his head in thought. "I kinda like the old coot."

Quinton's thoughts were elsewhere. "What's up with Booger and his vacuum?" he asked. When Everett didn't reply, Quinton continued, "Seems like anytime he's not around, it's because of some broken vacuum. Sounds like they need to get a new one or something."

Since they were nearing Quinton's duplex, Everett didn't want to take the time to explain Booger's mood swings. "His dad sells vacuum cleaners."

"Maybe he's fixing vacuum cleaners for his dad," Quinton said and opened the door to get out.

"It's hard to say," Everett said and pulled away.

Booger's Homecoming debut had nearly arrived. Tommy was providing moral support by watching Booger repeatedly play "Classical Gas." He had watched Booger countless times but continued to be mesmerized by how fluidly his fingers moved over the guitar. Tommy was anxious for everyone to hear. Booger was simply anxious.

After Melody's birthday party, word had gotten around that Booger had learned to play the guitar. But until actually hearing him play, it was impossible for anyone to imagine his level of excellence.

"I don't know," Booger said after finishing the song for the fifth time. Earlier that day Mr. Tobin had given Booger a recording of the school jazz band playing "Classical Gas."

"Look," Tommy said, "the song starts slow. Once you start playing, you'll forget about the crowd. Don't worry about the jazz band; their job is to match you." Tommy had just made that up, but Booger appeared to believe it. "You could play this song blindfolded."

"Let's try it," Booger said.

"Try what?" Tommy asked.

Booger reached for his dresser drawer and pulled out a bandana. "Tie this around my head." After Tommy had secured the bandana, Booger sat motionless for several seconds and then began. He started slower than normal, struggling at first to find the strings and frets. Slowly he got used to sightless playing and eventually picked up the tempo.

When finished he softly said, "I guess I'm as ready as I'll ever be."

Amazed, Tommy softly said, "It's game time."

Tommy's dad knocked lightly on the door. "We need to get going," he said. They exchanged rolling-eye expressions. Neither wanted to ride to the game with a parent, but since neither Tommy nor Booger could drive and the guitar practice had caused them to miss a ride with Clyde, they had no choice.

Booger snapped the latches on the guitar case, and they headed for the door. Booger's dad had already walked out. Miss Anderson was waiting for them on the porch. They couldn't drive yet, but they'd be riding to the game in her GTO. Not having a driver's license had its advantages.

Homecoming

STEEPED IN TRADITION, HOMECOMING IS the most well attended game of the year. Codger's Corner was packed. Speculation about play call for the game at hand was debated and the telling of legendary plays of past Homecoming games were repeated with ample embellishment. Memory enhancement reaches a new zenith during the exaggerated recollection of past games. Men with graying, receding hairlines and bellies pouring over their belts expound on the star roles they contributed to super-teams that exist primarily in their memory alone. The Will Rogers quote, "Things ain't what they used to be and probably never was," is never more true than during the Homecoming pregame confab at Codger's Corner.

Venus Merle, nee Storm, had seen to it that her husband Milton Merle followed through on his therapy. It had been years since he'd been seen sneaking around in the middle of the night and snatching women's undergarments from clotheslines. His relationship with the Codgers had gradually grown to inner-circle status and was confirmed when they'd given him a nickname. Nicknames are generally endearing and indicative of a person's personality. The Codgers' new handle for Milton was "Midnight."

He still didn't have his own chair under the legendary sycamore tree on Codger's Corner but was no longer ostracized by the courthouse curmudgeons. And since he was the only person in Colby who had actually played college football, the Codgers listened when Milton offered an opinion on the game.

Milton and Venus arrived at the game in a golf cart he'd picked up after being inspired by Monkey's spear-adorned contraption. Milton's cart had also been modified. He'd removed the fiberglass top but left the braces. Venus had custom made a canvas cover and painted a powerful-looking

Indian chief on each side. And on the back, in memory of the liberal arts college that had called Colby home from 1880 until 1934, and where Milton had played football, Venus had painted a beautiful Will Mayfield College logo. She'd painted number 45 on the front, Milton's number in both high school and college.

Milton's athletic ability had been recognized and oftentimes resented because, during his career as a Peeping Tom, no husband had been able to catch him in a footrace. Four years earlier, however, Milton had finally endeared himself to Colby by running down a villain who, out for revenge, had tried to kidnap a cheerleader and in the process terrorized the town.

At that time he was making regular visits to the Fairview VA hospital and getting counseling for his nocturnal excursions through clotheslines in pursuit of women's panties. Some said that Milton's cure was mostly his marriage to Venus and his no longer needing to leave the house in search of women's apparel. Regardless, Milton was no longer lurking around town in the wee hours of the morning.

When people suffer a physical ailment and then are cured, the change is easily seen and believed and even celebrated. But a psychological ailment is different. The treatment is obtuse, and the results and eventual cure, more difficult to discern and see. And in many cases, such as Milton's, the former illness has too often affected others in a negative way. Unfortunately, those memories linger long after the cure. Milton and Venus's arrival added a new dimension to the already diverse crowd.

Milton had never owned a car; he'd never had a job since the war and lived off of a disabled veteran's pension. Venus had driven him to his treatments in Fairview; that's how they'd first gotten to know one another. And except for when they were in the cart, she continued to be the one behind the wheel anytime they drove anywhere.

"Well, fizzlesticks," Rabbit said when Milton and Venus pulled up in the cart. "Would you look at Midnight's rig?" It was the first time Milton and Venus had taken the cart out since adding the modifications; they'd chosen Homecoming for the debut.

They pulled up beside Monkey's cart and parked behind the Codgers, who were seated in discarded desk chairs that had been placed under the sycamore tree exclusively for them. Coach Heart, still one of the holdouts regarding Milton's cure, had yet to provide a chair for him. Getting a chair was a rite of passage of sorts, and Milton's passage would take some time since Coach Heart was sure that Milton's lingerie collection included items which had belonged to his wife.

"Boy oh boy, that'n might be better'n Monkey's, don't cha know," Bem said.

"Jeeminy," Monkey said, somewhat defensive. "It don't have no spear."

Before making further comment, the Codgers moved slowly toward the cart and began the requisite examination. Rabbit pointed at the side of the canvas cover and the beautiful rendition of a fierce Indian chief and said, "Yours doesn't have a picture of an Indian." And for the comment, Rabbit got a look from Monkey. Rabbit shrugged. "Just sayin."

Venus defused the exchange by saying, "Your cart was the inspiration, Monkey. We copied your idea, but I wanted Milton's to be different, not necessarily better. They both support the team." Venus refused to refer to Milton by his new nickname.

Monkey coughed, which meant he was about to speak. "Like I said," he began, "you gonna drive it in the parade?" The Homecoming parade, which traditionally occurred on the Saturday following the Friday night game, always included an eclectic array of floats.

Monkey had been looking at Venus when he asked the question, so she answered. "Sure. How about we drive them side by side?" Milton nodded agreement with Venus's answer.

The crowd that had parted to make way for Venus and Milton filled back in and began to gather around the carts. Codger's Corner had become a quasi-reverent area. It was somewhat of a perch between the bleachers and equipment shed where the Codgers watched every practice and game; they'd become unofficial mascots. The corner was a destination for many to gather before going into the stadium. For some, they simply wanted to do a head count and make sure that all of the Codgers were in attendance, and that none of them had succumbed to old age. All of the Codgers assembled under the tree before the game meant that all was well with the world of Colby football; their presence provided continuity from year to year.

While most of the locals rendezvoused at the corner and then left for their seats, those who had moved away from Colby and had returned for Homecoming lingered to hear what the Codgers had to say about the team. Rabbit, the only Codger to have excelled at high school football, turned and looked toward them and asked, "What's your prediction, Midnight?"

Milton's face brightened; he clearly appreciated the question and Rabbit's interest in his opinion. "With the kid from Fairview, we're certainly two-dimensional," he replied and then paused in thought. "But we won't show much tonight."

"Yeah," Rabbit nodded agreement, "I think you're right, but anything could happen." He made an "I don't know" with his hands and said, "I'm just sayin.'"

The Homecoming game was traditionally scheduled with Drake, the smallest nearby school with a football team. Drake's population was less than Colby's, but not by much. But it was smaller, so Drake was to Colby what Colby was to Fairview. Colby was expected to win the game, as they usually did, which is why Drake was always chosen as the Homecoming opponent. But they weren't to be taken lightly, and the coaches knew it.

People from Drake rarely came to Colby to shop or for any other reason. If they couldn't find what they needed in Drake, they went directly to Fairview. So, even though the two towns weren't separated by a significant distance, there were cultural differences. Neither was necessarily superior to the other, but the students at both schools liked to think that they were.

"The team I see at practice isn't the same team that takes the field on Friday night," Milton continued.

"I've noticed too," Rabbit agreed. The other Codgers nodded agreement too.

"I think Coach Heart's strategy is to hold out until Fairview," Milton said.

"Fairview," Rabbit said. "It's always nice to beat Fairview. Beating them this year would be a double treat." Again, all of the Codgers nodded consensually.

RIDING TO THE GAME IN Miss Anderson's car was akin to being elevated to celebrity status.

"Cool car," someone shouted from the line of students streaming into the stadium.

"Put the top down," said another.

Miss Anderson was nearly as much of a draw as her car. Male students and fathers of male students stopped to look at both the cherry-red GTO and its driver. Booger and Tommy slipped away unnoticed, leaving their celebrity status at the car.

THE PLAYERS WERE TAKING THEIR places on the locker room benches. Just like on the school bus, there was an implied seating chart. A junior varsity player who'd inadvertently sat on the wrong bench got hip-checked onto the floor. He scooted back a row.

Caleb was making the rounds with his helmet. For reasons that even Mr. T couldn't explain, Caleb's helmet was such an olfactory shock that it made eyes water. He'd sneak up behind a JV player and stick the open helmet in their face. When the coaches came in, Caleb took his seat near the front and morphed angelic.

Mr. T had once called the locker room a giant petri dish. One of the standout memories for past players was the locker room stench. It was a mixture of aerosol deodorant, bacteria-laden pads, nervous breath, and dirty socks amplified by warm, damp air from the showers and no circulation. It was probably toxic.

The only door to the dressing room swung open wildly, and Coach Heart made his pregame entrance. His expression was a mixture of determination, focus, and insanity. He slammed his hands together and shouted, "Smells like a football team in here."

He began pacing back and forth in front of the blackboard on which he'd typically written the primary offensive plays for the game. And they would be the plays that had been practiced all week, which had been chosen based on scouting reports. This week was different. The bottom half of the board had plays, but on the top half Coach Heart had used the side of the chalk stick to write in bold letters: "1957—Notre Dame vs. Oklahoma" and "1926—Carnegie Tech vs. Notre Dame."

"Listen up, men," he said and then tapped the board with his pointer. "In 1957, the Sooners had a forty-one-game winning streak going. They were expected to win, they expected to win, and everyone except the Notre Dame Fighting Irish thought the Sooners would win. After all, the Sooners had a four-year winning streak going." He let the words soak in and then filled in the score, "The Sooners lost, 7–0."

He held the pointer vertically behind his back, almost emulating the pose George C. Scott had made in the movie *Patton*. "Ever heard of Knute Rockne?" he asked. All heads nodded. Every football player had heard about Knute Rockne and his unparalleled win record as a coach at Notre Dame. He tapped the board. "In 1926, Notre Dame went to Pittsburgh undefeated. Nobody had scored on them for eight games, and they'd beat Carnegie Tech the previous four years with a combined score of 114–11." Coach Heart grinned. "So sure that his team would win, Knute Rockne chose to attend the Army-Navy game in Chicago rather than travel with his team to Pittsburgh." He then wrote the score of that game on the board. "Carnegie Tech beat Notre Dame 19–0. The loss cost Notre Dame a shot at the national title."

Coach Heart yielded the board to Mr. Franklin, who'd slipped in with little fanfare and looking normal. "There's a saying," he said and then paused. "'Keep some powder dry.'" He looked at Quinton. "We're gonna play to win, Quinton. But we're only going to use the plays we need to win." He pointed at the board. "Here's how we'll start the game. We'll adjust at halftime if we need to."

He didn't mention that the team wouldn't be running some of the plays they'd been practicing all year and had yet to put into a game, or the target of the metaphorical dry powder, which was Fairview.

"What's the most important game?" he shouted.

In unison and enthusiastically the team responded what they'd been taught to say: "The next game, Coach." Every player knew that the most important game of the year was Fairview, but they went along with it.

"And what's the most important play?" he yelled a little louder.

Again in unison, and a few decibels louder, "The next play, Coach," the team shouted.

"The Drake Gophers came here to win. Let's not be Oklahoma; let's not be Notre Dame," he said and then took a deep breath. The veins on his neck nearly burst through the skin when he shouted, "We're Fighting Indians, warriors, Colby's best!"

Coach Heart tossed the game ball to Flop. "Lead us out," he shouted, spewing spit in the process. Flop raced for the field, and everyone followed, nearly taking the door off its hinges in the process. Part of the enthusiasm was to take the field and get the game underway, but mostly their anxiousness to get on the field was to get out of the stench of the moldy locker room and into fresh air.

Flop ran manically toward the center of the field where the cheerleaders were holding a paper banner with a beautifully painted likeness of a proud, fierce Indian holding a crippled-looking gopher by the tail. Flop raced through the banner at full speed, destroying what a member of the pep squad had spent hours creating. The rest of the team followed, grabbing bits and pieces of the banner that remained wrapped around two PVC pipes painted to resemble long willow branches made into spears.

No doubt the parents of the pep squad artist had been sitting in the stands and admiring their child's rendering of Drake's mascot when Flop made his feral entrance. It was an honor for their child to have been selected to spend the past several evenings studying each detail of the cougar and getting it perfect. And it was an honor for Flop to have been chosen to lead the team onto the field and be the first to rip through the effigy of Drake's ferocious mascot. Flop's visceral destruction of the beautiful piece of art brought the spectators to their feet and a proud smile to the face of the pep squad artist's parents—tradition.

Everett and Clyde, the Bookends, were standing apart from the frenzy of players jumping up and down, pounding each other on the shoulder pads, and helmet butting. Their pregame ritual was more staid and private. For one thing, it wouldn't make good sense for them to body bounce with boys, some of which were half their size. But more importantly, they needed to focus. The execution of the plays depended upon their split-second moves and reactions to the moves of those across the line. While the smaller players usually received the praise by the general public, the true football aficionados recognized Clyde's and Everett's extraordinary God-gifted skill.

Clyde shook his head in disgust. "Can't believe Coach doesn't want us rushing the quarterback."

"He can't throw," Everett replied. "By not rushing we have a better chance of stopping the run and forcing him to throw."

"Yeah," Clyde said, "and then Flop gets to make all of the tackles."

"Another thing," Everett added, "we might throw the Fairview scouts off."

"But look at those guys," Clyde said and pointed across the field at the Drake players. "We could blow by any of those clowns."

"Or we could stop any of them from running," Everett replied.

"Who do you think will be king and queen?" Clyde asked, changing the subject.

"I don't know, probably Quinton and Sunny," Everett said. "Quinton's new, and everyone likes the new kid; and plus, he's the quarterback. Or it could be one of those pudgy brainiacs who always bust the curve in biology. And I just can't imagine anyone but Sunny being the queen." He paused a few seconds. "I hadn't really thought of it."

Clyde chuckled. "Sounds to me like you've given it a lot of thought." Everett grinned.

Everett scanned the crowd looking for his parents. College football coaches had been seen attending Colby games and already asking about Everett and Clyde, who were only sophomores. The college coaches were prohibited from making direct contact with the high school players, but they were allowed to speak to parents. Everett spotted his parents, and next to them, a pair of men who weren't from Colby—no doubt coaches on an observation visit.

Out of the corner of his eye, Everett noticed LB and LR standing against the field-level fence. They looked his way and waved. Everett elbowed Clyde. "There's Libby's dad and her uncle."

"They're huge," Clyde said.

"They both played for Missouri," Everett said.

"Who's that standing next to them?" Clyde asked.

Everett took another look and noticed the two men that Clyde had seen. "They're both wearing Mizzou caps."

"Think they played at Mizzou too?" Clyde asked.

"That or recruiters," Everett said.

"We need to tell Coach," Clyde said. "Maybe he'll let us make a couple of sacks."

Coach Heart cut the boys off when they began to petition him. "I know who's here," he said. He grinned and patted them on the shoulder pads. "Let's see how it goes."

PAST PLAYERS LINED UP MIDFIELD and were recognized. A couple of them looked like they could still suit up, but most of them had filled out considerably. Coach Heart and Mr. Franklin had warned the players about staying loose during the extended Homecoming pregame ceremony.

Quinton kept his arm loose by throwing short passes to Flop. Booger was catching the returns, as it's forbidden for the quarterback to receive passes during pregame warm-ups. Clyde and Everett were stretching, anxious to take the field and start hitting. Tommy was kicking into the practice net until time for the Homecoming court to march out.

The previous placekicker had graduated, so Tommy had worked hard all summer practicing kicks in hopes of securing a starting position at varsity. He realized placekicking wasn't held in the highest esteem but simply wanted to see his name listed along with the rest of the band of boys on the starting lineup.

Once the has-beens had been sufficiently recognized and marched off the field, the Homecoming court was introduced. Pairs of seniors marched to midfield and were introduced. Bulbs attached to instamatic cameras flashed throughout the crowd during each introduction, blinding those standing nearby but doing little for the quality of the photo.

The University of Missouri claimed to have originated the tradition of Homecoming when they'd hosted their rival game against the Kansas Jayhawkers in 1911. Of course there were the Texans with their giant egos claiming Baylor had started Homecoming in 1909. In reality, the Baylor event was simply a game with a preceding parade which they later named "Homecoming" after Missouri had coined the idea. The real spoiler was the University of Indiana, which had quietly promoted a homecoming event of sorts surrounding a football game in 1908. They hadn't called it Homecoming but had in fact invited past alumni to return to campus during a football weekend. Missouri was the first to bundle it all together, brand it, and crown a king and queen. Like many other things American, such as Disney entertainment, great presidents, Lindbergh's first flight instructor, and the world's only mite-resistant vineyard rootstock, Homecoming had originated in Missouri.

Frank Fritz watched and tried to grasp the concept of athletic competition and the notion of a mascot to aggrandize school spirit. He'd listened, at first with feigned interest, to Everett talk about practices and the game. Everett had gotten Fritz's attention when he'd mentioned that Quinton had been nominated for Homecoming king. In the name of making an earnest effort to understand racial integration, and learn something about this football game that apparently was Everett's main purpose in life, Fritz had decided to attend the Homecoming game.

The fence surrounding the field is always lined shoulder to shoulder with people standing and wanting to get a closer look. There were a couple of feet open on each side of LB, LR, and the two men wearing Mizzou caps; evidently nobody had wanted to stand next to the two Fairview nephilim. Fritz, never comfortable sitting and too short to see over anyone, was not easily intimidated. He had chosen the only open spot along the fence, next to LB. It was a providential placement. LB and LR were resting their forearms comfortably on the top rail of the boundary fence, which Fritz's chin barely cleared.

Fritz smiled proudly when he heard LB comment to his brother, "There's Everett; he's a solid kid. He and that other boy are the heart of this team." Fritz was amazed at how much bigger Everett and Clyde looked with their football gear on. Together, they were about the same size as his Volkswagen.

The Mizzou recruiters looked down at Fritz and then at LB and LR; all four men shrugged and ignored the diminutive fellow who'd squeezed in between them. So Fritz stood confidently among the leviathans and listened while they talked over him as if he wasn't there.

"They're obviously the biggest, but they're also two of the fastest guys on the team," LR said and then shook his head in amused disgust. "But because of their size they're on the line; it's automatic."

"Can you imagine either one of those guys at running back?" LB asked.

Fritz's curiosity about the game had been sufficiently boosted by the eavesdropping experience, and then he heard something that shocked him to the core. When Quinton headed toward midfield for the coin toss, LB said, "That Quinton kid is probably the brains of the team."

"Yeah," LR agreed. "Smart, athletic, good ball sense; he'll probably make it to the next level."

"And he's a good kid," LB said.

"That new boy, Greg Golden, is probably a better athlete," LR said, "but he's not the quality person that Quinton is."

"Quinton's smarter, for sure," LB said. LR nodded agreement.

"Next week is gonna be interesting," LB continued, referencing the game between Colby and Fairview.

Fritz hadn't missed a word.

Colby was able to maintain a two-score lead on Drake by running only the traditional high school run plays. Booger and Caleb took turns running the ball left and right behind Clyde or Everett. Flop got one short pass and ran it for a first down late in the second quarter.

At halftime the boys were too aggravated about the play calling to give much thought to Quinton being named Homecoming king. Quinton's queen was a brainiac girl who'd evidently won because Sunny had split the vote with another cheerleader. Fortunately, most people held the same credence for the Homecoming court as Fritz, and after a few frustrated frowns, the fan focus returned to football.

Late in the third quarter, Colby took a three-possession lead. During the quarter break, Mr. Franklin watched the crowd while Coach Heart fielded complaints from the team about not running any of the plays they'd been practicing. Mr. Franklin joined the huddle and said to Coach Heart, "They're leaving."

Everett and Clyde, thinking he was talking about the recruiters, turned to look. The men they'd thought to be recruiters were still in the stands. "Who's leaving, Coach?" Everett asked.

"Fairview scouts," Mr. Franklin said. Everett and Clyde then noticed the gaping space along the fence where LB and his brother had been standing.

"Here's what we're gonna do," Coach said and then explained. During the fourth quarter, he let the junior varsity play on defense and allowed the varsity to run the plays they'd been practicing for Fairview. The varsity scored during each series of downs. Fortunately, the JV allowed Drake to score an equal number of touchdowns, so the score wasn't lopsided.

Nearly half the Colby crowd had left along with the Fairview scouts. Those who'd remained had begun making casual conversation. Other than the Codgers, few, if anyone, had figured out what was taking place or noticed the new plays.

Fall Festival

THE HOMECOMING FOOTBALL GAME HAD drawn a sizeable Colby crowd, but the Fall Festival was the social affair that drew people from all corners of the county. The entire weekend had become a magical mix of attractions that pleased everyone, a rare occasion. Friday night's game was Homecoming, but Saturday's events were called the Colby Homecoming Fall Festival. While Friday night's focus was on football, that wasn't the case on Saturday. Every organization in the county came to town and either set up an exhibit at the park, participated in the parade, entered the talent competition, or just socialized; there was literally something for everyone.

Mrs. Koch, the town matriarch, had reluctantly agreed to be the parade's grand marshal. She'd lost her husband a few years earlier but not her passion for improving the community. She detested grandstanding, however, and it had taken a team of community leaders to coax her into participating in the parade. "It's enough that you're going to honor George," she'd said, referring to the bust in honor of her late husband, which was to be unveiled during the afternoon's festivities.

Mrs. Koch had insisted that she see the bust for the first time along with everyone else. And if there was only one thing to know about Mrs. Koch, it was that she usually got her way. She'd provided the bust's artist with photos of the town's past patriarch. Since she and Mr. Koch were rarely photographed separately, most of the photos had featured her at his side. The rare photos of Mr. Koch without her were of him sitting in his chair with his dog, Scout, on his lap. Scout had passed away on the same day as his master. Mrs. Koch was in for a surprise.

Tommy and Booger would generally be seen together just before the marching band took position. They'd been in the marching band together since sixth grade, when their position had been in the middle of the row where the least experienced members marched so that their mistakes weren't as noticeable to the watching public. This year they'd both earned an esteemed end-row position, equivalent to first chair, which meant they could linger on the edges until just before time to march. But Booger was nowhere to be found.

Tommy and Melody were talking. Melody was looking around, preoccupied, concerned for Booger. "Who you looking for?" Tommy asked.

"Booger." She frowned. "I haven't seen him all morning." Tommy knew where Booger was but didn't let on. "Working you think?" she asked.

"Probably," Tommy said. In truth, he was sure that Booger was home practicing. Booger was playing along to Mr. Tobin's recording, making sure his timing and tempo were perfect. And sometimes practice seemed like work, so Tommy didn't consider it lying to allow Melody to be misled.

Melody's worried frown morphed into one of disgust. "You don't seem too worried about him," she said. She'd stopped scanning the crowd and was looking deep into Tommy's eyes. She was cradling her french horn with her left arm, and her right fist was planted on her canted hip. Her voice remained soft, but her posture was screaming.

"I talked to him last night," Tommy said. "This type of stuff bothers him. Seeing the veterans in their uniforms brings back memories of Johnny," he continued, making it up as he spoke.

Sheriff Dooley flipped on his red lights and let go a short blast from his siren, and the parade was underway. Melody took her position at the end of a row of trumpets; Tommy joined the rest of the snare drummers.

Tommy was flooded with mixed emotions. He was anxious for everyone to hear Booger play and get past this vacuum ruse. And Booger had finally gotten comfortable with his ability to play and was ready to let others hear him. It wasn't that he was seeking the limelight, but he knew many worried about his mental condition, and he understood that playing in the contest would send a signal that he was doing fine.

But Tommy was concerned that Booger's guitar playing skills would suddenly gain him the attention of all of the girls, particularly Melody. Melody had always had a soft heart for Booger.

The drum majorette blew her whistle. "Time to focus," Tommy said, as much to himself as to the line of percussionists for which he was responsible.

The grand marshal traditionally led the parade, but Mrs. Koch had insisted that the armed services go first. In honor of her late husband, who'd served as a pilot in World War I, she requested a WWI veteran being in the parade.

"Fish would be perfect," she'd said. Fish, highly thought of by Mrs. Koch's late husband, had subsequently agreed to dig out his WWI uniform and ride, not walk, in the parade.

Years earlier, extending beyond the memory of most, Solomon had been confused with salmon, and he'd been given the nickname of Fish. A fair number of people, when asked his real name, would first tilt their heads in thought before coming up with it, if they remembered it at all. Even though Fish's legal name wasn't easily remembered, the fact that he'd served with Sergeant York was legendary.

When the news that Fish was going to be in the parade began to circulate, the memories of him convincing Sergeant Alvin York to march in the 1960 Colby Homecoming parade were recalled by those old enough to remember. Too many of the high school kids had to have Sergeant York's significance explained. Brother Russell Ralston took advantage of Fish's connection by mining two sermons from the conversion experience of the famous farm boy, Medal of Honor recipient, and crack shot from Pall Mall, Tennessee. Arnold's Theater had gotten a copy of the movie starring Gary Cooper as Sergeant York and played it earlier in the week to a sell-out crowd.

It had been suggested that Fish ride in Monkey's golf cart. "That hairball contraption with the pole that's supposed to be a spear?" Mrs. Koch had asked when she'd gotten wind of the plan. The nature of the question had been a tip that an alternate plan was needed, and that's when Venus had offered Milton's cart.

Milton drove while Fish held on to the back of the seat with one hand and made his customary clinched fist and extended index finger with the other. It was the same sign he customarily made before saying anything. And the same sign a mother would make to a misbehaving child. But it was Fish's sign, and everyone understood it.

Over the years he'd outgrown the uniform, but then had settled back to nearly the same size he was at twenty, when he'd served in the Meuse-

Argonne offensive with his late buddy, Alvin. Few people had any rela-
tional concept of World War I. There'd been very little media coverage of
the brutal savagery of trench warfare and widespread use of mustard gas;
few knew. Throughout the day a thin stream of emotional tears trickled
down Fish's face. Due to the chilly breeze, others had the same, but their
tears were physiological.

Several veterans who'd served in World War II, Korea, and Vietnam
followed. The vets from 'Nam wore camouflaged flop hats instead of helmets. But there was a marked generational difference between the Vietnam veterans and the older men that went beyond the differences in their
headgear.

New this year was the riderless horse representing those who'd served
and didn't make it home. The horse had been a suggestion by Booger's
dad, in memory of Booger's brother, Johnny, who'd died in Vietnam. The
Boy Scouts traditionally marched behind the veterans anyway and had
been volunteered by their leaders to take responsibility for the horse in
every sense. The Scouts worked in teams. One team, made up of older
boys, led the horse, and the younger boys picked up the horse's left-behind
lumps of used oats. Mr. Tobin had gone into a neck-vein-popping fit when
he'd heard a horse would be ahead of his spat-wearing marching band.
After the Boy Scouts' role had been explained, his diastolic pressure had
fallen safely into the double digits.

Mr. Tobin was known for his demonstrative facial expressions. During
the course of a simple conversation, his head would swivel wildly about,
his eyes would widen and squint, and his lips would smile, frown, and
pooch almost simultaneously. Without a doubt, he had the most developed facial muscles on the planet.

The day Tommy first spoke to Mr. Tobin about Booger playing the
guitar in the band, his face had clearly expressed doubt and suspicion,
but he'd agreed to a private audition. After a couple of weeks of coax-
ing, Booger had agreed to meet with Mr. Tobin one evening after football
practice. He began the audition by playing Beatle songs. During "Yesterday," Mr. Tobin had expressed interest. When Booger began the rift to
"Day Tripper," however, Mr. Tobin's expression was at first surprise and
then disapproval. Mr. Tobin had probably gotten hung up while thinking
about the song's lyrics, which adults had been convinced were about drugs
and sex.

When Booger finished the Beatle songs, he had paused to fine-tune his guitar. Mr. Tobin, thinking Booger was finished, began making comments. "You're certainly proficient," he said but then frowned. "But I'm not sure how we'd integrate a guitar into the band." He was rubbing his chin and contorting his face when Booger began playing "Classical Gas." Clearly stunned, Mr. Tobin's jaw dropped and his face froze; the only movement was a slight twitching and orbiting of his eyes. He suddenly changed expressions, as if to have been struck with an epiphany. "Homecoming," he said and then began to think aloud while developing the idea for Booger's debut.

Just before the parade had begun, Mr. Tobin was more anxious than usual. Most thought it because of the horse, but that wasn't the cause of his angst. He'd convinced a small detachment of the concert band to enter the talent contest. They'd practiced with Sunny, and together they'd learned "Classical Gas." Unknown to them, except for Sunny, they'd been learning a version of the score written to accompany a guitar. They'd complained that the score sounded incomplete, and Mr. Tobin had to repeatedly convince them that it wasn't. But that morning a couple of the band members had expressed reluctance to follow through on the festival competition. Sunny was pleading with them while Mr. Tobin tried to focus on the parade.

Fish and Milton Merle followed behind Dooley's squad car—one famous for his service in World War I, and one infamous for his nocturnal women's undergarment swiping. Both men were still trying to forget that for which they were famous.

"Who's that?" a little boy standing with his mother asked.

"He's a war hero," his mother whispered.

The little boy, fascinated, held up his finger emulating Fish. He then changed to a salute when the veterans marched by, some with canes and others with weapons, some with smiles and others with grimaces. The observant boy pointed at the horse being led behind the men in uniform. "There's a horseless rider," he said. His mother smiled but didn't correct him.

Mrs. Koch was too old to walk the two mile length of the parade but not too old to sit on top of the backseat in Miss Anderson's red GTO. Mrs. Koch was wearing elbow-length white gloves and the now famous red dress she'd worn at her husband's funeral. She waved proudly knowing she represented the memory of the famous George Koch.

The red dress had at first been a small scandal because grieving widows typically wear black. The dress was a reminder to everyone that she wasn't typical and that, while she grieved her loss, the funeral was a celebration of her late husband's life. And the funeral had been that, a celebration replete with aviation celebrities. The Colby Curls gals were the only holdouts to the scandalous nature of Mrs. Koch's apparel. The rest of the town understood. Truth be known, the beauty salon gossips were probably jealous of her spunk.

"Cool car," yelled the little boy when the GTO crept by. He was particularly drawn to the GTO's mag wheels.

"Who's the old lady in the red dress?" asked his little sister. The mother put her hand over her daughter's mouth and glanced at Mrs. Koch, who couldn't possibly have heard the little girl's innocent question over the rumble of the GTO's glasspack mufflers.

The Homecoming court was next. Quinton and the brainiac were riding in Melody's Malibu; Mr. Hinkebein was behind the wheel. The brainiac was clutching a football with one arm and waving with the other. Quinton was holding a broom with both hands and sweeping it through the air; *Neue Besen Kehren Gut* was inscribed on the broom handle.

Since being passively introduced to Colby by Fritz, the proverb had taken on a variety of meanings. Fritz had discovered the proverb on the old sign he'd acquired with the broom making equipment. The band of boys had seen it when they'd helped him unload the heavy machines. Coach Heart had heard it from them and subsequently adopted it as the team's motto when Quinton appeared on the scene. *A new broom sweeps clean.*

For Coach Heart, learning of the proverb on the cusp of Quinton's appearance was providential. He used it to move the boys to thinking of Quinton's addition to the team as a new era in Colby football. It wasn't that Quinton was a one-man team, but his addition completed the team. For the first time in many years, Colby had a complete package and the chance to go undefeated. The last game was with Fairview. He had the boys looking forward to the game that in previous seasons was the most dreaded contest of the year.

At first, most in Colby only understood the literal translation: a new broom works better than an old broom. Eventually, however, many began to grasp the deeper meaning.

No matter one's interpretation, Quinton looked odd swinging a broom back and forth. The inscription on the handle was too small for anyone to read, so the metaphor was lost to most—not that it really mattered. The men were preoccupied with the Malibu, and the girls were wondering how the homely girl with a mouth full of braces got the most votes for Homecoming queen. The significance of Quinton's broom went unnoticed.

As it turned out, the younger Boy Scouts with horse dropping duties had the best deal. Every time someone would cheer, the horse would flinch and shake his head wildly, making him difficult to hold. By the parade's end, he'd made several attempts to nibble on the fingers of his holders. It's possible the horse's cantankerous behavior was caused by constipation. Much to the joy of the boys chosen to gather the discarded lumps of oats, the horse failed to produce the menace feared by the marching band.

Colby's Homecoming and Fall Festival easily drew the biggest crowd of the year. And a statewide election was a few weeks away, which explained the men in suits milling around and shaking hands with anyone with a pulse.

While the parade was the kickoff to the day's festivities, unveiling the bust in Mr. Koch's honor was planned to be the main attraction of the afternoon's events. The politicians expected to get the chance to address the crowd during the recognition of the now famous George Koch. Just as Mrs. Koch was in for a surprise at the unveiling of the bust, the politicians' day wasn't going to go as they'd expected.

Those responsible for organizing a weekend community event fuss, fume, and fidget while the rest of the town ambles about enjoying themselves. Things never go exactly as planned, and adjustments are made on the fly. The parade was supposed to be finished and the last float through by 11:00, but it was past 11:30 when the last entry, a pickup loaded with 4-H kids from a small town a few miles outside of Colby that had little more than a post office, reached the school.

The rules for float entry had gotten very liberal. Originally, all floats were complicated designs replete with several square yards of chicken wire stuffed with colored tissue paper adorning a themed display. But the rules had been relaxed, and few floats exhibited any measure of creativity. For example, the Optimist Club always had a giant octagon with an "I" and an "O" in the center and "Friend of Youth" underneath. The Lions

Club, whose symbol is just a big L, always had a ten-foot-wide pair of spectacles symbolizing their drive to collect discarded spectacles.

Gradual change is incipient and easily goes unnoticed until a point is reached at which the balance has clearly shifted. And so it was with Colby's Homecoming parade floats. The Goolsby twins had been the first to enter what eventually became known as a nontraditional float. Years earlier they entered their lawn mowing business in the parade and had shown up with nothing more than a riding lawnmower and trailer; one drove while one rode perched in the tiny trailer. Everyone had sympathetically accepted the anomaly.

There'd always been horses in the parade. Horses played a significant role in the westward expansion, and Missouri being the gateway to the west, it was only natural to have them in the parade, despite Mr. Tobin's insistence that they be placed behind those marching.

And then there was Larry, the guy who'd bought a farm just outside Colby and started raising Peruvian llamas. Nobody had ever seen a real live llama until Larry, known as the llama man. Larry had retired from his job as librarian in Lima, Ohio, where he'd become obsessed with Lima, Peru. Larry claimed that Lima Peru was the educational center for the continent, with universities that began in the sixteenth century, well before the United States was a country.

Larry's explanation of how he ended up on a farm just outside Colby was long, complicated, and different each time he told it. The only thing more uninteresting than Larry's explanation of how he chose Colby was when he'd expound on the virtues of llamas and the fact that they'd originated on the plains of western America before being hijacked and taken to Peru. Larry insisted that neither llamas nor their droppings had an odor.

Larry the llama man from Lima had eventually found favor with the local cattle farmers when he'd extolled the merits of llamas as livestock guardians. After one of Larry's llama's had demonstrated a propensity to chase coyotes, he'd explained how llamas are much like young boys; they behave best when isolated. Add a second llama and they'll spend more time entertaining each other than watching for coyotes.

When Larry entered his llamas in the parade, he started the cascade of livestock entries. The FFA chapter always had a member or two with what they were convinced was a prize bull or a particularly productive dairy cow, so then there were cattle entries. The parade committee had the temerity to draw the line at swine.

The First Baptist Adult IV Sunday School class was the first to enter a float that consisted primarily of a pickup truck, lawn chairs, and older people smiling and waving. It was called Adult IV because everyone in the class was in their fourth quarter. The parade committee couldn't have seen it coming. The Baptists had convinced the Ford dealer to loan them a new truck. They'd adorned it with tastefully designed posters bestowing the virtues of Sunday School attendance. The men were wearing suits, and the ladies, dresses, and all were sporting new-denture smiles.

Larry the llama man, the Goolsby twins, and the Adult IVs were pioneers of sorts. In five years the parade had nearly doubled in length. The Adult IV class continued to enter a beautifully decorated pickup; but now there were several pickups, some not even washed, loaded with members of organizations barely heard of. Eventually, groups with access to a pickup and a desire to ride in the parade simply dreamed up a name and entered. In some cases the pickups had no identification, just a load of people looking like they were on their way to the next job.

Farm kids, expanding on the Goolsby's riding lawnmower float, began to enter their tractors. At first the tractors had been washed and tires dressed, looking like they'd just been driven off the show room floor. Eventually tractors began showing up directly from the field, some still sporting equipment such as plows or discs caked with sod clumps.

About the only control the parade committee retained was determining a float's placement in the parade. Rather than create a set of float construction rules, which no doubt would have been popular with a few but unpopular to the most boisterous, they'd wisely spread the traditional floats, those on which people had actually given a modicum of thought and created something worth seeing, throughout the parade. For example, an FFA student followed the Lions Club float on an ancient backfiring and smoke belching John Deere.

A pickup truck loaded with men who appeared to have already started drinking trailed behind the Rotary Club and their logo float, a huge keyed gear. The pickup load of drunks had a handwritten sign dangling on one side that covered a large dent and read Beagle Club. Sheriff Dooley had made sure that the driver was sober, and since they had cases of candy to toss to the kids, he let the Beagle Club truck join in the parade.

As soon as the marching band finished, Melody and Tommy headed toward the Malibu; Mr. Hinkebein was waiting for them. He'd been elected mayor the previous spring and in that capacity was expected to run the bust unveiling ceremony.

"You can drive," Mr. Hinkebein said to Melody and hopped in the backseat. Riding in the backseat didn't carry the same stigma with adults as it did with teenagers. She left the top down, and the three of them headed toward the courthouse square. Tommy couldn't put his finger on exactly why, but having Melody's dad sitting in the backseat unnerved him.

A small group had already gathered in anticipation of the bust unveiling, but most were crowded around the Optimist trailer. The Optimists were famous for their fried fish and hush puppies, but the crowd gathered around their corner of the courthouse lawn was much larger than usual.

Odi Portman, a member of the Optimist Club, had been to Wisconsin on a fishing trip the previous summer and had eaten fried cheese balls. He'd mentioned them to Patty Pope at the Houn-Dawg. Patty's supplier said he could get them on special order but she'd have to order a case at a time. She'd suggested to Odi that the Optimist Club try them at the Fall Festival and if people liked them she'd add them to the menu.

Odi had been in sales at Colby John Deere for eons, so most Optimist Club members thought he knew a thing or two about selling. But Odi's real goal was to convince Patty Pope that she needed to offer fried cheese balls at the Houn-Dawg, so he'd convinced the Optimist Club to offer free samples. He figured that if they gave away half and charged double their cost for the other half, they'd break even on fried cheese balls, sell more fish and sodas, and come out ahead. Plus, the whole town would be talking about the cheese balls, and Patty would be convinced.

The free samples were a hit. Word spread quickly—free fried food at the Optimist Club trailer. The balls allocated as free samples were depleted before everyone had a chance to test the new delicacy. Sheriff Dooley came close to drawing his weapon when the members of the Beagle Club, more intoxicated than they'd been at the Houn-Dawg following the previous week's shooting match, threatened to turn the Optimist trailer over if they weren't served the free fried stuff.

Odi had the good sense to give them each a corn dog and told them they were a new flavor. The new flavor was actually the result of freezer burn. Odi had first thrown the dogs into the trash after digging them out of the deep freeze, along with the rest of last year's leftovers, to make room for the cheese balls. When he saw the Beagle boys approaching, he dug them out of the trash and tossed them into the fryer.

Sheriff Dooley was arguing with the raucous group when Odi piled the half-fried breaded hot-dogs-on-a-stick onto a cardboard flat, stepped out of the trailer, and handed them their free samples, as it were. It wasn't Odi's first festival or his first dealing with drunks. "You might not want to eat that," he whispered when Dooley took one for himself.

The Beagle boys were later seen barfing, but it's anybody's guess whether their illness stemmed from the mixture of beer and bourbon they'd consumed during the parade or the cotton candy they'd purchased after woofing down the dogs. They spent the rest of the afternoon sleeping in their pickup; Dooley had taken the keys.

One had to own or represent a business to belong to the Rotary Club, and they had strict rules on decorum. The Optimist Club did not, or so it seemed. The Optimist Club was best known for organizing youth sports in Colby. The money they'd raised at their infamous "Friend of Youth" lemonade stand had recently paid for lights at the baseball park so people could now simultaneously watch Little League ball games and get eaten by mosquitoes.

The legendary nature of the lemonade was twofold. Surrounding the stand were bushel baskets of fresh lemons that were shipped in from a lemon grove in south Texas. The lemonade was truly fresh squeezed.

The other part was less conspicuous; for an extra dollar slipped through the window, along with a wink and request for extra sugar, the crushed ice would come from a "special" cooler. The ice in the special cooler was more of a slushy consistency, since alcohol doesn't freeze as easily as water. One of the most closely held secrets in Colby was the actual proof of the ice. "Helping pay for the lights," men—many of them Baptists, no less—would say before paper-cup toasting each other in an effort to justify their covert imbibing.

Politicians far and wide realized too late the opportunity they'd missed by not attending Mr. Koch's funeral. They wouldn't make the same mistake twice. Word of the bust had spread, and the competition for political grandstanding was fierce; the governor's office had expressed an interest. Since Governor Hearnes was a Democrat, and Mr. Koch had been an ardent Republican, Mrs. Koch had said she'd have no part in a presentation at which a politician, let alone a Democrat, would be speaking.

The governor's office offered for Mrs. Hearnes, a recent recipient of Missouri's Woman of the Year award, to speak. Knowing of Mrs. Hearnes's volunteer service, and that she wasn't running for office, Mrs. Koch agreed.

The Codgers hadn't let the festival interrupt their daily ritual. As soon as the parade was finished, they gathered at the courthouse bench and were discussing nothing in particular when the governor's entourage arrived.

"Lookie there, why don't cha," Bem began.

"Tootie's in the lead, and then there are two more patrol cars," Fish said.

"Fizzlesticks," Rabbit said. "Anybody can see that. What do you think is going on?" he asked.

"Probably the governor and his wife," Jupiter Storm said. He'd just walked up. "You didn't know?" he asked the Codgers. They shook their heads. Jupiter tucked in his shirt and puffed out his chest. "Mrs. Hearnes is going to speak at the unveiling."

Monkey spit and then asked, "Mrs. Koch know that?" Jupiter shrugged. "Guess you don't know everything," Monkey added.

The Beagle boys hadn't heard either. When they saw the three patrol cars, lights ablaze, they tumbled out of the pickup and scurried away. The Codgers, each on their second "lemonade," glanced first at their slushy mixes, then at each other, and, unfazed by the governor's entourage, shrugged and kept crunching.

GOVERNOR AND MRS. HEARNES, ACCOMPANIED by two highway patrolmen, strolled through the exhibits while final preparations were being made for the unveiling. Leon Goolsby and Irvin Enderle were working the Optimist Club trailer when Mrs. Hearnes walked up to the window. They both experienced a sudden onset of tremors when Mrs. Hearnes ordered lemonades for herself and the others. They both momentarily lost control of their bladders when she winked and said, "I'd like extra sugar in mine." They had the good sense to give her what she'd requested rather than comply with the secret code. Besides, she hadn't offered an extra dollar. In fact, there wasn't any indication that she expected to pay at all.

"Politicians," Leon huffed after Mrs. Hearnes and her honor guard had walked away.

EVERYONE WAS GATHERING FOR THE unveiling. Gooche's, Hinkebein's, and all of the stores on the square had Closed signs in their windows. All of the boys except Booger had gathered at the stone. Tommy and Melody were standing on the stone, Melody on top and Tommy on the step. "I thought you said Booger was working," she said.

"He was," Tommy obfuscated.

"He feeling okay?" she asked.

"I think so," Tommy said, masking his excitement for what would occur after the unveiling.

"You don't seem very concerned about him," she said.

Tommy didn't answer and, looking for a diversion, pointed toward the stage where the talent show would soon be taking place. "Look, they're lifting a piano onto the stage."

"Yeah," Melody replied sarcastically. "I heard that Sunny and the jazz band are going to play something." She paused long enough to roll her eyes and then continued, "Like she needs to draw more attention to herself."

Mr. Hinkebein approached the temporary podium situated next to the covered bust. Joseph Williams, known by most as Joe-Bill, and Mr. Webster were seated on one side of Mrs. Koch, and the governor and Mrs. Hearnes were on the other side.

"It is my honor and privilege," he began and then went on to thank everyone for coming. His role was basically to talk until the crowd settled and then introduce first Mr. Webster and then Mrs. Hearnes. Several made last-minute stops at the lemonade stand before joining the throng gathered in front of the courthouse. Once Mr. Hinkebein had everyone's attention, he introduced Mr. Webster.

After first nodding at Mrs. Koch, Mr. Webster said, "Mrs. Koch asked me to say a few words. And if I've learned one thing about Colby, it's that when Mrs. Koch speaks, you should listen," which moved the crowd to laughter. "When I was given the chance to move out of company headquarters and become a plant manager, I was very excited. Being a plant manager had always been my dream. But during our first drive-through of Colby, Gloria and I were less than enthusiastic. And I think you can see why." Again, the crowd returned a laugh. "But then we were introduced to the Kochs, who made us feel more than welcome." He turned to Mrs. Koch and nodded. "After living here for four years, I can say that our earlier concern about the town was unfounded, because starting with the Koch's and to a person, we've always felt welcome." The crowd became very quiet. "George Koch exemplified the Colby culture. Celebrating George Koch's character is a celebration of the culture of Colby. And it has been my honor to have been asked to pay tribute."

Cheers and whistles followed his comments.

Mr. Hinkebein returned to the podium. "Thank you, Carter," he said. "Now please join me in giving the First Lady of Missouri a big Colby welcome." The crowd cheered but not as enthusiastically as they had for Mr. Webster or after the previous night's football victory.

"It's my honor and privilege too," Mrs. Hearnes began, copying the words Mr. Webster had used. "Today we honor not only a citizen of Colby but a citizen of Missouri, the Show-Me State. A man who truly exemplified George Washington's saying 'Facta Non Verba,' which means deeds not words. Both Georges were men of integrity, compassion, patriotism …" She continued with the longest string of adjectives ever heard in Colby and finished with President Kennedy's famous quote, 'Don't ask what your country can do for you, but what you can do for your country.'"

Melody, having grown weary from standing, had taken a seat on the stone's step. "Let me know when they get ready to do the unveiling," she said. Tommy stepped to the top so he could better see. He saw Booger talking to Sunny and Mr. Tobin. Booger looked his way, and they made momentary eye contact. Booger grinned.

The crowd started clapping. "What's happening?" Melody asked.

"Mrs. Hearnes is finished," Tommy said. "Your dad's about to do the unveiling."

"Let me see," she said. Tommy tried to wait until Booger and Sunny were out of sight before yielding the top step to Melody, but she politely but firmly pushed him out of the way.

"It's now my honor and privilege," Mr. Hinkebein again said.

"There's a lot of honor and privilege going around today," Melody said. Tommy had thought the same thing but hadn't said anything, not wanting to be critical of Melody's dad.

"Booger's on the stage with Sunny," Melody said. "What's up with that?"

"I guess he's helping her," Tommy said, looking aside so as to not give anything away.

"She just casts a spell and boys bow at her feet," Melody said, reminding Tommy of why he hadn't been able to tell Melody about Booger and Sunny's plan.

As soon as Mr. Hinkebein finished his well-rehearsed, accolade-laden speech, he motioned for Joe-Bill to remove the drape and reveal the much anticipated bust. People began clapping before the bust was visible. Mrs. Koch's response shouldn't have been a surprise. She first cocked her head like a dog hearing a siren and then touched her gloved index finger to her quivering chin. It was clear that she was emotionally touched, but the tenor of her emotions wasn't clear. The clapping slowly subsided, and the crowd awaited her first words.

"Prodigious. Absolutely prodigious," she said and then snapped her chin sharply in what most considered a nod of approval. She stepped next to the bust and ran her hands along the lines of the stone, which shaped an excellent likeness of her late husband's face. While Mrs. Koch patted Scout's stone head, Melody and the boys turned to face Everett for the answer to an unspoken question.

Everett had gotten used to being depended upon to translate, the price he paid for expanding his vocabulary. "It can mean she thinks it's exceptionally good or extraordinarily odd." Melody huffed, a sign she wasn't satisfied. "Specifically," Everett began, "prodigious is essentially the opposite of ordinary." He shrugged and pointed across the street at Mrs. Koch, who continued to stroke the bust and was now surrounded by a horde of people waiting to get their chance to touch it. "She basically said the thing was definitely not ordinary."

Mrs. Koch had met Mr. Koch while working as Colby's first librarian, fifty years earlier. Her vocabulary was unparalleled. Everett's explanation of Mrs. Koch's choice of adjectives was accurate.

Melody, Tommy, and rest made their way through the crowd to get a closer look at the bust. When they got near Mrs. Koch, they heard her make her first comment to Joe-Bill. "I see you still don't follow directions." She'd provided Joe-Bill with photos and had made clear the pose of Mr. Koch she liked best, which was the pose she'd expected to see.

Joe-Bill, at a loss for words, responded with the first thing that came to his mind. He'd reached an age where he no longer cared what people thought, and said about anything that came to mind. "That's the same red dress you wore to Mr. Koch's funeral." He meant it as a compliment.

She stiffened and stood board-straight erect. "It fit the occasion," she countered.

"So does the bust," he said, meaning the sculpture and not Mrs. Koch's anatomy.

Mrs. Koch grinned and reached for Joe-Bill with embracing arms. She air-kissed him on both cheeks, bowed slightly, and returned her gaze to the bust. A thunderous applause spread through the crowd.

"Unprecedented," Everett said. Those within earshot smiled and nodded agreement.

A photographer, sent from the *Fairview Daily* to get photos of Mrs. Hearnes, overheard Everett's comment and then recognized him as one of the football players featured in the preseason football insert. The *Daily* did an exposé each year with photos, bios, and stats on the area's most promising players. The photographer, a sports fanatic and ardent Fairview fan, approached Everett, who was standing with the others.

"So, ready for the game?" the photographer asked and looked at Everett with his head tilted to one side.

Everett looked the guy up and down and had to hold back a laugh. The photographer was dressed in quintessential newspaper reporter attire: short-sleeve cuffed shirt, loose-fitting pleated trousers that were too short, and an archaic hat that looked like something Joe Friday from *Dragnet* would wear. "It's going to be different this year," Everett told him.

"Pretty confident, huh?" the photographer responded.

Everett pointed toward Quinton. "We have a new quarterback."

The photographer gave Quinton a side-glance and then returned eye contact with Everett. "Yeah, he was almost good enough to play at Fairview."

Clyde took a step toward the photographer, but Everett held him back. "Save it for the game," Everett told him. Clyde stepped back, but his pulse had clearly quickened. Everett gently put his hand on the photographer's shoulder, leaned over, and whispered into his ear.

The photographer laughed. "I'll have to see that," he said. "Mind if I quote you?" he asked.

"Sure," Everett replied, full of confidence.

"What'd you tell him?" Clyde asked after the photographer scurried away. The rest of the boys gathered to hear what Everett had said.

Everett looked at Quinton. "I meant it too."

Quinton returned Everett's gaze and then checked Clyde's expression. "Somehow I believe it," Quinton softly replied and then told the rest of the gang what Everett had said.

Metamorphosis

"Test, test, 1-2-3," cracked Mr. Tobin's voice though the speakers set up for the talent contest. The crowd turned to see the Colby High Jazz Band, Sunny at the piano, and Booger seated center stage with a microphone situated next to his acoustical guitar.

"Ladies and gentlemen," Mr. Tobin continued, "this year's talent show will kick off with a piece that the jazz band has been working on since the start of this school year." He carried the mic over and put his hand on Booger's shoulder.

"What's going on?" Melody asked. She and the band of boys looked to Tommy for an explanation.

"Remember the existential vacuum that Booger told us about?" They nodded yes, but their perplexed expressions remained. "And Booger'd say he needed to work on his vacuum?" Again, nods.

Mr. Tobin continued. "Randy," he said, calling Booger by his real name. Booger said something, and Mr. Tobin leaned down to hear what he'd said.

Booger's whisper came through the mic for all to hear. "It's Booger," he said.

Mr. Tobin's face flushed. He faced the crowd. "I stand corrected," he said; the crowd responded with laughter.

While Mr. Tobin continued, Tommy finished. "This is what Booger has been doing when he said he was working on his vacuum." He paused for a response but realized that they still didn't understand. "Learning to play the guitar, and specifically 'Classical Gas,' filled his existential vacuum." Still, they didn't understand. Frustrated and out of time, he said, "Just watch and listen."

Mr. Tobin went on, "Booger didn't want anyone, even some of his closest friends, to know that he was learning the guitar." He paused and glanced nervously at Booger. "He has his reasons. Anyhoo," Mr. Tobin said and then wiped his forehead with a pastel-colored handkerchief, "unbeknownst to the jazz band, Booger and Sunny have been working on the same piece." He then turned to the band and said, "And that explains why you've been working on the music written for guitar accompaniment."

Melody's expression was one of hurt. "Why didn't he want me to know he was going to play in the festival?"

"He wasn't sure he'd be able to do it," Tommy told her, but in reality the reason was that both he and Booger were afraid of Melody's reaction to the duet being played with Melody's arch nemesis.

Mr. Tobin went on ad nauseam to explain the challenge of working on a piece of music meant for accompaniment but not having the accompanying member with which to practice and collaborate.

The consensus around Colby was that Mr. Tobin was a master with the baton but not so much as an orator. His preludes, also known as his "diatribes," were lengthy and relatively substance free. In this particular case the consensus was wrong, but no matter. The only people listening were Booger's friends and close relatives of the jazz band.

By the time Mr. Tobin finished, the Optimist Club had collected several extra dollars for their special lemonade and the winking patrons had returned to view the talent show kickoff. People were admiring the bust, talking about the parade, and arguing strategy for Colby's last and most important football game of the year, the annual matchup with Fairview.

Mr. Tobin finally finished his "and-um" laden introduction, turned to the jazz band, and tapped his baton on the music stand. People had learned to pay attention at the sound of the baton's tapping. Mr. Tobin signaled for Booger to begin.

Booger played the first few chords, and anyone who regularly tuned in to KXOK recognized the tune. After the first few bars Sunny joined in, but the sound of the guitar remained prominent. Conversations that hadn't already drawn to a close ceased without finish. Even those who weren't familiar with the song immediately appreciated the melodic tune. All eyes focused on Booger. Booger was focused on his hand left fingers moving rhythmically up and down the fret board with an occasional glance at his right hand fingers strumming the strings.

Tommy scanned the crowd and noticed several people checking their forearms for goose bumps. Melody was holding her tear-streaked face with both hands. "The two of them together," she began, "it's beautiful." She leaned into Tommy and sobbed.

The band of boys stood shoulder to shoulder, touching slightly, so close and so taken by Booger's performance that they'd later be too embarrassed to accurately reminisce about their precise emotional state at the time.

Melody stopped sobbing long enough to ask, "How'd Sunny get him to do it?" she asked.

"He asked her," Tommy replied. He left off the part where he actually made the call for Booger.

Tommy was stunned when Melody said, "That was so sweet of her to play with him."

Melody was transfixed with both Booger, or Boogs as she called him, and Sunny. Tommy had watched her focus on Booger during the parts of the song when the guitar was most prominent and then shift her eyes toward Sunny during the short guitar pauses when Booger would seem to momentarily pass the melody to Sunny and the piano. The Codgers were all standing; they wanted to see as well as listen.

The applause lasted for more than a minute. Tommy's hands became numb clapping; he finally gave Melody a one-armed hug as an excuse to stop. Caleb was the first to speak. "He's good enough to be in a band." The others, holding their emotions in check, only nodded.

Male members of the audience exchanged glances and silently offered others a chew. Unabashed tears were flowing freely among the ladies. Sunny's cheerleader friends were holding their faces much like Melody, but since they were in a group, their emotions manifested with ankle hops, group hugs, and a variety of solo gyrations.

Tommy thought the involuntary response by girls in times of intense emotion interesting, possibly contagious. He'd seen the phenomenon many times, usually during the close calls or injuries at football games. Watching them caused him to momentarily forget about Booger's performance and think forward to the football game with Fairview.

Those with Optimist lemonade took frequent sips to hide their trembling chins. Those with empty cups were in line to get more. Tommy heard Mrs. Hearnes say to Mrs. Koch, "Extraordinary, absolutely extraordinary." Mrs. Hearnes then turned to admire the bust and placed her hand on Mrs. Koch's frail shoulder. "This town is full of inspiring people rich with character and talent."

Mrs. Koch touched the bust and smirked. "And Republicans, most of them."

Mrs. Hearnes, not to be outdone, politely responded. "I didn't say they were perfect." The two ladies exchanged understanding, genuine smiles and graciously but inaudibly agreed to a truce.

BOOGER HADN'T GIVEN ANY THOUGHT to the response to his debut. And he certainly didn't anticipate the throngs of elementary-aged girls waiting for him behind the stage. He spotted Melody and the band of boys standing near the stone. Having never been in the limelight, he felt awkward, trapped.

While the two of them were still standing at the top of the stage steps, Sunny, having experience with well-wishers, whispered, "Take your time, keep smiling, and tell each one of them thanks." She patted him on the shoulder and pushed him gently; he stumbled on the first step and then signed autographs for elementary kids on his way to the stone. By the time he reached the stone, his heart was palpitating. He wasn't sure if it was the crowd that had caused the anomaly or the fact that Sunny had kept her hand on his shoulder since leaving the stage.

There was a moment of awkward silence once they reached the stone. Boys aren't accustomed to showering each other with compliments for such things as playing a musical instrument or even singing for that matter. Sure, hit a roadside sign with a rock from a moving car and there are high fives all around. Skip a rock until it nearly completes a ninety-degree curve, and a bruised rotator cuff from celebratory shoulder slaps is the likely result.

And since Melody had gotten her Malibu, which was a much sportier car than Sunny's Fairlane, Sunny had stepped up her flirting with the band of boys. The boys, unaware that they were no more than pawns, relished the attention from Sunny.

Sunny had put the boys into a trance by simply approaching them, so Melody spoke first. "That was amazing, Boogs."

"Thanks, Melody," Booger replied and then continued with a comment that transfixed Melody's mental state. "I owe it all to Sunny. She talked me into playing in the competition."

Sunny, oblivious to Melody's now seething jealousy, broadened her smile, exposing every single perfect tooth, did a body giggle, and said, "It was all you, Boogs," and then made matters worse with a cordial kiss on the cheek.

Melody was only able to control her temper and avoid flying into a rage by keeping in mind that Sunny had in fact taken the time to practice with Booger and encourage him. Sunny, in spite of being the perfect girl, did have positive attributes. But written on Melody's face wasn't a show of appreciation.

Following Booger's cheek kiss from Sunny, Caleb unintentionally brought some needed levity to the situation when he made a feeble attempt to employ a new word. "Prodiginous!" he said and then smiled, proud of himself.

Everyone knew what Caleb meant but was nonetheless amused by his mispronunciation. Even Melody cracked a momentary smile. Caleb's expression was timely; he didn't have a clue that Melody was exuding enough negative energy to power half of Colby and that his single-word comment had possibly saved the top of her head from blowing off.

"I'd love to stick around," Sunny said, "but my mom is waiting for me." She gave Booger another peck on the cheek and said, "Come by the house later on. I'm sure my mom would like to tell you how proud she is." Booger, unable to speak—no doubt trying to retrieve a swallowed tongue—just nodded.

EVEN THOUGH MELODY HAD SURPRISED them all weeks earlier with her keen interest in seeing Clyde's Chrysler on the track, nothing could have prepared the boys for what came next. When under duress, people often do and say things that are out of character, things which they'll eventually regret.

Exceptionally ignorant feats involving automobiles are generally carried out by male members of the human species, but there are always exceptions. The mother of all exceptions was about to spring forth.

Melody's still-intense eyes locked with Tommy's. "I think we should do it tonight," she said and then smiled a devious smile that put Sunny's to shame.

Tommy's mind raced. He recalled the weekend retreat the church had held when all of the kids his age were huddled into small groups and spent the weekend in one giant sleepover in the musty and fungus-rich church basement. A rosy-cheeked youth pastor from a church in Fairview had visited Colby First Baptist. He'd spoken on the biblical verses addressing chastity, and then each group returned to a moldy room to discuss the scripture's personal application. Tommy's group's discussion had focused more on football than sexual purity. But in the end they'd all made their vow and gotten their bracelet. The boys had all removed their bracelets, along with all forms of jewelry, for football; Melody was wearing hers.

Before Tommy or the others had a chance to mentally develop Melody's suggestion, she clarified, but the extraordinary nature of her intention remained exponentially astonishing. She looked at Booger, the true motivation for her suggestion, and stunned them all with, "Let's drive through the tunnel."

Caleb was on the road to wearing out his new word. "Prodiginous—for sure," he said. Everett still hadn't corrected him, and the others, still in a state of shock, hadn't noticed the repeated mispronunciation. Caleb's eyes took on a call-of-the-wild, untamed appearance. He began moving and twitching about, no doubt trying to think of something more to say, but unable. The others tilted their heads as if they'd just heard a dog whistle, clearly knowing but not fully comprehending what Melody had just suggested.

"The town will be packed," Melody went on. "Sheriff Dooley and Tootie will be busy here. It's perfect." Coincidentally, Sheriff Dooley was fussing with the Beagle boys and pointing toward their pickup, apparently suggesting they leave. Melody motioned toward the Optimist trailer. "See," she said.

"I don't know," Clyde said, assuming she was talking about taking the Chrysler.

"That's fine," Melody said. "We can take the Malibu." She grabbed Tommy by the arm and looked at Booger. "You in?"

The hyperactive Fairview youth minister had covered countless bases with the boys on what to be on guard for in the unlikely event that they encountered a sexually aggressive girl. "They're out there," he'd said. None of the Colby boys had ever seen one, and each of them secretly looked forward to such an encounter—if for no other reason than to employ the tactics set forth by the fidgety youth pastor. But the boys weren't equipped to handle a challenge set forth by a girl that involved a driving stunt.

Melody's suggestion was perceived more as a challenge. The boys were mentally staggering and processing the notion of driving not just to but through the tunnel. Had the suggestion come from Caleb, they all could have easily laughed it off. But in this case, the escapade had been suggested by a girl previously considered demure.

Everett, the voice of reason, spoke up. "With the town full of people, how do you suppose we get your car situated onto the tracks without being seen?"

"Easy," Melody said, full of confidence. "We get onto the tracks on the other side of the tunnel." The boys were looking at her with unbelieving stares. "Remember that little trail that crossed the tracks?"

Still dumfounded, there was no response. Riding the rails to the tunnel had been discussed countless times, but Everett and Clyde had convinced the others to wait until after football season just in case the antic led to problems that might jeopardize their athletic eligibility.

"I'm in," Caleb said, to nobody's surprise.

Melody had unwittingly put the boys in a precarious spot. She'd essentially taken the alpha-male spot by first suggesting the rail ride and then by offering her car as the vehicle. The unhinged look on her face was such that she'd go it alone if the others didn't follow. In essence, she'd challenged their manhood; anyone not willing to join her in the escapade would forever be branded a coward or worse yet a pansy. Although the specific attributes of a pansy were uncertain, pansy was considered more offensive and effeminate than coward.

Nobody wanted to be outdone by a girl and run the risk of being labeled a pansy, so the rest of boys quickly but unenthusiastically responded affirmatively. "We can't all fit in the Malibu," Melody said with a hint of mischief and sent Clyde a grinning glance.

Clyde shrugged. "I guess we can see if the Chrysler will fit through that opening that leads to the crossing." He rubbed his stomach. "But I need to get something to drink first. I think I ate too many of those cheese curds."

Everett nodded agreement. "Me too." Both of them had gotten several free samples on the condition that they walk around making satisfied sounds with a full mouth and pointing first at the curds and then at the Optimist stand. The ploy had worked with regards to sales, but a gastrointestinal episode was in store for both of them and whoever else would be riding in the Chrysler.

"Hey, Quinton," Melody said when Quinton walked up. "Where have you been?"

"Helping Mr. Fritz set up a broom display," Quinton replied.

"You missed Booger playing the guitar," she said.

"I heard the guitar player," Quinton said and then faced Booger. "Was that you, man?" Booger nodded. "You're good, *really* good."

The rest of the boys fidgeted nervously while Melody filled Quinton in on the plan to ride the rails to the tunnel. To save face they'd verbally agreed to Melody's plan, but deep inside, each of them was wishing another would introduce some reason for not doing it. The prevailing feeling was that tunnel talk was better than action.

"Really?" Quinton said repeatedly while Melody explained. "What happens if we get caught?" he asked.

"That's just it," Melody said. "We won't. Everyone will be here tonight. Sheriff Dooley, his deputies, and Tootie will be occupied with yahoos like those Beagle Club drunks." She paused for a breath. "There's more where those came from."

"But what if something happens and we do get caught?" he asked again. Tommy and the others smiled; it seemed that Quinton was making headway. "I don't know," he added and looked to the others for confirmation.

"Everyone else is going to," Melody said, playing the peer pressure card. Before Tommy or any of the others could give Quinton a sign that they hadn't necessarily agreed, Melody turned and faced them. "See," she said and then swept her open hand toward the bewildered and helpless man-boys.

"Who's driving?" Quinton asked.

Melody pointed at Clyde. "We're taking the Malibu and Clyde's Chrysler."

Quinton looked at Clyde. "You're not worried about getting caught and not being eligible for the Fairview game?" Clyde's shrug could have been interpreted as him being unsure or indifferent. Quinton took it as indifferent. "Well, I guess if you're not worried, then I shouldn't be."

"Exactly," Melody said.

And then Quinton added something that caused Clyde's sweat glands to go into overdrive. "I guess if we get caught only the driver will get into trouble."

"We're not gonna get caught," Melody whined. Tommy looked at her and wondered what had caused the behavioral metamorphosis.

"My dad doesn't want me driving after dark," Melody said. The boys, still reeling from the swift decision to break any number of laws by driving their cars on the railroad tracks, didn't immediately respond. "That means we need to do this before dark."

"Can you get the Chrysler?" Everett asked.

"Sure," Clyde said. "My mom has her lawn chair in front of the stage. I'll take her some cheese curds; she won't move for hours."

"Where are you gonna say we're goin'?" Tommy asked.

"The tunnel," Clyde said. "I told her all about the tunnel after we'd walked through it. I'll just tell her the truth."

Flop's twitch became more prominent. "You're gonna to tell her we're goin' to drive through the dang tunnel?" he asked.

"I'll leave the part about driving through the tunnel out," Clyde said.

EVERETT, FLOP, AND QUINTON FOLLOWED Clyde. They stopped by the Optimist trailer and got another order of cheese curds and a large lemonade. "On the house," Mr. Enderle said. Being a star football player had its advantages.

On the way to where Clyde's mom had parked herself in an oversized lawn chair, the boys passed the portable toilets that had been brought in for Homecoming. Clyde would have stopped and used one if he hadn't been carrying the cheese curds and lemonade. And since he didn't stop, Everett didn't either. Both of them would be sorry later on.

Melody, Tommy, and Booger were putting the top down on the Malibu when the rest caught up with them at the Houn-Dawg. "Don't even start," Clyde said. "We're not putting the top down."

"I thought you said that Burt had looked it over and thought it'd be okay to put it down," Caleb protested.

"He did," Clyde admitted. "But we don't need to be drawing any extra attention right now." The rest of the boys, apparently in agreement, nodded.

Melody, Tommy, and Booger crowded into the front seat of the Malibu and led the way. Rather than head directly for the tunnel, Melody made a trip through town, passing Sunny's house along the way. She honked and waved. It was then that Tommy began to understand Melody's behavior.

Tommy remained partially perplexed. Why would Melody be jealous of Sunny spending time with Booger? His mind raced; Melody frequently asked about Booger and occasionally became visibly distraught when Booger was at home and not out with the boys. Booger was flying his palm in the car's slip stream, apparently oblivious to the role he'd played in Melody's sudden hormonal imbalance.

When they reached the edge of town, Melody kicked in the four-barrel and let the Malibu accelerate hard for a few seconds. She gave Tommy a menacing look, increasing his concern about her mental state. He stopped thinking about Melody and Booger and focused on making sure she kept the car between the ditches.

Clyde and Everett, being about the same size and having eaten equal quantities of cheese curds, began to suffer the consequence for their over-indulgence simultaneously. Their choice was to either hold it in and risk the noxious gas painfully expanding their colons or let it out. They both chose the latter. And in an effort to retain the solids and only emit the gas, they both relieved the pressure silently and without the typical celebratory gestures that accompany male flatulence.

Normally the odor of flatulence isn't repulsive to the guilty party, but in this case the potency was such that everyone's olfactory senses responded violently. Neither Clyde nor Everett was aware that the other had done the same. The onset was sudden.

Quinton poked his head out the rear window. "It wasn't me," he said. Caleb silently did the same on the other side. To speak was to breathe, so he didn't mutter a word.

Flop, having claimed shotgun and then getting hip-checked to the middle of the front seat between Clyde and Everett, started gagging.

The thick stench lingered. Everett and Clyde were sporting grins, and the others were cupping their hands over their noses. "I guess we know who the culprit is," Caleb said, "And it's not me."

"Cheese curds," Clyde said.

"Dadgum," Everett said. "It's worse than when Caleb eats that burnt gingerbread."

"Did you know that farts are mostly nitrogen and carbon dioxide?" Everett asked no one in particular. Nobody responded, probably not wanting to risk having to take an extra breath. "But," Everett said and held up a finger, "particularly potent flatulence contains methane and is explosive."

"Don't anyone light a match," Quinton warned.

Quinton's warning caused laughter, which resulted in momentary loss of sphincter control, and another wave of human-produced methane filled the car's interior.

Flop, his gagging subsided from the first episode, uncovered his face long enough to blurt out, "Put the danged top down before we explode!"

When they reached the turnoff for the tunnel, Everett stopped the car. "You'll have to unzip the rear window," he said and then turned and saw that Quinton was one step ahead of him and holding his nose with one hand while unzipping the window with the other. Flop had his T-shirt pulled up over his head.

Clyde worked the top-down button a little at a time and slowly lowered the top. Unknown to the others, Clyde and Burt had put the top up and down a couple of times, lubricated the hinge joints, and made sure it folded correctly. The boys jumped out, breathed in the untainted air, and admired their topless ride.

"Cheese curds?" Quinton asked. "Really?"

"No more cheese curds," everyone said in unison.

Torpedoes

THE ONLY PROBLEM WITH HAVING the top down and following Melody was the dust, but Clyde was happy to endure it in order to get fresh air and avoid being the first to get onto the tracks. When they reached the forest access road that led to the tracks, Booger hopped out and opened the gate. Sitting in the middle has its advantages, Tommy said to himself. He recalled the snake they'd seen when walking along the same path.

"Close it behind you," Booger shouted in the direction of the Chrysler. Clyde eyed the opening in hopes that it was too narrow for the Chrysler. Melody pulled forward to make room for the Chrysler; unfortunately there was ample room on both sides, and the drop-top barge easily passed through.

As soon as Booger got in, Melody gunned it to the tracks. "Get out and help me get lined up," she said. Booger and Tommy, one on each side, gave Melody instructions while she carefully inched the Malibu forward and backward until the tires were centered on the rails.

The Chrysler crew had gotten out to watch. "You two need to stand downwind," Caleb said to Clyde and Everett.

"Hold on," Clyde shouted toward Melody. "Let me get my tire-pressure gauge." He returned to the Chrysler and got the gauge he wore in his shirt pocket while working at Burt's Sinclair. "I'll let the tires down to about 15 psi; that should make 'em drape over the rails and stay on better."

"Remember," Caleb said, "don't hit the brakes. Just creep along." Since riding the rails had been Caleb's brainchild, he'd appointed himself resident expert on all matters rail riding.

"I'll move forward and make room for Clyde," Melody said. She slipped the car into drive momentarily, and as soon as the car began moving forward, she put it back into neutral and let it coast to a stop.

"Thing of it is," Caleb said, "stay off the brakes. They'll pull the front tires one way or the other and come off of the track. And keep your hands off the wheel; just let the track guide the tires."

Fearlessly, Melody stood in the seat and looked back at the Chrysler; she was holding something. Clyde and Everett were still standing off to themselves. "Here's a Monkees tape," she yelled.

"A Monkees tape?" Clyde asked.

"Yeah," she shouted enthusiastically, her hands cupped megaphone-like around her mouth. "When we go through the tunnel, we'll play 'Last Train to Clarksville.'"

"Did you just think of that?" Tommy asked.

"Are you kidding?" she asked. "I bought this tape specifically for this day." Tommy was once again perplexed. He then realized that Melody had given the tunnel trip considerable thought prior to the Sunny event. His uncle Cletus had warned him about the complexity of the female mind and cautioned him not to try and figure girls out.

Since the Chrysler was so much longer, it was a little more trouble getting on the tracks at the narrow crossing. "Maybe we shouldn't take the Chrysler," Clyde said. "What if we can't get it off at the lower crossing?"

"Don't be a pansy," Melody said and unwittingly invoked a teenage boy's most feared label.

"Dadgummit," Everett barked. "She'll fit. Keep inching back and forth." Once the Chrysler was sitting on the rails, Clyde hopped out and let air out of each tire, carefully measuring the psi while doing so.

"Don't get too close," Melody told Clyde. "Your car is heavier and might not stop as fast as mine."

Okay, Tommy thought. That made sense; she hasn't completely lost it.

Clyde and Melody coaxed the cars toward the tunnel. "Don't touch the brakes," Caleb kept saying.

"Caleb," Clyde said, "enough about the brakes."

Caleb sat still for a few minutes and then stood in the seat and held onto the windshield with one hand, beat his chest with the other, and shouted, "Ungowa!"

Clyde grabbed Caleb's belt. "Sit down, Tarzan," he said and pulled Caleb down into the seat.

They were less than a hundred yards from the tunnel when a bang, similar to that of a cherry bomb, came from under the Malibu. "What the hell was that?" Caleb asked, using his favorite cuss word.

"I don't know," Clyde said. "You're the expert, remember?"

"Was that my tire?" Melody shouted and fought the urge to grab the wheel. She shifted into neutral and watched the steering wheel begin twitching.

"Don't touch it!" Caleb warned.

The Malibu slowly rolled to a stop. Everyone had to jump out of the Chrysler and hold it back to keep it from ramming into the stopped Malibu.

The boys investigated the track where they'd heard the explosion and found what appeared to be the shredded remains of a giant firecracker. They'd learn later that the railroad used small explosive devices, called torpedoes, to warn that a train may be coming from the other direction. In this case the torpedo had been placed on that side of the tunnel as a warning to railroad personnel riding a small inspection cart that the Colby Spur train had passed through the tunnel and to proceed with caution.

"Dadgum it all!" Everett said repeatedly while the boys, using sticks they'd found near the tracks, poked at the mysterious shredded paper fragments.

Meanwhile, Melody was looking at her left front tire and stating what the boys had already discovered. "Tire's flat. Now what?" she asked. Tommy sensed that Melody had come to her senses and was beginning to realize the weight of their predicament.

"That's exaggravating," Caleb said. Everyone frowned momentarily but knew what Caleb meant with yet another invented word.

"Hey, Caleb," Quinton said. "The train doesn't run on Saturday, right?" He was no doubt bewildered and wondering how he'd gotten involved in this misadventure.

They all looked at Caleb, who had first presented the train's schedule when concocting the idea of rail riding through the tunnel. "According to the schedule it doesn't," Caleb said unconvincingly. Quinton's question and Caleb's less than certain answer introduced more than a thread of doubt and fear.

Booger, who'd been quiet most of the afternoon, which was normal for him, asked the obvious question. "Got a spare?"

Melody turned her palms up and shrugged the girl sign for, "I don't know."

Tommy snatched the keys from the ignition and popped the trunk. He flung back the trunk carpet to reveal the spare tire and jack. Clyde and Everett, the only boys who had their driver's licenses, were immediately expected to know what to do. Clyde was the obvious choice since he worked at a filling station that fixed flats.

"Let me have the jack," Clyde said after everyone had stared at him for nearly a minute. He attached the jack to the front bumper and began quickly ratcheting the jack one click at a time. He stopped before the weight of the car was completely off the flat tire. "Loosen those lug nuts," he said.

"What if it comes off the track?" Flop asked, for which he got skull-burning stares but no answer. For a few minutes the only sounds were that of nearby crows and the methodical click-clack of the jack. Melody began to pout.

Clyde stopped working the jack to catch his breath. "Hey, Everett, make sure that spare has 15 psi." Everyone leaped to help Clyde check the spare's pressure.

Once the tire change was completed, the two-car rail-riding caravan was ready to proceed, albeit with a bit of the wind let out of their proverbial sails. Walking through the tunnel had been done with the tinge of fear that accompanies things new and potentially dangerous. Driving a car through the tunnel with the possibility of derailment, and now the chance of a tire blowing out, added exponentially to the fear factor. The adventure had lost its luster, and what had started out as fun had become something to endure.

The angle of the setting sun illuminated the fall foliage that framed the tunnel's opening. The car began to maintain a steady speed without being put into gear. Just before reaching the tunnel entrance, Caleb said, "Remember—"

Melody cut him off. "I know, don't touch the wheel or the brakes. I got it." Her patience had vanished along with the air in her front tire.

They slowly entered the tunnel. "Okay," Melody said once the darkness had fully enveloped them. "This was not a good idea." No one argued. "How far back is Clyde?" she asked.

Tommy and Booger looked back; their eyes had yet to adjust. "I can't see anything," Tommy said.

"The other side isn't far," Booger said, the tone of his voice calm, as if he was a veteran at rail riding.

"You sure?" Melody asked.

"Uh-huh," Booger lied.

"You're full of crap!" she said. No one spoke for several minutes. The only sound was that of the idling motor and an occasional rubber-on-steel squeak when the tires adjusted to anomalies in the track.

Once they emerged from the tunnel, Melody's spirit was renewed, and she pushed in the Monkees tape and began singing along to "Last Train to Clarksville."

Booger elbowed Tommy and pointed back. Tommy looked; the Chrysler was only inches away. "You might want to speed up a little," Tommy said.

Melody looked in the rearview mirror and saw the Chrysler. "Tell them to slow down," she squealed.

Tommy climbed into the backseat, stood on his knees, and, looking back, yelled, "Slow it down."

Everett raised himself above the windshield of the Chrysler. "Clyde has it in neutral. We've been coasting since the tunnel."

Clyde leaned his head out from behind the windshield. "Tell her to speed up a little."

The Colby Spur, for nearly a mile leading to the tunnel from town, is an incline of between two and three percent, imperceptible while walking but enough to keep a car moving. Due to the laws of physics, and in this case gravity, the Chrysler, the heavier car, moved slightly faster down the incline plane.

Booger picked up on it first. "We're going downhill," he said.

Melody pulled the tape out of the player. "What? You sure?" she asked.

"That's how they built it," Booger said.

"Did you know that before?" she screamed, once again frustrated and losing composure. "How far before it levels off?"

"I don't know," Booger said. Tommy was still on his knees in the backseat looking back and forth between the Chrysler and what lay ahead.

Tommy looked at the speedometer; it read a little over ten miles per hour. Before the tunnel they'd crept along so slowly the needle wasn't registering. The crossing where they'd planned to get off was slowly approaching, but since they risked derailing if they used the brakes, it felt like they were flying at lightning speed toward the planned exit point. "We're not going to be able to stop," he said.

"What?" Melody shrieked. "What do you mean we're not going to be able to stop?"

"At the crossing," Tommy clarified. "We're going to have to ride the rails all the way to town. The crossing there is wide enough to use the brakes."

"What if we get caught?" she asked. Tommy didn't answer.

He looked back at the Chrysler, made an "I don't know" expression with his arms, and yelled, "We'll have to go into town and get off there."

Everett slowly eased down into the seat and muttered, "Dadgum."

THE TIE YARD AND RAIL-SIDE bulk fuel station area is the grungiest place in Colby, and it's a magnet to drunks and general troublemakers. That's good and bad—good because it made it easy for Sheriff Dooley to keep watch over the unsavory element attending Homecoming festivities, and bad since that's where the Malibu and Chrysler would end their rail ride. Meanwhile, Dooley was cruising Colby, making frequent passes through the tie yard and bulk stations.

"HOW FAR IS TOWN?" MELODY asked again.

Tommy shook his head. "I still don't know."

"It's got to be shorter than taking the road," Booger said.

"But we're going slower," Melody reminded him. "Has the sun set?" she asked; her eyes were glued on the track, and she was holding her hands inches from the steering wheel but resisting the urge to grab it with each corrective twitch. Changing the tire had taken much longer than normal due to the challenge of jacking the car without it sliding off the rails and it was getting dark.

"It's down," Booger confirmed.

"What time is it?" she then asked with an anxiety-induced higher pitch.

"Calm down," Tommy told her, for which he received a threatening glance.

After they'd gone a few hundred yards past the crossing, the cars began to slow. Tommy watched the speedometer needle slowly sink to below five miles per hour. The Chrysler was catching them again. Melody put the Malibu in and out of gear in order to maintain a good distance between the two cars.

"Looks like we're slowing down," she said.

"You're doing great," Tommy said, hoping to calm her nerves.

Showing signs of momentary sanity, she said, "Dad will be looking for me if I'm not home before dark."

"I wouldn't worry about that just yet," Tommy advised her and received another wrinkled-brow glance.

"Tell him you had a flat," Booger suggested, trying to help.

Melody frowned. "What if he asks where?"

Tommy shrugged and suggested, "Tell him we all drove to the tunnel and you had a flat on the way back."

Booger giggled. "Exactly."

"I'm not going to lie," she said.

"It's not really a lie," Tommy said.

They'd all become so engrossed in the cover story that they failed to notice the Chrysler about to hit them from the rear. Clyde tapped his horn and nearly launched them out of their seats. Melody moved the shift lever to D.

ARNOLD AND RITA HINKEBEIN WERE standing near the square when they saw Sheriff Dooley slowly cruising by. Mr. Hinkebein waved him down. "Hey, Dooley," Arnold said. "Have you seen Melody lately? She's driving the Malibu."

Dooley shook his head. "Not lately, Arnold," he said. "The last time I saw the Malibu was at the Houn-Dawg. It was parked next to Clyde's Chrysler."

"If you see her, tell her we're looking for her."

"Will do," Dooley said, and then asked, "Want me to turn on the lights and put a little scare into her?"

Arnold grinned. "Sure."

"You two are bad," Rita said but didn't protest the harmless prank.

THE RAIL RIDERS WERE LESS than a quarter of a mile from town. "What do you think?" Melody asked.

"About what?" Tommy asked, not sure if she was wondering about how to get off the tracks or contemplating a lie.

"Getting off the tracks," she said with a hint of audible panic. "We're coming up on the crossing, and if there's a car coming, I'll have to hit the brakes."

"If you do that then Clyde will too, and more than likely both cars will run off the tracks," Tommy warned.

"That'd be better than hitting another car," she said, again making sense.

"Let's just hope for the best," Tommy said.

"Leave your lights off," Booger suggested. "It'll make it easier to see if another car in approaching the crossing."

Tommy glanced back at the closely trailing Chrysler. Clyde made the "I don't know" palms-up sign. The crossing was less than a hundred yards away.

Booger was in the backseat standing on his knees. "It looks like there's a car headed toward the crossing," he said.

"What should I do?" Melody asked, her hands less than inches from the wheel. "What if we go off the track?" She and Tommy's eyes locked for a split second. Tommy's heart ached seeing the fear in Melody's eyes.

"Make sure it's in neutral," Tommy said, trying to act calm, but he was anything but.

"It is," she shrieked. "But Clyde is really close."

"If the car doesn't slow down, it should beat us to the crossing," Booger reported. They emerged from the trees less than thirty yards before the crossing.

"Hurry up!" Melody shouted in an effort to will the approaching car to speed up.

THE BEAGLE CLUB BOYS HAD parked on the other side of the train yard and were scattered out among stacks of ties relieving themselves. Dooley had seen their truck and suspected what they were up to. He'd returned the truck keys and told them to go home and sleep it off. He shined his spotlight on the nearest one, and momentarily hit the button for his red lights. The Beagle boys scattered, leaving their vacant truck idling alongside the road. Amused, Dooley chuckled and continued on his patrol.

THE SLOWLY CREEPING MALIBU WAS within ten yards of the crossing, and it was going to be close. "I can't watch!" Melody screamed and covered her face. For several moments she'd successfully fought the urge to grab the wheel, but when the time had come to do so, she freaked out.

Fortunately, the car coming from town cleared the crossing just a few feet before the Malibu arrived. Had Tommy been able, he probably would have hit the brakes. But instead he grabbed the wheel, turned the car sharply to the left, and guided it safely off the tracks and onto the road to Colby. He then tapped the accelerator just enough to keep the Malibu moving, making room for the Chrysler.

Once stopped, Tommy and Booger stared at each in disbelief. "That was close," Booger managed to say.

Both cars were shrouded in a cloud of dust caused by their sliding turn off of the tracks onto the tie yard road. Melody was already crying when Dooley appeared from around a stack of ties. He saw them and flipped on his red lights like he'd promised.

The Beagle boys, who'd run from the other side, saw the red blinking lights ahead of them, staggered to a stop, and then raced back to their waiting pickup to hightail it home.

"Hey, guys," Dooley said when he walked past the Chrysler. The boys sat in silence and awaited their fate.

"Coach is going to kill us," Everett whispered. Flop, sensing the furious nature of Clyde, jumped into the backseat.

Dooley approached the Malibu, and when he saw Melody crying, he started apologizing. "I'm sorry, Melody," he said. "I didn't mean to scare you."

"I ... guess we're in big ... trouble," she said through sobs.

"Well," Dooley said. "Your parents are looking for you. I'm sorry if the lights upset you."

"We had a flat," she said.

"I don't think you'll be in trouble if you explain," he said. "They're on the square watching the talent show." He looked across at Booger. "You might want to get back there. The winners will be announced before long. From what I've heard, you're in the running."

On the way back to his patrol car, Dooley swept the Chrysler passengers with the beam of his giant flashlight and then stopped. The boys braced for the worst. "That flat tire really has her upset," he said. "You boys be careful," he warned. "There are some losers in town tonight." He was no doubt referring to the Beagle boys, who were at that moment whooping and hollering through the Seven Sisters.

The Chrysler boys raced to the Malibu as soon as Dooley pulled away. "Dadgum," Everett said. "What the heck?"

"What'd he say?" Clyde asked, looking perplexed.

"He didn't have a clue where we came from," Tommy said, grinning.

"We did it," Caleb said. "We did it." High fives were exchanged, and Flop did a backflip from off the Malibu's door. He landed on his feet but then fell backward and lay in the gravel beside the road squirming and laughing.

They'd all but forgotten about Quinton being new to Colby until he said, "I'm hoping what we just did wasn't normal."

Melody was still sobbing. "My parents are looking for me," she said.

"Here's the story," Tommy began. "Melody's car had a blowout on the way to the tunnel."

"What if someone asks if we drove through the tunnel?" Clyde asked.

"I can't imagine that anyone in their right mind would ask," Quinton said. "Who'd even think of doing something like that?" The rest exchanged knowing grins.

The town was packed; they parked as close as they could to the square and went looking for Melody's parents. Tommy wanted to be there when she first spoke to them. The Hinkebeins were admiring the bust and talking to Mrs. Koch when Tommy spotted them. "There they are," he said.

"What's wrong?" Melody's mother asked and looked suspiciously at the boys. She took Melody into her arms. "Sweetheart, we've been worried about you. What happened?"

"We had a flat," Tommy said.

"Sort of a blowout," Booger said.

"Where?" her dad asked.

"Out by the train tunnel," Melody barely got out before running to her dad and hugging him.

"We changed it," Clyde said. "The blown tire is in the trunk."

Tommy was thinking the least said the better and was relieved when Clyde didn't elaborate. He got Caleb and Flop's attention and made the zipped lip motion.

Melody's mom gave her dad a hard look. "You've been talking about getting new tires," she said.

"Yes," he agreed and continued patting Melody on the back. Her dad thanked each boy for changing the tire and then turned to Clyde. "I'll drop by Burt's to get a new set of tires next week."

Melody's mom put her hand on Booger's shoulder and gave him a ten-der motherly smile. "Your performance was the best yet," she said. "Your mother would have been so proud."

Miss Anderson interrupted Mrs. Hinkebein's shower of adoration. "Where have you been?" She sounded exasperated. She was closing fast; Booger's dad was in trail. "You disappeared. We've been looking for you for hours."

An epiphany of sorts washed over Melody while she watched the adults congratulate Booger on his performance. She examined the faces of the other boys; they looked stressed and tired. She slowly realized that she'd used them to vent her loathing of Sunny's participation in Booger's performance. And that rather than detest Sunny, she should be appreciative of Sunny's friendship and support of Booger. She'd made the afternoon about her, and it should have been about Booger; she'd stolen his limelight and nearly gotten him and all of her friends in serious trouble.

She watched as more and more people approached Booger and waited their turn to congratulate him. "Don't squeeze too hard when you shake his hand," someone in line said. "Those fingers are golden." She knew what she had to do.

"I'll be back in a minute," she told her mom.

"Where's she going?" Tommy asked while watching Melody disappear into the crowd.

"Probably the potty," her mom said. The mere mention of the word caused an involuntary response in all of the boys, and they headed for the row of portable toilets. They left Booger standing with several more people waiting to speak to him.

"I'll bet Booger pees his pants," Caleb said while they were making their way through the ambling crowd.

Melody had to go too, but she had a more pressing matter to take care of first. While searching the crowd, she realized that her resentment of Sunny was selfish and petty. Her mind raced with the multitude of evil things she'd oftentimes wished upon Sunny, such as hair loss, skin lesions, nose and chin zits, belly fat; the list went on.

Sunny was sitting near the stage with her mom watching the final act setting up to perform. Melody was out of breath from running when she reached them. "I'm so sorry," she said, catching Sunny unaware.

Sunny graciously stood, held her upturned palms at her side, and looked angelically at Melody. "For what?" she asked, mystified.

Melody, still pumped with adrenaline from the tunnel trip, flat tire, and power-sliding track exit, thought fast. She realized that Sunny had no idea of the evil that had been wished upon her. "I'm sorry," Melody began, "for not catching you sooner and telling you how much I appreciate you playing with Booger and encouraging him."

Sunny smiled and waved it off. "Oh, it was fun," she said. "The music was really hard, but I'm glad that I had a reason to learn it." She clasped both hands with modesty, tilted her head slightly, and smiled her award-winning smile. "Booger is a sweetie," she singsonged and then paused, looking around in thought. "I think we've gotten to be good friends," she said.

A few hours earlier those words would have stung like a thousand hornets, but instead they caused tears of joy to spill forth from Melody's bloodshot eyes. The two girls hugged.

The boys, still standing in line at portable toilets, had watched Melody run through the crowd and approach Sunny. They couldn't have known what was going through her mind, but the embrace surely caught them by surprise. Totally focused on bladder control, they gave it no further thought and shrugged it off as yet another mystery of the female gender.

THE TUNNEL TRIP WAS A secret that Melody and the band of boys kept to themselves until graduation. Over the years they'd learn of others who'd done the same and, like them, chosen not to tell. Some things are better left untold.

THE FOLLOWING WEEK MR. HINKEBEIN stopped by Burt's to get his opinion on the Malibu's tires. "They're all low," Burt told him after checking the pressure. "Looks like about fifteen pounds in each tire," Burt said. The men exchanged glances. "Strange," Burt said. They shrugged and gave the identical low tire pressures no further thought.

Mr. Hinkebein frowned. "I'm sure that I had the tires checked last week when I filled up." Burt shrugged; he'd heard that line before.

"Take a look at this," Mr. Hinkebein said and pointed at the blown spare lying in the trunk.

"Good thing she wasn't going very fast," Burt said.

"Why's that?" Mr. Hinkebein asked.

"Blowouts on the front cause the car to swerve and sometimes run off the road."

Mr. Hinkebein nodded amazement. "Well, looks like I'm just in time."

"How about a set of radials?" Burt asked.

"Sounds good to me," Mr. Hinkebein said. "I want the safest tire you have."

Invincible

THE GAME AGAINST FAIRVIEW WAS traditionally the last game of the season. The rivalry stretched back more than fifty years, when the two towns were of similar size and the teams evenly matched. Over the years Fairview, adjacent to the Mississippi River and Eisenhower's interstate highway system, had grown exponentially. Colby bragged about quality not quantity, another way of saying its population growth was virtually stagnant. Eventually, the quality claim failed to manifest itself on the football field. Due to the disparity in school size, the annual game ceased to be competitive. As a compromise between those who wanted to keep the tradition alive and those who were tired of getting beat every year, the game became a biennial event. In recent years, the best that Colby could hope for was to keep the score close. In light of the recent off-field events, there was every reason to believe that Fairview would run the score up as much as possible.

The Codgers were manning their desks under the sycamore tree and waiting for Monday's practice.

"Well, this is the last week of practice," Rabbit said.

"Yeah," Monkey agreed.

"I'm just sayin'," Rabbit replied.

"Sayin' what?" Monkey asked.

"Since Friday is the last game, this is the last week of practice," Rabbit said, his intonation remorseful. Since the last week of practice would end with the Fairview game, the Codgers found hopeful conversation a challenge. They had confidence, but their years of experience caused their confidence to lack depth.

They were exchanging sympathetic expressions when Milton pulled up in his cart. He always waited for the newspaper before coming to practice.

"What's in the paper, Midnight?" Rabbit asked after Milton shut down his cart.

Midnight pulled a pair of duct tape-repaired reading glasses from his shirt pocket and put them on. "Well," he said and then cleared his throat, "the FDA recalled a million cans of tuna because of mercury contamination."

"Ah, fizzlesticks," Rabbit interrupted. "A little mercury never hurt nobody."

"How'd the mercury get in the tuna can?" Bem asked.

Midnight looked over his glasses and continued, "Ten thousand women marched in Washington DC celebrating the Nineteenth Amendment."

"Now that'd be somethin' to see," Rabbit said. "How many portable toilets you think they had to haul in?" The rest of the Codgers belly laughed and then moaned of joint pain caused by the laughing.

"But that's not the best," Midnight continued. He held up the sports page for them to see, but none of them could read it from where they were sitting. Their natural reaction was to squint, but of course it didn't help. "I'll read it to you. Bookends Book a Bet," Midnight began and then continued to read the short article about Everett and Clyde's promise for the Fairview game.

"Jeeminy," Monkey said. "That oughter get 'em fired up."

"It also says the forecast is for rain," Midnight added, laid the paper aside, returned his glasses to his shirt pocket, folded his arms, and leaned back.

"They can't forecast the weather that far ahead, don't cha know," Bem said.

WHILE THE CODGERS DISCUSSED THE Bookends' bet and weather phenomena and debated a variety of mythic means of weather prognostics, including Benjamin Franklin's Poor Richard's Almanack, the coach was preparing the players for the first practice of the last week of what had been an undefeated season. Due to superstition, he didn't dwell on the perfect record.

"It's the last game," Coach Heart spit shouted from in front of the locker room blackboard. "It's the most important game." He was spraying everyone in the first two rows with spittle-laden fragments of the chewing tobacco he'd gotten rid of just before coming into the locker room. "It's the game that will determine if our other wins this season meant anything." He paused, either for effect or because he was trying to think of something inspirational. "You've given people a reason to believe we can beat Fairview." He slapped the football and then wiped his chin with the cuff of his sweatshirt. "The question," he said and pointed the football at the players, "is if this team thinks it can win."

Coach Heart's attempt at motivation rarely hit the mark and was usually diatribes to endure. And it was one of those times when sitting in the front row wasn't a privilege. Everett, Clyde, and Quinton had already decided they were going to win.

Everett and Clyde's double vow had caused a stir. Unlike recent years, most in Colby were now looking forward to the game even though it was traditionally lopsided against them and always dreaded by the players. To add to the drama, the Bookends had made their double vow public. The *Fairview Daily* paper had called their vow "farm boy theatrics," which only worked to fuel the so-called farm boys' desire to make good on their promise. It's not that they despised being called farm boys, but they did not appreciate the term "theatrics."

Coach Heart held up a copy of the *Fairview Daily* for all the players to see "Bookends Book a Bet" in large bold letters. He gave Clyde and Everett a scowl. "You've just given them unnecessary motivation." He was seething.

Everett, the one who'd actually done the talking, didn't back down. "It's not just talk, Coach," he responded in a respectful, submissive tone. Players rarely spoke during Coach Heart's Monday rants. And then Everett continued. He began slow and ended with a crescendo. "Vince Lombardi says that if you're good enough, you can tell the other team your play and then execute it anyway. We didn't exactly tell them a play, but we told them the result." He paused for a breath and then stood, turned to face the team, jabbed a fist into the air, and yelled, "And we're gonna do it!"

The rest of the team came to their feet and shouted, "Hoo-ah!" a battle cry that Mr. Franklin had recently introduced.

"Hit the field," Coach growled. He and Mr. Franklin exchanged grins while the boys tore savagely from the locker room to the field to begin their warm-up drills.

After practice the players were gathered around the shed putting gear away and dousing themselves with cold water when the Codgers waved the Bookends over. Milton was holding the newspaper.

"Think you can do it?" Rabbit asked. He and the rest of the Codgers were still giddy from watching practice and discussing the chance that Colby might win.

Clyde and Everett and the rest of the team had done extra wind sprints as a result of the now famous bet. "It ain't right how they treated Quinton," Clyde told Rabbit.

"Clyde was speaking figuratively to that goofball reporter," Everett added, and judging by the looks on the Codgers' faces, they didn't understand what figuratively speaking meant.

"I'm just sayin'," Rabbit started, "a bet is a bet."

"That's just it," Clyde said. "It wasn't a bet."

"It is now, don't cha know," Bem said.

"Back to the question," Rabbit said. "Think you can do it?"

By this time the rest of the band of boys, Quinton, and several other team members had moseyed over to Codger's Corner.

Clyde, frustrated and tired of being hounded about the comment, didn't respond. Everett draped his arm across Clyde's shoulders. "Dang betcha!" he said.

"Look," Clyde said and then looked at each Codger with a fierce expression. "We'll only play these guys twice, this year and two years from now. We'll only get one chance at that goofball Golden Boy or whatever they call him." He paused and looked to the sky in anguish. "I don't know if we can protect Quinton the entire game, and I don't know if we can sack their slippery pipsqueak on the first play, but we're dang sure gonna try."

"You can do it," came a voice from behind. Fritz stepped out from the shadows of the gymnasium; until then, no one had noticed him there.

It took a few extra seconds, but the Codgers got turned around to confirm who'd spoken. Fritz had never been seen at a practice, but nobody else in Colby had that accent. Fritz walked a little closer.

"Fizzlesticks," Rabbit said. "What makes you so danged sure? What do you know about football?"

Fritz moved a few steps closer to the players but kept his eye on the Codgers. "It's not about futeball," he said.

"Last time I checked it was," Rabbit said and chuckled. Fritz ignored the sarcasm.

"It's right here," Fritz said, putting his finger first on Clyde's chest and then Everett's. Afterward he gently touched Quinton's chest with an open palm and then waved his open hand toward the rest of the team, who'd now gathered behind the Bookends. Fritz turned and faced the Codgers. "It's vat you can't see vit de naked eye dat vill make de difference." He paused in thought. "One must first convince oneself that one can. Wictory begins here," he said and pointed at his head, "and depends on dis unt dis," and touched his arms and shoulders, "but ist decited here," and pointed at his chest.

Fritz then turned so he could see the Codgers and the team. He patted himself lightly on the chest and in a barely audible tone said, "Heart. Dees boys haf heart." He then jabbed a finger at the Codgers and in an elevated voice said, "Dat's vat vins futeball games."

Nobody spoke for several seconds. Finally, Caleb broke the silence with an ear-piercing "Hoo-ah!"

"Hoo-ah!" yelled the rest of the team.

Coach Heart stepped forward and extended his hand to shake Fritz's. "Well said and right on." After shaking he patted Fritz on the shoulder. "Would you like to stand on the sidelines Friday night?"

Fritz gazed up at Coach Heart. "Vat is a siteline?" Everyone laughed. The boys headed toward the locker room while the coach led Fritz to the sideline and explained. For once, the Codgers were speechless.

FRITZ'S SPEECH WAS THE TALK of the hallway the next day. Clyde and Everett were glad to have people focusing on something other than the "bet." The heart speech had spread the responsibility for winning across the entire team.

The words "The most lopsided battle in American history?" were written on the board when everyone took their seats in Miss Anderson's class. It was a question. As soon as the bell rang, one of the brownnoser's hands shot up. "Pearl Harbor," the front-of-the-class-sitter said.

"I'll give you a hint," Miss Anderson said to the class, somewhat ignoring the first responder. "Remember, we're studying the Founding Fathers."

Everett and several of the girls raised their hands. Proving the girls' assertion that Miss Anderson favored the boys, she called on Everett. "The Battle of Brandywine," he said.

"That battle occurred before we were a country," one of the know-it-all girls said without having been called on and then looked toward Everett with a satisfied, smug expression.

"Let's wait to be called on before shouting out answers," Miss Anderson said. Taking into consideration that she favored the boys in too many instances, she didn't admonish the girl for talking without permission. "You are correct, however. Brandywine did in fact occur before we became the United States, but it is part of our American history."

She walked to the board and, while writing *Monongahela*, said, "I'm thinking of a battle that occurred twenty-one years before the signing of the Declaration of Independence." The class became silent, and the waving arms dropped.

Miss Anderson told in bloody detail about the battle of Fort Duquesne, where British and Virginia Regulars led by England's General Braddock and then twenty-one-year-old Colonel George Washington were soundly defeated by a French/Indian army.

Near the end of her explanation, she returned to the board and wrote *bulletproof* on the board. "Arguably the most significant event that occurred during the battle was the demonstrated invincibility of our future president," she said and then paused. "Colonel Washington had two horses shot out from under him, and his uniform was riddled with holes made by bullets, but he was never harmed."

She dropped the chalk and turned to face the class. "Years after the battle, it was learned that several French and Indian sharpshooters had been given orders to shoot only at Colonel Washington. After Washington and Braddock's retreat, the French and Indians were amazed and frightened by Washington's apparent providential invincibility." She let that fact soak in.

It seemed like only moments had passed when the bell marking the end of class rang. The students, amazed by what they'd just learned, ambled instead of rushed from class.

The Bookends, their vow now known by all, had been elevated to celebrity status. They walked together toward the locker room; students moved out of their way as if to be in awe, and most were.

"Invincible," Everett whispered to Clyde while smiling at the sea of parting students. "That's what we want the headline to be on Saturday." Clyde looked perplexed. Everett explained. "We'll make Quinton look invincible."

"And that will make us look good to the scouts," Clyde said, grinning.

"Win-win," added Everett.

"Yeah," Clyde said, "except unlike Washington's battle on the Mononga-hela, we're going to win."

Everett jabbed his fist into the air. "I'm charged," he said just before they reached the locker room door. "It'll be our first chance to go 100 percent and not have to worry about hurting anyone." Everett thought for a moment and then grinned. "I don't think I've ever hit anyone as hard as I can."

Clyde held the door for him and grinned. "Friday will be our time to shine."

MR. FRANKLIN OFTEN REMINDED THE players that scholarship comes before sport. Serving as both principal and assistant football coach, he had to balance his allegiance, at least through word. In reality, during the week before the Fairview game, there were no homework assignments for any class attended by a football player.

Quinton took advantage of the lull in schoolwork to get in some extra hours at Fritz's. Clyde dropped him off there after practice. Approaching the broom shop, Quinton noticed a new sign below the one reading "Neue Besen Kehren Gut." The new sign read "*Nur tote Fische Schwimmen Mit Dem Strom.*" Quinton had no idea what the words meant and was too tired from the last full-pad practice of the week to give them much thought.

"Hallo, Q. I see that Clyde brinks you again," Fritz said when Quinton stepped inside.

"Yes, sir," Quinton replied and then reached for his apron. Fritz always insisted that he wear an apron.

"Vy you don't get a license, Q?" Fritz asked.

Quinton worked for Fritz for a couple of weeks before they'd begun to converse about things not broom related. Quinton explained the insurance conundrum but then added, "But the insurance agent who handles Tommy's family's insurance called and told us how we can cut down on the cost."

"Unt how is dat?" Fritz asked.

"Good student discount," Quinton told him. "It will still cost a little more, but nothing like the agent in Fairview told us."

"How much more?" Fritz asked.

"About ten dollars per month," Quinton said. "I make enough here to pay for the insurance and gasoline."

"Did you safe any money vom you job in Fairview?" Fritz asked.

"I've never had a job before," Quinton replied.

Fritz stopped what he was doing. "Vy?" he asked but then realized the reason. "I see—color?" Quinton nodded.

Quinton stopped attaching broomcorn to a handle long enough to ask, "Can I ask you a question, Mr. Fritz?"

"So lonk as you can ask and verk at the same time," Fritz said. He'd said early on that he didn't like to talk while working but had slightly relaxed that rule. Quinton had noticed at first Fritz simply didn't like to talk. His reclusive nature was the result of something more than the slight language barrier.

"I noticed the new sign," Quinton said.

"Not new," Fritz corrected.

"I'd never noticed it," Quinton said.

"I just hung it today," Fritz said. Fritz was an extremely literal thinker.

"What does it mean?"

"Not simple to translate, Q, but the verds in English mean zumething like 'The ignorant go happily to der doom.'"

Quinton took a risk. "You must have had a reason for hanging it today, instead of yesterday, or the day before, or the week before."

"Keep verking," Fritz said. "I'll explain. Too many people know only vat they've been tolt by others. They don't see for themselves." He jabbed a finished broom in Quinton's direction. "Like you. In Fairview you couldn't get a jop because nobody taked de time to zee for demselves dat you're a goot verker. And you taked de insurance agent at his vert, but now ju know dat he vas vrong. You vere ignorant about insurance, but now ju know." Fritz was on a roll.

"And it's the same vit religion. The Jews know only vat the bearded rabbi tells them; the Catholics know only vat the pious priest says; the Baptists know only vat the chubby chicken-eating man says." Quinton had to muffle a snort.

"I have much to say, but I don't say much," Fritz continued. "I hear people say, 'I heard so and so say such and such,' and I sometimes vonder if anyone knows anything for demselves." Fritz removed his apron and hung it on the nail below his name, next to the nail marked "Q." "Come, Q, I show you zumthing."

Quinton paused an extra moment and admired the carved Q before hanging his apron and following Fritz to his house. The walls of Fritz's house were lined with bookcases. He narrated the arrangement of the books. "Here are books having to do vit de great generals and de vars they fought." He put his hand on Quinton's shoulder. "I notice dat de great generals are never attacked; dey usually fight for others—Patton for example."

"Dees books are on religion. I've noticed dar's a difference between religion and faith. Few religions are faith based. Most are based on behavior." This time he put his hand on Quinton's forearm. "Our behavior is too often controlled by our brain, but our faith is controlled by our heart. The heart is stronger than the brain." Fritz pointed at his head. "But first we must use our brain to train our heart. Books for the brain equal wisdom for the heart," he said. He looked deep into Quinton's eyes. "You know dis?"

The headlights of a car coming down Fritz's driveway shone through the windows and broke Fritz's string of reasoning. "That's probably my dad," Quinton said, his eyes sweeping the rest of the room. "Have you read all of these books?"

"All of dem once, and zum of dem twice or more," Fritz said. "Many of dem are in German, and dat makes for faster reading." He then smiled and pointed at himself. "At least for me." Smiles from Fritz were becoming more frequent.

Since Tommy didn't have any homework, he went to Colby John Deere after dinner to work on the truck. He hadn't called anyone to go along since he wanted time alone to think.

He opened the overhead door nearest the truck, removed the protective tarp, and started working. While his hands sanded away at rust spots, rather than realize the privilege of owning the coveted Gooche's Grocery truck, he allowed his mind to dwell on the negative and take another self-pity journey.

Clyde and Everett each had their license and a car. Melody had a drop-top Super Sport Malibu and was now friends with Sunny; it was anybody's guess how many boys from who knows where she'd meet through Sunny. And since Booger won first place at the music festival, he'd become an item, in spite of not having a driver's license. And he'd helped Quinton find a solution for getting his license. All I have is this rusty old truck that I can't even drive, Tommy thought, descending deeper in self-induced misery.

He was contemplating the chance that he'd developed an existential vacuum like Booger once had, when Melody's Malibu pulled into the lot. "I called your house, and your mom said you were here." Sunny and Booger were with her. "We stopped by the Houn-Dawg and got you a graveyard."

"Thanks," Tommy said and took a long draw of the concoction. The carbonation made his eyes water and nearly took his breath.

"I got a new tape," Melody singsonged and held up a Turtles *Happy Together* eight-track.

"Cool! New tires too," Tommy said with lackluster intonation. Her new tires were the expensive radials with raised white-lettered sidewalls.

"Want a ride home?" she asked and then raised her eyebrows suggestively. Since riding a bicycle at fifteen is verboten, as Fritz would say, Tommy had walked from home to the shop.

"Sure," he answered, still lacking his normal enthusiasm. "Let me close up."

Everyone hopped out and helped him put the cover over the truck's bed. "You okay?" Melody asked.

"Just tired," Tommy lied.

Back in the car, Melody gave Tommy a wink and then pushed in the tape. The Turtles began: "Remember me and you, I do. I think about you day and night, it's only right ..." She'd obviously cued that particular song and had it ready to play.

It was a dream situation, a proverbial light to shine in his moment of uncertain darkness; but Tommy's mind had clouded his heart with doubt, and he wasn't able to escape the doldrums and enjoy the moment for all its potential.

Epiphany

The Bookends challenge, combined with Quinton's success as quarterback and Colby's winning season, guaranteed a standing-room-only crowd. Fans—mostly mothers and wives, since the husbands were supposedly working—began lining up two hours before game time, an hour before the gate opened. Once the gate opened, the throng made a mad dash for the seats nearest the fifty yard line.

Large signs were posted in several places reading "You and Two Only," which meant that each person could save only two extra places. Nobody could remember the logic of allowing three instead of two or four, which would have made more sense. The only explanation was that the person making the rule was a suffering poet.

Since the bleacher spots weren't marked and there was no rule as to how much room you and two required, there was ample opportunity for fudging and fighting over just how much space was needed for three people. For once it was chic for ladies to claim large derrieres. They marked their spots with Fighting Indian stadium blankets—nothing less would do.

A threatening western sky meant the forecast for rain would prove to be accurate, which would change the dynamics of both the game and spectator apparel. Novice or normally fair-weather fans would show up with umbrellas and then be harangued by those sitting behind them. Experienced fans came prepared with hooded raincoats and ponchos and didn't tolerate umbrellas.

The civic clubs had been given permission to set up stands inside the perimeter. There was no shortage of food—fried, boiled, broiled, or otherwise. The Optimist Club had become known for their cheese curds. The special ice wasn't a menu feature but was frequently ordered and, for an extra dollar and a wink, served.

Music was blaring a selection of '60s favorites from the PA system. By game time it would seem that "Na Na Hey Hey Kiss Him Good-bye" by Steam had played a hundred times. The lyrics didn't make a lot of sense, but the rhythm and beat worked wonders for whipping the crowd into a pregame frenzy.

THE PLAYERS HAD BEEN TOGETHER since seventh hour. They'd eaten as a team, gone over the game plan, and then been told to get dressed and begin stretching. Each player had his personal routine. Some got their ankles taped; others stared into their lockers at posters of legendary players. The JV players hid their hairless bodies while the older, more mature players—proud of their physiques—pranced around in nothing but their jockstraps. Booger had a photo of his brother, Johnny, and held it reverently for a few minutes before dressing.

Caleb and Flop had started out by applying appropriate amounts of eye black on their cheeks but ended up smearing it all over, making them look satanic. Coach Franklin then convinced Coach Heart to apply the same markings to Everett and Caleb, who reluctantly agreed.

"Looks like rain, boys," Coach said. "That's to our advantage." The rain being to their advantage was debatable, but winning coaches always convince players that whatever phenomenon exists is to their advantage.

"Will we be able to change at halftime?" Quinton asked. He'd yet to play in a rain game at Colby and, since they had used equipment to begin with, wasn't sure of the protocol.

Everett leaned in close. "Don't worry," he said. "Like I said, they'll never touch you." Clyde, sitting on the other side, punched Quinton's leg and gave a confirming nod to Everett's whisper.

"We have some extra pants and plenty of socks," Coach said. He was being truthful about the extra socks, but the only extra pants that existed were being worn by the JV kids who dressed out but rarely played varsity and certainly wouldn't be on the field against Fairview.

"This is our house!" Coach Franklin began, using a worn-out football cliché. It worked; the players repeated it over and over and worked themselves into a frenzy. Just before losing control, Coach Heart removed his hat, the signal for the pregame prayer. "Take a knee," he said and then led them in the Lord's Prayer.

"Amen," he said and then shouted, "Booger, lead these freshly blessed warriors onto the field of battle!" Booger squeezed his head into his helmet, took one last look at Johnny, gently closed his locker, and moved to the head of the pack of adrenaline-pumped Fighting Indians.

MELODY AND SUNNY WERE GIVEN the honor of holding the paper pyramid depicting a wimpy rendition of Fairview's tiger mascot. Super Fan had reached an impatient zenith and was orbiting nervously between the pyramid and the locker room door. The rest of the cheerleaders and members of the pep squad formed two lines from midfield to the bench. The Colby crowd were on their feet and reaching for their ponchos. A light drizzle was barely visible through the reflection of the lights.

Traditionally, the starting lineup is announced one by one, and each starter races from the goalpost to center field and then trots to the bench. The coaches had agreed to change it up. "Ladies and gentlemen," the announcer said, "here are your Fighting Indians." Booger led the entire team in a confident, slow, steady trot toward midfield. Super Fan, confused by the change, was gyrating wildly and using his arms to make a circling motion, trying to get the team to speed up. After reaching the forty yard line, the players tore savagely through the paper pyramid and raced to the bench, high-fiving the pep squad along the way. Once gathered on the sideline, the players held their helmets high and began chanting, "Colby, Colby, Colby." The crowd joined in.

Melody, Sunny, and the rest of the pep squad cleaned up the remains of the decimated effigy while Clyde and Everett, co-captains, returned to midfield for the coin toss. Fairview won the toss and chose to defer their choice until the second half.

Fairview kicked off to Colby; Flop received and didn't waste any time surprising the Fairview fans, players, and coaches with his athleticism. Neither did Clyde and Everett; Fairview special teams players raced down the field sure that they'd be able to outmaneuver the two giants and make their way to Flop. The Bookends couldn't cover the entire field so a few Tigers got by, but by the time Flop was forced out of bounds at the fifty, the field was strewn with dazed Fairview players, who were slowly getting up from the damp grass and no doubt wondering if they'd just been hit by a freight train.

The light drizzle became a light rain by the time Indian offense took the field. The crowd were still on their feet; the Bookends were facing a defensive line determined to get to Quinton and foil the bet. The Tiger defensive ends, having sufficiently had their bells rung during the kick-off, weren't much of a threat. Clyde and Everett looked across the line to see the same faces they'd first seen at the Colby theater and then at the Fairview Chevrolet. "Game on," one of the Fairview players said and then snickered—another cheap cliché.

Offensive guards normally stand their ground or pull back, depending on the play; their primary job is to protect the quarterback. They're not eligible to receive the ball, so advancing downfield makes no sense except in special circumstances.

Clyde and Everett had approached the coaches with an idea for the first play of the game. Quinton, knowing he was going to be unprotected, immediately threw the ball toward the sidelines and out of bounds. Clyde and Everett launched forward, catching the defensive tackles by surprise and knocking them to the ground; they then proceeded to do the same with a pair of linebackers. The referee blew the play dead before the Bookends did any further damage.

The play had lasted less than five seconds, but four of Fairview's key defensive players were lying on their backs in the mud. The Colby fans, already on their feet, cheered even though the play resulted in no gain and loss of a down. Super Fan raced down the sideline and then dropped to his knees and slid along in the wet grass, jabbing his fists into the air. Shaken, the Tiger tackles and linebackers got to their feet; the backs of their uniforms were now smeared with grass and mud—proof that they'd been pancaked.

On the next play, Quinton released quickly to the sideline, where Flop was waiting undefended. To the surprise of the Tiger coaches, he caught the ball. Because of the wet field conditions, however, he wasn't able to maneuver his way through the Tiger defense and was brought down after a six-yard gain.

Realizing that Flop could catch, the Tiger defense adjusted. Expecting the adjustment, Coach Heart called for a handoff to Caleb. Caleb shot through a hole made by Clyde and advanced the ball all of the way to the ten.

The Colby crowd went wild. All eyes were focused on the field. The only concession stand still doing business was the Optimist trailer, where, on account of it being first and goal on the ten, dollar bills and winks were exchanged with increased velocity.

A wet field usually favors the defense in a goal line stance. Offensive players lose their ability to cut sharply and fool the defense. Pass plays at the goal line are high risk and seldom used at the high school level. Colby kept the ball on the ground and after three plays had moved the ball only two yards to the eight.

The kicking unit trotted onto the field. Tommy had never kicked in the rain. Coach Heart grabbed Tommy by the arm and motioned for Quinton and Flop before spitting a long stream of tobacco juice. Since it was raining, he probably figured nobody would notice. "Look, Tommy," Coach said, "the field is wet, but the ball will be dry." He pointed at the referee who was drying the ball with a towel. "Kick it like you always do."

He swatted Tommy on the rear and sent him on his way and then grabbed Quinton's shoulder pads and Flop's face mask. "Fake the kick." He locked eyes with Flop. "Run a corner route and get open." Flop already had his mouthpiece in and just nodded.

Only Quinton and Flop knew that Coach Heart and Coach Franklin had called for a pass play. After the snap Quinton held the ball until Tommy's foot was only inches away, and then he stood, found Flop in the corner of the end zone, and made the pass for six points.

Tommy, not knowing about the fake and already in a kicking motion, ended up flat on his back in the mud and missed seeing the completed pass.

Men screamed like women until overtaken by coughing. Women hugged. The Codgers were almost in need of resuscitation. Super Fan raced into the end zone and lifted Flop off his feet. The rest of the team closed in. The referees had to blow their whistles to clear the field.

The Colby coaches, now full of themselves and drinking in the cheers, corralled Quinton, Tommy, and Flop. "Same play," Coach said, "except this time we're goin' for two." Again, he grabbed Flop's face mask. "Nice catch, Flopper." He jiggled the face mask for affect. "This time run a crossing route." Coach turned toward Quinton. "We practiced this. Think you can hit him on the run?" Quinton nodded confidently. Coach turned to Tommy. "Good job on the fake kick. They took the bait." Tommy got high fives from the bench as if he'd known about the fake and played a significant role in the touchdown.

The crowd hadn't sat down since kickoff, and some had never taken a seat. When the kicking unit returned to the field, the roar of cheers increased to a deafening rumble.

It's difficult to fool well-coached teams twice. The Fairview coaches had identified Flop as the go-to receiver and assigned a pair of secondary defenders to him. Quinton's pass was on the mark, but Flop received a crushing blow the moment the ball reached his hands; he couldn't hold on to it.

Clyde and Everett had helped him up. The three of them, covered in mud, trotted toward the bench. Quinton's uniform, except for his knee where he'd kneeled to hold the ball, was pristine.

Tommy got ready for the kickoff. Coach Heart's warning about the wet ball was heavy on his mind. The field was so wet he couldn't accelerate as well as on dry ground. He thought too much and instead of launching the ball downfield squibbed it less than twenty yards. A Fairview player chose to pick the ball up rather than lie on it and secure it. He was rewarded for his action by being hit hard by both Clyde and Everett; the player, shaken, never returned to the game.

The crowd continued to cheer, but Tommy knew the cheers weren't for him. All the negative thoughts that had clouded his mind while working on the truck were returning. Doubts began to flood his mind, and he questioned his ability as the placekicker. He looked down the bench at the JV kicker, a small pencil-necked kid who was years away from his first shave, and realized the team had no other option.

The Tigers, knowing that Clyde and Everett would be coming for Golden with everything they had, chose a play that called for a quick release. The Bookends couldn't tackle the quarterback if he didn't have the ball. They were half right.

An eerie hush fell over the crowd when both teams lined up. Photographers were balled up on the sideline at the line of scrimmage; it was the play of the season. Golden was quick but the Bookends were too. Golden took the snap, dropped two steps back, and launched the ball in a high arc downfield.

Clyde and Everett's uniforms were already slick with mud; they shot through the slots between Fairview's guard and tackle and reached Golden a split second after he'd released the ball. They hit him with such force that he fell to the ground and slid nearly ten yards in the now muddy mess of a field. Clyde and Everett stopped momentarily and stood over Golden on their way back to the huddle. They exchanged helmet-to-helmet eye contact but made no visible celebratory movement. Everett looked down at Golden's crumpled body and said, "You pusillanimous punk." The nearby referee threw a penalty flag.

The Tiger trainers were called to the field to attend to Golden, who was crumpled in a muddy mess and gasping for air. Fortunately, he'd only had the wind knocked out of him and wasn't injured.

The Colby fans' cheering reached a new crescendo, bordering on vicious. So focused were they on seeing Golden get sacked that nobody on the Colby side, including Colby's secondary, noticed the Fairview receiver racing downfield and getting under the high-arcing pass. After making the catch, he walked into the end zone untouched. They'd tied the game in one play.

Coach Heart threw his arms into the air, called the referee over, and asked what the penalty was for. "Unsportsmanlike conduct," the referee said and pointed at Everett.

"What did he do?" Coach asked. Coach Franklin was making sure that Everett and Clyde kept their distance.

"He called the Fairview quarterback a name," the referee answered.

"A name?" Coach Heart asked, showing more than a little emotion. "What name?"

"He called him a … well, I can't remember exactly what he said," the ref said. "Some kind of a punk."

"Punk? Really, Gerald?" Coach asked, calling the referee by name.

"He used another word too, Coach," the referee replied.

"What word?" Coach asked. "Profanity?"

"No, I don't think so," the ref said. "I'm not sure what the word was."

"Can you do that, Gerald?" Coach asked. "Give them fifteen yards because one of our players called their player a punk?"

When the ref blew his whistle, picked up the flag, and waved off the penalty, Fairview's coach rushed the field and demanded an explanation.

Eventually the refs got the game under control. The Tigers PAT was good and, after possessing the ball for less than thirty seconds, were leading by one.

Mr. Franklin, keeping with his advice to focus on the next play, didn't ask Everett what he'd said. He was probably enjoying the disruption caused by whatever Everett had said.

The field was reduced to a quagmire, and Golden was significantly shaken, but Colby, down by one, was still riding high on having drawn first blood. The two teams fought it out to the end of the first half, repeatedly punting on fourth down.

At halftime Coach Heart paced back and forth in front of the blackboard. Once all of the players had squeezed in, he turned to them squinting and said, "I'm proud of you men." He made direct eye contact with several players. "We're down by one, but I can assure you that Fairview feels like they're down by twenty." He wrote some statistics on the board. "We're beating them offensively. And that's what they're hearing about right now." He grinned. "On paper, we're winning." He rested his fists on his hips. "Let's keep taking the game to them. They'll make a mistake." He held up a towel. "Anybody need dry gear?"

"No way," Clyde said. "Let's not change anything; it'll be bad luck."

"That's right," Everett agreed. "I like the mud."

"Hoo-ah!" roared the team, and they stormed back onto the field.

By the fourth quarter, Flop had gained nearly a hundred yards receiving but scored no more touchdowns. Both teams had gotten the ball inside the twenty several times but in the wet conditions had stalled and gotten no further. Super Fan, cold and wet, had both hands shoved into his wet jeans pockets but continued to jump up and down and run in place during each play. The rain dripped off of the bill of his St. Louis Cardinals baseball cap.

Tommy hadn't been in the game since the botched kickoff. He hadn't necessarily been benched; there just hadn't been the need for a kicker. He'd watched Caleb and Booger carry the ball countless times and listened to them being cheered in spite of their futile attempts to fight their way through the Tiger's secondary. Flop made one catch after another only to be forced out of bounds, but the crowd cheered just the same.

Quinton didn't look natural. His pristine uniform was an aura in a sea of players with uniforms so mud caked that it was difficult to discern for which team they played. The Bookends had kept their promise, and the game had so far gone according to plan except for one thing—the score.

Late in the fourth quarter, Flop caught a pass at the ten and was able to keep his feet in bounds before being hit hard by a Fairview cornerback. He was okay, but having had the breath knocked out of him, he required the help of the trainers to make his way to the bench. The trainer set him beside Tommy. Tommy watched Flop wince and hold his side in pain. He'd played a great game. Tommy, much like the whisker-free JV players, had only watched, and that was eating away at him.

Fairview held Colby at the ten. It was fourth down with only seconds on the clock. The coaches turned to Tommy. Tommy was engrossed with Flop's condition and hadn't been paying attention. One of the JV players elbowed him and pointed toward the coaches. Tommy could see them frantically waving for him, but like being in a dream, he saw their lips moving but couldn't hear their voices. An ethereal sensation swept over him.

Coach Heart got Quinton, Flop, and Tommy into a separate huddle. "It's just like an extra point," he said, foregoing any mention of mud or dampness. "There's no option this time," he added. "Tommy," he shouted, "you *will* be kicking the ball; Quinton is going to hold, just like always." He grabbed Tommy's helmet and looked deep into his frightened eyes. "You'll have plenty of time; they'll drop back to defend the pass." Coach glanced across the sideline at the other coaches. "They're watching us right now." Again he made no mention of the mud or that the reason he thought Fairview would drop back for a pass was because Tommy had muffed the last kick. He swatted Tommy on the rear. "Just like an extra point, except no pressure."

The crowd was eerily quiet. Unnerved, Tommy walked onto the field for the first time since muffing a second kick to start the second half. Colby had called time-out, so there was no rush. He scanned the sideline fence and saw familiar faces; everything seemed to be in slow motion. He looked toward Codger's Corner and noticed the Codgers were all on their feet. He found Melody; she looked fearful.

"Just like kicking an extra point," Tommy said to himself. He'd done it several times that season.

Right before the snap, Fairview called a timeout, no doubt an attempt to give him more time to consider the consequence of the kick. Tommy took the time to pray. He wasn't sure what to ask for, but he was pretty sure that praying for a win wasn't appropriate. He just wanted the moment to pass. He was surrounded by the team and the stadium was packed, but he felt alone.

During the second timeout, the rain stopped and the clouds began to break up; the referees got another dry football from the sideline. Tommy scanned the crowd and found his parents; his mother was holding her hands as if to be either in prayer or hiding a face fraught with fear. His dad was smiling proudly; his look exuded confidence. Tommy fed on that visual sign of assurance. Booger and Caleb, not part of the kicking team, stood together on the sideline. They'd already removed their helmets, and Tommy could see their sweat-drenched, and mud-streaked faces looking toward the goalposts.

The referees blew the whistle signaling for play to resume. Tommy signaled that he was ready; he focused on the dry football and watched it sail from the snapper to Quinton, whose uniform, except for the knee, was still as clean as when he'd first stepped foot onto the field. Quinton received the snap, and Tommy kept his eye on the ball until his toe made contact; the momentum spun him around, but he stayed on his feet, albeit facing the wrong direction. He heard the roar of the Colby crowd and knew the kick had been good. By the time he got turned around, the ball had sailed well past the uprights and the team was on top of him.

The field goal put Colby ahead by two. The Colby crowd cheered, stomped, and threw hats, popcorn, and seat cushions into the air. Clyde and Everett hoisted Tommy to their shoulders and carried him to the sideline. The crowd began chanting, "Tommy, Tommy." Super Fan ran to midfield with his arms extended like they were wings and did figure eights on the fifty yard line.

The game wasn't over; Colby still had to kick off. Rather than relish the moment, Tommy went directly to the practice net and began making practice kicks. "Act like you been there before," he remembered the coaches saying. The kickoff team took the field, and as soon as they were in position, Tommy trotted to the ball and kicked it with all he had. This time it flew deep into Fairview territory, his longest kick of the season.

The crowd began chanting modified lyrics to Steam's hit single, "Na-na-na-na, na-na-na-na, hey-hey-hey, go start the bus."

The Fairview team that took the field late in the fourth, down by two, was not the same team that had taken the field earlier that evening. It was clear that to them the game was fete-accompli, and Colby had the lead.

The coaches had Quinton stand a few yards apart from the rest of the Colby Indians. Quinton's spotless uniform was a clear reminder to Fairview that the quarterback they'd passed over was truly invincible. The only thing dark on Quinton was his skin. Super Fan was standing on one side of Quinton with his thumb to his ear, fingers waving, and tongue sticking out toward the other team.

On the other side of Quinton was a tiny but sturdy-looking man. It was Fritz.

The Colby bleachers were emptying; the fans crowded around the sideline and watched Fairview make three failed attempts to move the ball. Out of timeouts, the clock slowly spelled their demise.

PARENTS, GRANDPARENTS, AUNTS, UNCLES, BROTHERS, sisters: everyone rushed the field and gathered around their favorite player. Kids with footballs raced around. Some were making what they dreamed were touchdown passes, but most were attempting field goals. None of their kicks were high enough to clear the goalpost crossbar, and a few bounced off the heads of departing fans who weren't paying attention, but they were mostly Fairview fans, so the parents let them play.

Photographers raced to Quinton and quickly snapped photos of him standing with the Bookends, the picture a contrast of the pristine, invincible quarterback and the Bookends that would become legendary. The nephilim waited until the photographer was finished before congratulating Clyde and Everett. "The Mizzou guys were here," LB said. "They wish you guys were graduating this year." They turned to Quinton. "They were impressed with you as well."

Everett tried to keep eye contact with LB while being swarmed by Colby fans wanting to offer congratulatory pats on the back. He looked down and smiled at each person and then back at LB. Finally, LB waved and mouthed the words, "Libby said call."

The Fairview newspaper headline would read, "Invincible Quarterback and Lucky Kick Result In Colby's Slim Victory." The *Colby Telegraph* would read, "Indians Tame the Tigers."

Tommy was surrounded by his family and the Hinkebeins. "Nice kick,"

Melody said before giving him a hug and then quickly following up with, "Yuck, you stink!"

People lingered until the lights began going out. Finally, Coach Heart whistled for the team to hit the locker room. He caught up with Everett and Clyde. "Everett," Coach said, "what did you call Golden?"

Everett told him. "A what?" Coach asked. Everett repeated the word.

"It means spineless, cowardly, and timid. Sorry, Coach," Everett said.

"It could have cost us fifteen yards, Everett."

"I know. Sorry," Everett repeated.

"How'd you say it again?" Coach asked. Everett told him again, and Coach repeated it a couple of times. "Good one," Coach said and then slapped Everett on the shoulder and ran ahead to the locker room.

The players were exchanging high fives and chest bumps until seated on the locker room benches. Every uniform was a muddy mess, some from game play and others from postgame celebration.

Coach walked into the locker room and waited until he had everyone's attention. "Game ball," he said and held the football high.

"Tommy," the team yelled in unison.

The unanimous response caught Tommy by surprise. Surely others were more deserving. Flop had taken countless unprotected hits to make catches. Clyde and Everett had kept their vow and protected Quinton while hammering Golden. They hadn't technically sacked Golden on the first play, and in fact he'd thrown a touchdown pass, but the impact of the hit had made their point. And who was to argue with them?

"He kept his poise," Coach Heart said. "Everything we all worked for came down to one kick." He paused and made momentary eye contact with several players. "I don't think anyone in this room would have traded places with him." He looked at Tommy. "T-Man, the game ball is yours."

The anointing of a nickname, which fortunately didn't stick, and receipt of the game ball pushed Tommy into sensory overload. He felt faint. "Thanks, Coach," he mustered and then asked, "Got a marker?"

"A marker?" coach frowned.

"I want everyone to sign it," Tommy said.

"Gather around," Coach said. "Tommy wants everyone to sign it."

By the time the players arrived, the Houn-Dawg crowd was spilling out onto the parking lot. Honking cars were making the loop. Anyone passing through Colby at the time and not knowing about the game would have sensed widespread pandemonium.

The crowd parted each time another player arrived. Playing time made no difference. If one was on the team, they were held in high esteem. Colby understood the contribution that each player made, including those who only practiced and seldom played. But the player in possession of the game ball was exalted above all others.

Patty always made a big deal out of the player who received the game ball. Knowing what was in store, Tommy made his way to the game ball table; Melody, Booger, and Sunny joined him. The whole thing made him uncomfortable. He didn't like the attention and certainly didn't feel like he deserved it. Through watching professional football games, he was aware of the disdain that players who'd fought to move the ball down the field felt about the kicker who prances out onto the field and pops the ball through the uprights and then gets all of the credit.

He wasn't dwelling on the undeserved accolade. He was holding the game ball, but his mind was on something more important. He marveled at the unlikely mix at the table. Two girls, one with the coolest car in the county, and the other arguably the most beautiful girl in the state, choosing to sit at a table with two fifteen-year-olds who couldn't drive and weren't even particularly good at football.

Patty brought Tommy his usual, a cherry freeze, and asked the others what they wanted. "Everything is on the house for those sitting at the game ball table," she said and squeezed Tommy and Booger on the shoulder. "Great game, boys."

Tommy's uncle Cletus and Penny inched their way through the crowd. "Way to go," Uncle Cletus said and patted Tommy on the back. "That's surely more fun than driving a car through the tunnel," he said and then winked.

Tommy, Melody, and Booger froze. "Isn't that what you all have been talking about doing?" he asked. The relevance of his tunnel driving comment didn't register with Sunny.

"That's right," Sunny chimed in and pointed wiggly fingers in Tommy and Melody's direction. "Didn't you guys walk through the tunnel a couple of weeks ago?"

"Yeah," Melody agreed, her eyes meeting Tommy's. "It was kind of creepy." The mention of the tunnel had jostled Melody's memory. She looked up at Tommy's uncle Cletus and asked, "What's that written smack-dab in the middle of the train tunnel?"

Tommy noticed Penny give his uncle a particularly affectionate look when Melody asked about the words scribbled on the wall in the deep recess of the tunnel.

"You mean in the darkest part of the tunnel where you can barely make it out?" Uncle Cletus asked.

"Exactly," Melody said, her expression showing surprise that he actually knew.

"Let me think … Et Lux in Tenebris Lucet," Uncle Cletus said, saying the words with perfect intonation.

"Wow," Booger said. "How'd you know?" Uncle Cletus shrugged.

"He knows more than you think," Penny said.

"Impossible," Sunny remarked. "I already think he knows everything." To which Tommy's opinion of Sunny rose exponentially.

"But what does that mean?" Melody asked.

"And light shines in the darkness," he answered. Penny leaned her delicate head onto his massive shoulders. Already emotional from hearing that their initials were still there, the reminder of the Latin phrase tipped the scale, and a lone tear slowly made its way across the bridge of her nose. Colby was small, and everyone knew Penny Lane and Cletus Thornton's story.

Uncle Cletus's wisdom and Penny's display of affection rendered the kids speechless. The providential implication of the words, written eons earlier on the tunnel wall, cast the kids into a momentary contemplative funk.

After a few moments of silence at a table surrounded by celebratory laughter, Melody asked, "Did you write them?"

"No, no." Penny laughed. "Those words were there when we were your age. And they'd been there long before we discovered them."

"Now you have me curious," Sunny said. "Who do you think wrote them?"

Penny, looking skyward, smiled pensively, shrugged, and then said, "Nobody knows."

Tommy suddenly realized he had it all: his best friend Booger, Melody, the Fairview game ball, and the most coveted possession of all—the truck. Now that football season was over, it was time to get serious about restoring the truck. There was a lot of work to do before he turned sixteen.

"Hey, Boogs," he said, half mocking how Sunny referred to him. "Wanna help me with the truck tomorrow morning?"

"I do," both girls chimed in before Booger could swallow his french fries and answer. The boys exchanged grins.

The crowd cheered when Clyde stuck his head in the door. Tommy waved when Clyde, Everett, Flop, Caleb, and Quinton squeezed into the packed dining room. "Let's give them the table," he said.

"Hey, Mel," Sunny said. "Why don't we cruise the loop in the Malibu?"

Tommy knew by the way Sunny had shortened Melody's name that the girls had become friends.

THE NEXT MORNING TOMMY WAS waiting when Melody pulled up in the Malibu and honked. They swung by Booger's house before picking up Sunny and then headed for Colby John Deere to work on the truck.

Tommy raised the hood to show off how he'd repainted the engine compartment to its original color. He started the truck and let it idle, showing how smooth and quiet it was since the valve job. Booger was more interested in watching an idling engine than were the girls.

"I'm gonna reupholster it," Tommy said when he noticed Sunny looking at the stuffing spilling out of the truck's worn bench seat.

Melody showed Sunny the drawing she had for the door art and how it would be positioned on the door and then pointed out the rust spots that needed sanding. Tommy and Booger began removing rotten tongue-and-groove planks from the truck's bed. After an hour or so, they all took a break and admired the progress.

During the break Tommy started thinking out loud about the long list of things he needed do before the truck was ready to license and drive. "How long before you turn sixteen?" Sunny asked.

"Only eight months," Tommy replied.

"Think you can get everything done by then?" she asked.

"I hope so," Tommy said and then thought, *Only eight months!*

Sunny hopped up, dusted off her jeans, and said, "We need to get to work. You'll be sixteen before you know it."

Strangely, Tommy believed her.

He and Booger finished removing the bed boards while Melody and Sunny made girl talk and sanded away on the rust spots. He elbowed Booger and nodded toward the girls so Booger could see the rust dust smudges on their faces. "Don't tell 'em," Booger whispered.

"What time you have to be at work?" Melody asked and then wiped the sweat from her forehead, further smearing the rust smudge.

"One," Tommy said. "You?"

"Same."

Tommy looked at his Timex; it was already past eleven. They'd worked on the truck for over two hours. "I guess we should be going," he said and tossed everyone a shop towel. He and Booger exchanged smiles when the girls only used the towels to wipe their hands and not their faces. Tommy circled the truck looking at the freshly sanded areas and the now floorless bed. "Wow, it would have taken me weeks to get that much done by myself. Thanks a lot."

"Look at you," he heard Melody say.

"Me?" Sunny replied. "Look at you."

Another round of girl giggles erupted when they took turns looking in the truck's side mirror. "Here," Melody said and handed Sunny a tissue. Sunny's attempt at cleaning the smudges off wasn't any better than Melody's. The two girls took turns looking in the truck's mirror, exchanged "I don't care" shrugs and another round of girl giggles.

"That was fun," Sunny said. "I think I ruined my nails, but who cares?" She stood next to Booger and draped her arm across his shoulder. "We get the first ride."

"After me," Melody piped up.

Melody let the others off first before dropping by Tommy's house. "Want a ride to Gooches?" she asked.

"No thanks, I'll walk. It's not far." Tommy didn't want to turn Melody into his chauffeur, and the walk to Gooche's was only a few blocks.

"Get there early and we can meet at our spot," she said with her trademark smile now framed by a rust-smudged face. Tommy was perplexed by Melody's indifference to the smudges. He didn't understand why, but there was something appealing about her smeared face. "See ya there," he said.

AFTER WOLFING DOWN A PB&J sandwich, he headed for Gooche's. The sky was clear, but there was a winterish bite to the air. He turned up the collar on his jacket and jabbed his hands deep into his pockets. Anxious to meet Melody, he broke into a half skip.

Less than a block from the square, he noticed cars parked in the spots reserved for those taking their driver's test. It won't be long, he thought. Melody was sitting on the stone looking his way and holding two RC Colas. A red headband covered her ears and forehead; her auburn hair waved in the late-autumn breeze. Tommy couldn't quite make out her smile from that distance, but he knew it was there. He was enjoying the sensation that seeing her caused when he tripped on a crack in the sidewalk, which had been there since his paperboy days. He jerked his hands from his pockets, caught his balance, and looked back at the cracked section vowing to have it fixed when he became mayor.

He turned back to Melody in time to hear her say, "Catch this, clumsy," and then see a MoonPie flying his direction. It was one of the new kind with the peanut butter filling, his new favorite.

Epilogue

KEEPING WITH TRADITION, BOOGER, CALEB, Flop, Quinton, Everett, and Clyde gathered near the stone. It had been several months since they'd last gathered. The Codgers, across the street on the courthouse bench, had taken notice. Another football season was underway, and after the previous year's undefeated season, the Codgers' hopes were high and expectations were beyond reason. Colby had won the first game with Drake the night before; the year had promise. But the gang hadn't gathered to talk football. The Codgers too were aware of the special nature of the day.

Mizzou wasn't playing this weekend, so Quinton was able to return to Colby for the big event. Quinton's grades had qualified him for a scholastic scholarship to the University of Missouri. Mizzou's football recruiters, impressed with Quinton's overall athleticism and experience at several positions while playing for both Fairview and Colby, had suggested that he "walk on," which meant they weren't confident enough with his skill level to offer him a football scholarship right away, but if he joined the team and did well, a scholarship the following year was a possibility.

Tommy's fully restored Gooche's Grocery truck came into view. His dad was driving and parked the truck in a spot reserved for those taking their driver's test. Tommy and Melody jumped out and trotted to the stone. Tommy's dad headed home on foot; it was bad luck to have one's parents linger while taking the exam.

The Codgers knew what was taking place but, having lost a good deal of their sensitivity with age, were more interested in the truck than the owner's pending driver's test. They ambled toward the truck and were doing the tire-kicking circle when the driver's exam van pulled up. One by one the exalted brown-shirts emerged from the ominous van. Each one stopped to feast their eyes on the vintage pickup before going into the courthouse and preparing their test-taking lair.

The hour finally arrived; Tommy's longest year was over. It was time. The band of friends walked him to the door, just as they'd done with each other several times in the past year. To the others, the massive doors didn't seem as intimidating as they once had. To Tommy, the courthouse entrance, with its giant, creaking oak doors, never looked more foreboding.

So far the driver's exam record for the group was perfect; everyone had passed on their first try. "No pressure," Caleb said, meaning just the opposite, for which he got an elbow from Melody and a glare from Everett. They watched Tommy disappear into the cavernous courthouse and then returned to the stone to begin the wait.

Flop and Caleb's birthdays were only a few weeks apart; they'd taken the test on the same day. Neither had a car and rarely drove their parents' cars. Flop backed into another car while trying to parallel park within a week of getting his license; Caleb's parents' car, a not-so-vintage VW minivan covered with psychedelic art and holding an engine that belched more smoke than a coal-fired power plant, was possibly the one vehicle that had less appeal than a bicycle. Fritz had convinced Quinton to take the exam and then helped him fix up a convertible VW, which he couldn't take to Mizzou; freshmen weren't allowed to have cars.

Quinton was telling them about the college football experience when test takers began to come out of the courthouse and head for their cars. It was several minutes before Tommy finally emerged grinning ear to ear and with every brown-shirt in trail. They followed him to the pickup and slowly circled it. They didn't appear to be inspecting the truck; their posture indicated adoration rather than scrutiny. Other test takers, anxious to get the practical test out of the way, stood next to their vehicles and nervously waited for the brown-shirts to stop ogling the pickup.

Melody and the boys watched from the stone. From their view it looked as if the brown-shirts were flipping coins to see who got to ride in the truck. Finally, Tommy and an examiner got into the truck and pulled away. Sunny, also home from Mizzou, and making a pass through town, saw the gang gathered around the stone and joined them.

While trying to impress the examiner with his double-clutching skill, Tommy rolled through a stop sign. Tommy will never know if the examiner—so engrossed first with the truck and then Tommy's down-shifting technique—didn't notice, or if he let the rolling stop pass.

Tommy's next stop was Velma's counter, where for fifteen dollars he crossed the great divide. Booger, Melody, and Sunny crowded into the cab with Tommy; the rest piled into the bed. Tommy's first road trip was to the Craggy Creek Bridge.

CPSIA information can be obtained at www.ICGtesting.com
Printed in the USA
LVOW042221011112

305525LV00002B/4/P